River of Time

River of Time

Melissa Hamm

Library of Congress Control Number:		2010906130
ISBN:	Hardcover	978-1-4500-9383-5
	Softcover	978-1-4500-9382-8
	Ebook	978-1-4500-9384-2

This is a work of fiction. Names, characters, places and incidents either are the
product of the author's imagination or are used fictitiously, and any resemblance
to any actual persons, living or dead, events, or locales is entirely coincidental.

This book was printed in the United States of America.

To order additional copies of this book, contact:
Xlibris Corporation
1-888-795-4274
www.Xlibris.com
Orders@Xlibris.com
79247

Tell me not, in mournful numbers,
Life is but an empty dream!—
For the soul is dead that slumbers,
And things are not what they seem.

Life is real! Life is earnest!
And the grave is not its goal;
Dust thou art, to dust returnest,
Was not spoken of the soul.

Not enjoyment, and not sorrow,
Is our destined end or way;
But to act, that each tomorrow
Find us farther than today.

Art is long, and time is fleeting,
And our hearts, though stout and brave,
Still, like muffled drums, are beating
Funeral marches to the grave.

In the world's broad field of battle,
In the bivouac of Life,
Be not like dumb, driven cattle!
Be a hero in the strife!

Trust no Future, howe'er pleasant!
Let the dead Past bury its dead!
Act,—act in the living Present!
Heart within, and God O'erhead!

Lives of great men all remind us
We can make our lives sublime,
And departing, leave behind us
Footprints on the sands of time;

Footprints, that perhaps another,
Sailing o'er life's solemn main,
A forlorn and shipwrecked brother,
Seeing, shall take heart again.

Let us, then, be up and doing,
With a heart for any fate;
Still achieving, still pursuing,
Learn to labor and to wait.

(Henry Wadsworth Longfellow, "A Psalm of Life")

PROLOGUE

August 14, 1978

It was a warm August evening. The woman could not get comfortable no matter what she tried. But then, she was only days away from delivering her baby and knew from her two previous pregnancies that this particular discomfort was normal. When the doorbell rang, she was happy for the diversion and told her husband that she would get the door.

When she opened the front door, she saw an elderly man and woman on the steps. She recognized them both. The man was Aaron Sizer, and he was with his sister, Lydia Campbell. They had both been living in the small town of Corsehill with their families for as far back as she could remember. There was a small trunk on the steps by their feet. She smiled at them, asking if they would like to come in.

"Thank you, Mrs. Blodgett," said Aaron. "We would like to speak with you and your husband, if we could. We have some things that we must discuss with you."

As she showed them into the living room where they greeted her husband, Mrs. Blodgett noticed that Aaron Sizer had picked up the trunk and brought it inside with him.

CHAPTER I

May 15, 2008

Lord! It was getting muggy! It was too early in the season for this sort of humid weather. Beth stopped to wipe her brow, swatting at the mayflies hovering around her face. She shrugged her shoulders, causing the body armor wrapped around her torso to shift ever so slightly, feeling the clamminess under it as it moved but dismissed the discomfort. It was something that she was used to after nine years on the job. It had been a wet week, with exceptionally heavy rain and thunderstorms, and she wondered if they were going to get another storm.

Beth Blodgett, a game warden, was also a tracker. She was here in this watershed property in Corsehill looking for a hiker who had been missing since the night before. She got the call earlier that morning and was assigned to a group of five other searchers. She was out ahead of the group, cutting sign. Beth could hear them coming up behind her and waited for them to catch up. She had picked up what she knew were the hiker's tracks from the description that she had been given of his footwear. It looked as though he was heading toward the river. Her gut told her that they were close to him. His tracks had been getting more erratic, and she could tell that he was tired and confused.

She followed the tracks a little further toward the edge of the river and found where he had stumbled over a log, and when he got up, she could see that he had hurt his leg. She turned to the others and told them that they were close. Moments later, they found him on the edge of a good-sized clearing along the river. His ankle appeared to be broken, and he was dehydrated. Beth radioed in their position, and they began to give the hiker preliminary first aid.

Soon they heard the dull *whump, whump* of a helicopter approaching to pick up the injured hiker. Beth looked up toward the sky and noticed that it had, suddenly, become darker. The air had that telltale blue-green tint that was the precursor of a violent thunderstorm. They hurriedly loaded the helicopter when it landed, and everyone stepped back out of the way. Beth took a look around the clearing and thought, absently, that it once must have been a sizeable field that, like every other open area within this watershed, was shrinking with each passing year as the trees encroached further and further into the opening. She saw, where she stood by the riverbank, a large rock that had been split in two, and she stepped up onto the nearest half to watch the helicopter take off. Her friend Tim was one of the pilots, and as she stood there, he looked her way and gave her a smile and the thumbs up as the machine lifted into the air. She gave him a quick wave and a grin and looked up again as she heard thunder over the sound of the helicopter. The rain began to come down, and she thought, briefly, that she was glad that the helicopter didn't have far to transport the victim, given the speed in which this front had moved in. She was surprised that they had flown at all in this weather and thought that maybe she wasn't the only one that had been caught by surprise with this storm.

Through the noise of the lifting helicopter, there was another sudden, loud clap of thunder, and Beth saw the air shimmer as her body began to tingle. She had the illusion of looking through watery glass as people and objects seemed to blur and melt together. Sound and movement became slow motion, and soon all that was going on around her disappeared as though she were wrapped up in an electrified cocoon with a thousand fingers gently poking at her. Her skin rippled with goose flesh and all sound ceased but for an electric buzzing, popping noise.

Suddenly, invisible hands seemed to lift her, and she was thrown backward toward the river. The raindrops sparkled like glitter falling around her as she floated through the air. Beth didn't feel fear, more of a sense of wonderment at what was happening. For an instant, she was reminded of a fairy tale, where the sorceress casts a spell, and with a wave of her hand, the air is filled with the sparkle and shine of magic.

The spell was broken as she landed hard in the water, and she struggled to the surface, gasping for air as the shock of the cold water on her overheated body sucked the breath out of her. The river, swollen from the recent rain, swiftly carried her along, tossing her about as though she were a piece of cork. Coughing and choking on river water, Beth looked around frantically for something to grab hold of as she struggled in vain to get her backpack off, fearing that it would weigh her down or get snagged and drown her. She felt her forehead connect with something as her body slammed into a rock, and she squeezed her eyes shut and ground her teeth together for a moment against the white-hot pain of it, willing herself to focus when she opened them again. Her head was spinning, and she knew that she was going to black out.

Fighting against unconsciousness and the searing pain in her head, Beth spotted a heavy tree branch lying partly in the river in front of her. It was rushing up at her and she forced herself to angle in that direction, fearing for a moment that she would miss it. She could hear the river roaring in her ears as she stretched her arm toward the branch, closing her hand around the very tip of it. The momentum of the current swung her body in, toward the riverbank, driving her once again into the rocks. She lost her grip on the branch and quickly wrapped her other arm around one of the rocks. Pulling herself in closer, she wedged her body into the rocks, feeling a wave of nausea wash over her as everything around her began to spin and then went black as she passed out, blood running from her forehead and mixing with the river water.

May 15, 1908

It was a bright, sunny spring day. Everything had that clean, fresh look that always comes after a spring rain. Liam stood in the chilly water of the river. He'd found a free hour and was spending it doing one of his favorite activities. Fly fishing in the river behind his house was the ultimate in relaxation. He could let his mind drift with the river, forgetting for a time the pressures of being a rural doctor. He'd been up almost all night with a difficult delivery. After a few hours of sleep, he went to check on the new mother and her baby and took care of a few things in town. Now he had a few moments to himself. He led a solitary life, surrounded by the people of this hill-town community in Western Massachusetts, but not always a part of them. He'd grown up here, but he had left for a few years for medical school and other things. But his heart was always here in these hills, and so he returned to help the people whose Scots-Irish ancestry he shared.

He had fallen in love and become engaged while he was completing his training in Boston. He brought Lily back with him and told her of his plans to return there for good to practice medicine. A few weeks before the wedding, she broke off the engagement, stating that she wouldn't be the wife of a poor country doctor and would not live away in the country. Even though he hadn't said anything to his family, it had hurt him deeply that she hadn't been able to accept his love for these hills and the people in them. She hadn't even tried. From then on, he had immersed himself in building his practice and taking care of his patients. Now, at thirty-three, he had decided that he was fine on his own, and he had chosen to be a doctor here over having a wife, believing that he could not have both.

He found his position as a country doctor rewarding and enjoyed the challenge of tending to the physical and sometimes emotional health of these people who were his neighbors and friends. He had known most of them his entire life and worked hard to earn and maintain the trust that they had placed in him as one of their own. Lily had been right; he wasn't getting rich here, but he did all right. And he didn't need to be rich. Sometimes his patients would pay him with vegetables for the winter or a side of beef or hay for his horse. Sometimes the payment was a promise. He accepted whatever mode of payment they had, be it cash or goods or services, knowing that these were good, hardworking people who would never let a debt go unpaid.

Something caught his eye, something that was out of place in the familiar landscape of the river. At first, he thought it was some log that had washed downstream during the quick rain that had come down earlier that morning. But then he realized that he was looking at an arm draped across a rock. Dropping his fly rod, he ran over and saw a body lodged against the rocks. Because of the clothing, he thought that it was a man, but as he leaned over the body, he realized that he was looking at a woman's face. She had a deep cut on her forehead, with blood seeping out and collecting in her hair. Putting his fingers to her neck, he felt for her carotid artery and found a pulse. Her skin was ice cold, but she was alive. It briefly crossed his mind that she was not dressed like any other woman he had seen before, but he was too busy assessing her injuries to dwell on it. He removed the strange pack on her back. When he went to feel her ribs, he noticed that she had some sort of strange belt around her waist and a gun in a holster! Her body felt hard. He opened a couple of the buttons on the front of her shirt and saw that she had something on under it that was acting like a shell around her body. Regardless of how strangely she was dressed, she was injured and needed his help. He picked her up and carried her across the grass to his house.

CHAPTER II

He sat watching her. There was something vaguely familiar about her, yet at the same time, he knew that she was no one that he had met before. He wondered where she was from and how she had come to be in the river, injured.

Looking at her, he thought that she was not unattractive. Not necessarily pretty either. She was interesting, he decided, with a somewhat narrow face leaning toward plainness. He studied her face, relaxed now in her sleep. He looked at her dark eyelashes, resting on smooth skin covering high cheekbones. Her mouth was somewhat wide, almost too wide for her face, but her lips were full and nicely shaped nonetheless. Her hair was a deep auburn color and was spread out on the pillow around her head in soft, curling waves. It had been up on the back of her head, and he had loosened it when he got her out of her damp clothes and into the bed, piling blankets on top of her for warmth. She looked to be in her late twenties, perhaps early thirties, with a slim, strong body. He noticed that her eyes were a deep rich brown when he had checked her pupils after looking at the cut on her forehead.

He had cleaned the area around the cut, which had been deep and jagged, then stitched it closed, taking small precise stitches to try to minimize the scar that she would have. Reaching into the bowl on the table next to the bed, he wrung out a cloth and cleaned the dried blood from her hair. Her shoulder was scraped up, but aside from cleaning the abrasions, there was little more that he needed to do for that. But it, and her head, would hurt when she woke up. He laid his hand on her cheek and found that her skin was warming up.

He got up and went to check her clothes. He had never seen anything like these before. Was she with some branch of the military? Surely not a woman. But there was a patch on the shirtsleeve that said State Conservation Officer and a silver badge on the front of her shirt that said Commonwealth of Massachusetts. He looked again at the belt that had been around her waist, with the strange buckle. He still wasn't sure how he got it to release, and what was the strange material that all this was made of? And what of the black shell that she had worn around her body? He picked it up. It was flexible but hard at the same time. It looked like it was some sort of protection for her torso, like old-fashioned armor. But it, too, was made of a strange material. And why would she need to wear something like this?

He reached for her backpack, telling himself that as her physician, he needed to know more about his patient. He opened the pack. It was made of a similarly strange material. Inside he found a black leather wallet. Opening it, he saw another badge like the one on her shirt. There was a piece of paper with her picture on it. She was wearing the same clothes. It said that she was Officer Elizabeth Blodgett and that she was a conservation officer with the Commonwealth of Massachusetts. The date of employment was September 27, 1999. How could this be? This was impossible! Attached to her backpack was a clear flat packet that had a map of some sort in it. He opened it and found that the map was dry. Interesting. He opened up the map and looked at it. After a bit of studying, he realized that it was a map of this area, only different. He looked at the legend on the edge of the map and saw that the date of printing of the map was 2001. What was happening?

He looked again at the woman. He was a man of science. He had to keep an open mind and consider all of the possibilities. Could she, somehow, have come from another time, from the future? But how? Or was this some manner of elaborate hoax? If that were the case, then someone had gone to a great deal of trouble. He reached for her clothes and began to go through her pockets. He found her compass. It didn't look like the compass he owned. He found a strange knife in a pocket on the side of her trousers. A woman wearing trousers? And why would she need to carry a gun and a knife? He found paper money and looked at the dates: 2002, 2001, 1998, and 2004. It was different from the money he was used to. There were coins as well, all with similar dates. Aside from her name, he was only getting more questions from this. He shook his head and put everything aside, turning his attention back to the bed.

She had come to a couple of times, briefly, then passed out again, lying still and pale in the bed. Now she had finally slipped into a normal sleep. He felt that she was no longer in danger, and with one last touch to the side of her face, he went out of the room.

When Beth awoke, she saw that it was dark outside. She moved her head and felt sharp pain. Lord! What a headache! She was lying in bed in a strange room. Where was she anyway? She propped herself up on her elbows to look around but laid back down again almost immediately; her shoulder hurt, and her head swam. She tried it again using her left elbow to prop herself up and slowly surveyed the room around her, moving her head carefully. The only light came from an oil lamp on the table next to the bed, bathing the space around her in a warm golden light, fading to shadow by the time it reached the corners of the room. The bed was a big spindle bed, similar to her own at home, with a quilt on it. In the shadows, she saw that there was a large dresser with a mirror above, a small table with a pitcher and basin, a bookcase with books stacked anyhow on it, and a wardrobe. Next to the wardrobe was a straight-back chair and above that were pegs on the wall. She saw her uniform and body armor hanging from the pegs, along with some other shirts. Her duty belt and pack were on the floor next to the chair, along with her boots. There was a fireplace with a small woodstove in it on one of the outside walls and two doors in the opposite wall. One of them was slightly ajar.

As she was looking at this door, it opened all the way and a man walked in. Beth guessed that he was around thirty, with a solid-looking build and probably not more than three or four inches taller than her five feet seven inches. A shock of thick sandy hair was falling down across his forehead, and she watched him reach up to absently brush it back with strong-looking fingers while he watched her study him. His face was youthful, with laugh lines beginning to form around his mouth and eyes, and he looked like someone who people would like at first glance. As he approached the bed, she noticed that his hair was sun-streaked, as though he spent time outside. His eyes were an amber color and he was, she thought, an appealing man.

He picked up the chair, putting it down next to the bed. "How are you feeling?" he asked. As he spoke, he leaned over, peering into her eyes one at a time. She pulled away slightly, and he said, "It's all right, I'm a physician. I fished you out of the river and brought you here."

She studied him warily for a bit. "I have a real corker of a headache, but I guess that I'm going to live." She saw him smile at her words. She continued, "What happened to me, and where am I? And who are you?"

He sat looking at her for a moment and then replied, "I guess that we should start off with introductions. My name is William Sizer. As I said, I'm a physician, and my friends and family call me Liam. And you are Elizabeth Blodgett."

She looked at him. Doctor William Sizer—why did she feel that she should know this man? Yet she knew that she had never met him before. And his voice—it was warm and smooth, the timbre gentle and fluid. It reminded Beth of a fine scotch whiskey at the end of a long cold day. It would start somewhere around the middle of your breast and warm you from the inside out. Clearing away the thought, she replied, "Yes, I am Elizabeth Blodgett. But where am I, and how do you know who I am?" She felt a nervous sensation prickling her spine.

He hesitated before answering, as though composing his thoughts. Finally, he said, "I'm not sure where to start. I have quite a few questions for you, but I guess that I should tell you what I know first."

He paused again briefly before continuing. "I found you lying in the river behind the house here early this afternoon. You were unconscious, wearing those clothes over there." He turned and indicated her uniform hanging on the pegs. "I don't know how long you were there before I spotted you, but it's around midnight, now. You've been out for hours."

"You have a bad cut on your forehead, and I've had to put twelve stitches on you to close it up. I'm sure that it's fairly sore right now, and it will be so for a few days. You took quite a knock on the head from something, so it will ache for a time, and you'll probably feel dizzy if you move too fast. You have a slight concussion. Also, your right shoulder is scraped up fairly bad as well."

Beth put her fingers to her forehead as he was speaking and gingerly felt for the stitches, wincing when she made contact with them.

The doctor went on, "As for where you are—you're in my house. I know your name because I found a card with your picture on it in your pack over there." Again, he nodded toward her uniform. He hesitated before saying, "I went through your pack and your pockets, trying to get some answers, and I apologize for the invasion of your privacy. Please don't be alarmed that you and I are alone here, but I think it's best not to have anyone else here until you and I have talked."

She had closed her eyes to help ease the pain of her headache. She thought to herself that that was a strange remark. Struggling past her headache, she thought that she had to keep her wits about her until she sorted out what was going on.

Doctor Sizer then asked, "What is your date of birth?"

Without thinking, or opening her eyes, she replied, "August 16, 1978. Why?"

Without answering, he asked, "What is today's date?"

Sensing a tension in his voice, she opened her eyes and looked at him. He was leaning toward her slightly, as though her answer carried the weight of the world. "Today is May 15, 2008. Why? The last thing that I remember is that I was standing next to the river watching the helicopter take off, just after noon. Now it's dark outside. What time did you say it was? Strange that no one has come looking for me. Again, where am I?" The prickly sensation came again along her spine—demanding, more insistent.

Beth pulled herself further up against the pillows, watching him quizzically. He was looking at her the same way. She thought to herself that she had better pull it together and think about getting out of this place. "What is it?"

Slowly, he answered, "You are correct about the day. Today is the fifteenth of May. But you are mistaken about the year. This is 1908."

"C'mon! Do I look like I'm in a mood to be messed with?"

"Pardon me?"

"Quit screwing with me!" She threw back the quilt and began to get out of the bed, trying to ignore the wave of nausea that came over her.

"You know what? I need to use your phone to call my dispatcher to let them know where I am. If I've been missing all afternoon then they'll be looking for me. I don't suppose, Doctor, that you notified anyone that I'm here?" She paused, breathing in sharply between her clenched teeth, trying to ease the wave of nausea and dizziness that now had control of her body.

He put his hands on both of her arms and pushed her back into the bed. She was amazed at how weak she felt. "You'll just sit back for now while we sort this whole thing out! I'm not sure who you need to 'call' or exactly what a 'phone' is, unless you're referring to a telephone. But the closest one of those is three miles away, at Perkin's Store in town. But something tells me that whoever may be looking for you will not find you. I have to make you understand what I think is happening. Please just sit here for five minutes! Please wait at least that long before trying to get up again! Besides, you're in no condition to go anywhere." With that, he got up and quickly left the room.

Beth watched his back as he disappeared thru the door and tried again to get up from the bed. She sat back down, gripping the edge of the mattress until her knuckles stood out white against her skin. Her head was spinning and her legs were wobbly. She took a deep breath and stood up again, fighting back the nausea and buzzing in her head.

She didn't know what was going on, but this "doctor" was obviously deranged! She had to get out of here. There were no buildings within the watershed where she had been searching, only cellar holes! How had she come to be here, in this man's house? How far away was she? He had said that Perkin's Store was three miles away. The watershed was about three miles from the center of town, as the crow flies, where the store was. But again, there weren't any homes in the watershed. There was nothing but woods and trails.

She made it to the pegs on the wall where her uniform hung and was reaching for her trousers, one hand braced against the wall, when she heard his footstep outside the door. Reaching down, she picked up her duty belt as she heard him enter the room. She turned and leaned against the wall, holding the belt in her left hand with her right hand on the grip of her pistol, which she then pulled out of the holster. There was a thunderstorm raging in her head, and her shoulder was throbbing.

Liam froze when he saw her turn and draw her pistol. He was carrying a calendar, some postals that he had received the afternoon before, and his journal where he entered all of his medical calls into. He held his hands out toward her, offering the items to her for inspection.

"Look here—these are all proof of the date. I assure you, there is no need for you to use your weapon here! I mean you no harm. I can only imagine what you must be feeling at this moment. I, too, am confused. Please! Let's sort this out together!"

Beth was frozen with indecision. He seemed as confused as she was. But this was science fiction stuff. People didn't travel through time in real life! On the other hand, who would go to all of this trouble to trick her? No one that she could think of. It was true that she had made some enemies while doing her job, but none of them would go to these lengths. Why would anyone try to put her on this way? She stared at him from across the room through the haze of her headache and nausea.

He was now silently pleading with his eyes. She looked again around the room. She didn't see any light switches or lamps or wall outlets in the dim light from the bedside lamp. Not even a clock radio. Nothing had a "modern" look to it, that was for sure. Her eyes came back to the man again.

"Put them down on the bed and go stand against the wall." Her voice was cold and hard.

He walked over to the bed and set everything down. Then he walked backward until he felt the wall behind him, keeping his eyes on her the whole time. She looked confused and frightened, but he was impressed with the control that she had over her fear. He knew, too, that she was in a great deal of pain.

She put her duty belt over her left shoulder and walked over to the bed, picking up the calendar. It was an old style, but the paper didn't look old. The month and year were May 1908. She picked up the mail and looked at the postage dates. May 10, 1908. May 9, 1908. The handwriting looked so old-fashioned. They were addressed to Dr. William Sizer, Maple Hill, Corsehill, MA. Last, she opened the cover of the ledger and began looking at the dates. It began with January 1908. The last entry was for "Mrs. Franklin King, a baby girl, 3:21 a.m." The date was May 15, 1908. She looked over at him. He hadn't moved.

He was staring at her. His throat sounded dry when he spoke, and he stopped to clear it. "I know. It seems impossible to believe. Everything that I have tells you that it is 1908. Everything that you carry tells me that it is 2008. One of us has traveled one hundred years. It's you, not I, that have done so."

Beth sat down on the bed with one leg tucked under her, unable to stand on her own any longer. She felt a ripple of goose flesh rise on her skin, and she shivered slightly.

"No. No, this can't be. This can't be happening." She closed her eyes and began to shake her head then thought better of it as the pain in her head was already bad enough.

"I'm afraid that it is." As he spoke those words, Liam felt a tug of fascination creep along the edges of his mind. He was a man who followed logic and fact. Yet here was this woman in front of him, and he could find no logical explanation for her presence. But the fact was, she was here. *What do we do now?* he wondered.

Beth exhaled heavily, thinking to herself that she must be dreaming, but knowing that she wasn't. What was she going to do now? Absently, she dropped the belt from her shoulder onto the bed but kept her pistol in her hand and looked down at her attire. It suddenly occurred to her that she wasn't wearing her own clothes. In fact, she wasn't wearing much of anything at all. It was a man's shirt, buttoned up to the top without a collar, like the one he wore. It came about halfway down her thighs.

He saw her looking at herself and quickly began to offer an explanation and apology, "I'm sorry if you're embarrassed by your attire. I had to get you out of your wet clothing, and that was the best that I could offer."

To himself, he was thinking how very appealing she looked in his shirt. He flushed slightly at that thought as he realized that she was, after all, his patient.

Picking up the calendar again, Beth absently replied, "It's fine. All the important parts are covered. Besides, what would it matter if they weren't? You've obviously seen the entire me."

Looking up at him, she said, "Anyway, I'm not embarrassed, but I think that you are. Don't be. I should tell you that if we are, in fact, a hundred years apart, men and women are much more relaxed around each other in my time than in yours. We don't feel the need to cover quite so much of ourselves. Like I said, the important parts are covered."

Liam stood there, feeling ill at ease with her frank speech. He was a doctor, a professional; he was seldom uncomfortable around his patients. Why was this woman making him feel so off balance? Besides, it wasn't as though he had never seen a woman's leg. It must be the gun, not her bare legs.

"Look, do you think that, perhaps, you could put your weapon aside now? We need to work together to solve this puzzle." Looking closely at her, he saw that she was pale as a ghost, the fresh incision standing out bright against her white skin, which was covered with a faint sheen of sweat. "Also, judging from your color, you're not as strong as you think you are just now. Please trust that I have no intention of harming you in any way. Will you lie back down for now? Let me bring you something to eat, and then we can get started on this."

Beth thought to herself that he was right. Her head felt like it was going to explode. Reluctantly, she nodded, winced at the new pain the action caused, and slid back against the pillows, pulling the blanket over her legs, thinking that if she played it cool and rested, the opportunity to leave would present itself later. But whatever else was going on, her gut told her that this was someone whom she could trust for now.

Out loud, she said, "Let's just say that I'm willing to discuss this a little further." She sat back, laying the pistol down on the bed beside her thigh, her hand resting on top of it. She watched the doctor walk out of the room before closing her eyes. Her headache was killing her.

Liam breathed a quiet sigh of relief as he left the room and headed downstairs to the kitchen. He lit the stove to heat water for tea and cut off a couple of slices from the loaf of bread that his sister, Naomi, had dropped off that morning. That brought a new problem to mind. What if Naomi had come in after he had come back with Elizabeth? She was over here regularly. He would have to tell Elizabeth about her and vice versa.

When the water was ready, he brewed the tea, added some ginger to it, and carried it and the toasted bread up the stairs. He walked into the room and saw that her eyes were closed. He thought that she was sleeping, but she opened them when she heard him step into the room. Seeing that her hand was still on top of her gun, he thought to himself that he couldn't really blame her for being so cautious. He would have to show her that he meant her no harm.

"When was the last time that you had something to eat?" he asked.

"I guess it's been about a hundred years." She gave him a sudden, unexpected smile.

For a moment, Liam stared at her as her appearance was transformed with that brief smile, and he realized how wrong he had been when he had characterized her face as plain. Framed within the tousled waves of her chestnut hair, all of her face smiled with the simple act of turning up the corners of her mouth. Her lips softened, her eyes sparkled, even her cheekbones seemed to take on new structure. He hadn't expected that and, realizing with a start that he was staring, smiled back at her.

Beth noticed that he had a warm engaging smile. "My last meal was breakfast this morning. Of whatever year you want to call it. And, in spite of how my head hurts, I'm feeling hungry."

"That's a good thing. You can eat first. Then we'll talk about how you could have come to be here."

Balancing the plate of toast on her lap, Beth took the cup and saucer that he held out to her, taking a cautious sip. Ginger—there was ginger in the tea, and it triggered a hazy recollection for her. She took another sip.

"This tea tastes familiar to me, like I've had it before."

Liam nodded. "You have."

"Why don't I remember it?"

"As I said earlier, you were unconscious when I found you. You came to a couple of times briefly. You were pretty sick—vomiting—because of your head injury. I gave you ginger tea to help your stomach."

Beth remembered now, dimly, leaning forward over a basin while he held it in one hand and her hair back away from her face with the other. She heard, through the haze of pain, his reassuring voice telling her that she would soon be better as he bathed her face with a cool cloth. She recalled him sitting next to her on the bed, holding a cup to her mouth. Again, that same calming voice telling her to take small sips, that she would be all right, as the warm drink soothed her throat and calmed her nausea.

"You did far more than simply brew some tea for me. Thank you." She gingerly touched her stitches, adding, "Thank you for everything."

Liam smiled back at her. "You're welcome. Now eat your toast, slowly, and finish the tea."

While she was eating, Liam asked her what sort of things she did that would require her to dress the way she had been when he found her. Or carry a gun, which she obviously knew how to use.

She smiled at the expression on his face. "Well. Where do I begin with this? First, I guess, I'll tell you that I am a police officer, a game warden. But, come to think of it, Massachusetts won't have game wardens here for another five years or so, provided that this really is 1908. And the first woman won't become one for about another seventy years, give or take. Nonetheless, that is what I am. Primarily, I enforce the fish and game laws. I catch poachers and protect our natural resources. Also, because we are all so adept at tracking and reading sign, we do a lot of search and rescue. That is, we look for people who are lost, or injured, or trying to evade capture. In my time, there are a lot of people who hike for recreation. Many of them are ill equipped for this. I was on a search today when whatever it is that happened to me happened."

She saw his expression and asked, "Why are you looking at me like that? Oh, wait! Let me guess—is it because I'm a woman?"

He nodded, looking skeptical. What she was telling him was unheard of. Scandalous, actually.

"Well! Let me tell you that many things have changed in a hundred years. Right now, you are on the brink of huge changes in the world. Women vote! Women are in the military! Women can work just about any job that they put their minds to. They are scientists, doctors, engineers, and construction workers. They head up large corporations or hold political office. Not just the odd, independent one here and there, but many women everywhere! Look at me—I'm a police officer, a game warden. I enforce the law and make arrests. But then, some women still choose to be homemakers, to have children and take care of their families while the husbands support the family. My sister is like that." With the thought of her sister, she paused.

Sensing what she was thinking, Liam asked, "How many siblings do you have? Are you married? Do you have a husband?"

"No, I'm not married. I have a brother and a sister. They are both older than me, I'm the baby." She paused before going on. "Doctor, do you think that I will see them again? Or my parents? What will they think happened to me? How will I get back to where I came from?"

"Please, call me Liam."

She had finished eating by now. Liam took her empty plate and put it on the table next to the bed. He sat back in the chair and crossed his ankle over his knee, folding his hands on his lap. He sat there for a moment, studying her. It occurred to him that much had changed since he got out of that bed this very morning.

"I really don't know how you got here or how to get you back to where you came from. This all seems like so much to contemplate. But we must look at it. Tell me exactly what happened in the last moments that you remember."

She began to relate the search to him and continued on about standing next to the river watching the helicopter lift off. "I'll explain a helicopter to you later," she told him when she saw the question in his eyes. She related how the thunderstorm had moved in so quickly and how the air felt alive around her. She paused and asked him if there had been a thunderstorm here this afternoon as well.

"Yes, there was. And it came on the same way as the one that you're describing. It came in quickly, but I don't think that it had the same intensity as yours. There were only a couple of rumbles of thunder and one, single loud crack."

Chewing on her bottom lip, she thought about it a moment. "Okay, so we both had a thunderstorm this afternoon. Obviously, there is one connection with that. I was thrown backward into the river. Does that mean that I was struck by lightning? Wouldn't I have a burn on me somewhere?"

Liam nodded.

"But I don't. I just cut my head open and hurt my shoulder. I'm sore, and feel like there are bruises popping up all over me, but I think that we can assume that those injuries occurred when I was in the river. So, how did I end up coming back one hundred years? You do believe that this morning I was alive and well in 2008, don't you?"

Liam nodded again.

"And I guess that I do believe that I am in 1908, for now. I don't have a choice, I guess." She continued on, "So it must have had something to do with the way that the air felt. Remember, I said that it felt—almost—alive around me? I had the illusion of being . . . cut off, I guess you'd say, from the others. And I remember that my fingertips were prickling too."

She rubbed her temples, wincing, as she got too close to her stitched wound. "Could you hand me my backpack, please? I have some pain reliever in my first aid kit. I should have thought of it sooner. This headache is really killing me."

"I could give you some laudanum, now that you're awake and have had some food."

Beth laughed and said "Absolutely not! Just my pack, please."

Liam looked at her curiously but got up and retrieved her pack. He was already finding that he could learn something from this woman. He watched while she fished out a kit with a red cross on it and took out a capped vial. She shook out two small white tablets and washed them down with the rest of her tea.

Turning to set the cup and saucer on the table, she grimaced, saying, "Ugh. Talk about your bad days."

"That," laughed Liam, "is an understatement! What were those? Aspirin?"

"Acetaminophen. Five hundred milligrams each." She handed the bottle to him. "Perfect for a headache. It's sort of like aspirin, which is widely used in my time. I know that aspirin hasn't been around here for that long, but it will show its worth in the years to come. It even helps to prevent a heart attack. But isn't laudanum still used primarily now? And morphine? Sometime soon, they will become strictly regulated when they are finally recognized as highly addictive opiates."

Liam looked thoughtful. "Laudanum is very widely used. It's prescribed for everything. Morphine too for that matter. I can't imagine that the decision to regulate either one will be eagerly accepted. I use them in my practice." He shook his head, putting these thoughts away for later.

"But let's get back to your situation. Something, obviously, occurred when you were thrown into the river. I agree that the way the air around you felt was probably what caused you to be sent here somehow. Maybe we should walk upriver and try to find the spot where you were standing. We could try to do it tomorrow, depending on how you are feeling, but I don't think that you'll be ready for that for a couple of days. But I'm not sure how, or if, we could reproduce what happened. Maybe we would have to wait for another storm."

Beth nodded and then was thoughtful for a moment. "I'm curious about something else. Where, exactly, are we right now? I know that we are in Corsehill. But I'm wondering how far downriver my body traveled after I became unconscious."

What she wasn't saying was that what was a watershed here in the southwest corner of town in her time had once been a populated and thriving area up until the late twenties when the properties were seized by eminent domain and turned into a reservoir and watershed for drinking water for a nearby city. There had been shops and mills along the river, utilizing the water for power. It was strange to think that she was sitting in a home that, in twenty years or so, would no longer be there, and that throughout her life, she had taken hikes in this area and climbed around the cellar holes of the homes that weren't actually under the reservoir. Perhaps even this one. She decided to keep these thoughts to herself.

"I found a map in that clear holder on your backpack," answered Liam. "I assumed that it is a map of this area, although I didn't really study it closely. I got sidetracked when I saw the date on it. Perhaps you could show me on the map where you were standing, and we can find the house from there. You're on Maple Hill Road now. I don't think that you could have come far, only because that pack of yours was on your back when I found you, and I think that it would have had you facedown in the water if you were floating unconscious."

Rubbing her temples again, Beth said, "I remember thinking as I landed in the water that I should get my pack off or it would drown me. I must've hurt my shoulder when I was struggling with it. I was getting tossed all over the place, and I was trying to keep my head out of the water at the same time. How lucky was I to be found by you, a doctor? What were you doing there anyway?" she asked as she dropped her hands back to her lap.

"I was fishing. I had a clear schedule this afternoon. All that I had to do was check in on Mrs. King and her baby and make a couple of other short stops. After that, I decided to cast some flies about in the river. I had only made a couple of casts before I found you." With that, he smiled at her and found himself absently hoping that she would flash that smile of hers again.

She thought, again, how appealing he was. "Well, I am sorry that I interrupted your date with the trout." With curiosity, she asked, "Are you alone here?"—then hastily added—"What I mean is, do you run your medical practice by yourself? Doesn't that keep you fairly busy?"

"It does keep me busy, usually. They are rare times when I can be fly-fishing in the middle of the day. But then I can't predict when there will be an emergency, so I don't keep regular hours. I learned long ago to take advantage of a few quiet hours. It isn't too bad, since I do live alone here. No one is inconvenienced by my schedule, other than the times when I have made plans with my family . . . my parents or my sister and her husband. But by now they're used to me and my practice."

Liam paused and took a deep breath before continuing, "That brings us to another, more pressing issue. My sister Naomi and her husband Bill live very close by, and she drops by frequently. It will only be a matter of time before you and she meet. We need to decide how to deal with that. Also, and more importantly, you will need something to wear. The clothes that you were wearing when I found you cannot be worn here. A woman in trousers would cause a scandal. And as fetching as you are in my shirt, that will not do either."

Beth smiled as she saw a faint flush of red creep up his neck and wondered what he had just been thinking.

He continued, "We may need to turn to Naomi to help us with that, as my knowledge of the finer points of women's clothing is limited."

Beth leaned back again and closed her eyes. "You're right. I hadn't thought that far ahead. But yes, we do need to address that before I can step out of this house. I suppose too that I'm going to need to figure out where and how I'm to live in this time—for however long I'll be here." She sighed tiredly. "As for your sister as well as her husband and your parents, I'll leave it to your judgment on how much to tell them about me. You know them, I don't. I would prefer that people not know how I came to be here. If I'm to stay around here for however long, then I would rather be treated like any other person and not an oddity. But you would know if your family could help us sort some of this out. As you said, Naomi, anyway, is going to meet me sooner or later. I can't hide away here in your house for the rest of my time here. I don't know what story you could concoct to explain my presence in your home to them. Or for that matter, wearing your shirt." She sighed again and briefly tugged on her bottom lip with her teeth. "When all else fails, tell the truth."

Liam looked at her and suddenly felt great pity for her. He could only imagine how she must be feeling. She had woken up in a strange place, where all that was familiar was gone. She seemed to have accepted what had happened and was coping bravely. He knew that her head was aching fiercely, but she was still managing to focus on getting solutions to the many issues created by this situation. He admired her courage and spirit.

Taking out his pocket watch, Liam said, "It's late, and I should have left you to rest long ago. Why don't we both get some sleep now and tackle this anew in the morning? The first order of business will be my family. Then we'll move on from there."

He reached over and squeezed her hand then let it go: a simple gesture of reassurance that he frequently gave his patients. Standing, he turned down the lamp on the table next to her, until the room was lit only by a dim glow. He then picked up the chair and placed it back against the wall. Picking up the dirty dishes, he said, "I still have many questions for you. And I know that once you have absorbed this, you will have just as many questions for me. I think that tomorrow will be a full day, so get some sleep."

Liam began to walk toward the door. Beth watched him walking away. "Where are you going to sleep? This is your bedroom that I'm in, isn't it? I have put you to quite an inconvenience, haven't I? I'm sorry. And thank you. The words seem so inadequate, yet I don't know what else to say. You didn't ask for any of this, I'm sure, and now I have become your problem. I will repay your kindness, I promise you." There was strong emotion in her voice.

Again, Liam felt for her. He sensed, not for the first time, that she was not a woman who was used to relying on anyone else for help. "I'm glad that I was there to help you." Liam smiled gently at her. "We'll work this out together. I'm as intrigued by it as you are. And don't worry about my sleeping arrangements. I'll be fine." With that, he turned and left, leaving the door ajar slightly.

She lay there, listening to the soft noises of him moving around the house. Soon, everything became quiet. Too quiet. There was no hum of electrical appliances, no glow from a clock radio. Just the dull ticktock of a clock somewhere else in the house.

The pain in her head had eased up some with the pain reliever. Lying alone in the dark, she thought about what had happened and felt herself start to panic.

"What am I going to do? What about my family?" she whispered to the dark. *They'll never know what has happened to me! How long will they search for my body and never find it? Will I ever be able to get back there?* She couldn't imagine never seeing any of her family or friends again. *What if I'm dead—what if this is some strange sort of afterlife? What am I supposed to believe?*

She felt a tear roll down her cheek, followed by another, and another, then a flood of tears. She sighed heavily and thought, *Knock it off. If you're going to get through this, then you had better face it head on and do your best. It can only get fixed if you fix it. Courage, Beth.*

Beth turned her thoughts to William Sizer. Where did she know that name from? She knew the name of Sizer; Aaron Sizer and his sister, Lydia Campbell, along with their respective families, had lived in Corsehill for as long as she could remember. They had been very friendly with Beth's parents and had been a part of her life up until their deaths. She recalled now, riding her bicycle with her sister to Mrs. Campbell's house for "tea parties" when she was small. Mr. Sizer had been a professor of biology and wildlife studies at the State College in Westford, and it was he who had first suggested to her that she consider a career in wildlife law enforcement. They had always been so pleasant to her and treated her as if she were someone special. They always called her Elizabeth instead of Beth like everyone else did. They and their families were very nice people. Hadn't their father been a doctor? Suddenly, it came to her. There was a section in the town library dedicated to Dr. and Mrs. William Sizer, donated by their children. Of course! She had walked past that plaque more times than she could guess at. So the doctor may not be married now, but at some point, he would find a wife; and together, they would have two children. With memories of her childhood and the people that she had known flowing thru her mind like a gentle tonic, she eventually drifted off to sleep.

Downstairs, Liam had spread a blanket on the settee in the front room that he also used as his office. It had been a long day, and he was tired. He tried to clear his mind and sleep, knowing that there was nothing more that could be done tonight. He hoped that no one came knocking on his door this night, needing his help. He didn't want Elizabeth to wake up alone in the house. She intrigued him so! Never had he met a woman like her, even when he had been away from Corsehill for those years. Were all women like that in one hundred years? Or was she unique even then? How long would she be here before she returned to her time? Would she ever return to her time? She spoke as though she would do what she had to in order to make the most of her situation here. Well, if that was the case, then he could help her with that. He and his family. Tomorrow, they would address that. He rolled onto his side and eventually fell asleep.

CHAPTER III

The following morning, Beth woke up slowly. For a moment, she was confused about where she was. It began to come back to her as she looked around the room and saw her clothes hanging on the wall. She gingerly sat up and looked out the window. The sun was just breaking over the tops of the trees. She lay back down, thinking. At least her headache had eased considerably. There was just tenderness around the stitches on her forehead. Her shoulder was sore but not too bad. As she gently flexed the rest of her muscles, doing a sort of inventory of her body, she found that there were some tender spots here and there, and she would probably find some bruises popping up on her skin as well.

Beth recalled her long conversation with the doctor the previous night and wondered if she would meet the rest of his family today. How would they react? What were they like? She thought of her own family and quickly pushed those thoughts aside, making herself focus on her current dilemma.

She thought about what life in 1908 would be like for her. How ironic for her that her parents, especially her mother, had instilled such an interest in the past in her. And also that her great-grandfather, as well as her great,-great-grandmother, had kept journals for all of their adult lives. She had read them all several times, and it had given her glimpses into everyday life of this era and later. It had sparked her interest so much so that when she went to college, she majored not only in criminal justice but in history as well. Maybe it wasn't so ironic. In thinking on it, it occurred to her that her parents had been nudging her in that direction her whole life. Could they have known somehow that this would happen to her? But how? Wait! She was in the past, they hadn't even been born yet. Maybe she left word to them somehow. Could that be? And they never said anything to her? But then how could they not? If they had told her about this, then it could have been prevented. She couldn't imagine her parents letting this happen to her. Maybe they never knew. Perhaps she would be able to find her way back and return in the same moment that she had disappeared. That was a possibility, wasn't it? The intensity of her headache was coming back. Pushing the blanket back with a sigh, she got out of bed and headed for the door.

She walked out into a hallway. There was another door across from the one she came out of. It was closed, and she assumed it was another bedroom. She was standing at the top of the stairs, and turned to look out the window in the hallway. She saw that she was looking down toward the river. The lawn sloped gently toward it from the house and there were a couple of chairs and a bench on the grass between two large apple trees. She went down the stairs, padding softly in her bare feet.

When she got to the bottom step and looked around, she saw that she was in a hallway with wide pine flooring that ran from the front of the house to the back, with an outside door on each end. She looked around and didn't see any light switches or electrical outlets in the plaster walls. To her left was a doorway. She peeked inside and saw that it was the dining area and kitchen. There was a big oblong table with six chairs around it in the front of the room. Walking into the room, Beth saw that there was a stand clamped to one end of the table for tying flies, and a wooden tray with feathers and hooks and colored silk thread in it. Some books and other papers were lying on the table as well. The table faced a couple of windows at the front of the house, and Beth walked over to look out.

A porch was running across the front of the house, with rose bushes climbing up trellises on either side of the steps. Looking past the porch, there was a dirt drive widening out and ending to her left in front of a sizeable barn with a cupola and weathervane on the roof and an open front carriage shed attached with a wagon and buggy backed in. It looked like there was an addition being built on to the other side of the barn. There was a dark bay horse grazing in a pasture beyond it. On the other side of the drive was a dirt road, separated from the drive by a strip of grass, a stone wall, and a line of maple trees. Looking at the road, Beth couldn't see any utility poles or electrical wires.

She turned back to the room that she was standing in. The front portion, where she stood, was obviously the dining area. The walls were covered with wainscot on the bottom half and whitewashed plaster above. The other end of the room was the kitchen, with old-fashioned looking appliances, and the walls were covered with the same wainscot as the lower half of the dining area. It seemed spartan compared to the kitchens that Beth was familiar with. There was a gas/wood cook stove, an icebox, and a sink with drain boards on both sides, along with a hutch built into the wall between the two back windows. She noticed another bigger hutch built into the wall between the dining and kitchen areas. This one displayed dishes with blue flowers on a white background, six or eight glasses, a set of candlesticks, and some bowls. Looking closer, Beth found that both hutches had been embellished with whimsical carvings of leaves and birds. They were beautifully done. In the middle of the kitchen was a sturdy oak worktable, its surface scoured to near white. Seeing the tray with her dishes from the night before sitting on the table, she smiled to herself, thinking that no matter what year you were in, most men never had a problem leaving dirty dishes until tomorrow.

There was another door on the inside wall in the kitchen area, and walking through it, she found herself at the back end of the hallway. Here, there were a couple of coats and hats, as well as a wicker fishing creel, hanging on hooks above a small bench, and some fishing gear leaning against the wall next to the back door. She looked out across a small back porch and saw the river on the other side of the lawn.

Walking across the hall, she looked through another doorway into the only other room on the first floor. This room was directly under the bedroom that she had slept in. There was a desk toward the back of the room and several bookcases built in around the windows, loaded with books. There was a fireplace halfway down the outside wall. Toward the front of the room were a settee, a wooden rocking chair, and a leather armchair. Next to the armchair was a round wooden table with several books piled on it. There was a braided rag rug on the floor.

Beth stepped into the room and froze when she saw Dr. Sizer sound asleep on the settee. She had assumed that he was asleep in the other room upstairs. She stood looking at him. He was lying on his back, with a surprisingly strong-looking arm draped across his eyes and a hand resting on his chest. The blanket was down around his stomach, and she noticed a light sprinkling of hair across his bare chest. Embarrassed, she quietly backed out of the room and went into the kitchen.

She leaned against the worktable in the kitchen and chewed on her bottom lip while she collected her thoughts. She really had evicted him from his bed, hadn't she? One more thing that she would put on her quickly growing list of kindnesses that she would repay to Doctor Sizer.

Not knowing what else to do, Beth went back upstairs and made the bed that she had slept in. Maybe the doctor would be awake by the time she had finished that.

She took her time tidying up and came back downstairs to find that the house was still quiet. Looking in the room from the bottom of the stairs, she saw that the doctor hadn't moved. By now, the sun was fully up. Well, she thought, I can return his kindness from last night by making some breakfast. How hard can it be to master a 1908 kitchen?

She went back into the kitchen and took a good look at the stove. She thanked her parents again for giving her such an interest in "old" things. Thanks to them, she might actually be able to manage here. After nearly a box of matches, she got the beast going and, looking around, found some coffee and started the pot going on the stove. She opened the icebox and looked inside. She smiled, feeling delighted that she was actually getting to use this stuff instead of just looking at it or reading about it. Inside the icebox, she found a bowl of eggs and a ball of butter. On the cutting board was the rest of the loaf of bread from the night before. She found a knife and cut some off.

Liam leaned against the doorjamb, watching her move around his kitchen. It had been nice to wake up to the smell of coffee. He smiled at the expression on her face as she figured everything out. Obviously, kitchens in her time were different. She stepped back from the stove, chewing on her bottom lip. He noticed that this was something that she did when she was thinking. She absently reached down to scratch the side of her leg, lifting the hem of the shirt while she did so. Once again, he admired the way she looked in his shirt. She had very shapely legs. He cleared his throat and walked into the room.

"That coffee smells good. Are you finding your way around all right? How are you feeling?"

Beth jumped and turned at the sound of his voice. "Good morning, Doctor! It's a little bit different from what I'm used to, but I'm bumbling along. Would you like some eggs?"

Liam smiled. "Would you, please, call me Liam?"

Beth smiled back and nodded.

They had eaten, and Liam was finishing his coffee, trying not to be too obvious as he picked the coffee grounds out of his cup. Beth was looking over some of the flies that he had been tying.

"Do you fly-fish?" Liam asked.

"Not really, but I enjoy watching the fly fishermen work over a good pool. I have always felt that I would learn one day. My brother and I used to angle for fish when we were kids. We went a lot with my dad or grandfather who was an avid fisherman, or sometimes we would just go after the little brook trout in the stream below our house. And of course, as a game warden, I'm around fishermen quite a bit. If you don't mind, I would like to go along with you sometime. I know that some men consider fly-fishing a solitary activity, so I'd understand if you don't want me to come along." She picked up one of his flies. "You've got some interesting combinations here. I'd like to see them in action."

Liam got up and walked around the table to where she sat and reached past her to pick up another fly. Sitting down next to her, he said, "This is one that I use quite a bit. The trout are attracted to it more than any other in the spring. And while I generally do cast flies alone, I don't mind company occasionally." Smiling, he said, "I can teach you, as long as you promise not to get better at it than me!"

Smiling back at him, Beth crossed her heart with her index finger and held up her right hand. They sat looking at each other for a moment in comfortable silence.

"Well," said Beth, "I guess that we had . . ."

As she was speaking, the back door opened and a woman's voice called out hello.

Liam looked at Beth and said, "Oh, no! Not yet!" as he jumped out of his chair to stand in front of her.

A woman walked into the kitchen, and Beth knew immediately that this was Naomi. Her hair was the same color as Liam's, and she had the same friendly features on her face. She was about the same height as Beth and obviously pregnant. Beth was unsure of what to do and looked at Liam standing in front of her, deciding to leave it to him.

Composed now, Liam said, "Naomi. Good morning. What brings you out and about so early?"

She was frozen in the kitchen doorway, clearly confused and looking slightly uncomfortable.

Liam took a step to the side and half turned toward Beth. He caught her eye and gave her a reassuring wink. She gave a short nod, as if to say, "Go ahead."

"I would like you to meet my friend, Elizabeth Blodgett. We have some things to tell you, so why don't you come sit down?"

Naomi opened her mouth to speak, but Liam interrupted with, "Please. Just come sit." She closed her mouth and nodded, then walked over to the table, sitting down across from them. Liam picked up the coffee pot to pour another cup, thought better of it, and sat back down next to Beth.

Liam asked, "Can I get you anything?" When she shook her head, he began, "I know what your first question is. Why is this woman sitting at my table wearing one of my shirts? Am I right?"

Naomi nodded, her face flushing red.

"She's wearing my shirt because I do not own a dress, and right now, neither does she."

Beth smiled and looked at him out of the corner of her eye. She did like his humor. Naomi looked more confused than ever.

Beth spoke up, "Naomi, we have a story to tell you, and I think that I'm going to need your help. I know that you don't know me, and I'm not making a very good first impression, but I hope that you and I can be friends once you've heard what we have to say."

Beth and Liam began to tell Naomi what had happened. Naomi sat silently through the narration, looking from one to the other with her eyes wide. When they were finished, she looked up at Beth's forehead, where the stitches were, as though for confirmation. Then she folded her hands on the table and cleared her throat.

"I believe you, of course. It's too fantastic for you to have made it up! And I agree that you probably shouldn't share this story with anyone other than our family. For all sorts of good reasons. And at some point, you should go back up the river to locate the spot where you went in. Maybe it will reveal something to you. But I also agree that you *must* have some decent clothes before you take one step out of this house!"

She turned to her brother, "Liam! Why didn't you come get me yesterday? I could have helped you both then!" She continued to chatter on, asking questions and giving her thoughts, all the while gently chiding her brother for not calling on her for help.

Beth snuck another look at Liam and saw that he was sipping the last of his coffee and patiently waiting for her to stop. She concluded that this was normal behavior from his sister and that he was used to it. So she leaned back in her chair to wait it out as well.

When Naomi finally paused to catch her breath, Liam asked, "What brought you over here so early? You still haven't told me."

"Oh, yes! Can you blame me for forgetting? Bill said to tell you that your lumber is ready at the mill if you want to go get it. I wanted to catch you before you got busy."

She turned to Beth and said, "Bill is my husband, and he has a saw mill beyond our house down the river a bit. Now let's discuss some clothing for you. What was this 'uniform' that you were wearing when Liam found you in the river? Did you say they were trousers? Like a man wears?"

Beth nodded. Naomi shook her head in shocked disbelief.

"I can loan you some of my clothes. In normal days, we would be about the same size, but I won't need those dresses again until Little Whosit and Whatsit are born. My brother tells me that I'm to have twins. Bill hates it when I refer to them this way. But I can't call them anything else until I know if I have boys or girls or one each!"

Beth laughed. "When are you due?"

Liam answered for her, "In about twelve or thirteen weeks. We'll all be relieved when that day comes!"

Naomi stuck her tongue out at him. Beth smiled at the obvious affection between brother and sister.

He went on, "Why don't I hitch Ned up to the wagon and go fetch my lumber? And Naomi, you could get some of those clothes for Elizabeth, and she can get changed while I'm gone."

He turned to Beth and said, "Barring any emergencies this afternoon, we can take a walk up the river, depending on how you feel later." Beth nodded. "Good, then let's get to it." He rose and turned to Naomi.

"Do you want to wait while I hitch up Ned, and I'll bring you over to the house?"

"Yes. That would be nice. I'll help Elizabeth clean up the dishes here. Let me know when you're ready to go."

Liam caught Beth's eye before turning to head out the door. He gave her a small nod and a reassuring smile.

Beth stood up and gathered their plates and utensils and brought them over to the counter. Naomi began to get up, and Beth said, "Sit, please. There's not much here, and I'm sure that it will only take but a minute for me."

"Thank you. I think that I will stay sitting. My back aches a little this morning, and I don't see it stopping for another three months or so."

She watched Beth work for a minute before asking, "What are kitchens like in your time, Elizabeth?"

Beth laughed. "Is it that obvious that I'm struggling with this? Kitchens, everything for that matter, have come a long way by my time. I'd offer you some coffee, but . . ." She tilted Liam's coffee cup toward Naomi, showing her the grounds in the bottom. "I don't think that I've quite mastered the pot on the stove method yet! And please call me Beth, if you like."

They chatted back and forth about cooking and baking. Beth told Naomi how much she enjoyed cooking and baking and described the differences in ingredients in the recipes that Naomi used and the products available in her time. Naomi offered to help her adjust, and Beth thought to herself, *She's just like her brother. What must their parents be like?*

Liam walked in to tell Naomi that he was ready to leave. Naomi turned to Beth and said, "I'll be back soon, and you can try on some clothes and get out of my brother's shirt."

They went out to the wagon, and Liam helped Naomi climb up, saying, "I forgot my kit. I'll be right back." He ran inside.

Going into the kitchen, he said to Beth, "Thank you for taking so easily to Naomi. She can be a little overbearing, but she has a heart of gold. She'll be able to help us. I'll be back in a little while." With that, he ran into the sitting room and grabbed what looked like two saddlebags off of the desk and went out to the wagon.

Beth watched from the window as the wagon turned onto the road and headed down river. She didn't dare go outside for fear that someone might come along and see her, so she finished tidying up in the kitchen and wandered out into the sitting room. She looked around and finished the assessment that she had begun before she saw Liam sleeping on the settee. The room was cluttered, but in a comfortable, homey way. It was obviously a man's house.

The mantle over the fireplace caught her eye. It had been carved with the same type of leaves and vines that were on the kitchen cupboards, but instead of birds, they were woven in and around hearts. She wondered who had done these carvings and whom they had been done for.

Wandering over to one of the bookcases, Beth looked at the books. Several shelves were devoted to medical books. There were also a few on herbs and plants, which she thought was interesting. She had taken a couple of courses in the uses of herbs and had found them very informative. Maybe she would be able to put some of this knowledge to practical use here. The other bookcase had books that he obviously read for pleasure. She recognized many of the titles as the "classics" that she had grown up with. She saw Charles Dickens, Mark Twain, Robert Louis Stevenson, H.G. Wells, and Hamlin Garland. There was a collection of Walt Whitman's poems and Thomas Hardy's *Far From the Maddening Crowd*. She smiled to see that he had some of her favorites in Sir Walter Scott's *Ivanhoe* and Blackmore's *Lorna Doone*. There were other authors and titles that she did not recognize but thought that, perhaps, she could borrow them from Liam later to read.

Naomi turned to Liam as the wagon pulled out onto the road. "I think that I will like her very much. Her story is incredible! I would be terrified, but she seems to be coping quite bravely. You really should have come and got me! Do you think that she is here to stay, or do you think that she will disappear as quickly as she arrived?"

Liam was thoughtful for a moment. "I don't know. I've been wondering about that myself. I doubt that any of us can answer that question. I agree that she is handling this well. I think that she's a very strong woman. But I think that we should try to help her adjust to her life here, for however long it is, and do what we can to keep where she came from a secret. But we'll have to tell Mother and Dad and Bill too. If she is to be a part of our lives, then they'll need to know the truth. How do you think that we should do it?"

"Probably," retorted Naomi dryly, "the same way that you told me. You were never one to mince words. You're lucky that I didn't deliver my babies right then and there from the shock of seeing a half-dressed woman sharing breakfast with you! And," she added tartly, "an attractive one, at that! Or hadn't you noticed?"

Liam stared straight ahead over Ned's ears and said, "Really? I hadn't noticed how she looked. I've been more concerned with her welfare. After all, I am her doctor and a gentleman." With that, he turned into the dooryard of Naomi's house.

Beth went back upstairs to the bedroom, and her eyes went to her belongings against the wall. She picked up her pack and opened it, remembering that she still had to dry out the contents. She took everything out one at a time and spread them on the floor around her. She always carried spare socks, underwear, and a tee shirt in a plastic bag in her search pack. She thought, *Who would ever have known how valuable these would turn out to be? They may very well be the last real underwear I see for a long, long time, if my understanding of women's undergarments in 1908 is correct!* She set the bag with them aside. She had a couple of energy bars that seemed to be intact in their foil package, and a plastic bottle of water. But the chocolate bar was beyond rescue. Her medical kit was packed in a waterproof container, but her small notebook was soggy, and her leather gloves would need to be laid out to dry. She would need to condition them with something to keep them from stiffening. She would have to ask Liam for some harness soap or something. She found the field kit for cleaning her gun and set that aside with the thought that she would have to strip down her handgun and magazines and give them a good cleaning.

She found her spare compass along with her cell phone and GPS. The latter two would be useless here, so she didn't even try to turn them on. Cell towers and satellites were still a long way off in the future. She pulled out a plastic bag with her digital camera and iPod in it. She carried her camera everywhere with her, and her iPod was something that she had with her on searches for those periods of downtime on long searches that they were given to rest. She would listen to her music and relax or take a nap while the opportunity was there.

Her matches were good in their plastic cylinder, and so were the two ballpoint pens and the pencil. She found her hairbrush and a hair clip in the bottom of the pack, along with a tube of hand cream. She set aside the mosquito repellant and the roll of fluorescent orange tape used for marking trails. She wondered how much of these items she should continue to use. It wasn't the first time that this thought had crossed her mind since she got there. She would probably have to pack away her uniform as well as the body armor, duty belt, and backpack, as everything was made of materials that hadn't even been invented yet. Anything plastic could not be used outside of the house; how could she explain it? She was keenly aware of just how different these everyday items from 2008 were from anything that was here in 1908.

She opened the small pocket on the outside of her pack and found an envelope inside of a plastic bag tucked in there. She pulled it out and recognized her mother's handwriting on it. Her hands were trembling as she held it, remembering that she had stopped at her parent's house on her way out to work (Lord, was it just yesterday morning?). Her mother had disappeared for a few minutes while she was talking with her Dad in the kitchen. They were both acting strangely with her and walked her out to her truck when she left. As she went to get into her truck, both of her parents hugged her hard. She pulled back and asked them what was going on. Her mother replied, "Nothing, honey. We just want you to know that we are very proud of the woman that you have become, and that we love you very much. Always remember that." Her father had put his hand on her shoulder and said, "Now go to work." They had watched her truck until she was out of sight of their house. Shortly after that, she had received the call on her radio about the search and didn't give it any more thought until this moment when she found the envelope.

She opened the bag and took the envelope out. She was turning it over in her hands when she heard Naomi call out that she was back. She set the envelope on the table next to the bed and went out to the head of the stairs. She called out that she was upstairs, and Naomi answered that she would come up.

Naomi sat on Liam's bed with her back against the pillows, watching Beth as she tried on one of the skirts and a blouse that she had brought over. She had giggled when she saw Beth's skimpy underwear, sparking another discussion on the differences between their times. Beth was describing some of the different clothing styles that were accepted for women while Naomi sat, laughing incredulously.

"I'm afraid that it's going to take me a while to get used to wearing a long skirt every day, never mind the petticoat and underdrawers," laughed Beth. "How are you able to get anything done while wearing these things? They seem so restricting. If I'm not careful, I'll be tripping on the hem every time I try to walk."

Naomi laughed and asked, "Just what are you planning on doing?"

"Well," responded Beth, "I don't really know. Normally, I run several days a week and exercise daily. I guess that I can keep up my exercises privately, but running will be out of the question, I suppose."

"You run? From what?"

"No, no, no!" laughed Beth. "I run for sport to keep myself healthy and fit for my work. I have to be in good physical shape for my job. You have to realize that, even in my time, I'm working at a job that is still predominately male oriented. I have to work hard to hold my end up! And there are some dangers associated with my line of work, between dealing with hunters and poachers as well as our search and rescue operations that often take place under less than ideal conditions."

"You like your job, don't you?" asked Naomi.

"Yes. I have found it very rewarding. I was looking forward to a long and good career." She looked over at her uniform. "Now I don't know if I'll ever have the chance to put that uniform on again."

Naomi got up and walked over to her uniform, taking the shirt down from the peg. She held it up and looked at it, then reached over to finger the trousers. She turned to Beth and asked, "Have you given any thought to what you will do here? We'll help you all that we can, you can be sure of that! But something tells me that you are someone who always needs a challenge, aren't you?"

Beth was amazed that Naomi had seen into her so quickly. "I've been wondering a little bit about that, in between trying to figure out what actually happened to get me here, provided I can't find my way back home again. I don't know what I'm going to do to support myself, never mind fit in. I suppose that I will be considered an old maid at my ripe old age of almost thirty, in this time. What do old maids do here anyway?"

Naomi laughed. "How is it that a woman like you is not married? Is there someone? Don't tell me that marriage is done away within one hundred years!"

Laughing, Beth responded, "No, there is, was, no one. Of course, people still get married, but not always. Some couples choose to simply live together without marriage. And so many marriages don't seem to be as strong in my time as they are in this era. Many marriages fail, and the couple divorce. I think that sometimes, people marry too quickly. And I think too that they sometimes give up too quickly. I guess I have been too busy with my career, although marriage always has been something that I wanted. I almost got married, several years ago, but we ended it. I assumed that there would be time later." She shrugged slightly. "Maybe I was wrong. Besides, it has been hard for me to find a man with the job I do. I have a friend at work who has told me that I am a very strong independent woman, and that it still scares a lot of men away. But that's who I am. I don't think that I can change that, and I've yet to meet the man who can handle it."

It's funny, she thought, *that I could open up about this so easily with Naomi after having only just met her.* She had never really discussed it with anyone.

Naomi was busy coming up with a plan. She had seen the way her brother had protected Beth by stepping in front of her when she first walked into the kitchen that morning. And she saw through his excuse to run back in for his medical bags. He never forgot his kit; it went everywhere with him. He needed a strong woman, one that was his equal, and it was time that he gave up being a bachelor. Besides, his practice was getting busier with the growing population in Corsehill and the neighboring hill towns. Maybe he should be thinking of an assistant. Naomi was thinking to herself that maybe it wasn't an accident that Beth had arrived there. Maybe she was sent with a purpose. And maybe her brother was part of that purpose.

Out loud, Naomi asked, "Do you know anything at all about medicine?"

Beth gave Naomi an odd look. *What a strange question*, she thought. "I've been trained in the very basics, as a matter of fact. Why do you ask?"

"I was thinking that maybe you could assist my brother in his practice," said Naomi. "That would give you employment and a way to get out and meet the people who live around us. And you would have Liam there to pave the way while you adjust. Although something tells me that you would manage just fine on your own! If he would agree to that, then we need only to solve your problem of where to live."

Beth considered Naomi's words for a minute. "I could do that, I'm sure. But please, let's talk about it with Liam first and leave it up to him! I don't want to be forced on him if a helper isn't needed." *Liam had been right about Naomi,* Beth thought, *she did tend to take charge.* She was thinking, though, that it would be far less frightening to have a familiar face at her side.

Giving herself a mental shake, she said, "That's enough about me and my problem. How do I look in your clothes?" She had been getting dressed while they talked, and now she twirled around for Naomi's inspection.

"You look grand! They fit you perfectly. There are more at my house that you can borrow until you get yourself situated. Do you sew?"

Beth nodded. Her mother had taught her to sew as a little girl, and she had been sewing quilts and clothing for the fun of it ever since. Granted, much of her sewing had been done on a modern Singer; but she could sew with neat stitches by hand as well, since that was the way that she finished all of her quilts.

Naomi answered, "Good. That will help. You can make some of your things, such as aprons and the like, with some fabric that I have. Now what will you do with your hair? You should put it up, like mine, on top of your head."

With that, Naomi began to chatter on about clothes and sewing while Beth sat down on the bed. Sitting behind her, Naomi began to brush out Beth's hair. This was how Liam found them when he came back.

He stood in the doorway of the bedroom watching the two women. They were talking away like two old friends and didn't hear him when he called out from the bottom stair. He watched Naomi brushing the auburn hair, watching it slide through her fingers and under her hands, and wondered at how it felt. In his mind, he recalled her pale skin when he had removed her clothing the afternoon before. He had been too preoccupied with her injuries at the time, but now he remembered how smooth it had been and wondered how she would look with her shoulders bare, her hair falling around them while he brushed it. He realized, with a start, the direction that his thoughts were taking him and reminded himself again that she was his patient. He couldn't recall ever having had these particular thoughts about one of his patients, and to do so now was both unprofessional and inappropriate.

He cleared his throat. "So here you are. I called out when I came in the house," he said. "Sorry, I'm so late in getting back. Harlan Johnson caught up with me at the mill and wanted me to stop by to see his youngest girl, who has a little fever."

Both women turned to look at him with surprise, and Beth got to her feet. Naomi looked at the watch pinned to the front of her blouse and exclaimed, "Goodness! Look at the time! I didn't realize that it was so late. I'll have to be going home to get Bill his lunch!"

She turned to Liam and asked, "Did you say anything to Bill? No, not yet? Well, we'll have to tell him this evening. Maybe, then, the two of you could come to supper? Good. Then we'll see you tonight. Now Liam, give your sister a ride home, hmm?"

With that, she brushed past Liam and down the stairs, still talking. Liam raised his brows at Beth and turned back down the stairs again. Beth walked over to the wardrobe and opened the door to look in the mirror.

"So this is the new me," she murmured. She spent a few minutes looking at herself before she braided her hair in a straight plait and went to the table by the bed to pick up the scrunchy that had held her hair back in a knot when she left for work the day before. She saw her mother's letter lying next to it. Securing the end of her braid, she reached for the letter and sat down on the bed.

Chapter IV

She wasn't sure how long she had been sitting there on the edge of the bed in the quiet room when she heard Liam come back in downstairs. She stood up and, still holding the letter, went downstairs. Liam looked up as she was coming down the stairs.

"You look different. Nice, but different," he said. Then looking at her again, he said, "Elizabeth, what's wrong? You're upset about something. Or is your headache back?"

Beth hesitated for a second, then handed him the letter. She was holding a chain in her hand with a locket and a cross on it. She was suddenly shivering, and Liam said, "Why don't we go sit out back in the sun while I read this?"

He led her down the hallway and out the back door into the yard. There were two chairs next to each other on the lawn facing the river, and they both sat down. Beth was silent, toying with the chain and staring off toward the river, while Liam read:

May 15, 2008
Dearest Beth,

> *We don't know where to start with this letter, although we've had almost thirty years to write it. We have known since right before your birth that you would be leaving us on this date. We know that it sounds incredible; we had a hard time believing it ourselves, at first. But we have accepted it over the years, because we were presented with too much proof that this is actually what happens. We have finally decided not to give you too many details, because we feel that your life should be able to unfold as it happens. You will already know too many things about the future as it is! We hope that we have helped you prepare sufficiently for your new life in 1908. We have enclosed this locket and cross. The two*

people who told us about you before your birth gave them to us. They told us that they were yours, and that you wore them every day of your life. We have held them for you, for this moment.

We debated telling you all of this in person, but felt that it would alter the course of events too much. Please don't be too angry with us, Sweetheart. This was a very difficult decision for us to make, but we're letting you go because we have faith that you will find the one happiness in your life there that you have not found here. Please trust the decision that we made not to prevent this. We know where you are, and how you will live your life. Remember all of your days how very much we love you and how proud of you we have always been, and will continue to be. May God bless you always—

Mom and Dad

Liam finished the letter, then read it again. He set it down in his lap and looked at Beth. She was crying softly. There were so many emotions showing in her face. Sadness, confusion, pain, anger, determination. He sat there quietly, then reached over and took her hand. They sat that way for some time. Finally, she gave a sniffle and held up the chain to look at it.

"I've never seen this before. How could my parents not tell me about any of this? Didn't they want me to stay with them? Even if this was inevitable, why didn't they give me the chance to say good-bye? It wasn't fair of them to make these choices for me! How could they just let me go? So much of my life is falling into place now, all of the things that they made sure that I learned. But how can they know for sure that this was the right thing? What else did they know? What will they tell the rest of my family? My brother and sister, and their families? I guess it's pretty well a sure thing that I won't be going back home to them. I wasn't prepared for this! How could they *not tell me!*"

Liam let Beth go on, venting her pain and confusion, until she ran down and looked at him, anguish on her face. He released her hand and reached over to take the chain with the locket and cross. He opened up the locket. Inside was a picture of her with four other people.

"Is this your family? You bear a striking resemblance to your mother and sister."

Beth looked over at the picture. "Yes, it is. We do look alike, don't we? My mother's side of the family tends to lean toward auburn hair and dark eyes. And people used to mistake my sister and me for twins when we were little girls, even though she's two years older than me. But we were that similar."

Liam asked, "Shall I put it on you now?"

Beth nodded, and Liam got up and knelt in front of her chair. He unhooked the clasp and, leaning in toward her, reached around to the back of her neck to hook it. His face was next to hers, and she could feel his warm breath on her cheeks that were wet with tears.

When he was done, Liam sat back on the grass at her feet. "I can't pretend to know your parents, but it seems to me that they want you to be happy, more than anything. For whatever reason, they seem to believe that this time is where you will find happiness. Were you unhappy there?"

Beth sat for a moment, thinking about his question. "No-o-o . . . not necessarily unhappy. I love my family more than anything, but there were times when I honestly felt that I had been born in the wrong time. My grandmother used to tease me, saying that I always had one eye looking to the past. I had mentioned that to my parents several times. There were times when I felt that I just didn't fit in with all that was going on around me. It's funny, but when I look back on it, I remember that they never said anything when I would say that. What they must have been thinking! And too, there were times when I've felt lonely, because of the career that I've chosen for myself. I've watched all of my friends have normal relationships and get married, but it's been difficult for me to do that with my job. But I wouldn't say that I was unhappy. Maybe just not completely contented."

Liam looked at her. "I realize that your career choice would be impossible for you right now, but what made it so different in a hundred years? That is, why should your occupation interfere with marriage and family? I thought that women had all sort of careers, and men didn't mind."

"Well," began Beth, "women in law enforcement aren't a terribly common thing even a century from now, although our ranks had been growing steadily for fifteen or twenty years. But take my agency. There are about one hundred game wardens, but only nine of us are women. Make that eight now," she grimaced. "Law enforcement is difficult on women, both mentally and physically. Particularly my type of law enforcement, which requires you to be so physically active. We have to constantly prove ourselves. Add to that the strange work hours and conditions, and the fact that I am either working alone in less than ideal circumstances or with a male partner. What man wants to be involved with a woman who works under these conditions? I'm armed (I also carried a shotgun in my patrol vehicle, and you found the knife in my side pocket), will place myself in harm's way deliberately on any given day, work all hours of the day and night, and I'm used to taking charge. Police officer's are—as a rule—a very independent lot, and I'm no exception. Even in 2008, most men don't like to have their women as independent as I am. Sooner or later, I scare them away, and then it's all over but the crying." Saying that, she smiled.

Liam was watching her while she spoke. She was so passionate about what she was saying. He thought, *here is a woman who took on a job that, seemingly, many men wouldn't be able to do.* And it seemed as though she gave up so much for it. He wondered if she had known how much she would be losing personally when she took the job.

"How long have you done your work?" he asked.

"I was just coming up on nine years. I took the exam for the job just before I graduated from college, and then I was accepted into the police academy at the end of that summer. When I graduated, I was sent to work in the Boston area for a year. I was engaged to be married then, but he broke it off after a few months, saying that he couldn't handle the job that I had. We had a terrible fight over it. He wanted me to quit. I told him that I couldn't, after all that I had worked so hard to achieve. I thought that he had always known that this was the career that I had wanted. I had talked about it so much with him, and I thought that he shared my dream. But then he told me that he never really believed that I would be able to do it, and that I would eventually let go of the idea and get a 'normal' job for a woman, whatever that meant."

Looking at Liam, she saw what looked like sympathetic understanding on his face. She shrugged her shoulders slightly. "So that was the end of that. Then I had the chance to come closer to home, and I took it. I've been working here in the Corsehill area ever since."

"So," said Liam, "has it been worth it, then? Have you found it rewarding in spite of the things that you have lost?"

"Oh, yes, indeed!" she exclaimed without hesitation. "There have been times when I have helped someone in trouble or taken care of an issue that they were having, and they have been so grateful. You must see that in your work as well. I'm sure that you know what I'm talking about. Or I've investigated something where I started out with very little information and then pieced it together like a puzzle, getting the bad guy in the end."

She was smiling now, and it made him happy to see that.

"I have had the opportunity to participate in and see things that I would never have had the opportunity to do otherwise," she continued. "I have even helped to deliver a baby! But there have been difficult things too. Things that have stayed a long time with me and then changed me a little bit when they finally left."

"But anyway," said Beth, "if what my parents are telling me is true, I guess that that part of my life is over, and I have to face a new future now. I can't imagine never seeing my family again. I know that they aren't dead. For that matter, they haven't even been born yet. But it's hard to imagine that they are physically gone from me. I never had a chance to say good-bye to any of them. Or to my friends." She sighed heavily and continued, "I don't have any choice but to adjust and move forward without them, I guess. But I'm not really sure, right now, how I'm going to do that. And I can't imagine doing any other kind of work than being a game warden. It's what I know." She sat back, worrying at her lower lip with her teeth.

Liam sat watching her. "Don't worry. You don't need to be alone through this. I'll help you get the answers that you're looking for."

He said it with such sincerity that Beth looked up at him and gave him a weak smile.

He took out his watch and then closed the lid with a snap. "You're looking a little tired. My guess is that your headache has returned, hasn't it? It has, after all, only been twenty four hours."

Beth nodded.

"So as your physician, I am prescribing that you relax for a while. We can walk up the river tomorrow or even the day after that. It's not going anywhere! Don't forget that we have a dinner engagement this evening, if you're up to it. Why don't you get some rest while I take care of some pharmacy and clerical work that I need to do?"

Beth realized that she was tired, and there was a dull throbbing in her head. She was glad that he had picked up on that. They walked into the house together.

"May I borrow one of your books? I noticed that you have quite a collection."

Liam nodded. "Of course. Do you like to read? I read most evenings, when I have the chance."

Beth answered, "I do. I read many nights before bed. I've been known to sit up all night in order to finish a good book!" She walked over to the bookcase and selected Lorna Doone, a favorite since she was a teenager. "I think that I'll go upstairs, if you don't mind. Thanks."

She was lying on the bed when she heard Liam come upstairs and unlock the door to the room across the hall. Curious, she set aside her book and went across the hall to the doorway and looked inside. Liam was seating himself at a long table below rows of shelves with bottles and containers on them. There was a microscope, as well as a Bunsen burner and various-sized vials on the table. She saw various medical implements on shelves around the room. There were more books and some papers stacked neatly at the end of the table. Here, in this room, all was neat and orderly. Everything was returned to its place after use. He had glass front cases and filing cabinets lining the walls.

"So this is what this room is," she said from the doorway. "I had assumed that it was another bedroom, but couldn't understand why you had spent the night downstairs."

Liam looked over at her in the doorway. "I thought that the settee would be more comfortable than this table." He smiled at her. "Besides, you'd be surprised at how many nights I've spent on that settee."

"Why? Do you often rescue strange women and let them spend the night in your bed?"

"Oh, only the odd one, here and there." It was nice to share this banter back and forth, thought Liam with a smile. She had such a quick wit. "I fall asleep there reading, and sometimes, I'm too lazy when I wake up in the middle of the night to drag myself upstairs. So I just stay there. One place is as good as the other." Then he added, "I thought that you were going to rest?"

"I was," she replied, "but now I'm blazing with curiosity about this room. Are you a mad scientist, or is this where you practice medicine?"

Liam smiled. "A little bit of both, I suppose. It's my pharmacy, mostly."

"Do you mix your own medicines here, then?"

"Some of them. I order what I can from the suppliers and mix what I have to. Someday, I would like to have a separate clinic where I can store all of this. Then I can split my time between house calls and having people who are ambulatory come in. I'll have an examination and treatment room, an office and a pharmacy, all in one place. I've been adding on to my barn as I'm able to. That's what the lumber that I picked up this morning is for. I'm only putting a couple of rooms on there, for now. Someday, I'll build in the field next-door to here. I think that it would be more professional, and I could provide my neighbors with better and more complete care."

Beth smiled. "You're way ahead of yourself, Doctor. These things are achieved on a great scale in the years to come. There are hospitals and medical centers all around, not just the ones available in the big cities, with high quality care 24/7. Sorry—that means daily, around the clock. Medical treatment begins in the field with firefighters and police officers like me or even more skilled emergency medical technicians who are trained to identify the medical emergency and begin treatment and follow through to the critical care received in the hospital from the doctors and nurses. It's really amazing how far it's come."

She paused. "But it's also become rather expensive. In fact, the cost of healthcare has become a big political issue. I wonder what the solution will be."

Liam looked excited. "That sort of care is just what I would like to provide to these people! They work so hard, they always have, and they deserve good care. It is expensive even now, but I try hard to keep the costs down, which is why I mix a lot of my own medicines. I try to incorporate herbs when I can too. I want my neighbors here in Corsehill and the surrounding towns to feel comfortable coming to me in a clean professional place, where I can treat everyone, yet they can still afford the treatment. This house is fine, but I have some things downstairs and some things in this room up here. I even have to store some things in the barn. It would be so convenient to have it all in one location, on one floor."

She smiled at his enthusiasm. She could picture what he was saying and was sure that he would, one day, achieve his goal.

It wasn't until Beth had settled down against the pillows on the bed and opened the book up that she remembered. She hadn't been able to concentrate on the book; she kept thinking about her family, when some recollection began to stir in the back of her mind. Her mother had always collected antiques and had instilled her love and respect of them in Beth. It had begun when Beth was a little girl. Her first memories of it were of her and her mother traipsing around the woods in Corsehill, including the very watershed that Liam's house was currently in. Her mother had an old map of the area, showing all of the houses from an old census, and they would seek out the old cellar holes and scratch around looking for old bottles and glassware. She called it bottle digging. Her mother would bring home their finds and wash them up. Then they would look up the bottles in reference books to learn what their specific use had been. She had grown up surrounded by old things. Beth would imagine a house sitting atop the cellar hole, with its yard and flowers. They would locate the foundations for the out buildings, and she would mentally strip away the trees that had since grown up, picturing how the homestead had appeared when it was occupied with people living their lives. Beth had first learned to love the woods and read animal signs from the hours spent looking for those cellar holes with her mother. These excursions were some of her most treasured memories.

One day, in this very same watershed, her mother was scratching the ground behind the foundation of a barn. They had been finding pieces of what looked like medicine vials and had found an old burner. Her mother often took her to this spot to dig around and had told Beth that it was once the office of a doctor. Beth had become bored and had wandered away to sit down on the stone wall, several feet away. She was about seven or eight years old. Pushing a stone aside on the wall, she saw the sun glint off of something. Reaching in, she pulled out a bottle with another smaller bottle upside down inside of it. Looking at it, she saw that there was a piece of paper rolled up and tucked inside of the smaller bottle. She dumped the small bottle out and, with a stick, pried out the piece of paper and unrolled it. Written on it was the name Elizabeth Blodgett, with a heart drawn next to it. She had called out, "Mommy! Look, I found my name!" and had run over to her mother with both bottles and the paper. Her mother had taken it from her and looked at it for a long time. Then she pulled Beth onto her lap and held her there. She rocked her back and forth for several minutes, not saying anything. Then she put the paper and bottles back the way that they had been and wrapped them carefully in her handkerchief before putting them in her backpack. They sat on her mother's dresser from that day on.

Now Beth understood. *She* had left those bottles for her mother. And her mother knew it the moment that she saw it. Lying on Liam's bed, she thought about how, ever since she was a teenager, she would draw a heart next to her name every time she left a note for her parents. Sometime, now in this era, she would write her name on a slip of paper and leave it in this manner, so that it would be protected until she found it all those years later. She began to understand how her parents had come to accept her life here. She must have left signs for them throughout the years. But that didn't tell them that she was happy; only that she was alive and loved them and was thinking about them. Yet they had said in their letter that they had "faith" that she would find happiness here. How did they know?

She must have drifted off to sleep with these thoughts because Liam was gently shaking her shoulder to wake her. "Elizabeth, it's almost five o'clock. We need to be getting to Naomi and Bill's house. How do you feel? Do you still want to go?"

Beth sat up and rubbed her eyes. "Five o'clock? How long have I been asleep? I doubt I'll sleep tonight." She stretched her arms, wincing a little at the stiffness of her muscles. "Yes, I do still want to go."

Liam said, "Your body is giving itself the rest that it needs. I looked in on you a couple of times. You were sleeping quite soundly. I'll be downstairs when you're ready to go. Do you feel like walking? There's a path along the river."

Chapter V

They were walking along the river while Beth told Liam what she had remembered. She omitted the fact that she knew whose cellar hole she had been at. She also shared the thoughts that had followed that recollection. In a manner that she was learning was typical of him, Liam waited until she had finished her narration before saying anything.

"Perhaps you left them something more substantial to read. We already know that someone, or two someones, will go to see your parents and tell them about you. Why couldn't they have given them a written record of your life here? Maybe you should keep a journal. I don't think that there are any rules as to how you need to proceed. Remember that your parents told you that they had decided not to give you too much information so that your life would 'unfold as it happens.' They have the same type of historical advantage that you have, Elizabeth. They know how your life will unfold, and it seems to me that they wouldn't knowingly let you continue into a situation that would hurt you."

They had stopped walking and were looking at the river. Beth turned to him and nodded. "You're right, of course. I hadn't thought about it from that perspective. I guess that I hadn't expanded my thinking enough. Thank you for your insight. And advice."

As they began to walk again, Beth turned to Liam. "You know, Liam, you can call me Beth if you like. You don't have to call me Elizabeth."

Liam looked at her. "Would you rather I call you Beth? In my mind, I was already calling you Elizabeth before you even woke up last night, after I found your name in your pack. So that's how I see you."

Smiling, Beth said, "It just sounds strange, that's all. I've always been called Beth by just about everyone. There were only two other people who called me Elizabeth. They were brother and sister . . ." Her voice trailed off and after a moment, she said, "Interesting."

"What's interesting?"

Beth smiled again at Liam, saying, "Nothing. Nothing at all. If you prefer to call me Elizabeth, then it's okay with me." She walked on in silence, wondering how many more of these little ironies she would see as time went by.

Beth enjoyed their dinner with Naomi and Bill. Bill had sat listening, his eyes wide, while they explained Beth's situation to him, occasionally inserting a question or comment. Beth liked him. He obviously loved Naomi very much, and she was equally devoted to him. There was an easy friendship between him and Liam as well. After many questions, he finally accepted their story, and Beth wasn't surprised when he offered her whatever help he could to make her transition easier. She was curious when Liam told them that he had a few ideas that he would like to discuss privately with her, and they left shortly afterward.

They walked in silence along the path by the river. The moon was shining brightly, throwing long shadows out across the water, and Liam suggested that they sit for a moment on a log by the river.

After they were seated, Liam turned to her and said, "Naomi told me when I brought her back home this noon that you have had some medical training. And you had implied it as well in our conversation this afternoon. How much do you know?"

"I've been trained in what is called 'wilderness first aid,' and I am what is known as a 'first responder.' It's very basic, at best, but what it means essentially is that I can assess and begin first aid on a patient while waiting for more advanced help to arrive and transport them to a hospital. Let me see if I can translate that to a practical use here and now." She paused and then went on, "I can treat people for broken bones and shock. I can splint a broken limb, and I know what to do immediately for something like a chest wound or an airway obstruction until better-trained medical personnel arrive. I can identify an allergic reaction and a heart attack and know what to do for either. I'm positive that I could sew up a laceration, if I were shown the right way to do it. As I said before, I have helped to deliver a baby, and I'm not at all squeamish. Why do you ask? Do I feel a job offer coming?"

Liam laughed. "Yes, Elizabeth, you do. Naomi planted the seed, and I've thought about it all afternoon and evening. Do you think that you could be my assistant? The hours aren't normal, but that sounds like something that you're already used to. I'll teach you what you need to know, and I don't think that I'm a bad boss."

Beth was silent for a minute. "I'll take it, but I have to come clean with you about this." At the confused expression on his face, she said, "Living here will be very good for me grammatically! What I mean is that I have to be honest with you about something. Naomi and I talked about this earlier today while you were away. She asked me then if I knew anything about medicine and suggested that

I become your assistant. I think that, in her mind, she already had me working for you. So it wasn't as much your idea as you may think."

Liam laughed. "Don't worry. I know my sister better than she does. I saw through her right away. But I could use the help, honestly." He paused, then said, "Let's discuss your hours and pay."

"Yes. How will we work out the nighttime emergencies? Will you want my help with those?"

"Absolutely. Usually, they're the real emergencies. And that brings me to the other thing that I've been thinking about . . . where you will live? Obviously, you can't keep living in my house with me. And if you are to be available to help me at night, you will need to be nearby so that I can get you when I need you. Correct?"

Beth nodded in agreement.

Liam continued, "Well, as you know, I've been adding onto my barn to make an office and examination room. Why don't I finish it off as a small apartment instead, and you could live there?"

Beth held up her hand. "But that office is part of your dream! Do you really want to put that off? Couldn't we find another place where maybe I could board or something? You're being far too generous with me!"

Liam shook his head. "No. This makes a great deal of sense. And my reasons for doing this aren't entirely altruistic. Look here, Elizabeth. You will just be on the other side of the yard when you're needed. It will be easier for me having you close by, so we will both benefit."

Beth stared at the river, quietly thinking over his offer. "All right," she finally agreed. "As long as you're okay with it. But what about the rent for my new quarters? How much do you want?"

"You won't have to pay anything." At the look on her face, Liam went on to add, "But if you would like, we'll count some of your work hours as payment. How does that sound?"

Beth stood up, facing Liam sitting on the log, and stuck out her right hand. Liam put his right hand in hers, and she firmly shook it. "It's a deal, then," she said. "But only if I can help you finish building it. After all, the sooner it's done, the sooner I have a place to live. And you can have your bed back."

The next morning after breakfast, they walked across the yard toward the barn. Beth paused and felt the hair go up on the back of her neck when she saw the stone wall just a few feet beyond the far side of the barn. She knew that this was where she had found her name in the bottles with her mother. Liam kept walking and talking about what part of the construction they would be working on. She rushed to catch up with him as he turned to ask her if she knew how to swing a hammer.

"I'll manage, don't worry," she said.

"Somehow, I believe you will," he laughed. "Well, here we are. Your future new home."

Beth walked past him to look at what he had done so far. He had framed in two good-sized rooms off the side of the barn.

"I know that it will only be two rooms, but if you like, you can take your meals in the house with me. Or you can use the larger room for kitchen and sitting room alike and the other for your bedroom. I have, on order, a hydraulic pump to bring running water into the house and was planning on running the water across to here as well, so we can add on a bath for you. We'll need to put in a stove so you will have a heater for the water."

Beth was impressed. "You have given this a tremendous amount of thought! And what you've done so far looks good. My brother is quite a builder and very creative like you. I wish he was here now to give you a hand." She thought for a moment. "And hot water certainly sounds nice. I have to admit that in just two days, I'm already missing a hot bath. In my time, people bathe daily—not weekly—with hot running water. They don't just wash up."

Liam was looking at her and shaking his head with wonder.

They worked steadily for a couple of hours, framing in a small bath off of the room against the barn. They had stopped for a break when they heard hoof beats approaching. Liam came out from around the barn, with Beth following. A young man of about fifteen rode into the dooryard, calling out for the doctor.

Liam approached him. "Amos! What is it?"

"Doc! My father is on his way here in the wagon with Wallace. He cut his leg open, clearing brush down. It's deep, and he's bleeding bad! Pa sent me ahead to make certain that you were here."

Liam sprang into action. "Go tell him we'll be ready for him."

Beth stepped forward and said, "Wait! Amos, is it? Will you take me with you?"

She turned to Liam, "I can start treating him on the way, just give me something to use to apply pressure on the wound."

Liam nodded, understanding coming across his face, and turned back to Amos. "It's all right, she's my new assistant. Let me get you my kit."

A short time later, Liam heard the wagon roll into the yard and ran out to meet it. Beth was in the wagon with Wallace. She had both hands clamped on his left leg above the knee with a thick bandage. He could see that there was blood seeping around the bandage.

Beth said, "It's very deep. I've got pressure on it to slow it down. I don't dare let go."

Liam nodded and climbed into the wagon. "Good work." Turning to the driver of the wagon, he said, "Joseph, you and Amos help me get him into the house!"

They carried him into the house and laid him on a plank placed across two sawhorses next to the dining table. Liam had arranged his instruments on the table on a metal tray. Beth had not let go of Wallace's leg the entire time. Liam injected the boy with morphine and began telling Beth what to do, watching closely to see if she was bothered in any way by the boys' injury. But she worked quickly and efficiently, following his lead; and together, they cleaned and stitched the wound.

When they were done, Liam said to Joseph, "He should be all right. Keep the dressing on it to keep it clean, that's the important thing. I'll be by tomorrow to check on him, and I'll change the bandage then. He's lost quite a little blood, so he'll be weak for a few days. Let him get plenty of rest and ask his mother to fix him plenty of greens to eat. They're good for his blood. Hold on for a minute, and I'll get you some burdock root."

Liam returned a moment later with a small pouch in his hand, which he handed to Joseph. "Brew it into a tonic, and have Wallace drink it. That'll help his blood too. I'll be by in the morning."

He turned and put his hand on Wallace's head and said, "Next time, aim for the brush, not your legs!" Wallace smiled weakly.

After they had left, Beth and Liam began to clean up. "You did a good job," said Liam. "That was quick thinking."

Beth looked over at him from where she was picking up the soiled bandages. "That's what I was referring to when I was telling you about my first responder training. It adds to the patient's chances. By the way, I'll need my own kit, don't you think?"

A couple of days after they had read the letter from her parents, Liam went upstairs to find Beth sitting cross-legged on the bedroom floor, taking apart the gun that had been in the holster on her belt. The sun was coming in through the window, and she sat in the sunbeam, the light making her auburn hair shine. He came in and sat down, watching while she expertly cleaned and reassembled it, wiping the metal down with a light coating of oil. She left it unloaded and then stripped the bullets out of the magazine and also out of the two other magazines that had been on her belt, making a neat pile of them on the floor next to her. She had cleaned and ironed her uniform, and it was hanging from a peg on the wall with a hanger. She had polished her badge and nametag. Her boots had been cleaned and shined.

Liam said, "You look like you're getting ready for inspection."

Beth looked up at Liam, with a thoughtful smile on her lips, and said, "I've noticed the picture of you with some other men on your desk downstairs. It looks like a Chief Petty Officer's uniform on you, if I'm not mistaken." At his nod, she asked, "When? Where?"

He was surprised that she would recognize both his uniform and rank and said so.

"You forget," said Beth, "I have a keen interest in history and particularly, military history. Maybe because I work—worked," she corrected herself with a grimace, "with so many men who had been in the military before becoming police officers. Their influence has rubbed off on me, I guess."

"I was one of three hospital stewards aboard the hospital ship *Solace* during the Spanish-American War and a little while afterward. I volunteered for a year while I was still attending Tufts Medical School in Boston. After my year was up, I went back to school and completed my training. I learned a great deal on that ship. It was quite an experience for me, in many ways."

Beth asked, "What were your specific duties? Do you mind my asking you these questions?"

"No. I don't mind. I ran the wards and pharmacy. I assisted with all of the surgeries and cleared men back to duty. As I said, I learned a lot from that year. Certainly more than I would have anywhere else. I learned quite a bit about traumatic injuries and, of course, tropical diseases like yellow fever and malaria. And I traveled a bit during that time and got to see places and things that I wouldn't otherwise have seen."

"Where were some of the places that the *Solace* took you?"

"Cuba, of course, and Puerto Rico. There were a great many trips back and forth between there and the States . . . Florida, Virginia, New York, and Boston. I managed to stay with the ship when she sailed for Europe in February of '99 and stopped in China and then Hawaii on the way to California, where I got on a train and came home, then back to Boston that fall to finish medical school."

"Wow. Talk about a whirlwind tour! You covered a lot of ground in that year. Not bad for a country boy."

Liam nodded, a slight smile turning up the corners of his mouth. Beth sensed that he had said all that he wanted to say about the experience and left it alone after that. They sat in a comfortable silence while she finished her task.

Eventually, she looked again up at Liam. "Do you have a small trunk that I can put all of my things into? It would probably be better if they were put away out of sight and safe." There was heaviness in her voice.

Liam had gone into the attic and found a small trunk and a smaller wooden box for her gun and brought them to her. She looked so sad as she packed everything away that he asked her if she would be all right.

Shrugging her shoulders, she replied, "I have worn this uniform practically every day for almost nine years. It's become part of my identity and helped define who I am. I feel as though I'm packing away a piece of myself forever."

Liam looked at her for a moment, understanding her sense of loss. He left the room, giving her time for her thoughts. She had not said any more about it since then. That night, Liam noticed that she had begun to keep a journal.

". . . I packed away my uniform today. I packed away a piece of myself. I recall the day that I graduated from the academy. It seems so long ago, and yet it seems like it was just yesterday, too. I'm so acutely aware of time now. Past, present, future . . . which one do I fall into? . . ."

The days went by quickly after that. Liam and Beth worked on finishing her apartment every opportunity that they could, and Liam took her with him on all of his calls, introducing his new assistant to everyone that they met. They had decided that they would tell anyone who asked that she was the sister of one of Liam's friends from medical school.

She took in the scenery everywhere that they went, noting how different the same roads that she had known all of her life looked to her. Some of the roads were new to her, no longer existing in her time. Now the roads were narrow dirt lanes and sometimes, quite muddy. She commented that she understood why people weren't eager to accept Henry Ford's automobile here yet, as the roads weren't conducive to motor vehicle traffic.

"But they will be and soon too! Trust me!" she had said, picturing the paved Main Street of 2008. "Even the dirt roads in a century are much improved over these." She waved her arm around her, indicating the road around her as they rode down Main Street, adding, "But it will never again be as picturesque as it is right now!"

Beth's mother had a collection of old postcards of Corsehill, one of which depicted Main Street at the turn of the twentieth century. Suddenly, she felt as though she had stepped through the looking glass, and the picture had become life. She was seeing these things that had appeared in those old black-and-white postcards—the graveled street with its proud maples forming a loose canopy overhead, the domestic charm of the houses with their potted ferns on the front porch, the lilac bush at the corner of the parsonage.

She was constantly orienting herself from the buildings that would still be there in a century. Two of these buildings, the lending library and Perkins Store, were in the center of Corsehill.

This was the same library that she had been borrowing books from her whole life, but here, it had only been opened a few years ago. She had spent many hours in this building growing up, taking part in summer reading programs as a child and using their resources for schoolwork in junior high and high school. As an adult, she had continued going there to take out books. It brought a smile to her face the first time that she had walked in with Liam as she noted that it had the same quiet air and fusty book smell that she had always known. She had been pleased to see that the gigantic oak table sat in the same spot in front of the large brick fireplace with the portrait of the library's benefactor hanging above. Here was a familiar place!

Perkins Store still went by the same name in 2008 and was still owned and operated by members of the Perkins family. But the contents of the store were much different then from what she now saw. They carried everything here from food to clothing to hardware. She wandered down the creaking floorboards through the stacks and shelves of merchandise. There were barrels of flour, meal, and sugar with the scales hanging among them. Bolts of fabric were stacked on shelves with sewing notions next to gloves, shoes, and boots. Jars of hard candy and bottles of soda were sitting on shelves. There were fishing poles and baseball gloves next to casks of oil for lamps and replacement chimneys for them. She saw tools and axes and screws and nails. At the back of the store were the butcher shop and grocery. It was a fascinating place, full of sights and smells, and Beth understood why these places had been called "general" stores.

It wasn't just in the buildings that she found things different. The land around her was so open now; much of it was rolling farmland with fields for hay and grazing. The landscape was dotted with woodlots kept for cutting firewood and timber. Ancient maple trees towered up along the edge of every road and field. As beautiful as they were, Beth knew that they served a practical purpose as well: providing sap every spring to be boiled down to maple syrup, a New England staple.

The Hollow, where she now lived with Liam in the southwest corner of town, was a thriving, working community—almost like a second smaller town within the town of Corsehill. In Beth's time, what hadn't been flooded there was wooded, where the hardwood trees had grown back into most of the fields and overrun the cellar holes of the homes that were now inhabited by her new neighbors. The roads were more like paths, and some had disappeared completely, either underwater or reclaimed by the forest. It was quite a contrast in her mind; and sometimes, as she rode or walked along, trying to take it in, it all seemed surreal to her. There were days when she half expected to wake up and find that it was all a dream.

Beth helped Liam in his pharmacy, where she would label the vials and keep the ledger while he measured and mixed the medicines. She was constantly asking about everything that they did, and he found himself enjoying teaching her and watching as she applied what she had learned. He would question her, in turn, about medical advances in the future; and she would tell him what she could about modern medicine and other things like helicopters, interstate highways, and computers. An easy friendship was developing between them.

As Beth spent more time with Liam, she became aware of the calm manner that he had about him. It came to her that here was someone who was comfortably on good terms with life. It wasn't that he never worried about things; but rather, once he made a decision, he moved ahead with it and didn't worry any more, as though he had this much self-confidence in his ability to see it through. It wasn't cockiness; it was more of an easy self-assuredness. She admired this quality a great deal in him.

Liam watched her closely for any more signs of the sadness that she had felt in those first few days, but she kept it to herself. He would see glimpses of it here and there in an unguarded moment, but she spoke no more about it. Beth had immersed herself in learning about her new life and the people around her. They would sit in companionable silence as he quietly read, while she faithfully wrote in her journal every night.

CHAPTER VI

One evening, they followed the path along the river together to see Naomi and Bill. Liam and Bill sat outside the kitchen door, drinking iced tea and talking about finding a suitable horse for Beth, while she and Naomi wandered through the kitchen garden that Naomi and Bill had just planted. Beth was telling her about the people whom she had met so far.

Naomi asked, "Will you be going to the Decoration Day ceremonies in town this Sunday? You'll surely meet more people then."

Beth shrugged her shoulders and asked, "Decoration Day?" Then she remembered that the name had been changed in the seventies to Memorial Day to honor veterans of all wars, not just the Civil War. The date too had been changed from May 30 to the last Monday of May. "I don't know," she said. "Will you be going?"

"Oh, yes," answered Naomi. "And Mother and Dad, as well as Bill's parents. Please come. You're part of our family now, so you won't be thrown out there alone!"

Beth smiled. As she had done that first day, Naomi had seen right into her. She wasn't ready yet to be without the safety net of the family nearby. The whole family, including Mr. and Mrs. Sizer, had been keeping an eye on her every time there were strangers around. They had been as accepting of Beth as Liam, Naomi, and Bill had been. She liked them immensely.

Liam spoke up from his seat by the door. "Of course you won't have to go alone! It's a fun outing. We'll listen to speeches and have a picnic lunch. The children play competitive games, and then there's music and dancing later. I think that you'll like it."

Beth said, "Music. That will be nice. I miss music." She went on to try to explain to the others about how music was readily available in her time, and how she listened to it every day. "Thomas Edison's phonograph and cylinders have come a long way!"

Since electricity was still a fairly new concept and hadn't really reached a rural area such as this, she was having trouble getting them to understand things like radios and television. She was laughing with them by the time she gave up trying to explain it. Beth decided that she would not even try to talk about her iPod.

Walking back home, Liam commented on how he heard music every day. "Did you know that you hum to yourself quite a bit while you're working? I've been enjoying it, although I don't recognize the tunes. Sometimes, I hear you singing too. While I don't pretend to understand all of the songs, I enjoy the sound of your voice."

Beth felt her face flush. She didn't realize that he had heard her singing. It wasn't anything that she had ever been comfortable doing in front of anyone.

He saw the color in her face and quickly said, "Please don't be uncomfortable with that! I truly do enjoy it, and it would be a shame for you to stop just because I said something!"

On Sunday, Beth put on the dress that she had borrowed from Naomi for the picnic. It was white with lace work and light blue trim. Instead of her usual braid, she put her hair up on top of her head. Liam was coming in from hitching up Ned when she came down the stairs.

He stopped in the doorway when he saw her and said, "You look lovely! You truly do."

Beth didn't say anything, just smiled back at him, feeling somewhat self-conscious.

He stood watching her before eventually asking, "Are you ready to go?"

Beth nodded, still smiling, as she went in to get the custard pie that Naomi had helped her bake to bring to the picnic. It had frustrated her that she'd had to turn to Naomi for help with something that she had been doing since she was a little girl, but she had found that the oven was defeating her after two pie crusts that were burned to a crisp on the outside and not nearly done enough in the center of the dish. In exasperation, she had stomped along the river path to rap on Naomi's kitchen door. Naomi had taken one look at the thundercloud on her face and the flour on her hands and, having a good grasp of the situation, gave her a baking lesson using an oven from 1908.

They arrived at the park in the center of Corsehill, and Beth marveled at all the people there. She looked around at her surroundings. The park consisted of a good-sized lawn of grass with a gazebo in the center and an area of ornamental gardens. A road lined with chestnut trees separated the lawn and gardens. This park was, of course, still there in Beth's time. But what was now a grassy lawn would, over time, become a playground with swings, a basketball court, and a ball field. She and the other children that she had grown up with had spent countless hours playing together there.

There was an air of celebration, and she felt the excitement of the day wrap around her as well. They found the rest of Liam's family, and Beth set down her pie and exchanged greetings with everyone. Children were running after one another, and there was a group of men playing music in the gazebo. The men were clustered here and there in groups, some talking about new livestock that had been born that spring on the farms, some were talking local politics. Some of the young men were discussing the upcoming Olympics in London. She overheard bits of Liam and Bill's conversation about Teddy Roosevelt and the ongoing construction of the Panama Canal as they were joined by a couple of other men.

Beth wandered idly among the crowd, taking it all in, listening to the snippets of conversation that she would pick up as she passed through the people. She heard women talking about their children or their households. Everyone had their good clothes on, and she noticed that all of the men had traded their everyday work clothes for pressed shirts and their good caps. Some of the younger men were wearing straw boater's hats. All of the little boys were wearing shoes, something that she had noticed that many of them did not usually do. They saved their shoes for special occasions. The women had left their aprons at home, and the girls all had big bows in their hair.

She recognized a few people whom she had already met while out on calls with Liam and cautiously returned their greetings, but kept moving. She saw Wallace Clark, still recovering from his leg injury. He waved shyly at her and turned to his mother sitting next to him. She looked up and saw Beth, then rose from her blanket on the ground and approached her. For a quick moment, Beth felt herself panic. She thought, *What if I say something that gives me away?* She took a steadying breath and waited.

"Miss Blodgett? I'm Mrs. Clark. I'd like to thank you for helping fix up Wallace. My husband and boys told me how you rode out to meet them with Amos and give Wallace aid. I was hoping that you would be here today so that I could thank you in person." They chatted for a couple of minutes more before Beth said good-bye to her.

Before she walked away, Mrs. Clark said, "Please feel free to call for a visit any time. I imagine that it can be hard relocating to a new area."

She smiled warmly, and Beth found herself returning the smile with the same warmth. *That wasn't so bad,* she thought to herself.

Turning away from Mrs. Clark, she bumped into Liam. He put both hands on her arms to steady her as she said, "So! You're following me, hmm?"

Liam laughed, "I just thought that you might like a tour guide. You don't need to head off on your own into the masses. I did promise to help, remember? You're so independent!"

"Okay, okay!" replied Beth. "I give up! But only for now. Lead on, protector!"

Together, they strolled around the park, while people called out greetings to Liam everywhere that they went and he kept up a running commentary about everything and one that they saw, telling her where they lived or how they made their living. Beth saw a young couple that she knew she had not yet met, but they were very familiar to her.

She turned to Liam and asked, "Do you see that couple over there?" as she nodded toward them. "Would you please introduce me to them?"

Liam gave her a curious look but nodded and headed toward them. As they walked over, Beth was looking them over closely. The woman was in her early twenties and had the same auburn hair as Beth. She was slim and pretty, wearing a white blouse with a high collar and a light blue skirt, with a wide darker blue belt around her waist. The man that she was with was tall with thick dark hair and an open, friendly smile. They looked up as Beth and Liam approached them.

The man spoke up as they approached. "Hello, Doc. How are we doing today?"

"I'm doing well, Frank."

Liam turned to the woman and asked, "How are you, Miss Brigham?" He went on, "I would like to introduce my new assistant, Elizabeth Blodgett, to you. Elizabeth, this is Ethel Brigham and Frank Burdett. Frank lives out in the Devil's Half Acre, a mile or so beyond Bill's sawmill."

Liam noticed, with a start, that this woman bore a strong resemblance to Elizabeth. They both had the same color hair and eyes, the same tilt of the head. He looked from one to the other, realization dawning on him.

Beth smiled at them while her heart beat a quick tempo in her breast. Ethel smiled back at her with deep brown eyes. They exchanged pleasantries and chatted for a bit about the town. Ethel told Beth that she too did not grow up in Corsehill, but Boston. She said, "But I have fallen in love with this town, and I think that you will too once you have been here for a little while." Her smile was genuinely sweet, and Beth felt a lump in her throat. Then they said their good-byes and moved on.

Liam looked over at Beth and asked, "What's going on? She's your relative, isn't she?" It had only just occurred to him that she would have family here now.

Beth nodded. "I recognized them from photographs. Those two are my great-grandparents. My mother's father was their son. Of course, he won't be born until 1915."

Beth and Liam simultaneously turned to look back at the couple. Ethel was gazing lovingly up at Frank while he was leaning over, speaking softly to her.

Beth looked at Liam and raised her eyebrows and said, "They may or may not even know it yet, but they will marry each other this fall, on October 11," while Liam said, "Hmmm."

They turned away and began to walk again.

Beth said, "They'll go on to have four children—a girl and three boys—before they're done. Although their youngest child, a son, will ..." She stopped talking, a frown on her face.

"Their youngest son will what?" asked Liam.

"Never mind." She had been about to tell him how one son would die at twenty-two years as a pilot in World War II. But she couldn't tell about any of those things. Her parents had been right, she already knew too much about the future! It was ironic that her great-grandparents would be here on Decoration Day, so happy and carefree. After her son died in the war, Ethel would become the Gold Star Mother in Corsehill for every Decoration/Memorial Day. How this day would change for her!

"Liam, there are things that I can't tell you. Things that I wish I didn't already know!"

Liam thought for a moment, watching the emotions play across her face, before speaking. "Maybe you could change some of these events. Did you think of that? Maybe you could spare your great-grandparents from what I'm guessing will be a painful experience. Maybe that's why you were sent here."

"Liam, I have thought about that a great deal! It's been on my mind quite a bit. But 'for each reaction, there is an equal and opposite reaction.' And it's true. There must always be a balance. If I were to change the outcome of some event, it would alter the course of history in too many ways. While a certain event could be prevented or changed, it would probably also set off a chain of events that couldn't be predicted. How could I know that the new outcome would be better than the one I knew about and changed? Besides, some of these events that I have been thinking of bring about huge changes to the world. Some of these changes are bad, but also, some real good has come from them." She paused. "The choice is not as easy as it may at first seem."

They had stopped walking and stood facing each other. Beth put her hand on Liam's arm as if to emphasize her point. "Besides, historical evidence suggests that, at least for some of these events, warnings did come but were ignored. For all I know, I may have been the one to send those warnings. Or maybe someone else like me. How do I know that I'm the only one to ever travel back in time this way? What makes me so special?" She shook her head. "All these questions, and too few answers!"

Liam had been watching her closely while she talked. She was so animated and felt so strongly about what she was saying. He put his hand over hers, then tucked it into the crook of his arm and began to walk again.

"You're right, Elizabeth. When you put it that way, the answers don't seem so easy. This is a burden, isn't it? And, unfortunately one that you will have to learn to live with, because I doubt that it will go away." He exhaled heavily. "And it hardly seems fair. But you'll get through it, because you're a strong woman. I will, gladly, share this burden with you if it will help. Please think about that."

Looking around, Liam said, "We have forgotten, for the moment, where we are. This probably isn't the best place to be having this discussion." He replaced the serious expression on his face with a warm smile. "Am I safe in assuming that there's nothing looming on the horizon that needs to be dealt with right now?"

Beth smiled back at him and nodded.

"Then I suggest that we settle down and enjoy the rest of the festivities. But don't forget, I'll help you sort this out."

They ate and listened to all of the speeches. Beth was fascinated at hearing the actual words of Civil War veterans, men in their sixties and seventies who had answered the call of their republic forty plus years earlier.

The activities began after the speeches. The young children began to play tag. There was a baseball game going on with the young men. Some other men had begun to pitch horseshoes. Liam and Bill went over to play, and Naomi and Beth went along to watch. Beth had brought along a small blanket for Naomi to sit on.

"I will be so relieved when Little Whosit and Whatsit decide to show up. I'm so tired of having to be picked up and put down like a sack of flour!" exclaimed Naomi as Beth helped her sit on the ground. "And I would dearly love to know who said that expectant women were beautiful. Clearly, whoever it was has never been expecting! Beautiful is the last thing that I feel!"

Beth laughed. "You are beautiful! Just ask Bill. It's written all over his face every time he looks at you. And you know it!"

They sat watching the game for a while, chatting back and forth about where Beth could shop to get some clothes of her own, as well as fabric to make a few things.

"But to be honest," said Beth, "I've hardly had time to think about it, I've been that busy working with Liam and learning everything. But the apartment is almost finished, and that will give me more free time. Although I can't say that I've minded the work at all."

Naomi laughed and said, "This would be a good excuse for me to get some new clothes. That dress looks better on you than it ever did on me! You look very attractive today, or hadn't you noticed some of the looks that you've been getting?"

At the look on Beth's face, Naomi said, "You are a very attractive woman."

"Naomi," said Beth, "I'm really not. I'm actually kind of ordinary. There's nothing remarkable or outstanding about me."

She had never been comfortable with compliments about her looks and was feeling somewhat ill at ease. She had never read fashion magazines or paid attention to the latest fashion crazes. She liked what she liked and usually paid no attention to the rest. But that didn't mean that there weren't times when she felt like a plain Jane, particularly when she would be out somewhere with other women her own age around her. They would wear the latest fashion and hairstyles with such ease, their makeup so well-done. She didn't even know how to buy cosmetics and usually had to have her sister or one of her friends come with her.

"Don't you see it?" asked Naomi. "You carry yourself with a confidence that makes you attractive. While this may be unsettling to some men, I think that there are others who are intrigued by it." *Including my brother*, she thought to herself.

To hide her discomfort, Beth looked away from Naomi. She saw a man of around twenty-five or -six heading in their direction. He was attractive in a male model sort of way, with thick black hair, blue eyes that were pale as ice, and—as he smiled a greeting to two men watching the horseshoe match—she wasn't surprised to see perfect teeth. To say that he was aware of his looks would be an understatement, and he carried himself with a confidence that could be more appropriately described as cockiness.

When he neared where they were sitting, he said hello to Naomi, inquiring about her health; and then he turned his charm on Beth, saying, "Miss Blodgett, isn't it? Please allow me to introduce myself. I am Martin Harrison. I've been hearing about Doctor Sizer's pretty new assistant. You must be her." He reached out his hand and took hers and held it.

Beth listened to him, thinking to herself that there was no way that he could be a local boy; he must be one of the summer residents from the Boston area who were so fond of Corsehill. She felt a quick stab of panic as it occurred to her that she wasn't ready for this kind of attention yet. Forcing this thought aside, she looked him in the eye and said, "Yes, I am," and sat looking at him, waiting for him to make the next move. Just then, she heard Liam's voice behind her.

"Martin, how have you been? Back for the summer?"

Liam had been about to pitch his horseshoe when he saw Martin Harrison approaching Elizabeth and Naomi. Without stopping to wonder why, he blindly pitched the shoe, allowing the others to win the match. He walked over to Beth and Naomi just as Martin was speaking to Beth.

Beth turned to look at Liam and saw that his smile did not reach his eyes. She thought to herself that Martin Harrison must have a reputation, if Liam felt the need to come to her rescue so quickly.

Liam and Martin were making small talk while Martin continued to hold Beth's hand in his. Firmly, Beth pulled her hand away and gave him a slight smile when he looked away from Liam and at her.

Not quite ready to give up, Martin said, "Just a moment, before you leave. There will be dancing later. May I count on a dance with you?"

Beth paused and said, "I'm not sure how late I will be here, so I can't commit to anything. But thank you for asking, Mr. Harrison." It was somewhat unsettling to be receiving this attention from him in front of an audience.

As the four of them walked away from Martin, Bill turned to Liam. "Why'd you toss our match like that? We probably could've won this one if you'd paid attention to what you were supposed to be doing."

Liam simply said, "Sorry" as Naomi gave Bill's arm a squeeze.

Beth barely took it in as she went over the scene in her mind. It had not occurred to her that anyone would be interested in her that way here. She'd already begun to think of herself as an old maid. But this gave her something else to think about. Would there be any harm in allowing someone to have an interest in her? But she couldn't really become involved with anyone unless she felt that she could trust him enough to share the secret of where she came from with him.

The bright sky was turning to dusk, and the music began. Liam asked Beth if she would like to stay for it.

She pulled herself away from her musing. "Oh, yes! I would very much like to hear it!" was her enthusiastic response.

They said good-bye to the others in their party who were now heading for home, leaving Beth and Liam alone on the grass. They wandered over to the gazebo, where the musicians were warming up on their instruments. Beth watched them with interest. She had been looking forward to this all afternoon.

She turned to Liam and shared her thoughts with him. "I have, honestly, been missing music. Do you think that I'm too old to learn to play an instrument? Does anyone here teach music?"

Liam smiled at her. "I do believe that if you decide that you want to learn to play music, then that's what you should do. Which instrument were you considering?"

"I have always wanted to learn the violin. Although I'm not sure that I have the time right now." She went on to add, laughing, "Or the talent!"

They talked on comfortably while they listened to the music. After listening for a little while, Liam asked Beth if she danced.

"There isn't much of this particular type of dancing done in my time. It's evolved into something else," said Beth. She waved a hand toward the dancers. "But I love the grace and style of this, and to answer your question . . . yes, I can dance."

She turned to him, hands folded demurely in front of her. "Why, Dr, Sizer," she said, batting her eyelashes at him, "are you asking me to dance?"

Liam gave a quick laugh. "You, the coquette! That'll be the day!" Still smiling at her, he offered his arm and led her out among the other dancers.

As they began to dance, he said, "You do realize, of course, that since we have stayed for the dancing, you will have to dance with Martin Harrison. There's no polite way out now." Casually, he asked, "Or did you want to dance with him? I was having a little trouble reading you earlier. I wasn't sure if it was his attention that you were uncomfortable with or if it was with the rest of us watching you."

Beth looked up at Liam, surprised that he had seen so much. "I guess that it was a little bit of both. You don't like him very much, do you?"

"I neither like nor dislike him," said Liam, evasively. "But you haven't answered my question. Did you want to dance with him? I couldn't tell."

Mimicking Liam, Beth said, "I neither want nor don't want to dance with him." Liam threw back his head and laughed, and Beth laughed with him.

"I guess that I deserved that!" The music came to an end, and another piece started up. Then softly, he said, "Well, you're on your own with this, then. Because here he comes."

Beth heard a voice at her elbow. "So you decided to stay after all. That is my good fortune!" said Martin. To Liam, he said, "May I cut in, then?"

Liam turned to Beth with a wink and smile and said, "Thank you for the dance. I'll see you shortly." Beth smiled back at him as he turned to go.

She and Martin began to dance. Martin said, "I'm glad that you chose to stay, Miss Blodgett. How long have you been here in Corsehill?"

They talked on about the town as they danced. Beth found him to be a very good conversationalist. He asked how she had come to Corsehill, and she gave him the story of Liam and her "brother". She had been saying it so much now, that she was beginning to believe it herself. She smiled at the thought.

"You have a very pretty smile, Miss Blodgett."

Beth laughed, and said, "Thank you, Mr. Harrison. I should try to smile more often, then." She couldn't believe it! She was flirting with this man! The music came to an end, and Beth realized that they danced on through two songs.

"Thank you for the dance, Mr. Harrison. But I really must be getting back." She stepped back from his embrace.

Martin replied, "The dance was all my pleasure, I assure you! May I call on you sometime, Miss Blodgett? I have enjoyed our time together. I would like to say that I have found conversation with you to be quite refreshing. You intrigue me."

Beth was evasive. She had enjoyed his conversation, as well. But she still wasn't sure about this handsome overconfident man, or the wisdom in getting involved. "Well, thank you for the compliment, Mr. Harrison. But I really am quite busy. I'm still getting settled in and learning my job as Dr. Sizer's assistant. So I must decline."

He looked genuinely disappointed. "I won't take that as a no, but rather as a 'possibly at a later date.' You will hear from me again, Beth."

It surprised her that he wasn't taking no for an answer, and her reply was short. "You can take it as you wish, Mr. Harrison, but I really am quite busy. Again, thank you for the dance." She turned and walked back to where Liam was talking with an older man.

As she approached the two men, she heard Liam say to the other man, "Here she is now." He turned to Beth. "Elizabeth, this is Mr. Bemis. He owns the livery stable here in town. He has a horse for sale that he thinks might be right for you. Would you like to stop in tomorrow?"

Beth greeted Mr. Bemis warmly and agreed to stop by the next day with Liam to take a look at the horse.

After leaving Mr. Bemis, Liam and Beth sat to listen to the music and watch the dancing. It wasn't long before Beth was asked to dance by another young man. And after that, another. She finally found her way back to Liam's side.

Liam asked, "Do you have enough energy left for one more dance?"

Smiling and a little embarrassed, Beth said, "Who'd have thought it? Being the new girl makes one popular, I guess."

"I'm sure that it has nothing to do with how nice you look today," commented Liam as they began to dance. Beth didn't answer him.

After a moment, he said, "You're very quiet, all of a sudden. Are you not feeling well? Would you like to go home?"

Beth smiled back at Liam and gave a short sigh. "No, I'm feeling fine. I just have some things to think about, but I would like to stay just a bit longer, if you don't mind. I really am enjoying the music."

Liam gave her hand a quick squeeze where he held it in his. "I'm enjoying the music too. And the company. You dance very well, by the way. I would have hated it if I found that you had two left feet after asking you to dance!"

Beth laughed. "I'll be sure to mention in my journal that my parents' dancing lessons when I was a little girl were well received!" She was silent for a minute before saying, "You know, your idea of keeping a journal was a very good one. I feel as though it's a means for me to keep in touch with them, with the idea that one day they'll read my words. I hope that they'll find the same comfort reading them as I get in writing."

Later, on their way home, Beth told Liam that Martin Harrison had asked to call on her.

"What did you tell him?" asked Liam, guardedly. "Do you want to see him again?"

Beth thought her answer out before speaking. "I told him no, although he didn't accept it. He told me that I would see him again."

At that, Liam snorted. Beth ignored him and kept talking.

"As for whether or not I want to see him again, well, I think that's irrelevant. Although he is a fine-looking man! But in the first place, I'm pretty sure that his interest in me begins and ends with the fact that I intrigue him, making me a challenge. But nonetheless, there isn't a woman alive that can't say that they haven't, at least once, enjoyed shameless flattery from a handsome man. I'm no exception."

Liam snorted again before saying, "Then, Elizabeth. What's bothering you about this, if you already know that you don't want to get to know him better?"

"Well," said Beth, "it's just that I couldn't become involved with anyone now even if I wanted to, unless I was prepared to tell him the entire story of how I came to be here. I just don't think that I'm ready to take the risk of telling anyone else right now. Maybe I never will be. It's bad enough that you and your family have to carry the weight of my secret! And I don't see how I could become involved with someone and not share this with him. It wouldn't be fair to not tell the truth about this." She paused before continuing. "So you see, it doesn't matter how I feel about Martin Harrison."

Liam thought for a moment before responding. "I was right before. This is a bit of a burden on you, isn't it? Although I'm not as certain as you that you could never become involved with anyone. But I do agree with you about Martin Harrison. He's not the right man for you."

Beth laughed. "I knew that you didn't like him! Just who would be the 'right man' for me?"

Liam just looked at her without saying anything. It had been the truth when he told Elizabeth that he had neither liked nor disliked Martin. But what he felt now was definitely dislike. Maybe he was being too protective of her.

Changing the subject, Liam asked, "Are you planning on telling your great-grandparents who you really are? Had you thought about it?"

"I hadn't thought about it until today, but no, I don't think that I will. Like I said, you all already know about me. And you've been wonderful! But I actually think that it would be too close, if you know what I mean, to have them know about me. Again, there are things that I know that would make it very hard for me to be that close to them. It will be hard enough as it is now." She sighed. "Do you think that I'm being cowardly about this?"

"Cowardly? No, just cautious. I think that you'll feel it, somehow, if the time is right to share more information. I'm not certain how I would proceed, if I were you. You'll have to trust your instinct."

"*. . . Today was Decoration Day, a day to remember the soldiers of the Civil War. It seemed so strange to me to be listening to and talking with veterans of that conflict. To hear their actual voices, not just read their*

words in some history book. This really is a fascinating time! And I met
Frank and Ethel Burdett there, although they aren't married yet. It has
been an exciting day for me! . . ."

The next morning, while making their rounds on patients in town, Liam and Beth stopped at Mr. Bemis' livery stable. Earlier, Liam had suggested that he handle the possible transaction with Mr. Bemis. As he had expected, Beth had bristled at the idea.

He had laughed and said, "You are so prickly at times, so quick to become defensive!"

"Liam, don't laugh at me. I know that I'm sometimes too quick to react to things." She paused and pulled at the corner of her bottom lip with her teeth. "But even though I'm from a different time, I am still from this place. I share the same blood with these people that you do, it's just a little further removed. I understand how they are and how they think, and I'll try not to do or say anything to insult Mr. Bemis. I'm as much a Corsehill Yankee as you and he are. And I can't help that I'm a woman, or that you men aren't ready to handle the idea that a woman has as much ability as a man! Besides, if I'm to survive, then I must learn to make it on my own here. And while I'm more grateful than you'll ever know for all that you do, you can't protect me all of the time. Nor do you need to."

Liam reluctantly gave in but added, "I'll be right there beside you anyway. Just in case!" As Beth opened her mouth to speak, he said, "But I'm sure that you won't need me!"

Pulling into the yard at Mr. Bemis' stable, Beth took a look around and saw that it was also a blacksmith shop. This was attached to the stable at a right angle, the big doors thrown open. Looking inside, she could see the forge with the bellows attached and an anvil standing next to it. There was a mammoth pile of coal in an open front bin built into one corner.

As she climbed down from her seat next to Liam on the wagon, she noticed a big brown hound lying on his side under a wagon in the stable yard. He rolled his eye to look at her and thumped his tail on the dirt in greeting but made no move toward her. She spoke softly to him and was rewarded with more tail thumping.

Three kittens were chasing each other beside the stable door, rolling and tumbling. Beth watched them for a moment, smiling as they ran sideways at each other and made funny little jumps, batting their paws at the air.

Mr. Bemis was busy with another man inside the stable and gave them both a nod. Liam leaned against the wagon to wait, hands hooked in his pockets and one ankle over the other, watching the kittens. Beth looked around the stable yard and, suddenly, walked over to the corner of the barn, looking at a point somewhere in the southeast corner of the pasture. When she didn't move on right away, Liam pushed away from the wagon and walked over to where she stood, her arms folded across the fence rail.

"What do you see out there?"

Without taking her eyes from the pasture, she lowered her chin to the back of her hands and said, "Do you see that small maple tree growing way down there, on this side of the stone wall in the southeast corner?"

Liam looked and nodded.

"I grew up down there. That's where my parents' house will be. It's at the end of a street called Wayland Road, which, obviously, isn't here now but will be in around fifty years or so. By then, the field beyond the stone wall has reforested, and it's heavily wooded all the way over to the res—the Hollow."

Thinking about her childhood, Beth said, "My friend Deidre picked up a terrible case of poison ivy playing around that stone wall when we were small. She was so sick with it that her mother had to take her to the doctor . . . it really wasn't good." She shook her head where it rested on her hands.

"And that sapling will become one of the biggest maples that I've ever seen. All of us kids on the street called it the 'climbing tree' because that's what it was used for. My brother and his friend built a huge tree house in it, and we spent a lot of hours playing there.

"It's still there in a hundred years, still going strong in the backyard. The tree, not the tree house." She rolled her head, resting her cheek where her chin had been as she turned to smile at Liam. "My brother's building skills weren't as finely honed at eleven years old as they became later, and I'm afraid that the tree house didn't last more than one or two years."

Liam looked from the sapling to Beth. It hadn't occurred to him that she had grown up here, in town. He had, for some reason, pictured her living in the Hollow.

"It must be a little disconcerting to look at that now, with nothing but the pasture there."

Beth nodded, a wistful smile on her face. She straightened and turned away as she heard Mr. Bemis coming out of the stable, leading a small mare for them to see.

Liam watched her expression as she turned away, feeling a momentary sadness for her and finding a sudden, urgent desire to see her happy. He could only imagine how she must feel, seeing these places that were both familiar and foreign at the same time. He turned his attention to Mr. Bemis, who was now standing in front of them with the horse.

She was a dainty little sorrel with four white stockinged feet and a white blaze down her face. Beth had been around horses a little bit growing up and knew the basics about them. She looked her over carefully, with Liam watching, and turned to him for his opinion on the condition of the animal, which she thought was good. He agreed with her.

Beth looked at Mr. Bemis and asked, "How much do you want for her, along with a saddle and bridle?"

Mr. Bemis raised an eyebrow at her and turned to Liam. "So, Liam, are you interested in the mare?"

Liam paused, looking somewhat uncomfortable. "Well, she'll be Miss Blodgett's horse. Why don't we let her work it out with you?"

Beth knew that this was not an easy thing for Liam, and she silently thanked him with her eyes. She hadn't been entirely certain that he would let her handle this transaction, and she turned back to Mr. Bemis and asked him again how much he would like for the horse.

He gave her a stern look before stating, "Not used to doing business with women. What's a woman know about buying a horse?"

Beth put her hands on her hips. "Well, Mr. Bemis, how's a woman to learn about buying a horse if she's never given the opportunity?" She gave him her best smile. "I need to have a horse in order to efficiently assist Doctor Sizer. It's as plain as that. Would you be willing to help with this?"

Mr. Bemis continued to look at her. She could see that his mind was turning over the prospect of helping the doctor's new assistant. That finally won out, and he stated a price to her. "That includes the gear and all."

"That's awfully steep, Mr. Bemis." She countered his offer with one of fifteen dollars less.

"How am I to make any money at that price? I'll take seven off, no more!"

"Take off ten, and you've made a deal," said Beth.

Mr. Bemis turned to Liam. "She like this all of the time?"

Liam smiled, knowing that Beth had just bought a horse. "Yes, sir, she is!" His smile widened to a grin with relief. "Annoying, isn't it?"

Mr. Bemis turned to Beth. Grumpily, he said, "Well, missy, you've got yourself a horse! You trade like a man!"

Beth beamed and took his hand in a handshake. "Thank you! I'll take that as a compliment!"

Driving away with the mare tied to the wagon and the saddle in the back, Beth turned to Liam and smiled.

Liam said, "That was very nicely done. You let him think that he was doing me a favor by helping you. Was that your plan all along?"

"In my other life, I learned to read people and figure out what made them tick. I could tell that Mr. Bemis respects you, so I appealed to him that way. He liked the idea of being able to help you by helping me, because he likes you and holds you in high regard."

"Don't you think that you took advantage of his feelings for me to get what you wanted?"

Beth turned to Liam with a quizzical look. "You could look at it that way, but he didn't have to sell me that mare. And he has, actually, helped you and made himself some money at the same time. It will be easier for you now that I have my own horse. So we all saved face, and we all came away with something. And I think that I made a new friend today."

Liam finally smiled back at her. "That's true. But just one thing . . . I don't think that he had a choice about selling that mare to you from the moment you decided to buy her. Once you make your mind up about something . . ." His voice drifted off. "What are you going to call her anyway?"

"I think that I'll call her Belle. She's a pretty horse and dainty too."

CHAPTER VII

Beth and Liam continued to work away on the apartment and finished it sooner than anticipated. She had two rooms: the bigger of the two serving as a small kitchen at one end and living room at the other and a tiny bath off the bedroom with a tub in it. She couldn't wait to soak in a hot bath! Between the two of them, with Bill's help, they had installed Liam's new pump, and she had talked him into putting a cistern outside to fill up with water that the sun would heat up for her baths.

They had put in a small stove and icebox at one end of the front room, along with a couple of small cupboards and a work surface next to the sink. Liam had built a hutch for her dishes in the kitchen, and bookcases for both the bedroom and the living area.

Beth had watched Liam while he built everything in his woodshop in the barn. She never tired of watching his hands expertly shape the wood and make it do its bidding. His strong fingers would glide confidently over the pieces of wood, following the grain, sensing the texture. She had commented to him that he could have easily become a cabinetmaker instead of a doctor.

"You have real talent, Liam. I wish that you could know my brother. He has the same ability with wood."

Liam smiled at her compliment while he continued to work the wood. "I'm not sure if I should take that as a compliment after hearing your tree house story!"

Beth laughed with him, shaking her head. "Hey! C'mon! Give him a break—he was only eleven! Honestly, he gets much better and actually makes a very good living from it. He made me a small blanket chest when we were both teenagers, with a beautiful carving on the front of it. He's received many compliments on it over the years, and it became one of my favorite pieces."

She suddenly felt a wave of homesickness wash over her and bent her head to look down at the curled wood shavings that the planer in Liam's hands had created. She absently picked them up, letting them curl around her fingers before releasing them to float back down to the workbench. The sun shone in through the dirty window, and the dust motes floated lazily in the light. The air had the sweet tang of fresh lumber with the soft undertone of the horse stalls and hay in the other part of the barn.

Liam watched her from the corner of his eye as his hands absently worked the wood, knowing what she was thinking by her sudden silence. There was no sound save the rhythmic, gentle scraping of the planer moving across the wood.

"I always thought that if I didn't make it as a doctor, then I could fall back on woodworking," he said after a moment. "I learned it from my grandfather. He built this house for my grandmother when they married, and he ran the sawmill that Bill and Naomi have now. He was an exceptional woodworker, and my dad gave me all of his tools when he died. There isn't a single time that I don't think of him when I pick up one of these tools. Or look at some of the special touches that he put into the house for my grandmother, like the sitting room mantle and the kitchen and dining room hutches. They're good memories of many hours spent with both of them." He smiled gently at Beth and said, "Thank goodness for memories, hmm?"

Beth nodded, fingering the chain around her neck. "More than you know. Isn't it funny how a single thing, not just objects, but smells and sounds too, can trigger such strong memories?"

Beth furnished her new home with things from Naomi and Mrs. Sizer, as well as a bedroom set that had been in Liam's attic. She had brought over the trunk from Liam's house that had all of her things in it and placed it at the foot of her bed. She opened it, for no reason at all, and pulled out her backpack. Opening it up, she was surprised to find her digital camera and iPod. She hadn't thought about them since she had got there. Wondering if they still worked, or if the batteries were dead, she found that her iPod came on with a touch. She put the earbuds in and turned to her camera. She remembered that she had only recently bought the camera and had been taking a lot of pictures to get used to it, as it was a little different from the one that she had replaced. This too came on with a touch of a button. Beth accessed the data chip and found pictures! Jumping up, she ran from her apartment with the camera and iPod in her hands.

"Liam! Come see what I've found! Liam!"

Beth ran across the yard and in through the back door of the house, colliding with Liam in the back hallway. He put his hands on her arms to steady her.

"What is it? What's happened? Are you all right?"

"Yes! I'm fine, but look at what I've found! It's my digital camera! I can't believe that I had forgotten about this—how stupid of me! And my iPod too!"

Liam was smiling at her excitement. He didn't understand any of what she was saying, but she was clearly happy about something.

"What's a digital camera, and what's an eye pod?"

"The best way to explain them is to show you. Look." She pulled him into the sitting room as she said this, where they sat down side by side on the settee. Beth put one of the earbuds from her iPod in Liam's ear, leaving the other in hers. She watched his face as he listened to the music, knowing how strange all of it was to him. He looked at her, incredulous. Smiling, Beth began to move her shoulders to the music, tapping her hands on her legs as she listened to the songs. She had a varied assortment of music on her iPod, ranging from pop to classic rock, blues, heavy metal, bluegrass, and classical pieces.

Still moving, she asked, "So what do you think?"

"What are you doing?" he asked loudly, thinking he had to talk over the music playing in his ear.

"I'm diggin' the tunes!" she laughed. "You don't have to shout. I can hear you. Don't you like any of this? If you like the music, then you can't help but move along with it, don't you think? Try it . . . it's good for you!"

After a few minutes of shuffling through the music, she turned it off and pulled the buds from their ears, smiling at the look on his face. Putting the iPod onto his lap, she said, "Listen to all of it later, and you can tell me what you think of it. But let's look at the camera. It's even more exciting."

"I don't understand how you can get all of that noise into this contraption! You'll have to explain it all to me."

"Noise! This isn't noise . . . it's sound! I'll have you know, this is a collection of my favorite pieces of music. It's representative of my personality." She snorted. "Noise!"

Liam smiled at her, watching her face as she playfully rambled on about his lack of appreciation for fine music, enjoying this lighthearted side of her. He put the buds back in his ears and turned the iPod back on, giving it another try. He had never seen anything like this before in his life, and he turned the small strange-feeling device over and over in his hands.

Beth began to scroll through the pictures on the display screen of the camera. She imagined how Liam must be feeling, looking at these strange objects. She showed him how to scroll through the pictures and handed him the camera.

"How does this thing work? These are photographs?" He looked at her with his eyes wide, the iPod forgotten.

"Yes, they're called 'digital' photos because they're captured on a computer chip and stored to be utilized later. Remember when I explained computers to you?" Liam nodded, and she continued. "Well, you take the 'data chip' out of this camera and plug it into your computer."

She took the camera from him and pressed the button, ejecting the oblong chip into her hand. She handed it to Liam to look at. He was fascinated by it, holding it up and turning it around.

"It doesn't weigh anything! And all of the photographs go on here? How many?"

"I don't remember how many I have on here right now, but there are probably quite a few. Maybe twenty or so. Anyway, you do what's called 'download' the pictures from this chip onto the computer, and then you can start all over again and fill the chip up with more pictures. You save them on your computer. If you like, you can print out any of the pictures that you want on paper to put in a frame or album or whatever. Or you can just leave them in your computer to look at whenever you want. They could even be transferred onto my iPod. The iPod works on kind of the same principle, as far as putting and storing the data on it."

She put the chip back in the camera. "Let's see what's on here."

Liam began to scroll through the pictures. There were pictures of Beth's family, pictures that she had taken at work of things that were happening, and of her co-workers. They came to a picture of Beth with some of her fellow officers when they had tranquilized and moved a bear. Beth remembered the day, in April, when they'd had to relocate a nuisance bear. She had asked the biologist from Fish and Game to take a picture of her and the other two officers while they were preparing to move the animal.

"Is that a *bear*? Are there bears around here in one hundred years? What are you doing with it?"

Beth laughed. "Yes, it's a bear. There are, actually, too many of them around here in my time! They have become a real problem, and we tranquilize and move many of them. That's what we're doing here.

"This bear isn't dead, it's been temporarily immobilized. In fact, we released it somewhere right around here. Although sometimes, we do have to kill them. We call it 'dispatching'. I guess that sounds better when you're talking to other people about it."

"Why would you have to kill it? Do you eat them?"

"The meat isn't too bad, if prepared correctly. Although I don't care all that much for it. There is a hunting season," said Beth. "But they aren't always killed for food. Poachers will kill them illegally in order to sell the gall bladders, teeth, and claws. Sometimes . . ."

Liam interrupted her with, "Their gall bladders?"

"Yes. There is a belief in some alternative medicines that the gall bladder of the bear is very strong medicine. It gets a lot of money. Generally, it's dried and ground to a powder. I don't know if there's any real proof that it serves a useful medicinal purpose, though. There's quite a market for all kinds of animal parts from wildlife all over the world. Tracking this stuff down and enforcing the laws pertaining to it are just a part of what a game warden does.

"In any event, my most frequent involvement with bears usually had nothing to do with hunting, by any means. They get struck by cars—I mean, automobiles—and are badly injured, so they have to be dispatched. Sometimes too, bears can become what we called 'nuisance' bears. That is, their behavior is threatening or dangerous to people. Occasionally, individual bears reach a point where we're unable to haze them into changing their behavior or moving. And unfortunately, we're left with no other choice but to shoot them. It's really too bad, because quite often, the bears' bad behavior is because of something that people have taught it. Often, people put out food to feed the bears, either intentionally or not. This easy source of food then imprints on the bear, and he or she will continue to return to that spot for the easy meal and will come to expect it. They can become very aggressive over time and also, more importantly, lose their fear of us. We have an unfortunate saying that 'a fed bear is a dead bear.'"

"So," asked Liam, "have you ever had to shoot a bear?" He already knew the answer but really couldn't believe it.

"Yes. Several times. But I have never liked having to do it. It has always left me feeling somewhat out of sorts. It's not, usually, the bears' fault."

Liam continued to scroll thru the pictures, and a few frames later, they saw a picture of a moose with a calf. "Where did you see that? That's a moose!"

"I know it's a moose," laughed Beth. "We have a breeding population of them right here. I saw her and her calf not far from here. A lot of the wildlife that used to be here but aren't now will be here again in the future. These pictures are your proof. Part of my job was to make sure that, as a resource, they are protected and their population is managed."

They came to some pictures of a family birthday party for Beth's grandmother. Beth took the camera from Liam and sat looking at one picture that she had taken of everyone, including herself, in her parents' living room. She had set the timer on the camera and jumped into the picture.

"I wish that I had the ability to print out some of these pictures. This one is great!"

Liam was looking at her family on the little screen and noticing the clothing that they were wearing. Everyone looked so different from people around here. His eyes kept going back to Beth. Her hair was down, and she was wearing trousers and a V-necked sweater. She had her arm across the shoulders of the woman that she identified as her grandmother, and everyone in the photograph was laughing. It saddened him that she had been taken so abruptly from these people that she was so obviously happy with.

"Tell me who all of these people are. I recognize your mother and father, as well as your sister and brother from the photograph in your locket. I know which one is your grandmother, but who are the others?"

"Okay—this one is my sister's husband, and this is their daughter. This woman is my brother's wife, and these two are their son and daughter. And the other man, the one with the auburn hair, is my mother's youngest brother, and that's her sister next to him. The elderly couple is my mother's aunt and uncle. My uncle is the last surviving child of Frank and Ethel's." Beth thought for a moment, her eyebrows drawn together, before saying, "You know, it's probable that you will deliver him into this world."

Liam looked with interest at them all, particularly at the elderly man, looking for some resemblance to Frank and Ethel. It was somewhat mind-boggling to him that he was looking at a man of around ninety who hadn't even been born yet. It occurred to him, suddenly, that Elizabeth must have this same type of sensation several times a day.

They continued on through the pictures, giving Liam glimpses into the life that Beth had left behind. There was one of Beth standing next to her all-terrain vehicle, with another officer next to his. She was holding her helmet in her hand, and her hair was a mess.

Beth looked at Liam and said, "This is a vehicle built for rough terrain. We use them to patrol off the road, where regular cars and trucks can't go. You have to wear a helmet to protect your head from injury in case you roll it over or flip it. That's what I'm holding in my hand."

"Why don't you just take a horse into these places? It seems that it would be safer, if you have to protect yourself from injury in order to ride these things."

"Most people don't have a horse or the ability to go to a livery stable to rent one," replied Beth with a smile. "In fact, there aren't even livery stables like Mr. Bemis' around anymore. Horses are more of a hobby, although they are still used for work, to a certain degree, out west."

Next, they came to an image of a man in a flight suit standing next to a helicopter. Beth said, "Remember a helicopter? That's what this is. This is my friend, Tim. He flies them."

"You mean, he gets into that thing and goes up into the air? Have you ever been in one while it was flying through the air?" Liam's eyes were wide with wonder. Beth nodded and laughed.

"What was it like?" he asked. "How does it work?"

"It's the most incredible thing!" responded Beth, gesturing with her hands. "You rise straight up off the ground, then fly through the air and watch the world slip by beneath you! Faster than any bird you can imagine, but noisy." Shrugging her shoulders and shaking her head, she added, "But I can't begin to explain the engineering or physics of it to you. Air displacement, of course, is part of it. But that's about all I can tell you about it. And you probably figured that much out for yourself."

She had taken a picture of some of her coworkers standing in front of her patrol truck with the state emblem on the side and the blue lights on top. "This is what some automobiles will look like. This is called a pickup truck, and it's what I drove at work to patrol my area."

Liam murmured, "The design on the side matches the patch that was on your shirt sleeve. All of these men are dressed like you were when I found you." He recognized a couple of them from the other pictures. "Were they your friends too?"

Beth nodded, smiling. He continued, "This makes it somewhat more real to me, seeing these pictures. Do you understand what I mean?"

Beth smiled at him. "Yes, I think that I do. You were having trouble visualizing all that I have tried to describe to you over these past few weeks. And this helps, doesn't it? Before this, it was just too much to believe. This must all seem like something from a Jules Verne or H.G. Wells novel! But I assure you, it's all real. It's the future, Liam, and it's exciting! Here, at the beginning of the twentieth century, we are standing on the threshold of so many, many changes! What you've heard and seen just now is only a small example of how far man will be able to go."

They finished going through the images, and Liam went back through them again, questioning Beth about things that he saw in the background of the pictures that were commonplace to her, but alien to him. Shaking his head, he finally handed the camera back to Beth.

"Incredible! Who would ever imagine that we would advance so far in just a century? What makes this camera and 'eye-pod' work?"

"They run off of what's called a 'rechargeable battery.' That means that, eventually, I won't be able to look at these photos anymore or listen to my music. A battery is a small cell that stores up electricity for a period of time and supplies power to a device, in this case, my camera and iPod. But they have a shelf life—they don't last forever. The batteries in these are rechargeable, which means that I can keep putting more electricity into them by plugging them into a constant source of electricity and 'recharging' them. But I don't have access to electricity here, nor do I have the charger cords that I need to plug them in with. I remember that I had recharged the batteries the night before I went on the search that brought me here, so they should last me a while. But eventually, they will die down and lose power."

"Where did you access the electricity from?"

"Every building in my time has electricity in it. You plug into wall outlets throughout the house. I know that it seems strange now, but electricity will find its way here and soon too. It won't remain a luxury that's only available in the cities for much longer. Electricity will be used for lighting, heating, cooking . . . all sorts of things."

"So life here must seem dull to you after where you came from." Liam shook his head again. "You must miss all of the things that you had and were able to do. Until today, I guess that I hadn't realized, fully, how much you have left behind."

Smiling, Beth said, "I miss the people, mostly. But I'll admit that I miss some of the stuff, too . . . my Nikes, my sweats, my CD and DVD collections, and my washer and dryer. I miss my laptop, my wristwatch, and hot showers. Take-out and supermarkets and my microwave. I miss answering my cell to a friend's call with, '*Hey! What's up?*' and then going to hook up for some wings." She paused and looked at Liam. Laughing, she said, "You don't have any idea what I'm talking about, do you? It sounds like I'm speaking a foreign language, doesn't it?"

Liam nodded, his eyebrows high and his mouth in a straight line.

"Well, sometimes, I feel like I'm in a foreign land. Do you know what I mean?"

Liam nodded again, a small smile on his lips.

"Do you know what else I miss? I miss being able to just cuss outright when something goes wrong. Everyone is always so *polite* here! Mostly, I find it refreshing. But every so often, I'd like to just let go. Like the other day, when I whacked my head in the barn."

Liam laughed, lifting one eyebrow at her. "*Ladies* don't cuss! And *gentlemen* don't cuss in front of ladies!"

Beth laughed with him. "I can cuss like a sailor. I'm ashamed to say that I could probably teach you a few new words!"

"Mmhmm. Of that I have no doubt." He was shaking his head, still laughing.

She laughed again, then paused, thinking. "And I really miss my old copy of Longfellow's poems. My Mom and Dad gave it to me, and I do miss that. But—no matter," she said with a wistful smile, shrugging her shoulders, not uncaringly but dismissively, as one would do with something that they have already accepted. "I'm adjusting. Besides, life then had become far too hectic. We have created too many things to occupy our time and attention. I prefer the pace of my new life, here. I'm busy, but there's a difference that I can't explain. And this is anything but boring for me! In fact, I find many aspects of my life here to be fulfilling. Like I said, it really is the people that I miss more than anything.

"And it's funny, but I've always been drawn to things from this time, and I had furnished my home with many things that were made or in use right now or even before now. I spent a lot of time with my family, searching for and buying what we considered antiques for my house. I also have a lot of things that belonged to my grandparents or great-grandparents. I have my father's parents' spindle bed, my mother's parents' mantle clock, and Ethel's bean pot. My grandmother gave me her mother's rocking chair. The list goes on and on."

Liam sat back in the settee, running his knuckles back and forth across his chin, his ankle resting on his knee. He was lost in thought, mulling over all that she had just told him. Beth held up the camera and snapped a picture of him. He jumped as the flash went off.

"What did you just do?"

Beth sat back and turned the camera toward him. "I just took your picture. See?"

There he was, captured on the data chip. "Just like that? That quickly? It looks just like me. I'm not posed, and it looks the same as this room! The colors and everything! This is incredible!"

"I have an idea," said Beth, standing up. She pulled a small table toward the settee and positioned the camera on top of some books. She bent down and looked at the view screen, then adjusted it some more. Setting the timer, she returned to the settee and sat down next to Liam.

"Smile. We're about to have our picture taken!" She was thinking to herself that one day, this camera would find its way back to her parents, along with this picture.

> "... I have noticed around me the talent in these hills. There are musicians, artists, seamstresses, weavers, woodworkers ... you name it, and they can do it. And they treat it all as commonplace; these are just the things that they do every day. There is no need for television or computers to occupy their minds. I am finding that my days are full of these observations. I watched Liam building my kitchen cupboards the other day, talking with me while he worked. He shaped the lumber into cabinets to store all of my possessions, and took the time to put special touches on them, like carving designs into the corners of each one, paying as much attention to our conversation as he was to his woodworking. It seemed so effortless to him, yet I knew the skill required in making these pieces for me, and I was impressed by his ability and touched by his thoughtfulness. Everyone here seems to be born with their own unique talent for improving the quality of life around them. I wonder what I can bring to this community ..."

Chapter VIII

_____

One afternoon, while planting the hollyhocks and lilac bush that Mrs. Sizer had given her for her dooryard, she heard a rider coming into the yard and heard Liam speaking with a man. Beth decided that he would call her if she was needed or come get her, and she continued to put the plants into the ground, enjoying the scent and feel of the warm earth. The sun was warming her skin, and she could hear the birds singing all around her. *This moment*, she thought, *is perfect. Sublime, even.* She closed her eyes and tilted her face toward the sun, a tiny smile on her lips, a light breeze blowing across her warm skin.

Liam was working in the barn when he heard the sound of approaching hooves. Walking outside, he saw Martin Harrison ride into the yard.

He rode up to Liam and greeted him, saying, "I've come to pay a visit to Miss Blodgett. Is she here? May I have a visit with her?"

Liam returned the greeting, replying, "Yes, she is. I think that she's around, in her apartment." He gestured toward the side of the barn. "As for visiting with her—well, that's up to her, not me." Smiling, he said, "Let's go ask her."

Liam stepped back into the barn to take off his tool belt; and when he came back out, Martin's horse was tied to the rail, and he was nowhere to be seen.

A voice startled her out of her reverie. "A penny for your thoughts?"

Beth started and opened her eyes, looking up from where she was sitting on the ground toward the man who had spoken. He was standing with the sun at his back, and she shaded her eyes with a grubby hand so that she could identify him. It was Martin Harrison.

"Miss Blodgett, you look as lovely today as you did when I last saw you." He extended his hand toward her asking, "May I help you up, or shall I sit down there with you?"

Beth smiled at him and, after wiping her hands on the grass next to her, stood up on her own. "My hands are pretty dirty, so I'll just help myself up, thank you." Remembering her manners, she said, "Mr. Harrison, how are you? What brings you out here today?"

"Please, call me Martin so that I may call you Beth. I told you that you would hear from me again. I hope that you don't mind. I was riding out this way, so I thought that I would take a chance that you would be here and agreeable to a visit."

Beth thought to herself that it was not as though she could turn him away, now that he was here! Out loud, she said, "Of course. May I get you something cold to drink? I have some lemonade that I made this morning."

As she finished speaking, Liam came around the corner. She felt both relief and annoyance that he was there. It flashed across her mind that she didn't need constant supervision or an audience, yet at the same time, she was relieved at having someone to guide her through this difficult game of entertaining the opposite sex in one's home in 1908. Frankly, she was at a loss at how to proceed without looking foolish or ill-mannered. After all, this was a male caller. Could she entertain him without a chaperone? Should she? Did it no longer matter at her age? What was the correct way to go with this? Whoever said that these were simpler days hadn't thought about this stuff, that was for sure! She would have to speak with Naomi or Mrs. Sizer about the finer points of guests in the home. Meanwhile, Liam was hovering there to rescue her as usual. How did people ever date in these times?

Liam spoke up, saying, "Why don't I bring out some chairs for us to sit on? It's a nice day for sitting outside."

Liam followed Beth inside as she went to get the lemonade. Once in the apartment, she turned to him, and her independent streak made her whisper, "You really don't need to stay, Liam."

He lifted one eyebrow at her, smiling, and whispered back, "I wouldn't miss it," as he picked up two chairs from the table and carried them outside to the bench by her door.

Beth brought out lemonade, and the three of them sat in the sun, drinking and making small talk about Corsehill. Beth noticed that Liam didn't say much and seemed to get more on edge with each minute. After about an hour, Martin said that it was time for him to be going. As they stood, Beth thanked him for his visit. Liam smiled and offered to walk him out.

Back in the drive, Martin turned to Liam. "I have to ask you something, Doctor. And the best way to do it is to speak plainly. What are your intentions toward Beth? Am I intruding where I shouldn't be?"

Liam appreciated his honesty but didn't know the answer to his questions. "Elizabeth is my assistant and my friend. I will tell you this, Martin. She has been through a lot. But she's not like any other woman that you will ever meet. She is strong and capable of making up her own mind. If she chooses to let you into her life, then I can only say this to you . . . don't hurt her. She deserves to be happy." Liam looked him in the eye and continued, "And if you deliberately hurt her, then you'll answer to me."

Martin looked at him for a long moment. He turned and mounted his horse, riding off without looking back.

Liam went to the corner of the barn and bumped into Beth as she was coming around. Without saying anything further, he curtly told her that he was going fishing. He turned and headed toward the back of the house to get his fly rod without waiting for a reply from her.

Beth went back to planting her flowers, but after Martin's visit, she was restless. The peace that she had felt earlier in the day had left her, and her gardening now seemed like a chore. She decided to walk over and see Naomi.

Naomi was baking when Beth walked into the kitchen, and Beth offered to give her a hand. She began to tell Naomi about Martin's visit that afternoon and of how Liam had stayed with them.

"I swear, Naomi, I never would have survived these past few weeks without Liam and the rest of you! There is so much that I just don't know!" She sighed. "I mean, what is considered proper? Should he have stayed with us, or would I have been all right alone? I'm all adrift here! This is all very frustrating to me!" She sighed again, a heavy breath, and spread her hands to Naomi. "I'm not used to relying this much on other people."

Naomi listened patiently, smiling while Beth talked on. She was picturing her brother charging around the corner of the barn to rescue Beth from Martin's clutches. She suspected that Liam's reason for coming to her rescue may have had as much to do with Beth's honor as his own possessiveness. She wondered if her brother even knew how he really felt about Beth. It was obvious to the rest of them that she was becoming very special to him. His eyes would constantly go back to her when they were together. And Naomi had noticed that he seemed to laugh so much more than before and was always doing things to make Beth feel more at home. But whenever she tried to talk with him about Beth, his answers were evasive. She was certain that, whether he knew it or not, Liam was falling in love with Beth. And fighting it all the way. She also suspected that was why he had taken off to go fishing now, which was something he did whenever he needed to think.

Beth finished talking and sat looking at Naomi, cookie dough sticking to her fingers. "Hello. Have you been listening to me? Earth to Naomi."

Naomi laughed, "Some of your sayings! They don't make any sense to me! Of course I've been listening to you!" She sat back, rubbing the small of her back. "Ohhh, these babies are giving me a pain! Now on with what you were saying. You're doing just fine. Really, you are. As you just said, Liam and the rest of us are here for you. Liam was right in coming around to sit with the two of you. Not that *you* need a chaperone, but it is proper for a lady to entertain a gentleman caller with a third party present or nearby. At least, the first few visits, anyway."

Beth got up to put the pan of cookies in the oven and to take another one out.

Naomi spoke to her back. "You know, I have known Martin Harrison for many years. He comes from a good family, but he has grown up privileged. He is, for lack of a better term, spoiled. He isn't necessarily a bad person, that is to say he's likeable. But he seems to look at things in terms of how he can benefit from them. Liam knows this, and I'm certain that was the main reason why he was there. Trust Liam, Beth."

Beth returned to the table and sat back down. "I do trust him. But I think that he feels obliged to take care of me because of the way that I was, more or less, dumped on him. And sometimes, it seems as though he's too protective. I know that he doesn't like Martin Harrison, but he didn't even give me a chance to make my own decision, and I'm not used to that. Then he took off so suddenly this afternoon, not that he needs to give me an explanation, of course. But it just seemed as though he was angry with me for ruining his afternoon or something. It wasn't my fault . . . I didn't ask him to stay! In fact, I told him that he didn't have to. Maybe my living there, on his property, isn't such a good idea. He's been living alone all of this time, and now here I am. Always there, always underfoot. It started me wondering if maybe I'm becoming a nuisance, or . . . or a burden."

Giving Beth a frank look, Naomi said, "Beth, you've been so brave since you came here. I envy that about you. You take all of your challenges and face them head-on. It surprises me, then, that when it comes to . . . matters of the heart . . . well, you seem to lose all of your courage and question yourself."

Beth busied herself reaching for a cookie. It wasn't just now that she was that way. She had always been like that with her heart. Always unsure, never on solid ground. She broke the cookie in two, handing one half to Naomi.

Naomi put her free hand over Beth's on the table. "But don't worry about these things! I think that you coming into our lives has been a good tonic for my brother. He was spending too much time alone, and you're keeping him busy enough so that he is coming back out of that shell that he had been creeping into." Smiling, she said, "You've got it all wrong anyway! He needs your help as much as you need his, so you're both benefiting from you living in that apartment! Now, how would you like to make us some tea to have with these cookies, hmm?"

Liam stood in the river, letting the water wash around his legs while he cast the line of the fly rod. His mind was unsettled, and he doggedly sifted through his thoughts. Why was he so uptight about Martin's visit with Elizabeth? He shook his head with annoyance. What was it about this woman that left him questioning himself so much? He wasn't used to second-guessing himself; it was something that he hadn't done since he was a schoolboy.

And he could tell that she had been annoyed with him when he came around to sit with them, although she hid it well. She could certainly take care of herself, and besides, she had said that she wasn't interested in seeing Harrison again. So why, then, had she offered him lemonade and sat visiting with him for an hour? But he knew that wasn't Elizabeth's fault. Martin had not left her with much of a choice. And he could tell too that she really hadn't known how to proceed once Martin was at her door which was, he told himself, the reason he chose to stay, even though she was irritated with him.

He mulled over his conversation with Martin. Should he tell Elizabeth that Martin intended to see her again? He knew that he wouldn't say anything. He thought about Martin's question of his intentions. He didn't know the answer to that, and it bothered him. He had only known her a few weeks, but already he'd found that he enjoyed her company immensely. But what if she disappeared as quickly as she had arrived? If he let himself become too attached to her, then where would that leave him? And no woman was going to rule his life! He had been through similar pain before, and he wasn't going to go through it again.

He felt a new flash of annoyance as he realized that his thoughts centered around her more than he liked. It seemed as though every thought that came into his head came back to her. All of a sudden, he longed for the life he had before she'd arrived, where each day was the same as the one before. He took care of his patients, sharing in their joys and sorrows. He saw his friends and family every day and was very much at ease among them all. Then he went home happy and free with his life. The need to get back to that life was urgent and irrational . . . and it filled his chest with emotion. And he knew why.

He was amazed when he realized how much he would miss her if she left after such a short period of time and knew now that if she were to leave, he would feel it. Up until now, he hadn't minded being alone, but he found the house to be strangely empty now that she had moved across to her apartment. He had become accustomed to hearing her humming or singing or moving around the house, and he already missed her presence there. He had gotten very used to sharing his meals with her or sitting in the quiet of the evening while they both read or she wrote in her journal. The house seemed too quiet now without her.

But what if she really was here to stay? Would she live on the other side of his yard for the rest of their lives? What did she want? Would she be content with things the way that they were now, or would she want someone to spend the rest of her life with? She was so independent. Did she still believe that she had to remain alone? What would make her happy? Sometimes, she was such a contradiction. There were times when he would watch her and see exactly what was on her mind. Other times, she flummoxed him completely.

He felt a tug on the end of his line, and watched the fly disappear under the water. He played the line, letting the fish think that it had caught a fly, and then he carefully set it. He reached for the net on his belt and scooped the trout out of the water. He smiled at the beauty of it, watching as the late afternoon sun caught at the iridescent colors as it turned in the net. Carefully, he removed the hook and slid the fish back into the river, holding it gently while he moved it back and forth in the water for a few seconds to make sure that he hadn't hurt it.

Beth had taken the path along the river from Naomi's house. She sat down on the same log that she and Liam had sat on that first night. It seemed so long ago, but it was only a few weeks. Gradually, she became aware of the sound of the water flowing past her; that eternal voice that never ceased its soothing chant. She watched the grass growing up from the edge of the river, bending with the water as it flowed past, and wondered how it managed to grow at all with the water constantly pulling at it. Why didn't it just uproot and float down river? The roots must be strong to hold it there like that and still allow it to grow.

She looked upstream to see Liam fishing. As she sat watching the timeless scene of man and river, she began to understand the peace that he felt here. The wild honeysuckle were blooming in a riot of pink on the far bank, and as she looked over at them, she watched a phoebe fly across her line of sight, following a drunkard's path as it chased after some flying bug for supper. The afternoon sun was warm on her skin as it traveled toward the western horizon, and she could smell the pure earthy scent of the water as it journeyed past her in the river. She turned her gaze back to Liam in time to see him catch the trout. Beth realized that he hadn't seen her sitting there, and she watched as he brought the fish in, a slight smile coming over his face as he stood looking down at it. She stood up and walked toward him.

He looked up and saw her as he released the fish. "Oh, sorry. Did you want to get a better look at it? I didn't see you there." He was still smiling. She was glad to see it. His whole face lit up whenever he smiled, and one couldn't help but smile back.

Stupidly, she said, "I've brought cookies." And then she held out the packet that she had brought from Naomi's. Then, "Weren't you going to teach me how to fly fish?"

He smiled again and laughed. "Are you going to be such a bad student that you have to bribe me with cookies? What kind are they?"

Beth laughed with him. Suddenly, some of the peace that she had felt earlier returned to her, and it felt good. "They're Naomi's molasses cookies. We've just baked them." She paused. "Do you want to be alone, or may I stay?"

"You can go, but leave the cookies," was his deadpan reply. He looked at Beth's face and started to laugh. "I'm just having fun! Of course you can stay. You don't need to ask! Come out here if you want that lesson!"

Beth sat down and took off her shoes. She stood and looked down at her skirt. Liam was watching her. He shrugged his shoulders and smiled, enjoying her predicament.

Beth grinned at him, delighting in the challenge. She reached down and grabbed hold of the hem on the back of her skirt and pulled it up through her legs, tucking it into the front of her belt and turning her skirt into long, loose shorts. She waded, barefoot and barelegged, into the river.

"Well, where do we start?"

He was still smiling. "Do you have any notion of how you look? I don't think that it's a fashion that will catch on. But I don't mind it!" He admired the shape of her legs again as she stood in the water at the edge of the river.

Beth laughed. "I can only work with what I have. And that's a lot that you know anyway! Wait until I tell you about shorts or short skirts. Or the bathing suits of my time. This is nothing, believe me!" She began to walk through the water toward him, stepping gingerly over some of the sharper rocks.

They enjoyed the next hour in the river while Liam instructed her in casting technique. Beth watched while he effortlessly made several casts. Turning to her, he asked, "Are you ready to give it a go?" Beth nodded, smiling as she took the fly rod from him. They both seemed to have silently agreed not to discuss Martin's visit.

Liam stood behind her while she cocked her arm back to the eleven o'clock position and sharply snapped the rod forward until her arm was at the one o'clock position.

"Remember, wait until the line forms a nice tight loop behind you before you send it forward again." Reaching around from where he stood behind her, he placed his hand over hers on the rod. "You're too impatient! Wait just another second or two."

He left his hand on top of hers while they made a few more casts together into the river. His other hand was resting on her opposite shoulder. Beth could feel the warmth of his touch and thought at how comfortable she felt with him. It was as though he had always been present in her life.

"When you get the fly where you want it on top of the water," he said, "let it drift a bit before snapping the line back again. And remember to lock your wrist."

He took his hand off of hers, but remained standing where he was, hands on his hips, watching over her shoulder as the fly drifted downriver. Suddenly, it disappeared. Beth jumped, and Liam said, "Wait! Be patient!" They stood together in the water, waiting. Beth could feel small tugs on the line that she held in her left hand. "Now, set the hook!"

Beth pulled back on the line in her hand, stepping back at the same time. She bumped into Liam and stumbled, putting her foot down on top of a sharp rock. She jumped again, backward into Liam, knocking him down before falling backward on top of him.

Falling backward into the river with her full weight on his stomach, Beth heard Liam breathe out a gusty "Oof!" as she knocked the wind out of him. She slid off and sat next to him, chest deep in the frigid water, still holding the fly rod.

Liam sat up, rubbing his stomach. He shook his head at her, and Beth watched as he reached up to push the soaked hair off of his forehead. He reached over to pull in the line from the end of the rod. The fish was gone and so was the fly on the end.

"Now I'm going to have to teach you to tie flies as well since the one that got away took ours with him."

"I'm sorry! Oh, I'm so sorry! Are you all right? I didn't mean to knock you into the water. I hope that I didn't hurt you! I guess that I was a little overeager. You're right, I am too impatient. And I'm sorry about losing the fish, and once you teach me how, I will replace the fly." She was somewhat embarrassed about her clumsiness and found herself babbling to cover up for it. She stopped when she saw that Liam's eyes were sparkling with laughter, and there was a broad grin on his wet face.

"Do you know, I don't believe that I've been bored since I met you!" he laughed. "All that I can say is that it's a good thing you brought along cookies!" He stood up and reached a hand down to her. They were both sopping wet, and Beth was shivering slightly.

She felt a sharp pain on the bottom of her foot as she stood up, and she winced. She placed a hand on Liam's shoulder to brace herself and lifted her right foot out of the water. Looking down at it, they both saw that it was cut and bleeding.

Liam helped her to the house and into the kitchen, where he pulled over a chair from the table and sat her down. He went and got his kit, then put a towel down on another chair, and had her put her foot on it. He examined and cleaned the cut for her, then lifted up her foot, and sat down, putting her foot on his lap.

He shook his head at her and said, "It seems that I am to be forever fishing you out of that river!"

Beth smiled, her teeth beginning to chatter lightly. "I'll try to return the favor, someday!"

"Thanks, I'll remember that. You're lucky that you don't need any stitches to close this. I think that you should stay out of that river; it has it in for you. The cut on your forehead has only just healed, and now you've sliced your foot open." He looked across at her and smiled as he began to smear honey on the open cut on her foot.

"Well, that's me. Stem to stern with scars." She was watching him with the honey, enjoying the feel of his gentle hands. They were slightly calloused from his woodworking, but his tender touch made up for it. Closing her eyes, she thought to herself that his hands felt like heaven on her foot and ankle, and she could come to enjoy a steady diet of that soft touch. She forced herself to shift her thoughts elsewhere.

"You know, until I came here, I never knew that honey had topical healing powers."

"Yes," said Liam. "It works well as an antiseptic." He wiped his hands on the towel and reached for a bandage. "I wasn't going to say anything, but I noticed when I was examining your injuries on that first day that you have quite a number of scars on you. It's unusual for anyone, let alone a woman."

"I guess that I tend to jump right into things a little too much, without paying attention to how I may hurt myself. That has always been a problem with me, even as a little girl, according to my mother. She was on a first name basis with the emergency room personnel." As she said that, her hand went to the locket around her neck as though to make certain that it was still there.

Liam saw a look of homesickness cross her face and quickly disappear, and he bent his head and began to wrap the bandage around her foot. His eyes drifted for a moment up her foot to her delicate ankle and shapely calf. He wondered what it would feel like to slide his hand over her ankle and along her calf, to touch the soft skin behind her knee . . .

Beth looked at the top of his head and at the water still dripping off of him. "Thank you, Liam. Thank you for helping me today." Startled, he looked up at her. "I mean, earlier with Martin. To be honest, I have never been very good with this whole 'courting' thing, even in my own time, never mind knowing what was expected in this day and time. I would have made a fool of myself if you hadn't been there."

Liam smiled at her. "Elizabeth, the one thing that I have found in you is that you have a tremendous ability to rise to any occasion. This wouldn't have been any exception. But you're welcome."

"Well, thanks for the vote of confidence. And thank you for the fishing lesson and for getting soaked for it and for bandaging my injuries. Again."

"Lucky thing for you that there's a resident doctor on the premises, the way you get hurt, isn't it?"

"About that, Liam." Beth paused, trying to pull the right words together. "Am I sometimes a nuisance to have around here?" At his quizzical look, she quickly rushed on, "What I mean is, you were so used to being alone, and now here I am. Always underfoot, so to speak, day in and day out."

"Elizabeth, what brings this about?"

"Well . . . you seemed so edgy earlier, when Martin came by. I thought that maybe you were irritated that you never really have your home completely to yourself anymore. It reminded me that I have changed your daily life considerably, and that I'm not the only one who has had to adjust to a new lifestyle, and I just want to say that I'm very sorry about that."

Liam thought to himself that she had no idea about the changes that she had brought. He was still figuring them out himself. He smiled and slowly shook his head. "Sometimes, Elizabeth, you confound me."

Without saying another word, he gently set her bandaged foot on the floor. Leaning forward, he laid a hand on the side of her face. Hesitating for the barest moment, he gently, softly kissed her cheek. Slowly, he pulled away from her, stood up, and walked out of the kitchen. She heard him climb the stairs, and he called back to her, "You should go get into some dry clothes."

Beth sat in the chair with her mouth hanging open. Realizing this, she shut it. "What was that?" she softly murmured to herself. "Now I'm more confused than ever! And he said that *I* confound *him*!" She got up and gingerly walked out of the house, crossing the yard to her apartment. All in all, she thought, it had been quite a day.

Upstairs, Liam began to strip off his wet clothes, smiling as he recalled all that had just happened. Even though he had fallen in the river and lost one of his favorite flies, he couldn't remember when he'd had a more enjoyable time fishing. He continued to smile as he pictured Elizabeth's face as he pulled away after kissing her. He wondered how long it took her to realize that her jaw was hanging open. He didn't know why he had kissed her. He hadn't planned on it. Or why he had almost kissed her mouth, changing his mind in the last instant and kissing her cheek instead. It just seemed like the thing to do. She couldn't have been more wrong about what had caused his earlier edginess. Sometimes, she read people's actions so accurately. And then other times, she was so far off the mark . . .

". . . I learned to fly fish today. Or, rather, I learned how not to fly fish. But, now that I know what I shouldn't be doing, I'm confident that I'll do better next time! I am also learning the finer points of 'courting'. Not doing so well there, either . . . "

The next morning, she crossed the yard to the house. It was Liam's turn to cook breakfast. They had decided early on that it would be easier if they each took turns cooking. They had one rule: they didn't complain about each other's cooking, or the complainer got to do it all. Liam had gotten the better end of the deal, as it turned out that after a few early blunders, Beth adapted relatively quickly to cooking in what she called an old-fashioned kitchen and was, by far, the better cook. But she never complained about his cooking, not wanting to end up with the job every day. They continued to share in this duty for breakfast even after Beth had moved into her apartment.

Liam had the coffee going for himself and hot water on for tea for Beth. She saw that the table wasn't set and began to get plates and cutlery. Liam was at the stove trying to burn their eggs.

Beth asked, "What culinary masterpiece are you preparing for our breakfast today?"

He looked over his shoulder at her. "Is that a complaint about my cooking? How's the foot today?"

Beth put her hands up. "Absolutely not! I look forward to every morsel. And my foot's fine, thanks."

Liam slid the eggs onto the plates that Beth held out to him. "Elizabeth, you asked me a question last night, and I didn't answer it for you."

They walked to the table together and sat down before he continued. "I don't mind having you around here. I'll admit that if someone had asked me if I wanted a full-time assistant before you got here, my answer would have been different. But now that you're here, I've been glad to have you, and you have been a tremendous help to me. Besides, it's been very educational for me as well. You've made me look at everything in a different light, and I appreciate that. I meant it when I said that I haven't been bored since you came here. I enjoy your company. So it's my turn to say thank you."

They looked across the table at each other for a moment, and Beth grinned. She took a bite of the eggs and immediately fished an eggshell out of her mouth. Holding it on the end of her finger, she looked across at Liam as she said, "You know, I prefer to have my eggs without the shells, thank you very much."

She saw that he was watching her with one eyebrow cocked up, knowing that he was recalling her early attempts at making coffee, and she hurried on to exclaim, "But these are delicious!"

CHAPTER IX

Beth was amazed at how busy she stayed. The days working with Liam were always interesting for her, whether they were out on calls or working at home. Corsehill and the neighboring hill towns at the turn of the twentieth century were vastly different from Beth's time. With the river and all of the streams feeding into it, industry was booming. There was a bedstead factory, a hat factory, several tanneries, a whip factory, and a chair factory, as well as other woodworking and furniture shops. In addition to Bill's sawmill, there was also a gristmill and a small woolen mill that turned out men's clothes. The local women did the finish work in their homes. With so much activity in the area, Beth found that Liam had plenty of opportunity to practice his medicine.

Each of these calls that Beth went on with Liam resulted in her growing respect for him. She watched him interact with the people around them, putting them at ease with his quick smile. He would calm his patients with his touch and voice as he examined and treated them. He sincerely cared about all of these people and would always inquire about what was going on in their lives and with their families. He never hesitated to pitch in and help wherever he could; and she could see that, for the most part, they liked and respected him immensely, and he was forever receiving offers to "take tea" or to "stop by just for a visit."

In addition to the local businesses, there were many small farms where families supported themselves on their property, growing and harvesting what they needed or bartering for things that they didn't have. While the men worked hard every day, Beth was even more impressed with how hard the women worked to keep their homes. She and Liam would often find the woman of the house hard at work. She would be preparing baked goods or churning butter each day. Washday consisted of an entire day's work. When an animal was slaughtered, she would be busy for days, processing every part of the animal to be used later in everything from food or food preparation, to washing, to harness repair. Nothing was wasted.

Her sewing basket was always filled with darning and mending. Old clothes weren't discarded; they were reborn into something new by her skilled hands. Floors were swept and mopped daily, stoves reblackened, and kitchens whitewashed routinely. Many homes had two kitchens: one for summer use and one for winter. Both had to be maintained. There were butt'ries and pantries that needed regular upkeep and stocking. The vegetable garden and hen house were also her responsibility and required regular attention.

Rugs were hung outside to have the dust and dirt beaten from them. Fireplaces and woodstoves were swept clean, and the chimneys from the oil lamps were collected and washed each day. Mattresses were turned and restuffed, and blankets had to be taken outside for airing out. Produce and meat must be preserved or cured before spoiling, and time had to be made for harvesting fruits and vegetables as they ripened. Yet these women always stopped what they were doing and offered tea and pie or cake to "Doc Sizer and Miss Blodgett" as though they had nothing else to do. How they managed this all while raising a family was a mystery to Beth, and she admired them greatly for their ability.

When Beth wasn't working with Liam, she would ride out on Belle just to poke around. Sometimes, he would come along; other times, she went on her own, always with a cautioning word from him to "be careful." Beth enjoyed these rides immensely. She took note of the wildflowers that bloomed everywhere. The lilacs, followed by the columbine, wild geraniums, and lily of the valley were in every yard or on the roadside. The iris that seemed to spring up overnight in the wet areas of every field that she passed were beautiful. Swamp pinks were blooming, and the mountain laurel was just beginning to show color. She took some measure of comfort in the sight of these flowers, noting that they were still present everywhere in this area in her other life as well. As always, spring was gently handing over to summer. There was a sense of continuity in that thought, and she enjoyed the transition as much now as she always had.

She took many walks as well into the fields and the woods surrounding them. Liam would go with her, and they would collect medicinal plants as they found them. Each one would be stored for future use: sweet birch, dandelion greens, wild garlic, nettles and dock, chickweed, wild mustard, horseradish, blue violets, and wild strawberry leaves, to name a few.

While they walked, Beth would use the opportunity to keep her tracking and observation skills sharp; and her head was always turning as she looked around, taking in everything. Liam was constantly amazed at the things that she would see and point out to him—things that he would have walked past without noticing. She was beginning to recognize the footprints of people and livestock that used the roads and trails in the area. She would point to a footprint and tell him who had left it and how long ago. She would tell him what had taken place in a spot where all he saw were scuff marks in the dirt. She taught him about the wildlife in the area and point out the sign that they had left behind or identify every bird that they saw or heard, describing its habits and how it nested. This was where she was in her element. Liam would watch her walk with her long, easy gait and realized that this was the environment that she was most relaxed in. In his mind, he would frequently superimpose one of the pictures of her in her uniform that he had seen on her camera over the Elizabeth that he saw here. It was during these walks that he could fit the two together so completely.

She also spent some of her off time helping Naomi, who was getting closer to her due date and feeling increasingly uncomfortable. Her friendship with Naomi had been growing steadily. Naomi, like Liam, never tired of hearing her stories from what she would call her other life. And Beth would take every bit of insight that Naomi could share with her about a woman's life in the time that she was now living in. They would talk easily of childhood in Corsehill and girlish crushes that they had gone through as teenagers. There was laughter, and sometimes tears, shared between them.

The Sizer family would get together often and always insisted that Beth join them. They would share a meal and conversation and often play card games. They taught her to play Euchre and Bridge, and she found that as she got better at these games, her competitive spirit came alive, making these lively, fun occasions.

Mr. Sizer had begun his profession as a teacher in Corsehill and was now the superintendent of the four schools in town, overseeing the teachers and curriculum, as well as seeing to it that each schoolhouse had teaching supplies and was maintained. Beth enjoyed her discussions with him regarding these schools, such as the direction that he wanted them to go in, as well as where the educational systems of the future would take students. Both he and Mrs. Sizer were kind, intelligent people; and more and more, she found herself grateful for the presence of this family in her life. While no one could ever replace the family that she had left behind, their easy acceptance of her helped to partially fill that void within her.

She managed to keep busy most evenings as well. Before, if she wasn't working at night, she would listen to music and read or watch a movie. She would get in her car or on her bicycle and run errands or visit friends or family. Obviously, these things had changed. She still read quite a bit, borrowing books from Liam. Or sometimes when she was in town, she would go into the lending library. She also began to sew again, making matching quilts for Naomi's babies using fabric that she had got at Perkins Store across from the library.

She found herself baking a lot, making a couple of loaves of bread a week that she shared with Liam and usually a batch of cookies or a cake. Sometimes, she and Liam would get called out for a nighttime emergency.

Beth would wind up most evenings by writing in her journal before turning down her lamp. While it allowed her to recap her day, it also brought thoughts of her family to the front of her mind as well, since she was using the journal as a way of staying in touch with them across time. This was bittersweet, as she was still adjusting to life without them, and she would quite often lie awake in the dark fighting back the homesickness that she managed to keep at bay all day.

She would think about her friends as well. How were they coping with her disappearance? Beth knew that while her parents and family were aware of what had happened, her friends and coworkers were not. She was quite sure that as far as they were concerned, she had simply disappeared. Some of her friends at work, experienced and capable searchers, would not give up easily on her and would continue to look for her. Would her parents share their secret with them? Should she try to get a word to them, similar to what she had done for her parents? She found herself tossing and turning many nights over this. She was reluctant to talk about it with anyone, because they had all been trying so hard to help her adjust and move on. Beth didn't want them to know how badly she missed her old life. She kept reminding herself of her parents' words regarding her own happiness and drew strength from them.

> " . . . Mrs. Dugdale's mock orange was blooming when I stopped to buy my eggs from her. The air was heavy with the sweetness of it and I watched a pure white petal float softly to the ground like a perfect snowflake. I told Mrs. Dugdale how it reminded me of home, as you had one growing in the yard. She told me that I could take a shoot from hers, which I've done, and I've planted it already, outside of my window. One day, it will fill my apartment with its beautiful scent and, always, remind me of home . . . "

As Beth finished writing, she recalled the day that she and her mother had hiked into this same area, buckets and spade in hand, to dig up some shoots of the mock orange to plant at home. It had begun to rain when they headed back, and she had lost her shoe in a mud hole on the way out. In spite of the mud and rain, they had both laughed at the silliness of it. Could those shoots have been from Mrs. Dugdale's bush too? Maybe. She remembered how quickly the shoots had grown into bushes, and they were blooming by the second spring. She smiled to herself at the reminder of home.

The next morning, after a breakfast of pancakes that Beth made, Liam asked her if she would like to ride into town with him to place an order for some pharmacy supplies at Perkins Store. It was a beautiful June day, and Beth said, "It beats the cataloging that I was going to do for you! Sure."

Liam saddled both horses while she cleaned up from breakfast, and they set out. Beth still enjoyed riding Belle and said so to Liam.

"What you all view as a necessity, I still see as a pleasurable experience. I have always loved riding horses. When I was a little girl, I wanted to be a cowboy in the Old West, riding a horse everywhere and toting a gun. My sister played with dolls, and I played with toy horses. It was a bitter disappointment to me when I was told that, generally, little girls did not become cowboys. No! I'm serious!" She said as Liam started to laugh. "I cried real tears! So it's funny that, as an adult, I became a police officer, walking around with a gun on my hip. The only thing missing was my horse. Now, I ride a horse everywhere but can't carry my gun. Life is funny."

Liam was still laughing. "Maybe the next time that you travel through time, you can go back to the 'Old West' and prove everyone wrong about little girls becoming cowboys. Just make sure that you bring Belle with you!"

Beth laughed along with him, reaching down to pat Belle on the shoulder. She grew quiet for a moment, recalling the afternoon that she and Liam had walked up the river to locate the spot where she had gone in while she was watching the helicopter. After some looking around, Beth recognized the flat rock that she had been standing on when she was thrown into the river. The rock was in one piece now, but she recalled that when she had stood on it, it had been split in two pieces. She wondered what could have happened to cause it to split like it had been in her time. What had been little more than a clearing then was a field now, but it was definitely the same spot. It was a little anticlimactic, as she had been expecting to see something that would reveal some sort of information or explanation regarding her experience, but there was nothing extraordinary about the spot on that sunny afternoon. The birds were singing, and the wildflowers were bending gently in the breeze, innocent and peaceful as the river flowed past, determined not to give up its secrets yet.

Coming back to the present, she asked, "What do you think the chances are of that happening to me again?"

Liam became serious. "I've thought about that quite a bit over the last few weeks. If it happened once, why wouldn't it happen again, if the conditions were right?"

"Do you mean to me, or are you talking about someone else? I mean, what makes me special? Maybe there are others who have been thrown about in time as well. Who knows?" said Beth. "In any event, I think that I'm here to stay. Remember my parents' letter? They pretty much came out and told me that this was where I would spend the rest of my life."

Liam was thoughtful for a moment. "I believe that the only thing that is sure is what has already happened. The future is still open, and anything can happen. I don't believe that every move that you will make for the rest of your life is already mapped out."

He drew a deep breath before continuing, as though he were diving into deep water. "But anyway, Elizabeth, you shouldn't even be here! In your time, I'm just a name on a headstone in a cemetery—a ghost. Here, in 1908, your parents haven't even been thought of, never mind you! We should never know each other."

"That's true for everyone that doesn't know about me, and we can discuss the science of this forever. But nonetheless, Liam," said Beth, shaking her head, "I . . . am . . . here! I'm thinking, feeling, living, and breathing! I'm as real as you are. And while it may still be considered an open future to you, the next century is already history for me. I already know of the events that will take place. To change them means that I'll change my own personal history. I don't know how this happened or why it was me that it happened to, but I don't know how to get back to where I came from. So I've decided to find the good here, in this situation, and accept it as my parents suggested in their letter to me. You know—just sort of let it happen. I could go out of my mind if I let myself worry too much about whether or not I'm only here for a short period of time! I have a life to live, whatever century I'm in, and I don't want to put it on hold while I wait for some sign of what's coming next. My life is now. Besides," she said with an impish smile, "I give myself a headache every time I try to figure out the paradox of which comes first: my birth or my death."

She shook her finger at Liam and continued, "That's the difference between you and me, William Sizer! You're always the scientist, always needing proof to follow a path to the conclusion. I, on the other hand, am no scientist. I'm willing to take one or two things on faith. I'm willing to accept that sometimes, some things are, simply because they are. You couldn't take a leap of faith if your very life depended on it!"

"Yes, I suppose you're right. Guilty, as charged." Liam smiled to himself. She was so independent; her words didn't surprise him. She was dealing with this on her own terms and moving on with her life. It was hard for him to fully imagine how difficult it must be at times for her to adjust to what life had given her—this thing that she never asked for. Maybe faith was the easiest way for her to accept it.

Beth didn't say any more, and the silence stretched on as they rode along.

Liam broke the silence, asking, "Elizabeth, are you happy here? Are you adjusting all right?"

Beth shrugged her shoulders, making a noncommittal noise, but said nothing further. She had chosen not to say anything about her homesickness, but Liam was always so keen on what was going on within her. She wondered how much he had seen of what she had tried hard to mask from him.

He pressed on, "Are you sleeping well at night? Are things keeping you awake? I've been noticing how tired you look some afternoons. Am I working you too hard? Maybe you've taken on too much too soon."

Finally, Beth spoke up. He was going to keep this up until she told him something! "Liam, I appreciate your concern. I really do! But look, I haven't really been here all that long. What, maybe six weeks? I guess that I'm still adjusting."

Liam continued to look intently at her; and after a moment, she puffed her cheeks, expelling a deep breath, and continued. "And yes, I do sometimes have trouble sleeping at night! I left behind a lot of people that I wasn't ready to say good-bye to. This isn't like losing one person that you care about. That's bad enough! But I lost everyone. Everyone! And I guess that I have to look at it as though they're dead, even though they haven't even been born yet, because I'll never see them again. And I mourn that loss. But time, I hope, will help heal some of that. So in the meantime, I try to work hard and keep myself busy. But I'll be honest with you. Sometimes, at night, when I lie alone in the dark, my mind wanders back home. I can't help it. I miss my friends and family."

She felt tears sting the back of her eyes, and her gaze slid away from Liam, not wanting him to see the tears that she had managed to hold at bay since that first night, but kept talking now that she had started. "And sometimes, it feels so overwhelming, all that I have lost. But I don't want to forget any of it. Not a single person, not a single event! So I'm trying to be patient for the day when I can remember these things without sadness. And I know that day will come for me."

Liam said nothing, not knowing how to respond to this flood of words that he had forced from her. Beth turned back to him and smiled, her eyes bright with unshed tears, her voice thickened with grief. "And there is nothing that you can do to help me with this, Doctor. This healing can only come from within, in its own time and fashion."

Liam reached across and took hold of Belle's bridle, sidling Ned up alongside of her. They sat looking at each other. Beth was fighting back her tears, and Liam was cursing himself for having pushed the issue with her.

Leaning over, he put his arm around her and pulled her close. "Look, I'm sorry—I never meant to push you—I'm sorry. I know that it hurts . . . I wish that I could make it stop."

This was too much for Beth, and the dam that held her resolve broke as she turned her face into his chest and let her tears flow. Liam held her close, not saying anything more. He knew that she was right, and only time would heal this. He pulled her closer as she wept great wrenching sobs that shook her body and tore the breath from her lungs, letting the grief that she'd been holding back pour out. He had never felt more helpless in his life.

He wanted to offer comfort but couldn't begin to imagine the enormity of all that she had lost. He put his hand on her hair, smoothing the loose strands back away from her face, and whispered softly, soothingly to her, "It's going to be all right. You're not alone, honey, you have me. There are so many people here who care for you." He kissed the top of her head, not realizing what he was doing, wanting desperately to ease the pain that he had forced her to admit to.

"I lost my brother when I was fifteen, and he was thirteen. We were such good friends. I don't know how we would've gotten through it if my family and me hadn't had each other. I can't tell you that I know exactly what you're feeling, with all that you've left behind, but I do know that it hurts." He continued to talk on in that soft voice, telling her about his brother and their life together.

Beth's tears finally subsided, and when Liam paused, she pulled her face back from his shirt. He ran his fingers along the loose hair at her temple and tucked it behind her ear, smiling at her.

She gave him a watery smile back and rubbed her wet eyes with her knuckles. Liam handed her the handkerchief that he always kept in his pocket. "It's clean . . . I promise."

"Thanks, Liam. A lot." She sniffled. "It's amazing how a good cry on a strong shoulder can help. Thank you for letting me. I know that I'll be all right, in time."

". . . I am constantly amazed at how quiet it is here. Have you ever noticed that it is never truly quiet where you are? There are always noises from airplanes, cars, telephones, lawnmowers, or whatever. Here, there are none of those unnatural noises. It's twilight now, and I'm sitting outside by my door. I can hear the birds, heading back to those little places in the trees and bushes that are their homes. There are Phoebe's nesting on the front porch, and swallows in the barn. Liam tells me that they have nested there for as long as he can remember. Where will they go when these buildings no longer exist? The bats have come out, and I can occasionally hear their tiny squeaks as they fly past me, drawn by the light shining thru the window behind me. I can hear Belle and Ned pulling at the grass in the pasture, content to be near me and with each other. I think that they are quite taken with one another, for they are never far apart. If one is gone, the other paces in the pasture until they are reunited. I believe that no creatures, human or animal, were ever meant to be alone . . . "

Chapter X

Beth had run into Martin Harrison a few times while she was in town. Several times in the store, she had turned around to find him standing there. They would chat for a moment until Liam would appear at Beth's elbow. On one occasion, Beth had gone into the library while Liam was finishing up other business in town. Martin had come in while she was there, and they discussed the book she was returning. Beth found that he was as well-read as Liam, which was saying quite a lot, as Liam was an avid reader, and she found herself enjoying their conversation about writers and books. But, as with the store, Liam soon appeared and announced that they had to get back to work. Liam and Martin were never rude to one another, but it was obvious to Beth that they would each prefer that the other were gone. She had to admit to herself that it was flattering and never said anything to Liam about it, as she assumed that he was simply trying to protect her because he didn't particularly like Martin. She had given up trying to tell him that she did not need protecting. He was going to do it anyway.

One day, on their way back from their morning calls, Liam told Beth that he wanted to stop in to see Bill at the sawmill. Beth knew that this was the hour that Naomi usually took a short rest, so she told Liam that she would continue on home.

As she was dismounting Belle, Beth heard hooves come into the yard behind her. Assuming that Bill had not been around, Beth turned, expecting to see Liam but found that it was Martin instead.

After exchanging greetings, Martin dismounted and asked, "Where's your watch dog?"

"Would you be referring to Dr. Sizer?" asked Beth. It annoyed her that he would make fun of Liam, and her tone was a little short. "He'll be along soon."

Beth turned her back on him and walked Belle into the barn to take off her saddle and brush her before turning her out into the pasture. Martin followed her inside.

Martin smiled at her as he pulled the saddle off of Belle's back. "Don't bristle like that, Beth. I'm just saying that it isn't often that I see you without him hovering somewhere nearby."

"Well," responded Beth, "I am his assistant. It would be a little difficult for me to do my job if I wasn't there with him."

Martin raised his eyebrows and cocked his head, asking, "Are you certain that's the only reason?"

Beth considered his words, deciding to ignore his insinuation. Holding the horse brush in her hand, she brushed her hair back with her forearm, exposing the scar on her forehead while doing so. She saw Martin look at it.

"Martin," she began, "I'm going to tell you something that I haven't shared with anyone outside of the Sizer family." She hesitated for a moment before plunging in. "I lost my family, and everything that was familiar to me in a freak accident. I was fortunate enough to have the Sizers welcome me into their lives. The doctor needed an assistant, I needed employment, and fortunately, I had the training that allows me to help him. Because of all that's happened, they are all extremely protective of me." She looked at him. "And I'm very grateful to them for it. So I would appreciate it if you wouldn't make light of it."

Martin had stepped closer to her while she had been speaking and now stood watching her. Without warning, he took her in his arms and kissed her.

Beth thought to herself that it had been a long time since she had been kissed like that, and she found part of herself enjoying it in spite of the warnings in her head about Martin Harrison. It was hot and hungry and searching. There was no mistaking how far he would be willing to take it, she thought, if she allowed it.

Eventually, he pulled back from her. Beth asked, "What was that for?"

"I've wanted to do that to you from the first moment that I laid eyes on you. I couldn't wait any longer."

Beth took a step back from him, finding her equilibrium again. "You didn't listen to anything that I said, did you? It doesn't really matter what I have to say right now, does it?"

It occurred suddenly to Beth that he had already known that Liam wasn't with her when he rode in, and that he had been waiting for an opportunity like this to present itself. And if he'd had any intellectual interest in her, or if he'd cared at all for her, he would have pressed her for more about what had happened to her family or how she'd received her injury. But he hadn't expressed any interest in what sort of accident could have done all that she had implied. Part of her was, of course, relieved that he hadn't pressed for more. But her ego was more than a little bruised that he wasn't interested in the events that constituted her life and made her the person that she was.

Already knowing the answer yet needing him to confirm it, Beth asked, "What is it that you really want from me, Martin Harrison? Why are you here right now?"

Martin gave her his most charming smile; and Beth thought, again, that he was far too good-looking. "We can talk some other time, Beth. Right now, I need you. I told you on that first day that I found you intriguing, and I need to know you more. Don't make me wait any longer for what we both want." He stepped toward her and, putting his arms around her, began to kiss her again with even more passion than before.

Beth tried to pull back, but his arms were holding her tightly. She pushed back harder, turning her face away from him. He wouldn't let her go. She drove her foot down hard on top of his and took advantage of his momentary distraction to push him hard with both hands, back and away from her.

She was angry now. "Have I given you the impression that you can just take what you want from me?"

There was a dark look of anger on his face, and he opened his mouth to speak when another voice spoke out. "No, I'm sure that you did not!"

Both Beth and Martin turned at the same time to see Liam standing in the door of the barn. He had the same dark look on his face as Martin. "I told you, Martin, that you would deal with me if you hurt her."

Beth saw that his whole body was tense, and his hands were balled into fists by his sides. Beth had not seen him angry before this, but there was no mistaking it now. The usual friendly look on his face had disappeared, and his warm amber eyes had grown cold.

She looked at Martin and saw the tightness around his mouth and a quick look of caution that flickered across his eyes. She stepped between the two of them.

"Gentlemen, let's talk about this like the responsible adults that I'm sure we are. Martin has misunderstood me, and I'm sure that he won't do so again."

Martin stepped past Beth. "I'm leaving anyway. I've never had to beg for a woman, and I won't start with you." Then, with a quick look at Liam, he turned back to her and said, "I am sorry if I have offended you." Turning away, he brushed past Liam. They heard his horse leave the yard at a gallop.

Liam stood in the doorway, sunlight shining in behind him. Beth stood where she was. Neither said anything for a long moment.

Finally, Beth asked, "How long were you standing there?"

"Long enough to know that things were going too far." His voice was terse, the words clipped.

Beth could still hear the anger in his voice. She knew that not all of his anger was directed toward Martin. She didn't know what to say to him to make his anger go away.

"Yes, he did go too far."

"Elizabeth, I warned you about him! Your own instinct told you about him! What happened to you? What were you thinking?"

Beth stood there, still not knowing what to say. How could she tell him that she *had* known how he was, but that it had felt good to have a man interested in her? Or that she had enjoyed that first kiss from him? It had been so long since she had been kissed like that, and darn it, it had felt good! That didn't mean that it was okay for him to try to take more from her when she said no. But this was a different time, different people. She had forgotten for a moment that women didn't date like they did in her time, and there was no such thing as a casual relationship with a man. Suddenly, she was ashamed of what had happened, knowing that she had sent out mixed signals and was to blame for it.

But it angered her too, that Liam should be demanding an answer from her for her actions. She was a grown woman, and even though she had made a mistake, she could take care of herself. It really wasn't any of his business. He had no claim on her!

"Liam, this is none of your business!" she snapped out. "I just . . ." She closed her mouth with a snap, not wanting to explain herself to him, nor wanting him to see how badly she had messed up. Without saying another word, she lifted her chin and walked past him and out of the barn. She needed time to sort out her jumbled thoughts.

Liam watched Beth walk away. He wanted to call after her but kept quiet, watching as she disappeared around the corner of the house. He had seen the anger flash in her dark eyes. He took his time fussing around in the barn as he unsaddled Ned and brushed out both horses, hoping that she would come back and talk about this with him; but at the same time, he was not really certain that he wanted to talk about it.

Beth found herself beside the river and sat down on the riverbank. She pulled up a fern and began tearing it apart, throwing the fronds into the river. She smelled the tangy sweetness of the crushed leaves as she sat watching them drift away from her on the water. Suddenly, she didn't want to think about what had happened. She didn't want to think about anything at all. Throwing the last of the fern into the river, she exhaled gustily and flopped down on her back, watching the clouds drift by in the sky. She lay with one hand under her head, willing her mind to go blank while she plucked at the grass next to her with her other hand. But it refused to.

Beth's mind drifted over dates that she had been on. They sometimes ended with a kiss. That was normal. While she had never indulged in casual sex, there had been a couple of men whom she had felt were very special, and their physical relationship had progressed while they had been together. Admittedly, she hadn't felt that way about too many men in her life since her engagement ended; and over the years, she had come to guard her heart very closely, waiting for the right man to give her love to. She'd had many male friends with whom she was very comfortable. She would greet them quite often with a hug and sometimes a kiss, but that was different. There was never anything sexual about it. But this that happened today with Martin had just been a mix of normal curiosity and sheer, raging hormones. She hadn't expected the kiss, but when it happened, she allowed herself to be curious and, for a moment, enjoy the sensation of it. She had forgotten, briefly, that she was not in her time. And since she hadn't immediately pulled away, Martin took it as permission to continue. She was embarrassed by her lack of insight. She had been more right than she knew when she told Liam on Decoration Day that she couldn't get involved with anyone. Not because of where she had come from, but for the simple reason that she had no idea of how it was done here and now.

And she was embarrassed that she had allowed herself to think that Martin may have actually been interested in her, Elizabeth Blodgett. All that he had wanted was a physical relationship and nothing else. He had just been playing with her, stringing her along all of those times that he had shown up where she was. All along, he had been waiting for an opportunity like today to present itself, where she was alone. Beth finally had to admit to herself that she had known this all along but simply hadn't wanted to admit it to herself.

Well, she thought to herself, *you were playing too, weren't you? You were enjoying his flattery instead of paying attention to your own good sense. So write it off as experience, and don't let it ever happen again.*

Going into the house, Liam went upstairs to his pharmacy, thinking that he would get some work done. But he kept finding himself looking out the window toward the river. He saw Beth lying on the grass and wondered what she was thinking. He saw again the play of emotions on her face when they stood facing each other in the barn. Had it been any of his business? He didn't know. What he did know was how he had felt when he had ridden into the yard and saw Martin's horse in front of the barn. He had been concerned for Elizabeth and went to the door of the barn when he heard their voices. He had turned away after that first kiss, feeling both guilty for watching them and angry over what he had seen, but then he heard Elizabeth struggling. He had come through the door in time to see her stomp on Martin's foot and break free. He didn't try to sort out all of the reasons for his anger. He only knew that the protective feelings that he'd had for her since he first fished her out of the river had increased even more since the other day when he had held her while she cried.

Liam exhaled heavily and again turned away from his work, running his hand restlessly through his hair. He stood at the window watching her, then gave up, and went downstairs and out the back door.

Beth lay on the grass, staring up at the sky and listening to the river. The soothing chant of the flowing water had done its magic and carried her anger away. There was movement next to her as Liam stretched out on the grass. He didn't speak but just lay beside her with his hands under his head.

Eventually, Beth began to speak. "I know that what I did was wrong. In this time. You think that I led him on, and I guess that I did. In my own time, it wouldn't have happened that way. I know that it wouldn't have. We call it dating, you call it courting. While it's the same, it's vastly different. I can't explain all of the differences. But he and I would have had the opportunity to communicate more openly before it came to this. Women, like men, are able to speak their minds a little more freely. But I'm ashamed of what happened today, because I didn't play by the rules of today. I'm sorry that you had to be involved in it, and I'm sorry that I may have caused you some embarrassment."

She lay quietly, and the silence stretched between them.

"But there's something else too," she continued as though there hadn't been a pause. "I believe that it's very possible that even if this had been in my time, there wouldn't have been anything that I could have done with Martin that would have brought about a different result. I never invited him here. Not this time, nor the last time. Naomi told me that he was spoiled and used to having what he wanted. I guess that this time, that was me. I think that we both know what for. He told me that I intrigued him. I wanted to believe that he meant *I* intrigued him, you know . . . the person that I am, but I know that I never completely believed that.

"Maybe I should have pushed him away more forcibly after that first kiss, but I didn't think that I needed to. I didn't think that he would try to go so far or that he would only care about what he wanted and not what I felt. I told you once before, I'm not very good at this. Some of my friends that I used to work with would tell me that I was too naive where men's feelings or intentions toward me were concerned. They would say that I needed to be hit over the head with a ton of bricks before I get the message. I guess that they would be right. But in spite of all that, I can take care of myself. If that means that sometimes I make bad choices, then so be it. I made a mistake, I'll admit that, but it was for me to fix."

Liam was still silent next to her. She continued to talk. "And I have to be honest with you. I'm no different than anyone else. It's nice to be on the receiving end of flattery. Sometimes, it can be somewhat intoxicating."

She fell silent again. A bumblebee buzzed around them, drawing the nectar from the clover in the grass. The river gurgled past and the breeze made the leaves rustle softly. The midafternoon sun was warm on their skin and the air, full of the smell of the grass and earth beneath them.

"When I rode into the yard," began Liam at length, "I knew that he was up to no good. I know that it was wrong of me to stand there for as long as I did without making my presence known to you. You're a grown woman, not a child. You don't need my supervision. And if I had spoken up sooner, it wouldn't have gone as far as it did. But you're right. He was determined to do what he did. If it hadn't been today, he would have made the opportunity some other time."

He paused for a moment. "I think that I was as angry with you as I was with him. I did think that you had led him on. But now I don't think that you intentionally set out to do that. As you said, you are from a different time, where things are done differently, and I don't doubt that at all. Maybe if I had given you a little more freedom with him all along and minded my own business, you would have been able to deal with it differently. But the fact remains that he did go too far, regardless of the reasons.

"In hindsight, you didn't handle yourself too badly, in the end. I guess that you were right, you didn't need me there at all. To be honest with you, I was impressed with what you did to him. I told you I believe that you have a knack for rising to the occasion. You were well on your way to putting him in his place. Maybe I was just being overprotective of you." He paused. It occurred to him that part of his anger might be stemming from seeing someone else do what he had found himself wondering about more than once. "Now it's my turn to ask you. Am I—sometimes—a nuisance to you? Do I not give you enough room?"

Beth finally pulled her gaze from the clouds in the sky and turned her face toward Liam. She found herself looking into his troubled eyes. Rolling over onto her side, she propped herself up on her elbow, looking down at him. She tilted her head and held her hand up with the palm out, fingers spread, toward Liam. He looked at it for a moment before taking his hand out from under his head and placing his palm against Beth's. She laced her fingers between his and squeezed his hand before letting it go.

"If you were standing in the door for as long as I think that you were, then you heard me tell him that I am grateful to all of you for the way that you protect me. And I meant that even though, I know, I'm always so independent." She smiled. "I doubt that I could ever begin to repay all that you alone have given me. Naomi told me that I should trust you. She was right. And I do, completely. While I don't need you to do my thinking for me, I value your insight and your presence in my life. So no, you are not a nuisance. You are my friend."

CHAPTER XI

Beth was sitting in the yard by the river early one evening, a couple of days later, sewing on one of the quilts for Naomi's babies. She was enjoying the feel of the fabric in her hands and recalled her pleasure in choosing the colors and designing the quilts and the pride that she had felt when Mrs. Sizer had admired her choices of fabric and handiwork.

The screen door slammed, and Beth looked up from her work to see Liam come out onto the back porch. He had walked down to the mailbox, or letterbox as they referred to it, and was coming back with his mail.

"How would you like to go to a ceilidh tomorrow night?" he called out to her as he crossed the lawn.

A smile came to Beth's face. A ceilidh, pronounced kay-lay, was a Scottish term for a kitchen party. There was music, storytelling, and dancing, along with food and drink. It was, literally, a party held in the kitchen area of most houses where, in the old days, most of the household activity took place.

Her response was enthusiastic. "I would love to! Where? I know the term, but I've never been to one or known anyone who has. I know that it was a custom brought over with our ancestors, but I never knew when people stopped doing it locally."

She was thinking that the custom had more than likely died out sometime between the thirties and forties, when so much upheaval took place nationally and locally. They had probably thrived during the prohibition era; but with the depression, which had brought so much upheaval to this part of town, and then World War II—with the influx of new people and technologies to the area—they probably just faded away along with much of the rest of the way of life that was around her now.

Liam was talking, and she pulled herself away from her musings. "So they don't do these here in a hundred years?" he was asking.

"Well, not by that term, no. People do, still, have house parties. But they don't go by the name of ceilidh, and they aren't quite the same party."

"What do you mean?"

Beth tugged on her bottom lip, thinking for a moment before answering. "While there is still the pride in Corsehill's Scottish roots, most of the residents here are not Scottish. There will be many changes over the next century that will bring people from other countries together geographically with different beliefs and practices. Towns like these will lose their cohesiveness with regard to everyone coming from the same background. People from all around the world will come here to America for opportunities and, in some cases, simple survival. They will bring with them their own customs and beliefs. Initially, they will settle into their own ethnic neighborhoods. But over time, they will start to marry people from different backgrounds, and society will begin to blend together. Many of the old ways will be lost or blended with some other custom, creating new ones, and the original ceilidh will disappear. They don't call America the melting pot without reason."

"So, how is it that you are familiar with the term, then? It sounds like it has faded from existence."

"It hasn't faded from existence entirely, just here. They are still held in Scotland, Ireland, and Nova Scotia, as well as other places. And I know about them because I'm from here and my ancestors before me for three hundred years. I'm proud of my heritage and have made sure that I know what life was like for my ancestors that came before me. There are, still, a few of the old families around town in my time, although I have to say not too many. Here, now, you can mention almost anyone's name. And someone will know that person and their grandfather or even great-grandfather and can tell you who they married and what they did or even where in Scotland and Ireland that they originated from. But people move around more in my time. That type of oral history, that connection to community, isn't too common anymore because no one stays around long enough to learn it. It's sad, really."

Liam sat in silence for a moment, contemplating her words. He had forgotten that her ancestors were the same Ulster Scots that he came from. She was a throwback from the lowland Scots that had helped to settle this country. Their ancestors had been, originally, from the lowland area of Scotland around Edinburgh and Glasgow, which was where the town of Corsehill had taken its name. In the 1600s, they relocated to the Ulster Plantations in Northern Ireland. Then in the early 1700s, they arrived in Massachusetts, where they temporarily settled in Worcester and Framingham. From there, they went out to what was then the western frontier, the hill towns. Life in Ulster had prepared them for their hostile surroundings in the wilds of western Massachusetts. They were the explorers, the border guards. And the rolling hills of this area reminded them of the homes that they had left behind. Elizabeth may have been born one hundred years after him, but they shared the same ancestral blood. In his mind, he saw her as a fighter, helping to settle these new lands. Living off this new land, a survivor. He smiled to himself. He had never pictured a woman in any manner other than that of the traditional woman's role. Somehow, that didn't quite fit her, and what he was picturing now suited her perfectly. She was an example of the women of the future America but also of the generations of resilient Scottish women who had come before her and helped tame this land for his generation.

"Hey, Doctor, what's so funny? What's with the smile?"

Liam came out of his reverie, looking at her, still smiling. "Nothing. Just a thought. But why does everything change so much in the next hundred years? This community has been here for two hundred years and hasn't changed all that much. What causes people to start moving around so much and leaving everything familiar behind them?"

Beth thought for a moment, putting her response together. "Well, why did our ancestors leave everything behind to come here? They wanted a new, better life for themselves and their families. It's not so different in my time."

"Yes," said Liam, "But why so many? It sounds like it has happened all around the world. What makes all of these people want to move?"

Beth chose her answer carefully. "The world becomes a much smaller place with all of the inventions and improvements that occur over the next century, Liam. Improvements in communication and transportation make it much easier to see the rest of the world. You can have a conversation with someone on the other side of the world using several different methods or physically get there in a matter of hours instead of days or weeks. And the technological improvements make it easier to live virtually anywhere that you want."

She hoped that he would be happy with this answer, but suspected that he would not. She couldn't explain to him the wars that would come in the next century, bringing about disaster that would force thousands upon thousands of people from their homes, or about all of the technology that would emerge from these wars. Or how people's attitudes and approach to life would change because of these events. She simply didn't know how to tell him of all of these things, never mind about the things that would happen right here in this community at the southwest corner of Corsehill. She couldn't tell him how or why they would be displaced from their homes without causing him the same pain that she felt with the knowledge.

Liam had been watching her face. "You're leaving part of this explanation out." He looked at her shrewdly. "I know that you are. But I know—'you have your reasons,' don't you?"

Beth sat looking at him for a moment, her lips pursed in thought. "Yes, I am. And yes, I do. But you're going to have to be satisfied with what I've given you. Okay?"

Liam reluctantly nodded, a slight smile on his lips.

"Good," she said. "Now, where is this ceilidh?"

He sighed and shook his head at her. "Oh. Right. I saw Clare Owen at the letterbox, and he invited us both to their place tomorrow evening, around six o'clock. We don't usually have ceilidhs until the winter to help pass the long nights, but Clare just got himself a new fiddle, and I think that he wants to give it a workout. I went ahead and told him that we would both be there. I thought that you might enjoy it. I hope that you don't mind my having spoken in your stead?"

"No! Not for this, not at all. Of course I want to go! Cool! This is so exciting for me!"

Liam smiled at her exuberance. "I hope that it doesn't disappoint you. You really are very excited about this, aren't you? 'Cool'? What does 'cool' mean?"

"'Cool' is just an expression of joy or excitement or wonderment. It's one of those words that you would use when no other word will fit, I guess. Sort of like saying, 'Cool! Did you see that?' at something incredible. Or 'Cool! This is nice!' at something good. Or 'Cool! This is so exciting!' Do you see?"

Liam looked skeptical. "If you say so. Does everyone say things like that in your time?"

"Oh, yes, and more!" Beth launched into a comparison of terms used in her time versus terms used here in his. In the end, Liam was laughing with her at some of the more ridiculous phrases.

"Honest!" said Beth at one point. "I can't make this stuff up!"

They were still laughing when Beth picked up her sewing and said good night, crossing the yard to her apartment under the opal blue of the twilit sky. Liam watched her walking away, realizing again how much he enjoyed being around her. He loved the way that she became so animated whenever he was able to get her talking about something that was on familiar ground for her. He would smile while she would talk with her hands, using them to emphasize a point she was making. Or the way her facial expressions would change to show what she was trying to describe to him. He was looking forward to her reactions over the ceilidh tomorrow night.

The following night, they were greeted with the sounds of people talking happily when they walked into the Owens' kitchen. Beth had baked a cake, and she now carried it over to the table that had been pushed against the wall. It was overflowing with food and pitchers of refreshing-looking drinks. She had never seen so many cakes and pies at one time. Liam had told her that everyone brought something to the party. She didn't doubt it after seeing this.

She sought out Clare and Mary Owen so that she could say hello and thank them for the invitation. She thought about what a striking couple the Owens were. Clare was a big, handsome man who took a great deal of pride in his appearance. Mary was a tall woman with pale blue eyes and lovely blonde hair. Liam told her that they had only been married for a few months and that Frank Burdett and Clare were close friends.

She heard a voice behind her. "Good evening, Miss Blodgett." She turned to see Ethel Brigham.

"Miss Brigham! How nice to see you again! How have you been?" Beth was thrilled at the unexpected pleasure of seeing her great-grandmother again, and it showed on her face. She hadn't seen either her or Frank since Decoration Day ceremonies at the end of May, a month ago. She settled in now beside Ethel on a bench to talk.

Corsehill, like all of the hill towns of western Massachusetts, was known for its wild blueberries. Local cookbooks devoted entire sections to blueberry recipes, and there were luncheons and socials centered on them. Beth remembered that her great-grandmother had been known for her blueberry teacake, a recipe which Beth and her sister had both learned at a very early age. It was the first cake that she had ever baked entirely on her own as a little girl in her mother's kitchen. She mentioned to Ethel that the blueberries would be ready for picking in a couple of weeks and that she looked forward to baking some pies and cakes. Ethel was telling her where the best berry picking in town was, when Liam came over with Frank. The four of them chatted with each other for a while before Frank took Ethel over to greet another couple that had just come in.

"I really enjoy the notion of being friends with my great-grandparents! It doesn't bother me so much now to think that I won't be telling them who I am," she had said to Liam after Ethel and Frank had walked away. "I do think that it's better this way. I just enjoy being around them and hearing their thoughts and just the sound of their voices."

Beth heard the sound of a fiddle warming up and turned to see Clare with his new fiddle, sitting on a chair in the corner. There was a younger man, whom she didn't recognize, next to him with a tin whistle and another, with a small accordion.

Liam leaned over to her and said in her ear, "You're really going to like this, I think."

"I already do!"

The music began, and Beth lost herself in the moment. She looked around, taking in her surroundings. The Owens house was fairly large. The kitchen area was spacious, laid out like Liam's, only much bigger. The large table had been pushed against the wall and groaned under the weight of food and drink. There were chairs and benches surrounding the room, and the middle of the floor was left open for the dancing that would come. There were about thirty people of all ages in the room. They had all stopped talking when the music started up.

Beth found that she recognized some of the tunes. Some were new to her, but she enjoyed them all. Clare would stop, and one of the partygoers would stand and tell a story. Beth happily took it all in. They would sing along with some of the songs, and when Clare played "Johnny Has Gone For a Soldier," an old song from the Revolutionary War, Beth found herself singing along.

Liam glanced at Beth and saw that she was singing, surprised that she knew the words to this old song. But then, she was always full of surprises. It was obvious how much she was enjoying herself. He looked forward to the dancing that was coming later, knowing how well she danced, and he anticipated the feel of her in his arms again.

The song ended, and Beth sat back, looking around. She saw all of these people, her neighbors, simply enjoying themselves here in this kitchen. They had none of the knowledge that she had of the future and of the pain that was coming. There were a few boys present, probably around ten or eleven years old. In less than ten years, they would go off to Europe to fight a war that they may or may not even understand. Some would not come home. Those that did would not be the boys that had left. Life for everyone here would change after that. These parties would fade into memory, and the world would become a much smaller place. The safety and security felt within these hill towns would be challenged and, eventually, fail. The happy sounds around her had faded, and she was lost in her own thoughts. They saddened her, suddenly, deeply.

Liam turned to look again at Beth and saw that her thoughts were no longer at the party. He guessed, correctly, that this song about a young man going off to war had triggered something for her. He knew that the 'burden,' as he had come to call it, was upon her again. It was weighing heavily this time, judging from the look in her eyes, the utter sadness on her face.

Sometimes, he could tell that what she was thinking of wasn't a bad event; it was more like she was in on a secret surprise. But other times, he knew that the events that she was thinking about were painful or disturbing, leaving her feeling very alone. This, he knew, was one of those times. He moved closer to her.

"It is a heavy burden. You still won't share it with me?"

Beth came back with a start. She smiled at Liam, thinking that he had so accurately seen into her thoughts, her very soul, once again. How did he do that? She had to work on her poker face.

"I can't share this with anyone. Not even you." Still smiling, she put her hand on his arm and squeezed. "I'm fine, really." But the sadness lingered in her eyes.

She looked around and saw that people were eating and drinking. "How about some of that cake, maybe?"

Liam looked at her for a moment, reluctantly accepting that she wasn't going to tell him anything now. He gave up and smiled back at her, covering her hand with his, and stood up. "Sounds like the best idea that you've had in a while! Let's go!"

While they were getting their cake, Ethel approached Beth again, this time with another woman beside her. She introduced her to Beth as Mrs. Harmon.

"Ethel was telling me that Mrs. Sizer said that you are a fine quilter," said Mrs. Harmon. "I was wondering if you might be interested in sewing on a quilt that we're making to raffle off at the agricultural fair this fall. We're hoping to raise funds to add on to the south schoolhouse."

Beth smiled at the woman, both pleased and a little embarrassed by the offer. "I would like that very much! But are you sure that you want me to, without even seeing my work?"

Mrs. Harmon put a hand on her arm. "If Mrs. Sizer recommended your work, I don't need to see it! She's a good judge."

They chatted on for a few minutes longer, and Beth got the particulars on how the square was to look. When Ethel and Mrs. Harmon took their leave, she turned to Liam with a beaming smile. Liam had overheard enough of the conversation to know what she was so happy about. He smiled warmly at her, knowing that the invitation to help meant acceptance.

After a short break, the dancing began. Beth forced her earlier dark thoughts from her mind. She and Liam danced and danced. Everyone was happy, laughing, and Beth found it contagious. She had never had such fun. There were waltzes, square dances, and reels.

As the last dance ended, she spun around in Liam's arms, her eyes shining with joy. He was happy to see that, at least for now, the sadness had left her eyes. Impulsively, he kissed her lightly on the forehead and held her close, not caring that they were in a crowded room and not wanting to let her go. He could feel her heart beating strong against his own.

Suddenly, he realized that he had never enjoyed dancing and listening to music as much as he had on this night, here with her. He had been to many ceilidhs before, and he'd always enjoyed himself. He never minded going to them alone, because his friends and acquaintances were there, but he knew that it was Beth's presence here with him tonight that made this one so much more pleasant. He wondered if he would still enjoy them if she were to leave this place and return to her time. How could he, after sampling life with her in it?

Beth let herself spin around in Liam's strong embrace as the dance ended and saw the pleasure that she was feeling reflected in his eyes. Her heart skipped a beat as she felt his arm tighten around her, drawing her closer to his body, and his lips brushed her forehead.

This is silly, she thought to herself. *Why do you feel so lightheaded over this? It's just a kiss on the forehead! What's the matter with you?*

Liam felt something at his elbow and turned to see that the hat was being passed for the musicians. He stepped back to fish a coin out of his pocket and dropped it in the hat. When he turned back, Beth had turned and was talking with two women. The party was breaking up, and it was time to go home.

Riding home, Liam turned to Beth and asked, "So how was your first ceilidh? Was it all that you thought it would be?"

Beth laughed. "And more! I haven't had this much fun in . . . well, years! Thank you for taking me! There is so much talent in these hills. It's impossible to believe that most of these people are self-taught. Between the musicians, and the singing voices, and the storytelling—it's incredible! I'm so impressed." She paused, and then continued. "It almost makes me look forward to the winter here, just to be able to go to more of these!"

Liam laughed. "You'll look forward to the spring even more, once winter arrives. We always end the winter with a sugar eat. Have you ever been to one of those?"

Beth shook her head. Liam went on to explain it to her. "Your great-grandfather is the best person for that. Frank always knows just when to take the maple syrup off of the heat and when to leave it on. It's quite a talent to know exactly when the sugar's right. It's great fun. You'll like that too." He thought to himself, *She really would, and I would enjoy seeing her enjoy it.*

"Yum, maple sugar! New England candy. One of my favorite things! When I was a kid I used to break the icicles from the sap off of the maple trees and eat them. I'm looking forward to it already."

Beth was in her apartment, setting bread to rise, when she heard someone run past her door. Wiping her hands on her apron, she ran out to look, seeing Levi Osborne. He had come up the river path from the direction of Bill and Naomi's house.

"Levi! What is it?" she called. The young man stopped and spun around to face her. He had a look of panic under the sheen of perspiration on his face.

"Miss Blodgett! You and the doc need to come quick! My father has crushed himself with the oxen down at the sawmill! He's in a bad way! Hurry!"

Liam had come out of the barn in time to hear him. He called to Beth, "Just get your kit! Are you up to running? We won't waste time saddling the horses!"

Seconds later they were running downriver to the mill. When they got there, they found Jack Osborne lying on the riverbank with Bill kneeling next to him. Bill looked up at them and shook his head. Beth could see that the man was dead before Liam confirmed it. There had been no hope for him.

They had been skidding logs across the river to the sawmill with oxen, which was a common practice. Somehow, Jack had fallen, possibly while jumping the logs—another common, but dangerous, practice. The logs had shifted onto him before he could get out of the way, pulling him down and crushing him. The internal damage had been too much to his major organs.

Beth stood looking at him while she felt her own breast heaving from the exertion of running all the way there. She had met him a couple of times, most recently at the Owens' ceilidh. He had a farm near Frank's in the Devil's Half Acre. The Osborne family consisted of five children, the youngest being two years old and Levi, the oldest. She thought to herself, as she moved to stand next to Levi, that life here could be very hard. Looking at him, she saw that he was watching in a kind of numbed shock, as though he couldn't believe what he was seeing. Without thinking, she put her arm around his shoulders and put her other hand on his arm, offering this small amount of comfort, a physical gesture that she never would have done as a game warden. She recalled how Jack and Liam had laughed and talked so easily with each other at the Owens', and she saw now that Liam had put a carefully neutral mask over his own features as he knelt beside Jack.

Much later, Beth and Liam walked quietly home. They had seen to it that Jack's body was brought home, and Liam gently told the rest of his family what had happened. Beth saw here where his duties extended beyond tending to the physical needs of these people, as he now focused on their emotional welfare. He had asked Beth to borrow a horse and bring the minister back to the Osborne farm while he stayed behind to speak with Levi and Mrs. Osborne.

Upon her return with the Reverend Watts, Beth was surprised to see that Liam stayed to help the family with the arrangements for burial. While she busied herself making coffee and tending to the younger Osborne children, she observed that both Levi and Mrs. Osborne included him in these matters; and no one, not even Reverend Watts, thought that there was anything unusual about that. It was, she thought to herself, another statement of the trust that these people had in their physician.

As word began to get out about the accident, neighbors trickled in to the Osborne kitchen with food and offers of assistance. As the house began to fill with women, Liam pulled Levi aside and spent some considerable time alone with him. Beth watched them as they sat on the low stone wall by the barn and saw that Levi seemed to be doing most of the talking as Liam sat listening to him, occasionally responding, but mostly simply allowing the boy to talk. She thought to herself that she understood a little bit of what Levi must be feeling. The bottom had just dropped out of his world.

Now as they finally took their leave in the fading twilight, they walked along in a shared silence; and Beth looked over at Liam, wondering what he was thinking.

As though reading her mind, he said, "I worry that young Levi won't be ready yet for this responsibility. He has always followed his father's lead and looked to him for guidance. He hasn't had to make any decisions for himself. Now he'll be responsible for his family and the farm, whether he's prepared to or not."

Beth nodded. "Well, I guess that we'll have to hope that not only did he always follow his father's advice but learned from it as well." She breathed deeply and said, "I've noticed, Liam, that people here are incredibly resilient. I guess that they have to be, simply to survive. But it's more than that too. There is strength in their spirit as well. Levi may flounder a bit in the beginning while he gets his bearings, but he'll do all right. He's a good boy."

After a pause, she asked, "How are you, Liam? This was a difficult call for you."

His response was simply, absently, "I'm fine."

They lapsed back into silence. Beth was thinking how frightening it was to not have any of the financial assistance or security that would become available to people over the next century. There were no employers offering life or health insurance and no pension programs, social security, or welfare. Instead, the cities had poor houses, orphanages, and pauper's cemeteries; although she guessed that people here in the hills were too proud to take anything like that. She supposed that they simply worked harder when they hit tough times. They had no choice. It occurred to her that she now had to apply this to herself as well. Her state pension had not followed her here.

"What do people do here, Liam, if they can't take care of themselves? How do they get by if they're no longer able to provide for themselves or their families?"

"Generally, they'll move in with family or, at least, send their children to live with family," responded Liam, tiredly. "Sometimes, that means that they have to leave the area. With these farms, if there is a son who is old enough—as is the case with Levi—then he'll have to take over the responsibility of his family and the land. But if there isn't anyone else, the women will often remarry as soon as they can. They haven't a choice, especially if they have small children. That's the way it is."

"Remarry? Just like that? I guess that I understand the practicality of it, but what about the love?"

Liam gave a short, hard laugh. "Sometimes, Elizabeth, there isn't room for love. Or the time. The world doesn't stop turning for someone's terrible misfortune." After a brief pause, he added, "You've seen life on these farms and how much work there is. It takes both man and woman to work a farm, run the household, and raise the children. That's just the way it is."

"So what if they haven't any family or don't get remarried? My God, what do they do then?" This aspect of life here was something that she hadn't seen or thought about until now.

"They struggle, as best they can." Then bitterly, he added, "And occasionally, unfortunately, the strain of it is too much. And people sometimes resort to taking their own lives. When they think that there isn't any other answer."

Beth was aghast. She had stopped walking and stared after Liam. "Suicide? Here? I thought that that was just a 'modern' problem of the future! Surely, people don't have to resort to anything as tragic and dire as that, do they? There must be other solutions, aren't there? You must be able to prevent this, somehow!"

Liam spun around, a dark look of anger and frustration on his face. "What would you have me do, Elizabeth? It's not as though people here will ask anyone for help! We are a proud, stubborn people. Take your blinders off! Don't you think I try to help when I think they might be having trouble coping with what life has given them? Down through the ages, suicide has been the route of many poor souls who let themselves believe that there was no other way to go, just because they wouldn't ask for help. It's a tragic, pitiful fact of life! And I cannot always prevent it!"

Beth was stung by his sharp retort and remained silent. The silence stretched out long between them as they continued to walk, each thinking their own thoughts. As she replayed their conversation in her mind, it occurred to her that it was she that owed him an apology. He'd had to deal with the sudden death of a friend whom he had known all of his life, someone for whom he hadn't been able to do a thing to save. Now he was worrying over how Jack Osborne's family would fare without him, especially Levi, and she was bothering him about the very thing that was foremost in his thoughts. Too late, she recognized the weight of these things on his mind. She was angry with herself for not picking up on it sooner. God knew she was familiar with just how easy it was to be affected by these types of events, particularly when you knew the people involved. But Liam was always so strong, so capable of handling anything, and she hadn't paid close enough attention to the signs. How could she have been so careless?

As they neared home, Beth spoke up. "Liam, I'm sorry that I was so critical. It was thoughtless of me to pester you about this right now. I am sorry."

Liam simply grunted and shrugged his shoulders, clearly still preoccupied and angry.

There was more that she wanted to say to let him know that she understood what he was going through, but as her mind was forming the words, he turned and headed toward the house, the set of his shoulders saying plainly that he didn't want any further conversation. She let him walk away, the words unsaid.

Chapter XII

She was dreaming of home. In her sleeping memory, Beth had traveled back to her parents' house, where her family had gathered for a celebration. Looking around, she saw all the familiar objects of home that had been there for as long as she could remember. She walked among them, feeling the warmth and security of their constant presence wash over her. She felt the love of her family all around her, and there was an air of comfort and acceptance that can only be felt among the people that one has known for a lifetime. It was so good to be with them! She didn't want it to ever end.

Suddenly, faintly, Beth could hear someone calling her name. Going to the door, she looked out and saw Liam standing in the yard. Only it wasn't the yard that she had grown up in. It was his yard, and she could see the river behind him. He stood looking at her, as though waiting for her to come out. Just waiting, patiently. She beckoned for him to come in, but he shook his head, and she knew that it wasn't because he didn't want to. Turning back, she saw her family standing behind her, watching her. They were smiling. The love was there, a tangible thing that was all around her. It came through to her, in her dream state, that they were saying good-bye to her, telling her to go. Putting her hand on the screen door, she pushed it open and . . .

She woke up, murmuring, "I'm coming, Liam." She lay there, lingering in that disjointed state between dream and wakefulness, unsure of where the dream ended or if it had ended. She could still hear Liam calling her name.

"Elizabeth?" Called Liam as he knocked on her door. "Elizabeth, get up! We have to go to the Fergusons!"

She sat up—awake now—and threw her blankets back, the dream already beginning to recede into those faraway, elusive corners of her brain, always just out of reach of recall. She willed herself to remember this dream for the contentment that it had given her, wanting to be able to remember it later.

—

She called out, "I'm coming, Liam! I'm up . . . I'll be right out!" She was wide-awake now and already getting dressed. These middle-of-the-night calls had happened enough by now so that she had the routine down. Liam would saddle the horses while she got dressed and made sure that they had both of their kits and were ready to go.

She wondered, briefly, as she hurriedly got into her clothes, whether Liam had had much rest tonight. She had seen him silhouetted in the light from his kitchen window as he sat in the yard by the river after they had returned from the Osbornes' that evening, his posture and body language saying that he wanted to be left alone. She knew that, had it been light out, he'd have been fishing, trying to clear his head. Still feeling guilty over her lack of insight earlier and worrying over him, Beth had paced back and forth in her apartment, unsure if she should go to him. Knowing from her own experiences that she preferred solitude immediately following these types of events, she decided that she would leave him alone for the remainder of the evening, and she resolved to speak with him about it at the first opportunity.

They left the yard at a gallop with the Fergusons' oldest boy, Clement, and didn't let up until they were in the Fergusons' yard. Mr. Ferguson met them at the door, holding a lantern high.

Nodding to Beth, he said, "Hurry, Doc. Lizzie has an awful pain low in her belly. And she's a fever!" Clement took their horses as they dismounted.

They both ran into the house. Liam took the stairs two at a time, with Beth following close behind. They found young Lizzie in bed, bathed in sweat. She was a lively little eight-year-old with springy red-blonde curls, whom Beth had seen playing with her brothers in the barnyard on occasion. Now she was lying on her side with her knees drawn up, crying and clearly in pain.

Liam sat down on the edge of the bed and gently took her hands, removing them from around her midsection. "Lizzie, I know that it hurts, but you have to let me take a look at you so that I can help you feel better." His voice was soothing and soft. Beth watched as Liam's voice worked its magic on Lizzie, and she looked trustingly at him as he placed a thermometer in her mouth.

Liam continued to speak soothingly in a hypnotic voice to her while he probed her abdomen. He exuded a calmness that was contagious, and Beth could see Lizzie and her parents relaxing as she felt the tension leave the room. After he finished his examination, he laid one hand on her forehead and gently squeezed her hand with his other. "Don't go away, Lizzie. I'll be right back."

He turned to Mr. and Mrs. Ferguson and asked them to step into the hallway. He motioned for Beth to follow. Once in the hallway, he reached over and took Mrs. Ferguson's hand and said, simply, "I'm sorry, but there's no other way to say this. Her appendix has to come out, right now. If we don't remove it, it will burst, and she'll get a serious infection and quite possibly worse."

Mrs. Ferguson let out a small cry, and her husband put his arm around her, nodding at Liam. "What do you need us to do, Doc?"

Liam went on to tell them that the kitchen table would be where he would operate. Mrs. Ferguson was to get water boiling, and the table was to be covered with a clean sheet.

Beth placed Liam's surgical instruments into the hot water for sterilization and got everything ready for the procedure. Mr. Ferguson came downstairs with Lizzie in his arms. He laid her on the table and stepped back. Beth could hear the pot boiling on the stove and heard the instruments moving in the water. Every so often, water would hit the top of the stove and sizzle. The room was becoming very warm, and the air was heavy with the steam from the boiling pots. Liam must have noticed as well and asked Mr. Ferguson to open the windows.

Beth laid a hand on Lizzie's head and patted her shiny curls. "It's going to be fine, Lizzie. Doctor Sizer is going to take good care of you. We're going to make you sleep, and when you wake up, this will all be over. I promise." She smiled at the girl, and Lizzie gave her a weak smile in return.

Beth looked over at Liam. He nodded, and she began to administer the ether through a cone to Lizzie while he took his instruments out of the boiling water and laid them out carefully. He was all business, concentrating on his work.

When Lizzie was fully under, he made his incision. The procedure went quickly and smoothly. Liam removed the appendix, which was inflamed. He looked further to make certain that there was no other problem causing the pain or her elevated temperature, then he inserted a drain in the wound and closed it up. He kept up constant conversation with Beth about what he was doing and why. She had been with him long enough by now to anticipate much of what he needed and was ready at each turn. Mr. and Mrs. Ferguson, along with their two boys, Clement and Albert, were watching from nearby—something that Beth hadn't gotten used to. But then she probably wouldn't get used to performing surgery on kitchen tables by the light of oil lamps either.

Lizzie had been returned to her bed. Beth and Mrs. Ferguson sat with her as she drifted in and out of consciousness. Mrs. Ferguson held the girl's hand and watched her worriedly.

Beth looked across at the woman, who was probably only a couple of years older than her, and smiled. "She'll be fine now. Really," she said, trying to reassure Mrs. Ferguson. "She'll be sore for a time while the incision heals, but that should be all."

Mrs. Ferguson looked up at Beth and seemed to focus on her for the first time. "I can't thank you and the doctor for what you've done! I was so very worried about her, and we didn't know what to do. She'd been complaining of a bellyache all afternoon. I feel just awful that she's suffered so!" These last words came out on a small sob.

Beth got up and walked around the bed to her, crouching next to her chair. She laid a hand on the woman's arm. "Sometimes, things don't reveal themselves right away. You had no way of knowing that this was her appendix and not simply something that she had eaten. And you knew enough to send for Doctor Sizer, so don't be so hard on yourself! And she's come through it just fine!"

Mrs. Ferguson smiled at her with teary eyes. "Thank you, Miss Blodgett. That makes me feel better."

Beth smiled back at her. She gave her arm another little squeeze before standing. She checked Lizzie again and found that she had slipped into a natural sleep. She walked out of the room, stretching her back as she went. She found Liam and Mr. Ferguson with the two boys in the kitchen. They had cleaned everything up and were now sitting at the table with cups of coffee.

Mr. Ferguson offered her some coffee, and Liam poured half a cup from the pot on the table and pushed it toward her. Then he pushed the cream and sugar her way, knowing that she didn't care much for coffee, but would accept it from the Fergusons rather than be rude. He also knew that she could only drink it with large amounts of cream and sugar. Beth smiled her thanks at him.

He gave her a small wink. "Is she sleeping now?"

"Yes. She seems comfortable. Her mother is still sitting with her." Beth filled the other half of her coffee cup with the cream and spooned in a rather large dose of sugar.

Liam leaned back in his chair, stretching his arms over his head. "Well, I'm going to go check on her one more time, then I think that we can head home." He turned to Mr. Ferguson. "George, you can come up with me if you'd like. I'm sure that you would like to see her." He stood up and turned to the eldest boy. "Clem, do you think that you boys could fetch our horses for us?"

"Sure thing, Doc!" Liam smiled at him, and the boy jumped up; and he and his brother ran out, racing each other to the barn. The door slammed as they ran out, and Beth could hear Liam and Mr. Ferguson climbing the stairs. Then all was quiet.

She sat alone in the quiet, sipping her coffee. The clock was ticking rhythmically on the shelf. She peered at it and saw that it was almost three o'clock in the morning. Suddenly, she felt tired and put her chin on her hand and closed her eyes, thinking about the dream that she had been having earlier. She smiled as she recalled the warmth that she had felt. It had been so real to her. It was funny, she thought, that instead of making her more homesick, it had actually done the reverse. It had eased some of that loneliness that usually crept into her heart most evenings.

And it was loneliness. She wasn't alone here, but she had no one with whom she shared a common history. There were no family or lifelong friends here to sit down and reminisce with, none of her friends from work that shared that unique bond that law enforcement officers had. She realized that these were the threads that gave the fabric of her life tensile strength. It was the people in her life and their shared memories that held it together. Suddenly, she recalled evening patrols when she would bring her supper into her parents' or grandmothers' kitchen and sit at the table visiting while she took her meal break, not yet at the stage in her life where she seriously considered that it might be the last time that they sat together that way. Or getting together with friends for a couple of beers and a pizza. These were things that were gone forever from her.

She was making new friends here, it was true; and one day, they would have memories to share. But for now, it was not to be, and that realization often left her feeling very alone. Somehow, this dream tonight had filled her heart with her family's love as though to say that even though they weren't together, the love would always be there, and they would continue to share their memories of her.

She was just starting to look at Liam's presence in her dream when she felt him gently touch her shoulder. She hadn't heard him come into the room.

"Would you like to go home, or are you comfortable there?" He was smiling down at her.

Beth started and looked up at him, feeling vaguely uncomfortable, as though he were able to read her thoughts and would know that she had been dreaming of him earlier and was thinking of him now. She felt a slight flush wash over her face and quickly asked, "Why don't you look as tired as I feel? She's doing well, then? Is it all right for us to leave her?"

"Yes. The hard part is over, and she has to rest and heal now. Her mother will see to that."

George Ferguson had come back into the kitchen while he was speaking, followed by his wife. They both thanked Liam and Beth again as they prepared to leave. Liam went over his instructions with Mrs. Ferguson, telling her that they would be back later around midday to check on Lizzie after she had woken up.

They rode out of the yard in silence, the clopping of their horses' hooves the only sound in the dark.

"Did you ever notice how quiet it always is at this hour? That in-between time of night and day," commented Beth as they rode along. "If it wasn't such an awful hour, I would intentionally experience it more often. It's easy to believe that you're all alone in the universe at moments like this."

Liam smiled in the dark, not needing to reply, wondering to himself what she had been thinking about earlier in the Ferguson's kitchen to make her so philosophical now and how it could possibly relate to the flush that had crept over her skin then. He expected her to say more, and when she didn't, they continued to ride in silence.

Liam's thoughts drifted back to the events of the day before. He was mulling over his reaction to Beth's questions after they had left the Osbornes'. He regretted the way that he had blown up on her and was trying to think of the words to explain his actions, but they were eluding him. Just as they had while he had sat listening to the river in the dark, feeling anger first with everything and nothing in particular, then deep sadness over Jack's death, and finally, regret and embarrassment over his boorish behavior toward Elizabeth. She was behaving now as though nothing was wrong, and he appreciated it. But it still didn't excuse his behavior, and he must find the right words to explain it to her before it happened again.

Eventually, Liam broke the silence. "You did a great job tonight. I'm beginning to wonder how I got along without you all this time. You really have quite an aptitude for this work. Did you ever consider pursuing this instead of becoming a game warden?"

"Never in a million years," laughed Beth, privately glowing with his praise. "Being a game warden was all that I ever wanted to do. To be outside, doing work that changed with the seasons. To challenge myself physically and mentally and push myself a little bit further than the average woman . . . that was what I wanted. Not that helping you with your medical practice isn't challenging—it most certainly is! And I'm enjoying the work even more than I thought that I would." It occurred to her as she said this that she was beginning to feel a contentment here that she had never really felt before, even with her old job.

She thought for a moment. "But there were so many other things about my job that were intriguing. Just the mystique alone that's attached to the game warden was too alluring to me! I have always felt proud that I could do a job that most women wouldn't consider doing. I had many friends who were game wardens in this state as well as others. We all worked the lousy hours, often in awful conditions, sometimes placing ourselves in danger. But we all felt that our work was that important. Not just for ourselves but for future generations too. We would all agree that it gets in the blood, like a disease." She laughed. "But not one that we would want a cure for!"

They rode the rest of the way in companionable silence. Beth let her eyes close as her head nodded forward, trusting that Belle would follow Ned and get her safely home. She smiled to herself, thinking how quickly Belle and Ned had adjusted to each other. Belle was always following Ned around the pasture and letting him take the lead in just about everything. And Ned, for his part, was always a perfect gentleman to Belle. She wondered if horses developed friendships.

They turned into the barnyard, and Liam spoke up. "I don't understand how you can sleep in the saddle!"

Beth laughed. "Not sleeping, just resting! Another thing that I learned in my other life, I guess. I would be called out on searches where it was 'hurry up and wait.' I would get on the scene, and then sit around in a staging area with other searchers while they decided where to send us. But then when I got sent out, I could be out for hours, and this was often after I had already worked a full day, much like these calls. So I learned early on to grab whatever chance I could for rest during those periods of downtime, because I may not have the opportunity again for a long time. The result was that I could take a catnap just about anywhere. I guess that the habit followed me here!"

"Well, just don't fall out of the saddle one of these times!" was Liam's laughing reply.

"How is it that you're so wide awake and ready to go? Aren't you tired?"

Beth had noticed before that Liam thrived on these emergency calls. He always kicked into high gear, and it seemed that he would get better under pressure. He probably would have made an excellent emergency room doctor in her time.

"These unexpected emergencies are where the real challenge is! They exercise my brain and ability. When I'm involved with an emergency, I guess that I get so immersed in what I'm doing that I don't feel tired or hungry. Sometimes, it takes me a while to unwind afterward."

Beth nodded in understanding, recalling what had happened after they had left the Osbornes. She commented, almost casually, "You have to be careful that you don't lose yourself too much in your work. Sometimes, the things that we deal with don't go away at the end of the day, they just hide away somewhere and can sneak up on you before you know it. Once they get a hold of you, they're a lot harder to shake off than they were to take on. You see or hear things that, at the time, your brain just files away, because you're intent on the task at hand and don't really have the time to think about it. But later, when you no longer have to be so focused on what you're doing, your brain sneaks it out for another look."

They had dismounted and begun to unsaddle the horses. Liam had paused while Beth was speaking and was watching her from across Ned's back. He felt that she was speaking not only to him, but to herself as well.

Beth had stripped Belle's saddle off and was brushing her coat, her back to Liam. She continued talking. "A few times, I've rolled up on scenes that were, well . . . not pleasant. Much like some of the calls that I've gone on here, with you. Someone was dead, or dying, or suffering, and I had to deal with it. People expected me to be strong, because I was a professional. And dealing with this stuff was my job. But sometimes, the victim was someone that I knew. Choices and decisions had to be made and acted on. I've had to investigate fatal accidents that involved people that I'd known, and I've had to shut out the parts of it that I couldn't change and focus on doing my job. And also, I've been involved with incidents that continued for several days. These events would become my world. Everything else in my life would be put on hold. I would be completely focused on the task at hand.

"But many times, after, when it was all over, I wouldn't know what to do with myself. It was difficult to get back into my regular routine. Then I would find that I had become irritable and restless. I would begin to have trouble sleeping. Something would be wrong, but I just couldn't quite put my finger on what. Over time, I've learned to recognize the signs, knowing that it's inevitable, and ride it out. But always, when it finally leaves, it takes away a little piece of me and replaces it with something else. Something a little harder and a little more brittle."

Liam had sat down on the grain bin and was watching Beth intently. It was almost as though she had forgotten that he was there. Almost.

Beth turned from Belle, leaning her shoulder against the mare's haunch, and looked at him. "Where you have to be careful, Doctor, in addition to all of these other things, is with the transference of grief. When you come into an emergency, people transfer their grief and worry to you, because you are a caring and involved person. And you accept it for the same reasons. You shoulder it without a word, because that's how you are. People don't even realize that this is what they're doing, so you can't blame them. But the grief that you take off of them still has to go someplace, and you have to find that place where it won't affect you. That's the tricky part, I guess—finding a way to help folks with their grief and pain and troubles without losing a part of yourself."

She drew a deep breath and let it out. "Do you know what I'm talking about?"

Liam sat for a moment, simply looking at her. He had never heard anyone describe it like that before, but he realized, she had hit the nail right on the head. This was exactly the way that he had felt at times. She had found those words that had been so elusive to him. He had never discussed it with anyone, because he hadn't known how to express it in a way that wouldn't make him appear peevish. And he never felt that anyone else could relate to it. He now realized that she had experienced some of the same things and understood what it could be like.

He nodded, a slight frown on his face. "Yes, I see exactly what you're saying. And I agree with you. People with professions like ours are about helping others when they need it the most. And it is our nature, I guess, to just keep trying to push the things that we don't want to dwell on down deeper. Even when they refuse to go. You're fortunate that you've learned this. I know that there have been times when I've felt the stress of some of the things that I've dealt with. And to be honest with you, it can be maddening."

"Like yesterday, with Jack's death?"

"Yes . . . I'm sorry that I was so short with you."

Beth saw the regret in his eyes and realized that on top of everything else, he had been punishing himself for his earlier behavior with her. She reproached herself again for her lack of insight when she had pushed him into an angry retort with her questions. She should have understood what he was going through and offered him her support, even if that meant simply being with him and keeping her mouth closed.

"Liam, that's just my point! What happened then was my own fault. *I* was out of line! You could no more prevent your reaction to me than hold back the ocean. I, of all people, should have seen it sooner. I should've been there for you, instead of pestering you and leaving you to sit alone in the dark with even more on your mind. And once I realized that, the damage was already done, and you wanted to be left alone. Please forgive me!"

Liam smiled at her, and nodded. "Elizabeth, there's nothing for me to forgive. It was a rough afternoon. And as you said, it's inevitable, and you just ride it out. But I wish I could say that I won't do it again. While that doesn't make it okay, I'm glad to know that you understand what's behind it."

Beth looked around her, slightly embarrassed at all that she had revealed about herself, but relieved that it had been something that Liam understood. "Just one more thought before I drop it. I've found that sometimes just talking about these things with someone who has had similar experiences helps to get them filed away in the proper place in your head. Burdens are easier when they're shared with someone who cares. So don't forget—I'm always here. You don't have to ride it out alone."

". . . I was up early this morning, just before sunrise. I made a cup of tea and sat on the bench outside of my door to drink it while the sun came up. I have always loved this time of day. It's probably the only time that I feel as though time stands still. It brings to mind the fall hunting seasons, and getting up and out of the house well before sunrise. Everything would be dark and quiet, and I would pour out my thermos of hot tea and wait for the world to come awake around me. The stars would fade out one at a time, while the sky grew lighter in the east, showing purple, then red and yellow in hues more beautiful than could be imagined. The birds would start to sing with the rising sun and I would watch the mist swirl up from the water, now warmer than the air. The geese would take flight, calling out to one another in their haunting echo, and my heart would sing with the beauty that that first hour had given me . . ."

CHAPTER XIII

Mrs. Harrison, Martin's mother, had sent for the doctor to come by the house. Beth hadn't seen Martin since the incident in the barn over two weeks ago. She thought about what she would say to him if she should see him on this call and hoped that he just wouldn't be there. That was the easiest way out. It was ridiculous to think that she would never have to see him again, but it would be nice to not have to see him yet. She was still feeling some embarrassment over what had happened. She was quiet during the ride over, pondering these thoughts, dreading their arrival. There were other reasons too that were causing her to brood over this trip.

But in spite of her nervous tension, Beth admired the house as they rode into the yard. It was called the Mountain House, and she had seen pictures of it in a book on the history of Corsehill. She remembered reading that it had burned down sometime in the 1950s. Her grandfather had been on the volunteer fire department at the time and had told her about the spectacular fire that it had been, visible from miles away. It had also consumed the town's only fire engine, which had been parked too close to the fire.

But there was more to interest Beth in this place. Her home in 2008 was at this site. She had purchased what had been called the caretaker's house to the old estate about two years earlier. It was all that was left of the estate that was here before her now. She had intentionally avoided this location and hadn't mentioned it to Liam, not quite ready to face it yet. She felt a wave of homesickness and regret come over her quickly, unexpected in its intensity, and she focused on the main house, forcing her eyes and thoughts onto something else.

Looking at the big house now, she saw a grand three-storied house in the Greek revival style with a wraparound porch on the first and second floors. It was white, with green shutters. Trumpet vine was growing up the rails, and there were large maple trees lining the circular drive. They rode around the side of the house toward the barn, where they dismounted. Beth glimpsed a backyard surrounded by a hedge. Peeking through the gated opening in the hedge, she saw ornamental gardens with a small teahouse and a formal rose garden. Simply put, it was beautiful, and she longed to stroll through the flowers for a closer look.

A young man of around nineteen or twenty met them outside of the barn, a black-and-white collie trotting at his heel. Beth realized that he was the musician playing the tin whistle at the Owens' ceilidh. She smiled at him in recognition as she bent down and offered the back of her hand to the dog to sniff.

"Hello," she said to the young man as she scratched the dog behind the ears. "I recognize you from the Owens'. You played so well! I enjoyed your music very much."

He blushed to the roots of his hair, saying, "Good afternoon, Miss. Thank you. I'll take your horse for you."

Liam smiled to himself as he watched Beth making a fuss over the dog, who was now presenting her with a stick. He could see that she had no idea that this young man was sweet on her. He had noticed at the ceilidh that she had drawn many admiring looks, and several were from this young gentleman, who was still looking at Beth.

"Jamey," said Liam, "how've you been? I didn't get a chance to sit and talk with you at the ceilidh. How are your folks and sisters?" While he was talking, he held the reins toward Jamey with one hand and turned to take his kit from behind the saddle with the other.

Jamey's eyes were still on Beth, who was tugging on the other end of the stick; and after a moment, Liam tapped him loosely on the shoulder with Ned's reins. With a start, Jamey looked around at Liam's smiling face.

"Is everyone well?" Liam was asking, one eyebrow raised.

"Yeah, Doc, they are," replied the boy, grinning at Liam while he took the reins from him. "Pa's still caretaking this property, and Ma's still keeping the house here. I'm helping Pa with the barn chores and the farming end of things."

Looking around herself while the other two were talking, Beth saw that there was quite a big orchard out beyond the garden behind the house, and she could see a chicken coop and a corner of the sheep pens behind the barn. There were cows in the field beyond that, next to where the caretaker's house sat. It occurred to her now that this was where Jamey and his folks currently lived. Even though it wasn't as large as it was in her time, and it lacked the big front porch that she had, she recognized it right away.

The house was white, with green trim like the main house. At some point in the future, the house would get aluminum siding put on it and an enclosed front porch. She had stripped off the siding and sided it with cedar clapboard and removed the enclosure on the front porch, enlarging it and leaving it with a simple railing and spokes. She had then painted the house yellow, with white trim. The upstairs had consisted of four rather small rooms, and she and the men in her family had knocked down the walls, added dormers, and made two bedrooms and a small office along with a good-sized bath. The kitchen was sunny and bright and looked out over the old fields, where there was a small beaver pond on the far side. She still had a few of the old apple trees as well, and she'd had them pruned in order to restore them to their original beauty.

With a resigned sigh, she tore her eyes and memories away from the small house and looked again at the grounds and farm around her. Everything was clean and well maintained.

Throwing the stick for the collie to chase and turning back to the two men, she smiled at Jamey again, saying, "Well, you and your dad do nice work. This is one of the nicest-looking farms that I've ever seen!"

His face flushed again with pleasure as he thanked her. Liam's smile came back.

They took their leave of Jamey and his dog and walked around to the front of the house, where Liam reached over and twisted the handle for the bell on the front door. Beth looked over at Liam while they were waiting.

"What are you smiling at?"

He looked over at her. "You really don't know, do you? You just don't see it."

"Know what? What are you talking about?"

At that moment, the door was opened by a plump woman wearing an apron and carrying a towel. She had one of the friendliest faces that Beth had ever seen, and it broke out in a broad smile when she saw Liam.

"Why, Liam! How good to see you!" she said as she wiped her hands on the towel and reached for his hand. "How are your folks? I've been so busy here since Mrs. Harrison and Mr. Martin came back that I haven't seen anyone! And how are Naomi and Bill? Naomi must be about due, isn't she?"

Liam smiled warmly at her. "Hullo, Mrs. Duval. They're all doing fine. Naomi's babies should be arriving in a few weeks." He turned to Beth. "I'd like you to meet my assistant, Elizabeth Blodgett."

Beth was saying hello when she heard footsteps approaching. She looked to see a handsome woman enter the foyer. She knew that this would be Mrs. Harrison, Martin's mother.

Mrs. Harrison extended her hand toward Liam, saying, "Hello, Doctor. How good of you to come out today." She turned a quizzical eye toward Beth. "Is this your new assistant? How do you do, Miss . . . ?"

Beth took her hand and said, "Blodgett. Beth Blodgett. I'm pleased to meet you."

Mrs. Duval had disappeared during the conversation with Mrs. Harrison. Liam said, "You sent for us, Mrs. Harrison?"

"Yes, Doctor. My son's fiancé arrived this afternoon from Boston for the summer and is not at all well. I was hoping that you could perhaps do something to help make her a little more comfortable."

Beth started at the woman's words. Fiancé! So all the while that Martin had been chasing her around, he had been engaged! The two-timing rat! No wonder he had put the pressure on her that day. He'd been running out of time! She pulled herself together with a mental shake. Mrs. Harrison was still speaking.

"She was scheduled to arrive next week but decided to come out early and surprise my son. She's upstairs resting now, if you would like to follow me?"

Mrs. Harrison headed toward the stairway with Liam and Beth following. Liam looked at Beth from the corner of his eye and saw that her face, usually so expressive, was carefully blank. He could only imagine what she must be thinking and feeling. He was immensely grateful that she had seen through Martin. He was entertaining a few ideas about what he would like to do to Martin and was fervently wishing that Beth hadn't stepped between them that day in the barn.

After a light tap on the door by Mrs. Harrison, they entered one of the bedrooms on the second floor. Beth noted that it was as big as her entire apartment. There was a pale young woman lying in the bed with a large basin next to her on the mattress. Beth thought that she would be—normally—very pretty, if not for her current washed-out appearance. Mrs. Harrison introduced her as Miss Louisa Waverly of Boston and introduced Liam and Beth to her.

Liam pulled a chair over next to the bed and sat down. "Good afternoon, Miss Waverly. I understand that you're not feeling well after your long trip. Tell me what you're feeling, besides the nausea."

Louisa looked at him, and then—quickly—at Mrs. Harrison. Her eyes briefly touched Beth on their way by. Beth thought that she saw apprehension in them. Liam caught it too.

Turning slightly in his chair, he said to Mrs. Harrison, "Would you please go ask Mrs. Duval to get me some water to wash with? Miss Blodgett will stay here with me while I examine Miss Waverly."

Liam turned back to Louisa as Mrs. Harrison went out the door. In his most soothing voice, he said, "Now then, Miss Waverly, you can speak freely with us. Is there something that you would like to tell us?"

Louisa was blushing and clearly uncomfortable. She looked utterly miserable. The silence stretched on.

Liam cleared his throat and said, "I can't help you if you won't open up to me. How long have you been feeling nauseous?"

Louisa was looking down at her hands, which were twisting the sheet lying across her lap. Her knuckles stood out white against her skin.

Beth was starting to get what Liam had already guessed. She tapped him on the shoulder. When he turned to look at her, she motioned with her head for him to get out of the chair. He got up, and she sat down, placing her hand over Louisa's clenched ones. Louisa began to cry.

"How long has it been, Miss Waverly? How late are you?"

Louisa looked at her with frightened eyes and whispered, "Three months. I didn't know what else to do, so I came here . . . to tell Martin."

Beth smiled kindly at her. "And now that you're here, your resolve is crumbling a little bit, isn't it?" Louisa nodded through her tears. "Well, you have to remember that your body is going through some big changes right now, and those changes will wreak havoc on your emotions. Is there no one in Boston that you could talk to about this?"

Louisa shook her head. "No. My mother passed away several years ago, and I just couldn't face my father alone. I thought that the best thing to do was to come here and tell Martin."

"And so it is. And you will have to tell him. Have you been sleeping at all, or has worry been keeping you awake?" she asked.

"I haven't slept well for the past few weeks. When I missed my first monthly, I thought that it was just because of what had happened between Martin and I." She blushed again. "That is, because it had been my first time, and I had bled then. But then, the second month came and went without anything, and I began to wonder. Then of course, there has been the nausea. I didn't have anyone to ask about it, and I've been so frightened . . ."

She trailed off and looked at Beth and Liam who was standing behind Beth's chair, her face going to a deeper red. "When I began to suspect that I was going to have a baby, I thought that I was being punished for what Martin and I had done. It seems that I let him talk me into it so easily! What you must be thinking of me!"

Beth smiled again at her. "Nonsense! You're not being punished! You obviously are in love with the man who will be your husband, are you not?" Louisa smiled and nodded. "Then don't worry. You just put the cart before the horse, so to speak. Believe me, you are not the first, nor will you be the last, to do this! Do you want to have children?"

Louisa smiled and nodded again. "Well, then," remarked Beth, "it's not such a problem after all, is it? Once you've told Martin, then you'll be wondering what all of the worry was about. But the important thing right now is that you take care of yourself and the child that you are carrying. You must eat right and rest and do everything that Doctor Sizer tells you to do. Understood?"

"Yes, I do understand."

Liam put his hand on the back of Beth's chair. She could feel the pressure of his fingers against her shoulder blade, and she knew that he was silently thanking her for having intervened with Louisa.

"Have you eaten anything today?" he asked. She shook her head. "Why don't I go find Mrs. Duval and see if she could put together some dry toast and tea for you. I know that you don't think that you want food right now, but the tea and toast will calm your nausea a bit. And then I can give you something to take that will help."

Louisa nodded, saying, "I feel good the rest of the time, once I get past the nausea. Today is the first time that it has lasted this long. I suppose that it's because I'm so tired and upset."

"I'll need to complete a physical exam on you, but not today. We'll let you rest a little bit first." Liam excused himself and left the room.

Alone with Martin's fiancé, Beth was unsure of what to say. Louisa was still holding her hand tightly, as though it were a lifeline. Beth let her continue to hold it, and they sat in silence. She was thinking about how it must have happened between Louisa and Martin, after her own experience with him. How easy it must have been for him to get what he wanted from this pretty young woman, not caring that it was her first time, and then leaving to come out here and pursue other women before getting married.

Finally, Beth said, "Miss Waverly—Louisa—I want you to listen carefully to what I have to say." She paused to clear her throat. "Always remember this . . . *You* matter! Your thoughts and feelings and desires mean just as much as Martin's. As his wife, you should be his partner. Don't let anyone ever tell you that what you want or feel is second to him! And raise your children with love and respect in their hearts, and that's how they will treat others. This is what you deserve, so don't settle for anything less. Okay?"

Louisa looked at her for a moment, then nodded, and smiled. "Thank you, Beth. I'm feeling better already."

At that moment, there was a light tap on the door, and Mrs. Harrison walked in, followed by Mrs. Duval carrying a tray with toast and tea. Mrs. Duval set the tray down in front of Louisa with a warm smile before leaving. Beth looked back at Louisa and gave her an encouraging nod, whispering, "It'll be all right," and stood up.

Mrs. Harrison approached the bed as Beth walked over toward Liam, who was standing outside the door writing on the pad that he always kept in his kit.

He turned to her, saying quietly, "We'll come back tomorrow, after she's had a chance to talk with Martin."

Louisa looked at Mrs. Harrison and said, "There is something that I must talk with you and Martin about."

Beth and Liam quietly left and went down the stairs. Mrs. Duval was standing by the door, waiting for them.

Liam turned to Mrs. Duval, handing her the slip of paper, and asked, "Would you please tell Mrs. Harrison that we'll be back tomorrow to see Miss Waverly? Please see that she follows this menu. It will help her feel better." He put his hand on the door and then turned back to Mrs. Duval.

"Do you know where Martin is today?"

Mrs. Duval replied, "He left late this morning for some business regarding the orchard. He should be back any time now. Is there a message for him?"

Liam hesitated, and then said, "No. No message. Thank you. Good day . . . and say hello to Mr. Duval and the rest of your family for me, won't you?"

Jamey saw them from the barn and led their horses out as they walked around the corner of the house. He held Belle, and then reached across to hold the stirrup for Beth while she mounted, thanking him and telling him that she looked forward to hearing him play again one day. He smiled, a slight flush tinting his skin at her praise while he told her that he would be happy to play for her any time. Liam smiled again to himself and shook his head.

As they rode away, Beth saw that the smile was back on Liam's face. "Okay. What are you smiling about now?"

"You still don't see it, do you?"

"See what? What's the joke?"

"No joke. Just a fact."

At that moment, they heard hoofbeats and turned together to watch Martin ride up to them at the edge of the Harrison driveway. A look of concern came over his face as he recognized the two of them.

"What is it? Is my mother ill?" he asked.

"No, Martin, it's not your mother," responded Liam. "But she did send for us. We were here to see your fiancé. It seems that she has arrived early." Liam sat watching Martin closely, waiting for his response.

Martin's gaze moved from Liam over to Beth. She looked at him, without any emotion, watching a red flush creep up his face as he asked Liam if Louisa was all right. Suddenly, the thought came to her that this man needed to grow up. He was going to be a father in a few months, and his behavior had to change. And for the sake of Louisa and his child, she couldn't simply ride away without telling him what he needed to hear. She knew that she had to be careful with the information that she shared with him about Louisa, as their interview with her was considered confidential. But she had to say something to this selfish man.

Beth turned to Liam. "Why don't you ride on, and I'll catch up in just a minute. Okay?"

Liam looked at her. She nodded, a small reassuring smile on the corners of her mouth. She watched as he rode ahead, then reined in Ned, and sat waiting for her outside of earshot. Beth turned toward Martin.

"Beth . . ." began Martin, but she cut him off with a wave of her hand.

"Martin, what happened between us before was both of our faults, so let's just forget about it and move on." Pausing, she looked away before swinging her gaze back to him. "But that's not what I want to talk to you about!" She took a deep breath and plunged in, before she lost her nerve. "Martin, it's time for you to grow up! Inside of that house is a very, very nice young woman, and she deserves to be happy. Your life is about to change, and this could be a good thing if you would just let it. My advice to you is that you let it. Step up now, and be a good man to that woman instead of just taking what you want!" She gave him a small smile as she said, simply, "Good-bye."

With that, she urged Belle to a trot and rode toward Liam, Martin staring after her.

They rode on in silence. Beth thought to herself how much she had liked Louisa. She hoped that Martin would put his selfish ways behind him and be a good husband to her. She thought again of how he had tried to have his 'last fling' with her before Louisa arrived for the summer. She could well imagine how he had talked Louisa into making love with him before he left Boston for Corsehill in the spring, leaving her pregnant and having to face the realization of it alone. Again, she thought how much she wanted him to do right by Louisa. Time would tell.

Eventually, Liam spoke up. "I'm sorry that you had to find out about his fiancé this way. You could've knocked me over with a feather! Are you all right?"

Beth looked over and gave him a deprecating smile. "Yes. I'm all right, thanks. I guess, though, that I'm still a little bit embarrassed by the whole thing between he and I, and this didn't help. But it explains one or two things, doesn't it? Like why he chased me, for instance," she said bitterly. "He was looking for a quick, easy fling before his fiancé arrived. Being new to the area, at my age, and without any family and all, I must have seemed like an easy mark to him."

Liam looked at her. She couldn't really believe that, could she? She was a lovely, incredible woman! Why didn't she know this? "No, I don't think that's it at all! I agree that he was looking for a fling, as you called it, but he didn't choose you for the reasons that you think. I think that he pursued you because you are an attractive, interesting woman. And he was drawn to that."

Beth gave an unladylike snort. "Yeah, right! Once again, I've trapped a man under my spell. It's a curse, really."

Smiling and shaking his head, Liam said, "I'm not joking! You really don't notice it, do you? You don't see how you are. But others do, believe me. For a smart woman, it's surprising how much you underrate yourself! What did you say to him, anyway, back there?"

Beth reined in Belle and sat, simply looking at him for a moment in surprised pleasure as the impact of his words echoed through her, not really knowing how to respond to them. He continued to ride on, and she nudged Belle back into motion before answering his question, letting the compliment go.

"I just told him that it was time for him to grow up. I hope that he does for the sake of his future wife and child." Giving him a sideways look, she added, "I noticed that you seemed to enjoy telling him that his fiancé had arrived."

Liam gave her a wide-eyed look before he broke into a wide smile. "I guess that I am guilty of feeling more than a little bit of satisfaction at the look on his face when he heard that she was here. It was juvenile, I suppose. I confess that I couldn't help myself. But you're right . . . he needs to accept the responsibility for his actions."

They rode on toward home in a companionable silence. At length, casually, Beth said, "You know, I used to live there, before I came to be here."

Liam twisted around in his saddle, gaping at her. "Where? The Mountain House? By yourself, in that big place?"

"Not in the big house. In the caretaker's house that the Duvals live in now. I moved in about a year and a half ago. It was a little run down when I acquired it, and my family helped me restore and redecorate it. The men did the construction end of it, and I like to think that I helped them a little bit, and we girls did the painting and decorating. It was quite a project and took about nine or ten months of steady work before I could move in."

"So," said Liam, "this was the first time that you've seen it since you've been here."

It was a statement rather than a question, but Beth answered with a nod, "Mm-hmm. I was really dreading it, but I like knowing that the Duvals live there now. Mrs. Duval and Jamey are such nice people, and it pleases me that happy, pleasant people live in the house that I will one day call home, if you believe that houses retain memories."

"How'd you come to own it? Why was it in need of so much repair?"

Beth thought her answer through, something that she found she did with much more frequency these days than she ever had before. She tried to keep the information that she shared with him as broad as possible. Carefully, she said, "The Harrisons will stop spending summers in Corsehill in forty-five or fifty years, and the property will be divided up and eventually sold off. The caretaker's house sat empty for many years before I was able to purchase it a couple of years ago. Like I said, it took a few months of work to make it habitable again. I admired that house for years, and it sits in a beautiful spot. Buying it was one of my personal goals."

Liam tried to put himself in her place, thinking how he would feel if he were to suddenly lose his house, which he had such a personal connection to his own family with. "I'm sorry, Elizabeth, that you were taken away from it so soon after moving in." He paused, uncomfortable, not knowing what else to say to her, the words he had said sounding inadequate to him.

But Beth was shaking her head as she said, "It's okay, Liam. Like I said, it helps knowing the people who live there now. It gives substance to the history that I know of the house and property. I'm learning to recognize the value of these ironies that I experience here."

Late that night, Beth heard the sound of thunder as she lay awake in her bed. It was still some distance away, merely a far-off rumble now. She got up and went out to the kitchen. Feeling a breeze through the open window, she opened her door and let the stiff breeze blow across her bare arms and legs as she stood barefoot in her pajamas, which consisted of a pair of drawstring cotton shorts that she had sewn for that purpose and the spare tee shirt from her search pack.

As the thunder rolled closer, the breeze picked up and turned into a wind. The curtains danced to it in the open windows, and she listened as it sang through the trees, watching the flashes of lightning illuminate their bending branches. She heard Liam's words echo in her mind: *If it happened once, why wouldn't it happen again, if the conditions were right?* The rain began to come down, and her heart beat faster with the falling drops.

Turning away from the door, Beth lit the oil lamp on her table and looked around her cozy apartment. The clock on her kitchen shelf told her that it was almost half past two. She saw the shelves and cupboards that Liam had built for her, her lips curving in a smile at the carvings in the corners of each cupboard. Her eyes continued to move, seeing the second quilt that was almost finished for Naomi's babies, and the square that she had begun for the raffle quilt. There was a plate of cookies on her table that she had baked earlier. She thought of the flowers that she'd planted in the soil outside and of her work with Liam, her life here with him and his family, the curtains in her windows that Mrs. Sizer and Naomi had helped her sew and then hang. She thought of Frank and Ethel, of the ceilidh, and of all her new friends. She reflected on seeing her home earlier this same day, now inhabited by the Duvals.

She recalled the dream that she'd had about her family. She'd had variations of the same dream a couple more times since that first one, but each time, the theme was the same. Her family were letting her go and, always, with love. She had never believed in things like psychic messages, but then she hadn't believed that a body could be thrown through time either. She whispered to the room, "There are more things in heaven and earth, Horatio, than are dreamt of in your philosophy."

She stood in the open doorway, surveying her home while the rain and lightning fell behind her, both hands clasped around her locket and pressed against her pounding heart, her thoughts now racing.

Liam woke to thunder. He was about to roll over and go back to sleep when it struck him. *Thunder! A thunderstorm!* He sat upright in his bed, looking out the window as lightning flashed. Would this be her chance to leave? Was she going to try? His heart began to pump faster as he jumped up and reached for his pants. He wasn't ready for this!

Barefoot and shirtless, he ran down the stairs and bolted out the door. He saw her silhouette against the light in the open door as he raced across the grass. Her back was to him, and he stopped in his tracks halfway across the yard—watching—waiting while the rain came down and the storm raged. He wanted to go to her or call out to her, to tell her, *Don't go! Not this time, not yet!* But he remained silent, knowing that this choice was hers and hers alone.

Suddenly, Beth turned with a jerking motion back to the open doorway. The lightning flashed, and she saw Liam standing in the rain. Her hands dropped to her sides.

He moved toward her, letting out a pent-up breath. "Elizabeth, are you . . . all right?" He had been about to ask if she was leaving, changing his question at the last moment.

"All right?" She sighed heavily. "Yeah, I'm all right." She looked at him, feeling the tension leave her body. "Are you? Come in, it's pouring out there! What's up?" She stepped aside to let him in.

"Well . . . I heard the storm, and then . . . I saw your light. And I wanted to make sure that you . . . were all right." He suddenly felt awkward, unsure of what to say to her. "It's a fast-moving storm."

"Yes."

"It will be over soon."

"Yes."

They watched each other for a moment. The lamplight shone on Liam's wet skin, and Beth couldn't help but look at it, admiring the shape of him—his wide shoulders and strong flat stomach. She wondered if that wet skin would feel slick under her fingers if she were to reach out and skim them across his chest. Realizing that she was staring, she felt her face flush as she pulled her eyes away from his body and up to his face, framed in his wet hair. And she realized that she needn't have worried, since he was staring at her in her scanty pajamas. A new tension entered the room, and Beth shifted from one foot to the other, clasping her hands in front of her.

Liam's gaze slid away from her. He cleared his throat. "Well . . . if you're all right, then I'll see you in the morning," he said, turning toward the door.

"Liam."

He turned and looked at Beth. "Hmm?"

"I did think about it. You know—I wondered if this could be . . . it . . . . you know, my chance." She hesitated. "Liam, I would never leave without seeing you, without saying good-bye." She hesitated again. "Do you think that I should've tried tonight?"

He looked away from her, intently studying the back of his hand where it rested against the doorjamb, his thumb tracing a pattern in the wood, before turning his gaze back to her. "All that matters here, Elizabeth, is what you want." Relief made him smile. "Good night, sleep well."

Walking away, he felt the relief continue to wash over him. She was still here! For a little while, anyway. He recalled the look on her face when she turned around in the doorway—the indecision, the anguish. He knew that if the storm had lasted longer, if she hadn't seen him standing there, if she hadn't been taken by surprise, then she would quite possibly be gone now. *If, if, if!* He shook his head. *Accept it, Sizer, she'll go, sooner or later."* He was sure of it now.

He knew that Beth missed her old life and all that had been taken from her, recalling the day that he had held her while she wept over that loss. And he thought too of the way that her face would light up whenever she talked about her work as a game warden or when she shared stories about her family and old friends. She was surrounded by constant reminders of all that she had left behind. How could she not try to go home to that life at the first opportunity?

He thought about the depth of his reaction when he thought that she was leaving. It was more than he had expected. He pushed it away, telling himself that he still had control of his heart. He had come to enjoy her presence in his life, hearing her thoughts, experiencing her humor. And the fact that he enjoyed looking at her and watching her move didn't hurt either. That he felt physical desire for her was something that he no longer questioned. But she was his friend and coworker. And she wasn't going to be here forever. Besides, his life was solitary, not meant to be shared with anyone else. He'd learned that with Lily. But he knew that if he wasn't careful, he could easily fall in love with her.

Beth watched him until the light from her lamp no longer lit his retreating back. The storm had moved on and suddenly, she was okay with it. The tension that she had felt with the approaching storm had left her. Not knowing the exact reason why, she realized that she had made her choice to stay. It wasn't by accident that she hadn't left. She went over to the table where she had left her journal earlier that night. Sitting down, she opened it and began to write.

". . . There was a thunderstorm tonight, the first since I came here. I heard its approach while it was still far off. I didn't know what to do. I wondered, should I go back to that spot by the river and try to leave? But

then I looked around my new home and thought of my life here, and of the new friends that I've made.

Please forgive me, but I didn't even try to leave! I don't know if I can adequately explain this, but I feel as though I was brought here for some purpose, and I don't want to leave until I've finished whatever this thing is that I was sent here to do. I just don't feel as though I'm done here yet!

I miss all of you, and my life there with you, but now I'm making a life here, too. I didn't have a choice about leaving then, but I did this time. For now, I've chosen to stay and follow this path a little further. To whatever end, however long it takes me . . . "

Chapter XIV

"Do you think that you could hold down the fort for a few days while I go away?" Liam had asked the question while they were getting ready to go out on their rounds a few days after the thunderstorm.

"A few days? Where are you going? That is, if you don't mind me asking." asked Beth.

"Do you remember when I told you about my service time on the *Solace*?

Beth nodded. "Sure. I remember."

"Well, some of the crew members get together for an evening each year in Boston, just to catch up with each other. Usually, I take the train in to the city, meet them for dinner, and rush to catch the midnight train back to Westford. It makes for a long day."

"Wow! That makes for a very long day for you," agreed Beth, thinking that train travel to and from Boston in 1908 was a trip involving many hours, not to mention the trip by carriage from Corsehill to Westford to pick up the train. "So since I'm here now, you would like to have a little more time there, right?"

Liam nodded. "I'd like to go in on that day, then spend that night, and the next, taking the train home the next morning after that. I thought that I could stop in and see some old schoolmates as well. Would you mind watching things here? Do you feel ready to do that?"

Beth replied, "Of course I don't mind. And I think that I can take care of things here! You don't need to worry about a thing. You should be able to relax with your buddies and not have to keep looking at your watch. Go! Have fun!" She smiled. "I was beginning to think that you never took any more than a few hours off at a time! When are you going?"

Liam smiled at her enthusiasm on his behalf. "Not until next week, but I wanted to make sure that you would be okay with it. Are you certain that you can handle things here?"

Beth laughed at him. "Are you? You're like a mother hen with your patients! I'm positive that I could handle any of the small emergencies. And couldn't I send for Doctor Ferris in Westford if there is anything critical?"

"Yes. I'll telephone him from the store when we go into town and ask him if he could help you, should the need arise." He paused, looking at her. "Thank you, Elizabeth. I really do appreciate this."

Getting together with his old friends was something that was very important to him, and he had been reluctant to leave her alone while he went. He was relieved to see that she was comfortable enough here now to be okay for a couple of days.

Liam had thought a great deal about this trip over the last few days. He knew that Beth was capable of handling things for the few days that he would be gone. That hadn't really been a question, as far as he was concerned. He had watched her skill level increase over the past weeks to where he knew that he could trust her ability to make the right decisions and carry them out where his patients were concerned.

His disquiet had its roots in the thunderstorm of a few nights ago. She had told him that she wouldn't leave without saying good-bye. But what if it happened the same way as the last time? What if she was simply taken without warning? What if he came home from Boston to find that she was gone, without a word? But he knew what she would tell him if he were to express his fears to her. She would say that she had a life to live and wasn't going to sit around waiting for some sign of what was to come next, just as she had said before, and that he should do the same. He had finally conceded to himself that her way of accepting it was the only logical way to proceed without going out of his mind.

Beth looked at him with a smile. She was a little nervous about being on her own after having Liam there at every turn. But she thought about how important it must be to him to see his old comrades, thinking of her fellow officers from her old job and all that she had been through with some of them. How nice it would be to have just one evening with them to reminisce!

"Liam, this is just a small way for me to repay you for all that you have done for me over the past couple of months. So don't worry any more about it."

They got going early on the morning of Liam's departure to get him down to the train, and Mr. Sizer came with them. Beth had a list of some things that they needed while they were in Westford, and Mr. Sizer was going to help her get them after they saw Liam's train off.

Liam went over all of his last minute instructions all the way down the mountain. "Liam, please! Stop worrying!" cried Beth. "You've gone over this a hundred times already! I'm good with all of it."

"Well, I just want to make certain that you'll be all right! I don't want you to be nervous without me there."

"You're making me nervous! I've got it." She waved her arm in the air. "You've covered everything from amputation to snakebite. Just what are you expecting to happen anyway?"

"You're laughing at me, aren't you?" asked Liam, the corners of his eyes crinkling up as he smiled.

His father answered before Beth did. "We're both laughing at you! Son, just go and have yourself a good time! It's two nights, so stop worrying. I don't know how to break this to you, but the people on this mountain managed before you came along." He put his hand affectionately on his shoulder. "Maybe not as well, but they did manage."

Beth smiled at both of them, a surge of affection welling up inside of her. There was a strong bond between father and son. It was obvious that Liam's father was proud of his son, and his words were not spoken unkindly. She thought, not for the first time, how fortunate she had been to have been found by Liam and welcomed by his family.

Beth looked at the train station with eager anticipation as they pulled up in front of it. She had always liked train stations, finding them to be wonderful, romantic places. This was her first trip to the Westford train station. It was no longer there in the future. Although the train did still run through the city, it didn't stop there to pick up passengers, and the train station had long since been torn down.

She looked at the long low brick building with its wooden platform as they walked up to it. Inside were long benches and the arched ticket windows at one end. There was a giant clock, probably one of the biggest that she had ever seen, on the wall opposite the ticket windows. A large slate was in the center of the wall opposite the tracks, listing all arrival and departure times. Consulting it, she found that all trains were running on time. She wandered around, taking it all in while Liam purchased his ticket. Mr. Sizer had seen someone that he knew out on the platform and had gone to say hello.

Liam turned away from the ticket window and looked for Beth. He watched her as she walked around the station looking at everything. Every time that they went somewhere new to her, she would take it all in and check out every detail. He smiled as he walked over to her.

Beth turned as she heard Liam behind her, smiling as she took in his appearance. He had on a suit and a shirt with a stiff white collar. He was carrying his hat in his hand, his hair was combed down flat on his head, and his shoes were polished. He looked nice and, overall, at ease in these clothes; but it wasn't how he normally looked. His hair was usually tousled from his fingers running through it during the course of the day, and he dressed in comfortable clothes for a day full of an assortment of activities. Usually a collarless shirt, sometimes with a buttoned vest over it with plain trousers and, most often, boots. But Beth was still amazed at how people dressed nicer for simple things like a train ride into Boston. She had learned that doing anything that wasn't considered everyday work required nicer clothes.

"Did you get your ticket? Are you ready to go?"

Now that it was nearing time for him to get on the train, she was beginning to get butterflies in her stomach. Before coming here, she had lived alone and worked much of the time by herself, but this was different. It sometimes felt to her as though she had landed in another world and had to learn everything new. Liam had been her safety net and guide more than once, and even though there had been times when she would have liked a little more breathing room, this was the first time that he would not be somewhere nearby.

"Yes. I'm all set." He looked closely at her. "You're a little nervous, aren't you? Should I not go?"

"Nonsense! I'm fine!"

Liam cocked one eyebrow and continued to look at her.

She grew a little uncomfortable under his unwavering gaze and spoke again. "But . . . it was just occurring to me that I have never really been on my own for more than a few hours since I came here. Suddenly, three days without you nearby does seem like a long time. It feels a little funny, if you know what I mean. But I'm okay with it, and I'm positive that I'll be fine."

For a quick moment, as he looked into her eyes, Liam was reminded of that first night when she braced herself against his bedroom wall and looked at him, gun in hand. She was so unsure and so determined, both at the same time. Now he couldn't resist taking her hand lightly in his and shaking it gently back and forth.

"I've gotten used to you being underfoot all of the time too." His words were softly spoken, and his eyes shone flecks of gold in the amber. "I'll be back before you know I'm gone." Then after a moment, "I'll miss you, I think."

He smiled softly at her, and for some reason that she couldn't understand, Beth felt the butterflies do a cartwheel.

They continued to stare at one another, neither saying anything further. The air between them seemed charged, and Beth wouldn't have been surprised to see sparks. The spell was broken when the whistle sounded for Liam's train, causing them both to start slightly, and he dropped her hand.

On impulse, Beth gave him a quick hug and kissed his cheek lightly saying, "Have a very good time. I'll be here to pick you up when you get back," before stepping quickly away from him.

Liam picked up his bag and followed her out to the platform, where his father was waiting for them. With a wave, he got on the train and settled into his seat, a slight smile on his face.

Beth and Mr. Sizer had a pleasant day in Westford, where he treated her to lunch before they did their shopping. This was only her second trip into this town. She had come once before with Mrs. Sizer and Liam. She and Mrs. Sizer had shopped for some 'necessaries' for her, as Mrs. Sizer had called them, while Liam had picked up a few supplies. As she had done on that first trip, she was looking from one thing to another. After having been in Corsehill for so long, this place seemed very busy indeed and quite metropolitan, with the automobiles competing for space with the horses on the cobbled streets lined with the new electric lights. Not for the first time, she commented to Mr. Sizer how fortunate he was to be living in this era when they were on the very brink of so many incredible changes.

The trip back up into Corsehill went by quickly while Mr. Sizer told Beth about growing up in Corsehill in the nineteenth century. And he shared stories about Naomi and Liam as children and about his other son, who had died at thirteen of diphtheria. He told her that he believed that was the reason Liam had chosen to become a doctor and remain in Corsehill.

"They were very close, as brothers sometimes are, and Rob's death hit him hard. He sat with him every minute, toward the end, seeing to his every need. He was angry for quite some time over how helpless we all had been with his illness. Those were dark, hard days for all of us. But mostly for him, I think. Now, he makes it his purpose to keep these people up here healthy. He's quite protective of them, as you have already seen."

"Liam told me about Rob's death," said Beth, putting her hand on Mr. Sizer's arm. "I'm very sorry for your loss. I understand what a very difficult time it must have been for all of you."

Mr. Sizer gave her hand a fatherly pat. "It's all right, my dear, it was a long time ago. We still miss him in our lives, and we always will. But we have gotten past the pain. I miss the man that he would have become." He patted his chest, saying, "But he lives here, in our hearts. One day, you'll find that you will be able to remember all of the people that were taken from you too soon, and the pain will be tempered by the good memories."

Beth smiled at his kind words, realizing that he had told her about Rob's death, so she would know that he understood some of what had been lost to her when she came to them. She felt tears catch in her throat as she gently squeezed his arm next to her. She wondered briefly if Liam had said anything to his father about the grief that she had shared with him that day, but she realized that he wouldn't have. That was a private thing between the two of them. It was simply that Mr. Sizer was as intuitive as his son and had used this time alone with her to make sure that she knew that they cared.

Back at the house, Beth brought in her purchases and put them away. Some of them were for Liam's pharmacy, and she catalogued all of them before storing them away in the cupboard upstairs. After coming out of the room and locking the door, she turned to go down the stairs. Following a sudden impulse, she instead went across the hall and stood in the doorway to Liam's bedroom. The urge to walk into the room was strong, but she resisted, not wanting to invade the only real private space that he now had in his own home.

She recalled her first days there, when she had stayed in this room while they finished the apartment for her. Had it only been a couple of months? So much had happened since then! Leaning against the doorjamb, Beth thought about what had passed between them earlier. Closing her eyes, she was back in the train station. She felt again the pull of his eyes, saw the color change as they turned golden and bright, and recalled how she couldn't look away but wanted to look deeper and deeper until she was part of him, seeing herself through his eyes. There was no denying that the air between them had been charged with a tension just like the night of the thunderstorm. She realized with a start that she was physically attracted to him. It was more than just recognizing that he was attractive; she had seen that in him on that first night and many times since. And she was used to working with men, so what made this so different? She thought again of the tension that had crept into the room the night of the thunderstorm. Chemistry? Could that be it? She'd frequently been alone with men where there could have been plenty of opportunities for intimacy, but it had never occurred to her to go there. They were her coworkers and, often, friends; but she had never felt that sexual pull. But Liam was her friend too. So it must be the chemistry this time. And what if they were to follow through with that tension that she had felt? What would happen if things didn't work out?

Besides, even though Liam had kissed her before, the kisses were more affectionate than passionate. They were always on her cheek or forehead. Never on her lips. He had never said anything to her to indicate that he would be interested in anything further. She had always considered these to be times when they had been caught up in the moment and nothing more. And she was probably reading way too much into what had passed between them at the train station anyway. Wasn't she?

Liam checked into his hotel with plenty of time to take a walk before meeting with his friends. He headed out into the street, noting that with every year that passed, the city had grown more each time that he came back. But the cobblestone streets and familiar old buildings of his schooldays were still there amid all of the changes. He pulled his watch out of his vest pocket, checking the time and made a beeline toward the Old Corner Bookstore on the corner of School and Washington Streets. There were a couple of books that he wanted to pick up for himself. But also, he recalled from his first conversation with Beth that she had a birthday coming up soon. There was a certain book that he wanted to get for her.

Sometime later, he emerged from the store, satisfied with the purchases that he had made. He took a roundabout route back to the hotel with his packages tucked securely under his arm. While he walked, he recalled what had passed between them at the train station and saw again Beth's expression while they had stood looking at each other, her hand in his. He had stood staring at her, thinking to himself that she was so beautiful, as though he was seeing it for the first time again. He had thought of little else during the train ride into Boston, thinking how nice it would be to have Beth there with him, taking in the sights of Boston and adding her own commentary on how the city would look in her time. He could picture her in one of her animated narratives, with her hands moving while she talked, and her expressive face showing how she felt. She had told him how she enjoyed going into Boston and that she used to go as often as she could. They had talked about places that they had both been, in their respective eras, and she told him of places that were just being constructed now, or would be soon.

Liam thought to himself that there were so many things to see and do in this city that he knew she would enjoy. It would be nice to bring her with him the next time, maybe take in a show and have dinner in a nice restaurant. He frowned as it occurred to him that she might not even be around in a year . . . she could leave as suddenly as she had arrived. There was no sense in making long-term plans where she was concerned.

Later that night, he and his shipmates were sitting back, enjoying brandy and cigars after their meal. There were seven of them, including Liam, who had served together as medical officers for that year on the *Solace*. They had reminisced and retold all of their old, favorite stories and were now catching up with each other on the past year of their lives, telling of work and children and home. One of the men, Toby Mason, had been Liam's cabinmate on board the *Solace*. It was he who put this gathering together each year; and Liam had written, telling him to book him a room, as he had an assistant and wouldn't need to leave early this time.

"So Liam, tell us about your new assistant," asked Toby, sitting back and looking at him. "He must be working out well for you if you don't need to rush out of here tonight to catch the train for those hills you call home."

"Yes, you are more relaxed now than I've ever seen you," added someone else.

Liam sat back, taking a long pull on his cigar before answering. After taking a sip of his brandy, he said, "Well, to start with, he is a she. My new assistant is a woman." He smiled. "A very capable woman named Elizabeth Blodgett."

"What made you think to take on an assistant?"

Liam sipped at his brandy, considering his answer, wondering how much information he should give these old, trusted friends of his.

He shrugged his shoulders. "She came to live in Corsehill and needed employment. She had the training, and my practice has grown to where I need some help. She's quick and bright, hardworking, and eager to learn what she doesn't know." Looking down into his snifter of brandy, watching the amber liquid as he swirled it around in the glass, he absently continued, "She's been a tremendous help to me. She's funny and kind and tough as nails when she needs to be. And she has more courage than I've ever seen in anyone." His voice trailed off, and he looked up at the faces around him. They were all staring at him.

"What?" he asked of them.

"How old is she, Liam?" asked Toby.

"And what does she look like?"

"Is she married?"

"What difference does that make?" he asked them as he shifted in his seat, knowing where this was headed and helpless to stop it.

"Just tell us, my friend!"

"She's twenty-nine. And no, she's not married. And yes, she's pretty."

His friends all gave each other knowing looks and then began to laugh.

Toby reached over and slapped him on the back, saying, "By this time next year, you will be married to this woman! It's about time you followed the rest of us into it!"

Liam felt his face flush, but he smiled as he shifted again in his chair. "I'm not the marrying kind. You all know that."

Amid the laughter and smiles, he was told, "We'll see!"

He was relieved when the talk moved on to other topics. He sat, smoking and drinking, thinking that they would understand if they knew the whole story. It would be nice, he mused, if she had come into his life through more conventional ways. Perhaps then they could have explored the possibility of a future together. *But no,* he told himself with a mental shrug, *that wouldn't work, either.* No woman wanted what he had to offer. He knew that. And he didn't want that anyway. And he would do right to remember it.

Chapter XV

Beth stayed busy over the next couple of days, and as Liam had said, the time went by quickly. There were a couple of Liam's patients who needed to be followed up on, and some prescriptions had to be delivered, which she and Liam had put together before he left.

She brought some cookies to Mrs. Dugdale when she went to pick up her eggs, and she stayed for tea. Mrs. Dugdale was a pleasant old woman who supported herself by taking in sewing and selling her eggs. She lived in a small cottage-style house that had an inviting dooryard with hollyhocks, sweet peas, dahlias, and a number of other types of old-fashioned flowers. Her chickens were always scratching contentedly in the garden, making their comforting clucking and whirring noises while they worked away. Beth always found her visits there to be soothing to her soul while she sat in the sun for an hour or so with the elderly woman. They would sip their tea and eat cookies while Mrs. Dugdale gently reminisced about her life, her old orange tabby cat curled up on her lap.

Beth had gone to spend some time with Naomi, helping her out with some chores around the house. As she worked, Beth talked with her about the night of the thunderstorm.

"Do you remember the thunderstorm we had a week or so ago?" She continued when she saw Naomi nod. "Liam and I both thought that the best way for me to get back to my own time would be to try to wait for another storm and return to that rock by the river. To wait and see if anything would happen. But when this storm hit, I found that I didn't even try."

"What made you decide not to?" asked Naomi, placing her hand over Beth's. "It must have been a difficult choice for you to make."

"I don't know, exactly. I was already awake and heard the storm coming, so I had plenty of time to think about it. I don't know—I got up and looked around my apartment, thought about Liam and the work he does, you and Bill, your folks, all of the people that I've met here . . .

151

"Then I turned around to look out the door and saw Liam standing on the grass. Right there, in the pouring rain! I think that he was wondering, just like me, if I was going to do it."

"What did he do? What did he say?" asked Naomi.

"Nothing. He asked me if I was okay. That's all. When I asked him if he thought I should've tried to leave, he said that all that mattered was what I wanted."

Naomi looked at her. "Did you tell him that you had decided to stay?"

Beth shook her head and shrugged. "No. I hadn't really realized that I'd made up my mind. It wasn't until he left that I knew it. I just don't want to leave, and there it is. I'm not ready." She lifted her shoulders again, dismissively.

Naomi impulsively hugged Beth, saying, "I'm selfish, I guess, but I'm so glad that you decided to stay here!" Suddenly, she gave a start and put her hand between them, on her belly. "Oh! Feel this!" she said, grabbing Beth's hand and putting it against her stomach.

Beth smiled with her, feeling a thrill run through her as she felt Naomi's babies moving beneath her hand. "It won't be long now! Feels like they're ready to take on the world!"

Naomi smiled at her comment, but Beth could sense nervousness beneath that smile. She picked up Naomi's hands, softly asking, "What is it?"

"Bill and I had about given up on the hope that we could have children. I still can't believe that it's finally happening for us! Now I'm anxious to have them here and hold them in my arms for real," she said. "I'm just so afraid that it's too good to be real!"

Beth and Naomi talked about what to expect when the time arrived and how she and Liam would be there to help her through it all. Beth told her how to breathe during labor and how regulating her breathing would help with her discomfort as well as ease the delivery of the babies. Mr. and Mrs. Sizer arrived and their conversation turned to more daily things. By the time Bill came home, Beth was getting ready to leave, and Naomi had begun to relax somewhat.

After Beth had said her good-byes and headed home, Naomi turned to the others saying, "How is it that Beth and Liam can be so dense that they haven't seen what they feel for each other? Sometimes, I want to shake both of them and tell them to wake up!"

Mrs. Sizer laughed, saying, "I know, dear, but leave it alone. Water always finds its own level, and they'll find theirs."

"Naomi, sweet, you must stay out of it," added Mr. Sizer. "Liam is fighting his feelings, and Beth simply hasn't realized her own yet. It's not surprising, given all that she's been through." He went on to tell them how he had observed the two of them through the window from the platform at the train station.

Bill came up behind Naomi and put his arms around her, putting his hands on her belly. "You can't force Liam anyway. He's too stubborn. And Beth will get there on her own. Once she does, well, Liam will have his hands full, I think!" They all laughed.

On the afternoon of the third day, Beth went to Westford to pick up Liam. She sat on a bench on the platform at the train station, reflecting on how life moved at a much slower pace here. What would be a fifteen-minute ride in a car from Corsehill to Westford took her over an hour with a horse and buggy. It had been difficult for her to adjust to working within that kind of time frame when she had first arrived, but now she found that the time spent getting from one place to the next was a good opportunity for her to let her mind wander. That was something that she had often found difficult to do in 2008, as time was something that there just was never enough of; and she was always rushing from one thing to the next, busily planning her next move before she got there.

She was pulled from her musing by the sound of the whistle from the approaching train. She rose from the bench and stepped out onto the platform as the train pulled alongside with much noise and steam. She saw Liam through one of the windows, and he gave her a wave. Her heart gave a slight lurch as she smiled and waved back, suddenly feeling an inexplicable wave of shyness. She felt her face flush as she tried to puzzle through her reaction at seeing him. She muttered to herself, "Blasted chemistry!" A moment later, he was beside her, and they made their way through the station toward the street in front.

"How was your visit?" asked Beth, looking at a point beyond Liam's shoulder, still not feeling like she had full control of her emotions. "Did you have a good time?"

"It was very nice! And since I had the extra time, I was able to meet up with some friends from school too. We had lunch yesterday, and I enjoyed seeing them. Thank you, again, for covering things for me so that I could go."

Liam helped her into the buggy and, after stowing his bag and packages behind the seat, climbed in beside her. He wondered if it was just his imagination that she slid about as far away from him as she could on the seat. "Were there any problems while I was away? Did you manage all right?" he asked.

"No problems," she said, staring over Ned's ears. "Everything was nice and quiet. I had myself a nice visit with your father and then with your mother when we got back to town. I finished up some work in the pharmacy and put away the stuff that I picked up the other day. I went to see Mrs. Dugdale for eggs and stayed with her for an hour or so. And I delivered the medicines to Mr. Locke and Mrs. Tibbets and had a nice chat with her as well. I ran into Mrs. Osborne with her two youngest children on my way back from the Tibbets'. She invited me back for tea, so I went. They seem to be doing all right. Levi looks tired, though his spirit seemed good. He's working very hard." She realized that she was almost babbling, telling him more than the question required. *Get a grip on yourself!* she silently chided.

"I'll stop in to see him in a day or so," said Liam. "Just to talk and see how things are going with him."

Beth nodded. "I went over to help Naomi for a while too. She's getting pretty nervous about the delivery."

"I'm not surprised. New mothers generally are. But I suppose too that she's just plain anxious to have them with her. She and Bill have waited a long time for children. She miscarried several times before this, and I think that she still can't believe that this time she's really going to have her babies."

"That's it exactly! How did you know? Did she tell you?" asked Beth.

Shaking his head, Liam said, "She's my sister, and I've been watching her closely. I know her. But don't worry. When the time comes, we'll get her through it just fine. I'm sure of it." He turned and smiled at her, but she didn't see it. "Now what else has been happening?"

"The only catastrophe that occurred was that Michael Tibbets socked Alvin in the nose over who would get to tighten the girth on Belle's saddle for me. I tightened it myself while they were brawling. Poor Mrs. Tibbets has her hands full with those two little boys!"

Liam laughed again. "All of the Tibbets' boys have always been brawlers. They're very hot-tempered. Their temperament matches their fiery red hair! How's Alvin's nose? Not broken, I hope."

Beth smiled in the direction of Ned and shook her head. "No. But his pride was injured that I had been there to see it. So I had to tell him that I thought that he was very brave for an eight-year-old for not crying while I examined his nose. It was obvious that he wanted to, very much. So," she said, "tell me all about your trip. How was everything?"

Liam told her about his friends from the *Solace* and his dinner with them. He described the hotel and the restaurant, then went on to tell her about having lunch with a couple of his classmates from medical school. He discussed their work in the city and how it differed so much from what they did up here in the hills.

They pulled into the dooryard at the house, and the buggy had barely rolled to a stop before Beth hopped down and took hold of Ned's bridle. "You go on inside, Liam. I'll take care of Ned for you so that you can relax after your trip."

Liam jumped down after her, putting a restraining hand on her arm. "Elizabeth, what is it? You're acting strangely."

Fussing with Ned's harness, Beth answered, "I'm fine. Really. Now go unpack and relax a little, will you?" She turned and was headed toward the barn with Ned before he could respond.

Liam stood watching her and shrugged his shoulders. What was wrong with her, all of a sudden? Three days ago, she was nervous about him leaving. Now that he was back, she seemed anxious to be away from him. He thought to himself, *Women! Who can figure them out?* He picked up his bag and went inside. Ten minutes later, he headed toward the river with his fly rod in hand.

Beth couldn't figure herself out. She had spent the last couple of months in close proximity with this man without a problem. Now he came back after just three days away, and all she could wonder about was what it would be like if he put his arms around her and kissed her . . . really kissed her . . . the way that Martin Harrison had. Just what was the matter with her?

She'd had to force herself past an iron grip of shyness that seemed to wrap around her at the station, and then again when they got home. She was behaving like a teenager with her first crush. All that she knew was that she had to pull herself together before she said or did something embarrassing to both of them.

Standing in the barn, brushing Ned out, she thought about Liam's standing here in this community. She knew that she had only been able to live in such close proximity to him without the local gossips carrying on because of the respect that people had for him. She had seen how hard he worked to earn and keep that respect. A large part of Liam's success with his patients came from the trust that they had in him. It would be wrong in so many ways for her to do anything that could jeopardize that for him and that included becoming intimately involved with him.

Beth reflected on her friendship with Liam. Her best friend had been a fellow game warden, a man whom she would entrust her very life to. They knew everything about each other's lives and could depend on one another for almost anything. But there had never been any physical desire between them, just a comfortably solid friendship.

She had never felt that close to anyone else, until Liam. But with Liam, there had been an instant rapport, and she felt even closer to him. There was a different, deeper sort of bond between the two of them, as though they had known each other forever. And now, she felt this pull of physical desire that she couldn't make go away. "Blasted chemistry!" she muttered again, shaking her head. But there was no way that she would hurt that friendship or Liam by doing something foolish based on her physical needs. Besides, he was her employer, for God's sake! And to get involved with him now would be improper as well as foolish.

She realized too that her thoughts were her own, and Liam didn't need to know how she was feeling unless she chose to tell him. The awkwardness between them today was of her making, not his. All that she had to do was get her feelings under control, and everything would be fine again. It seemed so simple when she looked at it that way. *So I'll just have to keep reminding myself to look at it that way,* she murmured to herself. *For my own sanity.*

With new resolve, she turned Ned out into the pasture, where Belle greeted him enthusiastically, as though he too had been gone for three days.

With a lighter heart brought about by her new resolve, Beth left the barn and headed around the corner toward her apartment. She heard hoofbeats coming down the road at a gallop as she headed across the grass. Turning toward the road, she saw Frank Burdett ride into the yard.

Absently, he put his fingers to the brim of his cap. "Miss Sizer! You and the doc need to come quick to Clare's house! He's hurt himself with dynamite!"

Beth was dumfounded. "With *what*? Never mind! I'll get the doctor and we'll head right out! Can you help with the horses?"

She turned and called the horses by name, and both horses ran toward the barn. Frank had dismounted and was rushing toward them as Beth ran around toward the river calling for Liam. Moments later, the three left the yard at a gallop toward the Owens' house.

They found Clare sitting in the kitchen, blood on the front of his shirt. His wife had towels pressed against his face, a look of both horror and concern on her own features. Setting his kit on the table, Liam pulled a chair close to Clare and sat down. As he lifted the towels to examine Clare, Liam asked Frank over his shoulder to tell him what had happened.

"We were clearing some land up back of the house, and we were dynamiting the stumps. Clare stuck his head out from behind the tree too soon and caught a piece of wood in his face!"

"I see that," said Liam. He tilted his head to look at Clare's face from another angle, taking in the injury. He reached for the syringe of morphine that Beth had filled for him and held out when she saw the piece of wood protruding from Clare's cheek. "Clare, this is going to smart just a little. I'm going to give you something for the pain, then we're going to clean it, and stitch it up."

Beth turned to Mary and asked her to start heating some water. She took out the forceps and other items that Liam would need to clean and stitch the wound and slid them into the hot water.

Liam injected Clare with the morphine and waited a moment for it to take effect. "What were you thinking, sticking your head around that tree, Clare?" The man shrugged his shoulders, with a sheepish look in his eyes.

Frank chimed in, "He wanted to see if the dynamite was working. I figured I'd wait for the boom to find out. But you know Clare, always has to be the first to know everything!"

Liam smiled at Frank's humor, knowing that it was true that Clare always had to be the first to know what was going on in the Hollow. He shook his head at Clare and said, "Don't you know that it was curiosity that killed the cat? Let's get to it, then. We'll get you fixed up."

With painstaking care, Liam pulled out the piece of wood, and then all of the smaller splinters, cleaning the wound thoroughly until he was certain that he had gotten every last piece of wood. With small, careful stitches, he closed the wound on the man's cheek. It began below his eye next to his nose and arched across his cheek toward his jawbone for about four inches or so. Knowing what his appearance meant to him, Liam had taken extra care with the stitches, but there was no avoiding the scar that the man would have. As it was, it would—in time—fade to a thin white arch. Eventually.

Beth and Liam cleaned up and left with Liam's promise that he would be back the next day to check on him. As they rode away, Beth turned to Liam. "I'm glad that you were back home before that happened! I know that I could stitch someone up, but I don't think that I could be as neat about it as you are!"

"Well," said Liam, "it was his face. People will see that scar."

"Yes. I noticed that you took the same care with my forehead. Did I ever, specifically, thank you for that?" As she said it, she put her fingers to her forehead, running them back and forth across the scar.

"As a matter of fact, not in so many words." Liam glanced up at her hand. "I always assumed that you just didn't want to talk about the scar."

"No." Beth shook her head, looking at him. "It's just a scar on the outside. I have lots of scars and don't usually give them too much thought. But every time that I look in the mirror, I can't help but notice what a nice, neat job you did for me. You didn't just close the wound. You repaired it too. And that takes skill, not simply the ability to stitch it closed. Thank you for caring enough about your patient to do all that."

They rode on. Liam thought to himself that whatever had been bothering Beth and causing her earlier tension seemed to be gone, and she was back to her old self. He was glad of that. Sometimes, she confused him to no end. He allowed himself to privately admit that he had missed her over the past few days. The sound of her voice, her thoughts, her very presence around him. Out loud, he said, "It was nice to get away, but I'm glad that I'm home." And he meant it.

Beth turned to him with a smile. "Me too." And she meant it.

The next morning, Liam left to go see Clare Owen. Beth wasn't really needed on this visit, so she had elected to stay behind and finish up a couple of things at the house before going to see Naomi. Mrs. Sizer was planning on coming over that afternoon, and Beth was going to stay with Naomi until she got there. Bill had asked them to keep an eye on her while he was at the mill. She knew that lately, he was only going to the mill at Naomi's insistence; and even then, it was only for part of the day. She smiled warmly at the depth of his concern for his wife and the impending birth of their babies.

Taking the path along the river, Beth walked with her kit slung over her shoulder enjoying the sights, smells, and sounds of a bright summer morning. The spiderwebs still carried drops of dew, sparkling like a hundred diamonds in the morning sun. The birds were warbling gaily all around while the ferns gently waved at her in the breeze as she passed by them. It occurred to her as she walked that she loved New England. She had traveled in her own time across the country. She had been to the mountains and the ocean and all sorts of places in between. But here was the place that would always be her anchor. The Berkshire hills of western Massachusetts—with their clear rivers and streams that attracted such abundant plant and animal life—and the hardwood forests and rocky fields were, she thought, the most beautiful that she had ever seen. She would never tire of the sight of the New England farmhouses and barns and the golden green fields separated by stone walls and old fences, proud that her American heritage went back almost three hundred years to this very place. She felt connected to the very soil beneath her, and it felt good. Here, now, she felt more connected than ever before.

As she walked through the back door of Bill and Naomi's house, Beth heard a low groan. She looked toward the sound and saw Naomi gripping the edge of the worktable in the kitchen.

"Naomi!"

"It's time, I think. They're early," was all that she said as she looked at Beth.

Beth ran over to her. "How long ago did your water break?"

"I don't know! A few minutes, I think." She groaned again as another contraction came over her.

Beth's mind raced as she recalled her first aid for childbirth. She wasn't supposed to be the one doing this! She was just Liam's helper! But she had helped deliver a baby several years ago with another officer. The baby had begun to crown when they got there, and the ambulance had arrived just as the delivery was complete. Well, there wouldn't be an ambulance, and it would have been better if Liam was there with her; but this was going to happen, regardless.

"Naomi, can you make it to the bedroom?"

Through gritted teeth, Naomi replied, "I don't think so!"

"All right, Naomi, hold on one second while I get some sheets and blankets for you to lie down on. We're going to do this right here!" With that, Beth ran from the kitchen and went to the upstairs hallway where she took clean sheets, a quilt, and pillows from the cupboard. She ran back to the kitchen and spread the quilt and sheets on the floor and threw the pillows down on top of them.

She turned back to Naomi and helped guide her down onto the makeshift bed. She prepared her for the birth, and then draped another clean sheet over her lower body. She put the pillows behind her and another under her hips, then washed her hands, and knelt back down with her, holding a stack of clean towels.

"I don't know what to do!" cried Naomi. "I thought that I was ready, but now I'm not so sure! What if something goes wrong? This isn't the way that this was supposed to happen!" Beth could hear the fear in her friend's voice and thought to herself that she wasn't kidding about that!

Taking a deep, calming breath, she said, "Naomi, relax and take slow, deep breaths like we talked about before. Your body knows what to do and so do your babies, so stay calm and go with it. I'm here for you, and we'll do this together. I know that it hurts, but if you focus on breathing steadily, it will help with the pain."

Beth spoke calmly to Naomi, but inside, she was a nervous wreck. This was her friend, and she was delivering two babies! And quickly too! She wished again that Liam were there, with his unflappable calm and soothing voice. She pulled herself together with a mental shake and thought to herself, *Courage, Beth, you can do this!*

At that moment, the door opened and Beth looked up to see Bill come in the room.

"Bill! Go get Liam! He should be on his way back from the Owens'."

Bill stood where he was, staring at Naomi lying on the blankets on the floor.

"Bill! Go! Now!" He looked at Beth and nodded and with another quick look at Naomi, turned, and ran out.

"Okay, m'dear, let's see how close your babies are to putting in an appearance!" With that, she gently pushed Naomi's knees up and apart and found that the crown of the first baby's head appeared with her next contraction.

"Naomi, each time that you feel the urge to push, I want you to push steadily until I tell you to stop. Then I want you to rest and breathe slow and steady until you feel the urge again. Do you understand?"

Naomi nodded, her teeth gritted.

And so it began. Beth continued to talk to Naomi, telling her to push or stop and always to breathe. While she was talking, she guided the baby's head while he slowly came out with the contractions.

"Okay, Naomi, you have to stop for a moment." Beth took a towel and cleaned away the mouth and nose of the baby. Gently, she put her finger under the umbilical cord and unwound it from the baby's neck. She placed her hand on Naomi's lower abdomen and gently pushed. Naomi cried out as Beth guided the baby's shoulders and he slipped out the rest of the way.

"Naomi! You have a son!" She felt a surge of emotion as she held the perfect pink little body in her hands. She tilted his head down slightly and lightly tapped the bottoms of his feet. Beth heard the door open as the baby began to cry. She looked up as she reached for a clean towel to wrap him in and was relieved to see Liam and Bill in the doorway.

"Welcome to the party, Doctor! We've saved one for you!" Relief was evident on her face and in her voice.

Liam ran to the basin and quickly washed his hands. He was beside her in an instant, reaching for the baby that was now wrapped head to toe in the towel, his squalling little face peeking out. Bill knelt down by Naomi's head, leaning over to gently kiss her forehead while he reached for her hand.

"Bill," said Beth, "get a cool cloth and wipe Naomi's face, will you? She's been working hard! And wash your hands!"

Beth smiled at Naomi. "We're halfway there! You're doing a great job of it!"

Liam said to Naomi, "Just one more time, sis, and then you can rest!" He turned to Beth and said, "You're doing a great job too so just keep going with it. I'll take care of the cord on this little one." With that, she delivered Naomi and Bill's daughter.

Beth laid both babies on Naomi's chest while Liam finished her delivery and, eventually, she and Liam went out and gave the new parents a few moments alone with each other and their babies.

Standing on the porch, Beth turned to Liam with a grin. He understood just what she was feeling and impulsively wrapped both arms around her, hugging her close, a broad smile on his face. There was nothing more satisfying to him, as a doctor, than helping to bring a new life into the world. He could feel her shaking slightly as she returned his hug.

"Elizabeth, are you all right? What is it?"

Beth stepped back, saying, "I'm okay now. But I have to tell you, I was scared to death! I was so afraid of making a mistake and hurting Naomi or the babies."

Liam smiled proudly at her. "You did a wonderful job taking care of my baby sister for me. Thank you!" He paused for a moment, "Do you know what I've noticed about you? You take a deep breath and plunge right into things. You always hold yourself together when you need to, no matter what. So it's all right to flake out afterward. I'm proud of the way you handled yourself in there!"

They both turned at the sound of horse and carriage and saw Mr. and Mrs. Sizer pull into the yard. Mrs. Sizer was disappointed that she had missed the birth of her grandchildren, but elated that they were finally here, and that mother and babies were all doing well. She ran into the house and immediately got to work. There was a flurry of activity as Naomi and the babies were moved upstairs to the bedroom, and the two cradles were set up near the bed. Liam did a physical exam on both babies, as well as Naomi, and pronounced that even though they had arrived almost two weeks early, everything was just as it should be. Naomi was very tired after her delivery, and was left alone with Bill to rest and nurse the babies for the first time. There was an air of celebration in the house, and Beth was happy to be included in the circle of this warm, wonderful family.

Eventually, Beth and Liam said their good-byes and headed for home, leaving Mr. and Mrs. Sizer and Bill to take care of Naomi and the babies, who had been named Percy and Pearl.

They walked together along the river road toward home. Liam led Ned behind him as he walked with Beth. Beth turned to him and asked, "So how's it feel to be an uncle?"

Liam grinned at her. "I hadn't really thought about how it would feel, but the instant that I took Percy from you, I realized that these babies have some of the same blood flowing in them as I do. It was . . . special, I guess. It took me a little bit by surprise, to be honest with you."

"I know how you feel. I had the same feeling with each of my nieces and nephews. Family—it's a good feeling." Beth felt a pang of homesickness deep inside. She missed those little kids!

Liam, sensing how she felt, put his hand lightly on her shoulder for a brief moment. Beth turned and smiled at him, appreciating the gesture. She was fingering the locket hanging on the chain around her neck.

But homesickness wasn't all that she was feeling. She recalled how she had felt when she watched Naomi holding both babies for the first time. She had felt a little bit envious. She realized again that, most likely, her opportunity for a family had probably passed her by. Most women here, now, were married with several children by the time they were her age.

With effort, Beth changed the direction of her thoughts and asked Liam, "How was Clare today? How did he look?"

"The swelling is still pretty bad, but then his face took quite a trauma. His temper is foul. He's short with Mary and didn't have much to say to me either. He's not going to be one of my better patients! But then I rather expected this reaction from him."

"Of all the places for him to get a scarring injury," responded Beth, "his face would be the worst. His looks are a matter of pride to him. Maybe, when the swelling goes down, he'll be better with it."

"Hmm, we'll see," was Liam's only response as they walked shoulder to shoulder.

In the days that followed, Liam and Beth began to spend more time apart. It hadn't been through any sort of agreement. They hadn't even talked about it. Beth just seemed to want some time for herself, so after her work was done for the day, she usually went off to visit Naomi or Mrs. Dugdale, or she went into her apartment. Some evenings, when she wasn't out on a call, she would indulge herself with a long, hot bath, surrounded by candlelight and the scent of lavender from the bath salts that she had picked up in Westford. She would soak in the luxurious water until it grew tepid, letting her mind drift wherever it wanted to go. Sometimes, her thoughts brought her around to what she was going to do, where she would end up. Other times, she came back around to Liam. It didn't occur to her that each time she thought about one, the other came into her mind.

She had managed to put her physical feelings for him into perspective. She had convinced herself that her sudden desire for him had grown from being around him all of the time. He was a man, and she was a woman. What did she expect? Their friendship was still there, they worked as well as ever together and got along just fine. But they both went their separate ways at the end of the day, instead of sitting quietly in the backyard by the river, or on the porch, talking while she sewed and he tied flies in the golden light of the summer evenings. She didn't sit on the riverbank watching Liam fish; she left him to his solitude and he to hers. She told herself that she didn't need his guidance like she had when she first arrived, and it was time for her to start spending time on her own, facing whatever the future held for her here. A melancholy mood had come over her, and she was uncharacteristically indulging herself in it.

Beth woke slowly. It was an overcast, gloomy morning. *It figures,* she thought, *that my birthday would be a gray day.* With a sigh, she threw back the covers and got out of bed. She hadn't mentioned that her birthday was approaching; why would she? This day was just like any other day. So what difference did the weather make? It occurred to her as she washed and dressed that she had been having a series of gray days. The birth of Naomi's babies had triggered feelings in her that she had not experienced before and never knew she had. She was feeling a vague panic over whether or not she would ever be able to have her own children. It was something that she had thought about before, but never worried over, thinking that she would have time 'later.' Suddenly, she was feeling that, in this era, there was no 'later.' Her opportunity had passed her by when she came to live here. Beth finished dressing and headed for Liam's. This was his week to cook breakfast.

Beth came in through the door to hear Liam cursing roundly. She looked into the kitchen and saw that he was at the stove. As she got closer, she saw that he had dropped the bowl of egg into the pan on the stove. Now bits of scrambled eggs were cooking where they had splattered on the hot stovetop.

"With grace like that, you ought to consider a profession that requires you to use your hands!" was Beth's tongue-in-cheek comment from the doorway. "And such language! What happened here?"

Liam looked over his shoulder and grimaced at her. He was glad to see a smile on her face. He had been worried about her these past days. She had been unusually quiet, lost in her own thoughts. Normally, they would always have plenty to talk about, such as how she had lived before she had come to be here, her family, or her job as a game warden. They would compare her childhood here in Corsehill to his, or discuss the work that they were both doing now, and books that they had both read. He had found himself greeting each day with a new enthusiasm, eager to spend time with her. But she'd had little to say lately, and he had the impression that he only had half of her attention, at best, during their conversations.

He had noticed immediately when she had become so quiet. It had begun around the time Naomi's babies were born, when he got back from Boston. He had tentatively questioned her a couple of times about it, but she didn't seem inclined to want to talk. He hadn't pressed her too much, giving her the space that she seemed to need. He thought to himself that it didn't require too much thinking to figure out that the babies, along with her approaching birthday, had triggered a wave of homesickness. It had settled on her like a cloak. It did surprise him a little that he had remembered her date of birth. But then he recalled everything else about that day that she arrived in his life, so maybe it wasn't so surprising after all.

Now grimacing over his shoulder at her, he said, "Breakfast is what happened. I dropped the bowl into the pan, and the rest is history. I'll have to clean this up and start over."

Still laughing, Beth said, "Don't worry, I'll help you!" She turned and picked up a dishcloth.

Liam reached over and took it from her. "Oh, no, you don't! You just sit down and drink your tea, please!"

Beth gave him a confused look as he led her to the table and pulled out a chair for her. Seeing her look, he gestured toward the table. She turned in her chair and saw a glass with roses that had been picked from the climbing bush growing up the front porch. She pulled the glass toward her and breathed in the fragrance of the clusters of double flowers, still showing drops of dew on the pale pink and white petals. Sitting next to the roses was a parcel wrapped in brown paper, with a ribbon tied around it. Beth turned her face back toward Liam, still confused.

"Happy birthday!" smiled Liam. "I'll bet that you thought no one knew, didn't you?"

"How? How did you know?"

"Remember that first night, when you woke up and I asked you when you were born? I remembered the date." At her surprised look, he said, "It was a memorable day, don't you think?"

"That," remarked Beth, "is an understatement."

He reached for the package on the table and handed it to her. "This is for you. Open it!"

Beth looked at the package that he put in her hands. Written across the front were the words "Happy Birthday, Elizabeth." Beth was deeply touched that he had gone to this amount of trouble for her birthday. She had been brooding terribly over the past few days, missing her family and friends, and feeling sorry for herself, thinking that life was passing her by in so many ways and trying to figure out what she was really meant for here. She hadn't realized that it had been so obvious, but she could tell by the way that Liam was watching her that he was hoping that this would help her feel better. She swallowed the lump in her throat as she untied the ribbon holding the paper in place. Her eyes were bright as she whispered, "Thank you," to Liam.

As the paper fell away, Beth found that she was holding a book in her hands. Not just any book. It was a leather-bound copy of the works of Henry Wadsworth Longfellow. Holding her breath, she opened the cover and read the inscription written inside, dated August 16, 1908: "For Elizabeth, Happy Birthday. I think that you will find 'A Psalm of Life' on page one hundred thirty three especially fitting now. It reminds me of you." It was signed "Liam."

Beth looked up at Liam, a queer look on her face.

"What is it? Don't you like it?" asked Liam.

"I know this book."

"I know that. You told me once that you used to read his works often and that you wished that you had your copy of his poems here with you." Liam looked confused. "Is something wrong?"

Shaking her head, Beth said, "Yes . . . No! What I mean is, I know *this particular book*! This very copy!"

Liam still looked confused, and she continued. "Let me explain. Growing up, my parents always had this copy of Longfellow's poems on a shelf in their house. It was older, the pages were yellowed and well read, but I know that it's the same book because of the inscription! I read it often, and as a little girl, I thought that it was funny that there was another Elizabeth that shared my birthday. I always wondered who Elizabeth and Liam were. Now I know! But I wonder how Mom and Dad came to have *this* book?"

Understanding dawned on Liam's face. He looked from Beth to the book that she was holding in her hands. He reached over and took it from her, feeling the skin on the back of his neck prickle. How could this be? He opened the book, seeing it with new eyes, realizing that—in a way—she had known him before they even met.

She had held this book and read his words, perhaps even run her fingers across his handwriting, throughout her life. He had been there with her, all along.

"When I moved into my own home," continued Beth, "my folks gave me this book, saying that it was more mine than anyone else's. It has been on a table in my living room ever since, where I have frequently picked it up and read it." She looked at Liam, tears in her eyes.

Liam, seeing the tears, said "Have I upset you with this? I had no idea that this would happen! I'm so very sorry!"

"No!" responded Beth, with a smile. She took the book from him, running her hand reverently over the cover. "Don't you see what you've given me? It's like finding an old friend again! This gift from you somehow ties everything together. The past, present, and future are all together with this one book. It is enormously comforting to have this book that has always been a part of my life here with me. I can't begin to tell you what you have done for me!" She stood up and hugged him hard. "Thank you! For everything—the book, the inscription inside, the flowers. All of it. I don't know what else to say!"

Liam smiled at the joy on her face, happy that he had been able to give her something that was so special. Earlier, he had felt somewhat uncomfortable picking the flowers and finding something to put them in, but he simply wanted to make her smile. Some inner voice told him that it was exactly the thing to do for her. Now he saw that it had been. "You're very welcome! I never thought that this book would give you this much pleasure! Now relax while I start over with breakfast." He turned back to the stove.

Beth opened the book to "A Psalm of Life" and read it, the words so familiar to her that she barely needed to read them on the page. *How many times have I read this poem?* she thought to herself. It pleased her enormously that Liam would find it a fitting parallel to her life here. She continued to smile as she looked out the window and sipped her tea, her hand resting on the open book. As the rain began to fall, she thought—suddenly—that the day wasn't so gloomy after all!

> " . . . *I am reminded of a poem by T.S. Eliot that I read in college,* Burnt Norton. *I can't recall many of the lines, but I remember some of it.* 'Time present and time past are both perhaps present in time future, and time future contained in time past.' *And,* 'What might have been and what has been point to one end, which is always present. Footfalls echo in the memory down the passage which we did not take toward the door we never opened into the rose garden.' *I don't have the ability to re-read the poem now, since it won't even be written for another twenty-five or thirty years. But I recall that the speaker sees the things that might have been, but never were, and sees that he is powerless to control these things that seem so unreal to him. And that past and present are all part of the same plan . . .* "

Chapter XVI

Beth had spent the morning cleaning, organizing, and inventorying the pharmacy, as well as bringing the ledger up to date. Having finished the job, she was heading across to her apartment to take care of a couple of her own things when she saw a rider coming down the road. As he turned his horse into the yard, she saw that it was Frank, and she broke into an impulsive smile.

"Hello, Frank! How are you today?" she called out cheerfully.

He smiled in return, saying, "Good morning, Beth. Can't complain. Wouldn't do me any good anyway," as he touched the brim of his cap. "Is Doc around?"

Shaking her head, Beth said, "No. But he should be back anytime now. I was just going to get myself something cold to drink. Would you like to join me and wait a bit for him? I know that he won't be long now." She didn't want to lose this opportunity to visit with her great-grandfather.

"I could wait a spell for him," he said as he dismounted and tied his horse in the shade by the barn.

Beth ushered him around to her apartment, where he took his cap off and stuffed it into his back pocket before taking a seat at her table. She busied herself with the pitcher of lemonade that she had made that morning and the loaf of spiced cake made the night before.

Frank looked around her neat apartment, his eyes coming to rest on the cabinets and shelves in the kitchen where he sat. He asked Beth, "Did Liam build all of this?"

Beth nodded as she turned and set two cold glasses of lemonade on the table, followed by two slices of the fragrant cake. "Yes, he did. I helped a little bit, but not much. Most of what you see was done by him."

Forking up a piece of the cake, Frank nodded. "I thought so. He's a fine cabinetmaker, like his grandfather was. If he wasn't such a fine doctor, I'd say he missed his calling."

Laughing, Beth replied, "He told me once that he thought that he could always fall back on this if he didn't make it as a doctor."

"Well," said Frank, between mouthfuls of his cake, "he needn't worry about quitting the doctoring business. He's a fine doctor, and we wouldn't want to lose him."

Smiling back at him, Beth said, "You like him, don't you?"

"Oh, aye. He's a good man and a good friend. And a good doctor."

Sensing now that Frank had something on his mind, Beth asked, "How's Clare doing, Frank?"

He pushed his empty plate aside and sat back, toying with his glass of lemonade. He studied the liquid for a long moment, and then abruptly looked up at her as though he had reached a decision.

"Not so well. That's what I stopped in to see Liam about . . ."

A voice came from the open doorway. "See me about what?"

Liam walked into the room and shook the hand that Frank had extended as he stood up. Beth got up to pour another glass of lemonade and cut more cake, offering another slice to Frank, which he accepted.

As they ate, Liam questioned Frank about Clare. The accident had occurred nearly three weeks earlier, and he had found the scar to be healing well when he examined it after taking the stitches out over a week ago. "Although," he added, "he wasn't in a very good mood."

"Yes," said Frank. "That's what I'm here to talk with you about. His face is healing just fine. But he's been mean as a snake to everyone that comes around. Won't go anywhere, just does the chores and goes back inside and shuts the door. It's not normal. Mary and me were hoping, maybe, that you could help."

Later that afternoon, Beth and Liam had gone over to the Owen farm, where they found Clare sitting alone in a small room off of the sitting room. According to his wife, he spent most of his time in there now, not wanting to see anyone. Liam had examined the new scar that resembled a bright red cord across his face.

"Clare, I know that this scar seems bad to you now, but it will fade to a thin line in time. It's healing very nicely."

Clare had only glared at him in response.

"You can't spend the rest of your days in here, Clare. There are people who need you, and you have responsibilities."

Clare pursed his lips and looked away. His wife came up behind him and put her hand on his shoulder. He shrugged it off. She backed away, clearly hurt and at a loss over what to do for her new husband.

—

Liam cast a sympathetic glance at Mary and said, "Clare, talk to me about this! We can help you through it."

Liam sat looking at Clare while the injured man glared at him. "You tell me, Liam, how I'm supposed to go anywhere with this scar on my face? I'll look like one of them freaks in a circus sideshow!"

With all of his willpower, Liam resisted the urge to look at Beth. He was certain that Clare had not given any thought to the fact that she had a scar of almost the same size across her forehead. He was so intent on feeling sorry for himself over how this injury would change his appearance that he had stopped caring about anyone else's feelings. He felt irritation rise within him over Clare's behavior. With effort, he pushed it down, remembering that he was supposed to be sympathetic and reassuring to his patients.

Beth stood silently to the side, leaning against the wall and watching the exchange between Liam and Clare. She saw Liam struggle with his irritation over Clare's words and actions. Clare had always been so proud of his looks. Now he would have to get used to a change in that appearance. She thought about the scar on her forehead. Surprisingly, she hadn't really given it much thought before now. She assumed that it was because there had been so much other stuff going on that she just hadn't taken the time to focus on it. True, she noticed it every day in the mirror, but she didn't give it any more consideration than that daily glimpse. It had never occurred to her that she could be considered 'freakish' or repulsive because of it. Although Clare's words were cutting, she didn't believe them. It was, simply, a scar. She drew a deep breath and pushed herself away from the wall.

"Excuse me, Clare, but I have something to say to you."

Clare turned his head and glared at her. Liam leaned forward in his chair, with his elbows on his knees.

Beth pulled out a chair and sat down facing Clare. Looking at him, she reached up and ran her fingers across her scar, feeling the soft new skin stretched over the hard cord of the healing wound as she did so.

"Do you see this? It's about the same size as yours, isn't it?" She didn't wait for his reply. "I too have a scar that I didn't ask for or expect. I suppose that it has changed my appearance, although I haven't really thought about it. But if I were to think about it, I guess that I would have to say this . . . scars are just marks on the map of your life. They show where you've been and what you've done. I actually have quite a few scars. I've never really worried about any of them. In time, this scar will fade to white and be barely noticeable. I expect that whatever it ends up looking like will give my face more character."

Beth paused, drew a breath, and expelled it. "Clare, you are still a handsome man! There's no denying that. And I know that you have always been proud of your looks, as you should be. But physical beauty fades and changes with time. The true beauty in any person is the beauty from within. That's the beauty that shows in the way that you carry yourself and the manner in which you treat others each and every day. Part of your particular beauty is the beauty that comes out when you make your fiddle come to life and lighten peoples' hearts with your music. I would love to be able to play the fiddle the way that you do! The beauty of your deeds is the mark that you make and what people notice and remember you for! It's this mark that will live on long past your time! Believe me when I tell you this!"

Liam sat listening to Beth's words, spoken with such conviction. Suddenly, he realized that she wasn't simply saying these things to Clare! This was what she believed and the way that she tried to conduct herself every day, and it was part of what made her the special person that she was. This optimism was one of the things that was so appealing and drew peoples' attention to her when she came into a room. It was as though he'd had a revelation, and for a moment, he was completely thrown. With some effort, he came back to what was being said in the room.

Beth continued to speak. "You can do what you want with what I've told you. All that I ask is that you think about my words." She smiled slowly, gently, at Clare. "This injury has changed you on the outside. You didn't really have a choice about that. But you do have a choice about what it does to the person inside of you! Remember that. Stop being so hard on yourself and the people who care about you."

Clare had remained silent. He hadn't made eye contact with her, nor did he acknowledge her words now. Beth stood up and looked at Mary, giving her a half smile. Liam rose from his chair. He placed a hand on Clare's shoulder as he walked past him and picked up both his and Beth's kits.

Beth, Liam, and Mary were headed out the door, and Beth's hand was on the knob. She stopped when she heard Clare ask, "How, Beth?"

Beth glanced at Liam before turning to Clare. "How . . . what?"

Clare cleared his throat and asked, "How do you not let that scar bother you?"

Beth thought for a moment. "Life's too short, Clare. I've learned that I can't burn up my energy fretting over something that I can't change. But I'm still in control of what I think and feel. The sun can't always be shining . . . learn to dance in the rain instead of hiding from it!"

She turned toward the door and then back to Clare with another thought. "You know, Clare, there are and will be people in this world who have accidents far worse than yours. Accidents that take away parts of them, leaving them maimed or crippled. You could have lost your eye, or worse, been killed. Think about that." She walked through the door and shut it behind her.

Liam and Beth walked outside with Mary Owen. She looked at both of them. "Thank you both for what you said to Clare. I don't know what else to do for him."

"There's nothing else that you can do right now, Mary," said Liam. "Clare is a proud, strong man. But he's also a smart man. I believe that he'll come around." He sighed, "I just don't know when."

Beth and Liam were quiet as they rode away from the Owens. Liam was thinking Beth's words over. Her outlook was just as he would have expected it to be—no matter what obstacles life threw in her way, she still had the freedom to choose how she would live; her thoughts and feelings were her own choice. He had been worried that Clare's insensitive words about scarring would hurt her. If they had, she wasn't showing it.

Beth was working hard to put down the irritation that she felt over Clare's words and actions. He had to realize that he was lucky to still be alive! She hadn't realized until now just how much importance he placed on his physical appearance. What she had really wanted to tell him was that having a scar on his face wasn't the end of the world and to get on with the life that was going on all around him. She huffed the breath out through her mouth and shook her head.

Liam looked over at her. "What is it?"

She shrugged her shoulders. "I don't know. I don't mean to sound insensitive, and I never would be in front of one of your patients, you know that. I meant everything that I said to Clare, but there was more that I would have liked to say to him. Things that wouldn't have been said so carefully. It annoys me that his vanity is allowing him to wallow around in this self-pity to the point where he's deliberately lashing out at people around him. So he made a mistake, and now he has a scar on his face. It's okay to allow yourself to feel bad about things. That's a natural reaction. I understand that as well as anyone, particularly lately. But soon you have to pull yourself out of it and get back to living your life, and he doesn't seem to want to do that."

"I know, Elizabeth. I was irritated with him too, with the way that he's treating everyone else. But you have to remember that his appearance has always been a big part of who he is. I do agree that it doesn't seem as though he has tried to come to terms with it yet. But I think that he was given a lot to think about today, and I believe that he'll come around. This is a big change for him, and he'll need time. Not all of us have the ability to see things with the same perspective that you can."

"That's true. I do have an edge on people there, don't I? For all the good it does me."

Beth let Belle fall half a pace behind Ned as they made their way down the road while her mind drifted over the future changes coming to their section of

Corsehill. She felt frustration well within her over not being able to say anything. Clare had injured himself permanently while improving this property of his. She sighed, muttering to herself, "And to think that all this is over land that won't be his to grow old on or pass on to his children." She shook her head.

Liam twisted around in his saddle to look at her. "What was that?" he asked, slowing Ned as Belle moved up alongside.

Beth could have kicked herself. She hadn't realized that she had spoken the words loud enough for him to hear! "Nothing. It was nothing."

"Yes it was. What were you talking about?"

"Liam, let it go, okay? Why can't you just believe that I didn't say anything and leave it at that?" Her voice was somewhat sharper than she had intended.

"Because you did say something, and I caught enough of it to know that it wasn't good!"

Beth rode along in stubborn silence. They were almost home now, and she would be able to escape into her own apartment.

"Elizabeth, I'm tired of this!" Liam said angrily. "I know that you were referring to something that hasn't happened yet."

"Oh, really?" She was getting angry too. They were both on edge after their visit with Clare. She turned to Liam, her dark eyes flashing with emotion. "How do you know that's what I was talking about?"

"I'm not stupid! I don't know why you feel that you can't trust me enough to share some of this burden with me. I know that it gnaws at you! Why won't you tell me?"

Beth shook her head angrily. "It's not that I don't trust you, so don't be absurd! Nor do I think that you're stupid! I'm just not going to share this with you. Everything will be different for you if you know the things that I know! You won't be able to look at anything in this world the same way ever again! Are you really sure that you want that?" She glared at him. "I don't think that you've thought this through sufficiently. So just quit bugging me about it!"

"I have thought this through, in spite of what you may think," Liam bit out. "I have eyes! I see what it does to you! I can guess at how it is!" He paused, "Besides, you can't just tell me about the good things without expecting me to want to know the rest."

They had arrived home while they were arguing, and Beth dismounted in the yard outside of the barn. "Just let me alone about this, Liam!" she threw back at him over her shoulder as she led Belle inside. "You can't bully me into anything!"

Liam paused for a moment before dismounting Ned, watching the stubborn set of her shoulders while she stomped into the barn. Bully her? She was so blasted independent! He dismounted and, before he changed his mind, stormed inside after her.

"Bullying you! Is that what you think I'm doing? I remember an early morning conversation not too long ago right here in this barn. You told me then that sharing with someone sometimes eased the problem. I agree with that. You told me that you would be here to talk to, should I need you. It works both ways, Elizabeth! This burden will be lighter if you have someone to share it with, and I'm offering to take some of it from you. You don't need to carry all of this weight by yourself!" He ran an agitated hand through his hair. "Dammit, you're my friend, and I care about you! Doesn't that mean anything?"

Beth continued to unsaddle Belle, her back to Liam. She said nothing.

The silence stretched on. With a disgusted grunt, Liam picked up a horse brush and walked back outside, where he quickly brushed Ned and turned him loose in the pasture. He stalked off toward the house. He had work to do, and he wasn't going to argue with her stubbornness anymore!

Beth brushed out Belle as she felt the anger slowly drain out of her. She knew that she had hurt Liam by refusing to talk and wished that she hadn't had to. If anyone could safely keep the information that she had, it would be him. The truth was, she trusted him with her very life. But did she have any right to tell him these things that would change his whole world? He seemed to think that he could take it, but then he didn't know the extent of what she knew. Which would hurt him more? Telling him or not? She didn't want to be at odds with him.

They had certainly discussed it enough, without her sharing any specific details. He wasn't stupid. He knew by now that much of what she knew wasn't encouraging. Maybe she could tell him . . . should tell him. He was right about sharing burdens. She smiled in spite of herself. Leave it to him to turn her own words on her. But she believed in what she had said to him that morning in the barn, and now she had to put up or shut up, as the saying went. She pressed her forehead against Belle's neck and buried her free hand in the mare's mane. She just didn't know.

Liam slammed in through the back door and threw his kit on the worktable in the kitchen. She was so obstinate! Why wouldn't she share this with him? He had to admit that it hurt that she wouldn't open up about it. He began to stalk about his house, walking a great circle from kitchen to dining area, across the hall, and into the sitting room. Through to the back of the room, back across the hall, and into the kitchen again, muttering all the while, "Bully her. I don't bully! Well, fine. If she wants to carry this weight by herself, then fine! I'm better off not knowing anyway. If she wants to figure out how to handle this all by herself, then I'll let her. She'll not accuse me of bullying her again! What do I know anyway?"

He picked up his fishing gear and reached for the door handle. Changing his mind, he threw the gear back down. He was wallowing in his anger over this right now and wasn't ready to let the soothing water of the river and the repetitive motion of fly fishing change that. He continued to pace around, grumbling over how wrong she was in her willfulness. He refused to consider that it might be for his own good that she refused to talk with him about it.

Several hours later, Beth walked across the lawn to the house. Letting herself in through the back door, she called out to Liam as she usually did. Not getting a response, she looked into the sitting room and found him at his desk, papers spread out in front of him.

"Hi. Um . . . is this a bad time?" she hesitantly asked.

Liam, still smarting from their earlier argument, set his pen down and leaned back in his chair, looking at her, his hands on the edge of his desk.

Ignoring the fact that his expression as good as told her that he didn't want to talk with her, Beth walked into the room and around to the front of the desk. She picked up a glass paperweight with an image of the *Solace* suspended in the glass and absently passed it back and forth from one hand to the other. She set it back down on the desk and began wandering around the room, collecting her thoughts. Stopping by the fireplace, she ran her hand down the side of the clock that sat on the mantle. She had never taken the time to look closely at it and now noticed that it had been made in Glasgow, Scotland. The ticktock, as it marked the passage of time, suddenly seemed very loud in the room. Putting her hand on the mantle, she turned back to Liam.

Clearing her throat, she said, "I know by now that I can trust you with anything. Even this. Especially this," she amended. She stepped away from the fireplace, taking a step toward him. "This is your last chance to change your mind. Would you like me to share the next hundred years with you?"

Liam looked at her for a long moment before he gave a short nod. He pushed himself back and rose from behind his desk, walked over to the leather armchair, and sat down. Beth sat down on the settee and, eventually, began to talk. Slowly, at first, the tentative words came, as though unsure of the way. But once she began, she couldn't hold anything back, and the words tumbled from her lips like rainwater to a stream, finding its inevitable way to the ocean.

She talked about natural disasters and how airplanes and flight would emerge from the Wright brothers' first flight. She told how the women's suffrage movement would finally gain them the right to vote, and how an eight-hour workday would become adopted in many places, and of the sinking of the Titanic. She shared the onset of the First World War and how the sinking of the *Lusitania* ultimately ended the isolationist policy of the United States.

"This war engulfed the whole world, no one was left untouched by it. Europe, the Balkans, Asia, Africa. It was fought everywhere. Poison gas was used for the first time in the trenches of this war. American boys by the thousands left to fight. Many never came home. Many of those that did were crippled and maimed. They all carried emotional scars. It was a horrible event that changed the world."

She related the murder of the imperial Russian family by the Bolsheviks and how the Turks tried to eradicate the Armenians because of religious difference. She told of the Spanish influenza epidemic that raged across America in 1918, killing thousands and quarantining entire towns, and of how the American servicemen brought it home with them from Europe when they came home from the war. She went on to tell of electricity and telephones making their way into every town—not simply the cities—and that automobiles would catch on and, eventually, become a necessity in every family.

She talked of prohibition and the 'roaring twenties' and the crash of the stock market, and how banks would fail, leaving so many with nothing. She told him of the dust bowl in the Midwest that resulted from overfarming the soil with the development of the tractor from the technology gleaned during the war, and how 'black snow' from the Midwest would rain down on people as far away as Boston. She related the plight of hundreds of families living in shantytowns begging for food and work and told him about the bread lines. She told him that this era would be known as the Great Depression.

She paused at this point, trying to choose her next words carefully. She looked at Liam. Typical of him, he had not interrupted her narration. He sat listening, with his fingertips pressed together in a steeple in front of his mouth, one ankle crossed over the other knee. His eyes never left her face.

"The president, Franklin Delano Roosevelt, created a program called the 'New Deal,' designed to put men back to work. Many of these men were veterans from the Great War. He initiated projects building watersheds and reservoirs. And one of the many programs that he formed was called the Civilian Conservation Corps, putting young men to work on various conservation efforts. It was a rousing success in terms of giving the people of a nation their working pride back. But there was a cost. One of the projects was the building of a reservoir here, in this part of Corsehill. It affected all of you here, in this hollow. You, Bill and Naomi, Frank and Ethel, the Owens, Mrs. Dugdale, all of our neighbors . . . all of you were forced to move from your homes and relocate. They gave you fair market value for your property, but the bottom line was that you had to move. This property became public land, open to what they would call passive recreation, and a large portion of it was flooded to provide water to the cities. What wasn't flooded became watershed."

Liam recalled to himself the map that he had taken from her pack and looked at while she had slept that first day. Now, he thought to himself, he understood. He was stunned.

Beth continued to talk on. "I have spent many hours in this area in my time. There are no houses or barns, just cellar holes in the areas that weren't flooded.

I've explored the cellar hole to this very house. The roads have turned into narrow paths, and the trees have all grown up around everything." Pausing, Beth looked into Liam's shocked eyes, saying, "I'm sorry Liam. But this is what will happen. It's how I came to be here, in a manner of speaking. I was looking for a missing hiker. We found him in what was left of the field upriver, by the big rock."

After giving him a moment to absorb what she had just told him, Beth picked up her narrative again, telling him that the Great Depression led to another event known as World War II. She told of a madman named Adolf Hitler and of his quest, along with Italy and Japan, to dominate the world. She described the attack on Pearl Harbor and how warnings came but were ignored, and America was taken by surprise on a sleepy Sunday morning in December. Again, the war had been going on for some time already, and America had been arguing over isolationism. Pearl Harbor resolved that argument. And again, thousands of American boys would leave to fight this war. And again, many would not come home. Or would come home scarred forever. She spoke of atrocities committed and of the attempts to exterminate the Jewish race. She told him of horrible acts of savagery beyond belief and of amazing acts of kindness and bravery. Millions would die. She related to Liam how this war, much like the First World War, would bring about incredible advances in science and medicine. Life would change drastically after this war, and the world would never be the same. The innocence of the nation was truly lost.

She paused for a moment and gave a heavy sigh. "Frank and Ethel will lose their youngest son, James, to this war. He was a pilot, which was something that he had always wanted to do from the first moment that he set eyes on an airplane. When America went to war, he joined the Army Air Corps. He was killed while flying. It will take Frank the better part of a year to get Jim's body back here to Corsehill for burial. I have read Frank's diaries. As you can imagine, this was a difficult time for him. For all of them." A single tear slipped out of her eye and rolled down her cheek.

"Jim had a sweetheart, and she came to visit the family after his death. She stayed on for an extended visit and fell in love with another of Ethel and Frank's sons. They eventually married and had four children of their own. These two were my grandparents, and one of their four children would become my mother.

"So do you see my dilemma in telling Frank and Ethel that their son will die? If his death is prevented, then it is a pretty good bet that my grandmother and grandfather will never marry. And my mother and her sister and brothers will not be born, which means that me and my brother and sister, as well as all of my cousins and their children will never be born. Not only would we cease to exist, but rather, we will never have existed at all. Everything that we have thought, or said, or done, or felt will never be known. It will all be erased."

Beth heaved another heavy sigh and remained silent for a moment before she continued with her narrative. She went on to tell of the baby boom after the war, how soldiers returning home were anxious to put the war behind them and start a family. They went on to college under what would be called the G.I. Bill and successfully rebuilt their lives and a nation torn down by the Depression and the war. She told of Korea, whose blueprint was laid out at the end of World War II, and how it would often, and unfairly, be referred to as the 'Forgotten War.' It led to the Cold War and the race for nuclear supremacy, causing people to build bomb shelters in their basements and backyards, and America almost went to war again at the Bay of Pigs in Cuba over nuclear weapons.

There was America's lengthy involvement in Vietnam, taking more young lives and continuing to create casualties long after it ended. She told how it divided a nation, sowing the seeds of hatred and mistrust. She spoke of the race riots and the assassinations of Martin Luther King Jr. and the Kennedys. She described man's first footsteps on the moon and the brief war in the Persian Gulf, which laid the groundwork for more violence in the future.

She finally reached the end with commentary on how America will begin to lose its cohesiveness in the latter half of the twentieth century and of the terrorist attacks of 9-11 in New York, Washington, and Pennsylvania, murdering hundreds of people and once again galvanizing the nation. And once more, heroes would rise to the top. She cried as she shared her feelings with him about that day—watching it unfold on the television—and the sense of horror and helplessness and, later, the anger that she had felt, worrying about friends that she had in New York and of attending the funeral for one of the many victims. America, again, would find herself sending her young men and women off to war in Iraq and Afghanistan.

"But through it all, over the next century, the human spirit will continue to rise up and persevere. The good continues to find its way through. It amazes me, really."

She finally wound down, her voice hoarse. She was all talked out and thoroughly spent. Several hours had passed since she had begun talking. Liam got her something to drink and, handing her the glass, sat down beside her. She drank it down and set the glass on the table in front of the settee. He put his arm around her and pulled her against him. She put her head down on his shoulder, her legs tucked up under her, as he put a leg up on the table next to her empty glass. Neither spoke, and they sat that way for some time, each lost in their own thoughts. Absently, Liam lightly ran his fingers up and down Beth's arm.

Liam thought to himself that she had been right; his world would never be the same. So many changes! Some were good, but so much death and destruction was on its way! How had she been able to keep this to herself all this time without going out of her mind?

—

Knowing now that she had been right about how this would change his perception of everything around him, Liam was deeply moved that she had chosen to share this with him. She was usually impulsive, yet this decision of hers had not been made in haste. He realized that she had given it a great deal of thought over these last months and that it had not been easy for her to bring this information to him today. It was a gesture of her trust in him. She hadn't done this to make herself feel better but, rather, to make amends with him because he had forced the issue; and she knew that she had hurt him by not sharing it with him.

He looked down at Beth and saw how tired she looked. He knew that she was still having trouble sleeping at night. He had noticed many times when he would stay up late reading or working that her light would still be burning long after he thought that she had gone to bed. Or the times when she was already up when a rider came for the doctor in the middle of the night. Now he understood the thoughts that would keep her awake in the quiet night. It wasn't just the homesickness. He was glad that she had shared with him, now he could help her share this burden.

Leaning his head back on the settee, Liam looked around the room. This house that his grandfather built had always been here for him. He couldn't imagine not being in it. Or of Naomi and Bill not having the sawmill. All of the families here in this hollow had owned their land for years. They had given birth, lived, and died on the same piece of earth for generations. It was all they knew. For many, it was all that they had. How would they start over without their farms or businesses? He tried to picture the area as Beth had known it, with nothing there but cold remnants of the lives being lived now. Just cellar holes and trees, without all of the houses and open fields and roads that were there now. He simply couldn't. But she had both images in her head. How did she manage to keep the two separate?

And what would these wars do to the people here, people that he cared about and took care of? How many would go to fight? How many wouldn't come back? She had said that no one in the world would be untouched. The world! All of those people! And what about Ethel and Frank's son? He realized with a start that he would probably be the one to deliver this baby into the world. How would he get through it, knowing that the boy would die in a war? Liam recalled the conversations that he and Elizabeth had had regarding the future, and now understood her comments about the changing of events. His mind raced as he contemplated the enormity of all that she had said. The possibilities were vast and unpredictable. They continued to sit quietly long into the night.

Chapter XVII

Beth was busy preparing breakfast when Liam came to her door the following morning. He had built a Dutch door for her, at her request, and she now had the top portion open. She was singing while she worked; and he paused at her door, resting his elbows on it as he listened to her, recognizing one of the songs from her iPod.

"...Today's the first day of the rest of my life. I'm gonna stop looking back, start moving on, learn how to face my fears. Love with all of my heart, make my mark, I wanna leave something here. Go out on a ledge without any net, that's what I'm gonna be about. I wanna be running when the sand runs out..."

She had picked some fresh blackberries and put them in a dish with a little bit of sugar. Now she was just putting French toast into the pan on the stove.

She turned when she heard him come in, giving him a bright smile. "How does French toast sound to you?"

Liam smiled back. It was his favorite, and she knew it. "It sounds good! You look well rested today. Did you sleep well?"

"As a matter of fact," she responded, "I slept very well!" Beth had woken up that morning on Liam's settee and had found that her shoes were off, and she was covered with a quilt. "Thank you for letting me sleep where I was last night."

"You were tired," was his simple reply. She had drifted off to sleep with her head on his shoulder, and he hadn't wanted to wake her. The truth was that he had sat with her sleeping next to him, well into the early hours of the morning, not wanting to break the physical contact with her, enjoying the feel of her body next to his as he dozed off and on with his arm around her. He was afraid that if he released her, she would slip away like water through his fingers. When he finally pulled himself from his thoughts and rose to go to bed, he had laid her down and covered her with a blanket for the remainder of the night, briefly cupping her face in his hand and leaving a gentle kiss on her closed eyes before turning away.

Liam poured his coffee while Beth put the French toast on the table with the berries and maple syrup. While they were eating, she looked over at him with a thoughtful expression. "I gave you a lot to think about, and I'm guessing that you stayed up with it most of the night. So what do you think about it all?"

"I think that it looks like quite a future, with a few rough patches thrown in. Some of it seems inconceivable, and I'm still taking it in. But if there's one thing that you have shown me, it would be that nothing is impossible. Your presence here is proof of that!" He paused, taking a bite of his breakfast. "And you were right, I will never look at anything around me the same way again!"

"I'm sorry, Liam, that I gave in and told you as much as I did. But once I started, it all just came out." She gave him a rueful smile. "Now I feel somewhat better about it, and you feel worse!"

"It's all right, Elizabeth! I insisted, and I don't regret hearing it. And now I understand your preoccupation. I don't know how you have kept this to yourself all this time."

"It's not all bad, Liam! There are some real shining moments, and we really are living at the start of the greatest century right now. The medical advances alone are incredible!" She went on to tell him about artificial limbs and organs, DNA testing, and experimentation with cloning.

Liam was thoughtful for a few moments. He sat back, toying with the remains of his breakfast. "You know Elizabeth, something occurred to me while I was thinking about all that you said last night. Not all of what happens over the next one hundred years will be new to the world. Much of it has happened before. We have already experienced natural disasters, wars, assassinations, racial issues, and economic depression before now. It occurs to me, then, that this is as inevitable as the sun rising. These things have taken place over and over throughout the history of mankind. I think that it's just our nature to bring much of this on ourselves. So I'm beginning to think that it wouldn't necessarily matter if we were to try to stop or change some of these future events. I believe that they would simply be replaced with another event of equal magnitude."

He held up his hand as Beth opened her mouth to speak. "I know that I didn't always agree with you on this! I remember trying to tell you that maybe you should tell Frank and Ethel about their son, but now I'm not so sure. The answer isn't as obvious as it seems at first." He returned the smile that had appeared on Beth's face and said, "I seem to remember you saying something like that to me once."

Beth watched Liam for a moment over the top of her teacup before she drank from it and set it down. "Liam, there will always be ordinary people all around the world who will continue to keep what's good alive. It too is human nature. They'll feed the hungry, heal the sick, and protect and help those in need, in a variety of large and small ways. There will always be evil in the world, and bad things will continue to happen. We can't stop most of them, even though we want to. But we can help those suffering from these bad things. And that will, hopefully, inspire future generations to do the same, like it always has."

"I suppose that's true," responded Liam. "Good and bad will always be together." He sat, thinking for a moment. "But what about the sadness that will go along with what you know? What about Jim's death? How do we handle knowing when and how people are going to die? Or lose their homes? It's a little bit more difficult to be so philosophical when they are people that you know."

"That's true. And I still don't know what to do about that. Like I said last night . . . changing Jim's history will change the history for all of my family." She shrugged. "But then, maybe it won't. Maybe my grandparents could still fall in love and marry even if he doesn't die in the war. Perhaps he would fall in love with someone else, and a new branch of the family tree would be created. Maybe I could orchestrate that. How far down that road should I travel? And do I have the right to make a choice that will affect so many other people besides just myself and him? I never said that it would be easy. And I'm not saying that I'll have all of the answers today, but I have faith that we'll get them." She smiled gently at him. "I'm sorry, but this burden is yours now too."

Liam could see that she was feeling much better after having shared this with him, as though her mind had cleared and she could sort it out. And she was right; together they could work out the answers. If she were to stay here. He kept this thought to himself.

He said, "As you once told me, loads are always easier to carry when they're shared." Smiling ruefully at her, he reached across the table to place his hand lightly over hers. "Elizabeth, I'm sorry that we fought over this. It was my fault for having let my temper get in the way. I see now why you didn't want to tell me any of this. But it is, truly, okay. I want to share this with you. You shouldn't have to carry it alone—no one could do it."

He stood up and began wandering around the room. "Tell me something, Elizabeth, if you can . . . What happens to all of us here after we have to leave this hollow? Do you know where I will go? And how much of this area ends up under water?"

Beth had anticipated these questions from him and was surprised that he had waited as long as he had to ask them. She had given it a great deal of thought while she had been picking the berries earlier.

"I don't know where you will end up living, specifically, or Bill and Naomi either. But I can say, with a great deal of confidence, that you will remain in Corsehill and have—as far as I can tell—a good, pleasant life." She was recalling the plaque in the library and Aaron and Lydia, his children, whom she had known as two good, kind people at the end of their lives.

"As for the rest of your question, well, I guess that I should show you." With that, she got up from the table and went into her bedroom, kneeling in front of the trunk at the foot of her bed. She returned with a folded map in her hand.

They cleared away their breakfast dishes and she spread it out on the table. Liam leaned over it, placing both hands flat on the map. Looking at it, he saw a large area shaded in blue, indicating water.

Beth leaned on the table next to him, their shoulders touching. "Look here, do you see Beech Hollow Road? And over here is the Albany Road."

Running her finger along a dotted line that ran off of Beech Hollow Road into the water, she said, "Here is Maple Hill Road or what's left of it. It's just a trail through the woods on this map. As you can see, it leads to the water, and you can see where the other end of it comes out here on the opposite side of the reservoir." Pointing to a spot on the road near the water, she said, "We would be right around here, I think. So in 2008, if you want to travel from right here into Corsehill proper—instead of following Maple Hill right up into town—you would have to go west first, to Beech Hollow Road, north, and take Albany Road east into town, essentially travelling all the way around the outside of the reservoir."

Liam continued to stare at the map, looking for the roads of the Hollow that were all around him now but, according to what he was looking at, had disappeared under water. "So where we are right now? Here in this house, doesn't get flooded, but becomes part of this . . . watershed?"

Beth turned her face toward him, lips pursed, and nodded.

"So all of these roads and the homes on them just disappear under all of this water—like they never existed?" He swept his hand across the map. "So they could make a reservoir? Just like that? Don't we fight back?"

"Well, in the end, you don't have a choice. It's a losing battle, I'm afraid. Do you remember what I told you about the Depression last night? No one had the money to fight the battle. It was taken by eminent domain, and you were all paid fair market value for your property and all of the buildings were destroyed. Or at least, that's the way the story goes."

He gripped her arm. "Destroyed how?"

"Liam, don't. Why torture yourself over this?"

"Just tell me, Elizabeth! I need to know."

Beth sighed, looking away. "They'll burn the buildings."

Liam stepped back, shocked. He looked around her apartment, her home that they had just built. He thought of his house. The thought of someone deliberately setting them on fire tore at his gut and left a hollow, sick feeling inside of him.

"I hate this!" The words burst from him, and he had begun pacing again, running both of his hands through his hair. "Are you telling me everything that you know? Is there more?"

Beth sat back down, looking at him and regretting what she had already told him. "Liam, I'm going to tell you the same thing that my parents said to me in their letter—you already know too much about the future, and you should just let your life unfold as it happens. You yourself suggested that the future is still open. Maybe that's true!" She smiled gently at him. "So stop looking for answers that I don't have."

Liam had stopped pacing and shook his head at her, saying, "You, with your secrets."

"I'm not being secretive, Liam, and you should know that now. I just believe that my parents gave me some good advice, and I'm passing it on to you. Our lives should be a surprise to us, not a planned set of events. I've already told you too much, and I'm sorry for that. But honestly, there isn't really anything more for me to tell about what direction your life goes in."

She put her chin on her hand and sat watching him. "You know, Liam, I remember coming back to this area several times with my grandfather and his brother, my great-uncle who you saw in the picture in my camera. They both said that the visits were bittersweet. Living here, now, I see exactly what they were talking about. They were both born out here—they were children when they had to move away. When we would come back here to visit the site of the old homestead, they would walk along what was left of the old road, through what had become heavy woods, and reminisce about what it had been like.

"Now, I can see the things the way that they remembered them. Down at the four corners, where the letterbox is—did you know, they used to ride their old white pig down the hill to the letterbox to get the mail? I can't wait to see that! I see the watering trough and the sheep pasture, the meadow slope where the wild strawberries grow, and the spruce grove where they would shimmy up the tree and take the top for their Christmas tree. And there's the asparagus patch and Cat Rock. They called it that because that was where they buried their farm cats when they died. I ride past the sap house out by Clare's, the schoolhouse where they used to cut across the fields to get to, and all of the other places that they talked about. They would tell me how open everything was. And it was always so difficult for me to picture all of the places and things that they would describe, because the landscape had changed so much. and all the structures were gone. Now I'm living in the place of their childhood memories. and I can see it for myself. But I also have my own memories of this place and how it looked for all of my life. And they were right—it is bittersweet."

She shook her head and shrugged her shoulders, looking at him. "Sometimes, I have trouble wrapping my brain around the two images."

Liam sighed and looked around the room as though hoping to find more answers there. Then abruptly, he said, "Let's clean this stuff up and get our rounds done early today! Then we can get some fishing in. What do you think about that idea?"

Beth laughed and nodded. She knew that Liam was still full of other questions and wanted to get away someplace where they could talk without being disturbed.

By midafternoon, they were both standing knee-deep in the river in a hole below Naomi and Bill's house. Beth had tucked the back hem of her skirt into her front waistband and was enjoying the feel of the cool water on her bare legs as the summer sun warmed her shoulders.

Liam didn't waste any time in questioning her about the things that she had described to him the night before. She patiently answered all of his questions regarding the next one hundred years. They discussed many of the events in detail, and Beth found that he would quickly grasp the significance of many of the causes leading up to a specific event. They also talked about changes that came as a result of some of these events, such as new laws designed to help keep people safe, or medical and technological advances. He wasn't critical as much as inquisitive, and Beth enjoyed sharing with him and hearing his thoughts. He didn't ask her any more questions about his own life, although she knew that he wanted to.

Beth and Liam talked about the current president, Teddy Roosevelt. Beth told him how TR would be considered one of the greatest U.S. Presidents.

"In fact," spoke Beth, "He will be memorialized on Mount Rushmore in the Black Hills of South Dakota, along with George Washington, Thomas Jefferson, and Abraham Lincoln." She went on to describe how, in around ten or fifteen years, their images would be carved into the rock. The project would not be completed until another fifteen or eighteen years had passed.

"I think that I would like to see that," Liam said. He thought for a moment. "Of course, by the time that it's completed, I'll be in my sixties."

Beth smiled. "So what? You'll get on a train and travel out there. Or by then, automobile travel won't be so difficult either. But a train would be easier. I'll go with you." She considered the timeline and added, "But I wouldn't suggest waiting too long after its completion, because that will be on the eve of World War II, and everything will change. The trains will be filled with troops and supplies moving around the country, and with rationing and all, we won't want to waste the gasoline to run the car or the rubber in the tires driving out to South Dakota on a tour. At least, not for a few more years."

"Hmm," was his response. She was implying that she planned on staying around and still being a part of his life for thirty more years. Liam wondered if she realized what she was saying to him. Probably not. He stood watching Beth while she cast her line into the river flowing in front of them. He smiled faintly as he saw her brow furrow while she concentrated on her casts. She was determined to master fly fishing which, by the way she was going, would take the next thirty years! His smile deepened as he pictured her all those years from now standing in this same spot, still trying to fly fish.

Beth felt Liam's eyes on her and turned to see him watching her with a smile on his face. She returned the smile, not feeling the need for words, as though they'd been together for years, then pulled a face at him and stopped casting.

"Keep laughing! I'll get this, don't you worry! I don't care how long it takes!"

Liam kept smiling. "I know. That's what I'm smiling about."

She resumed casting.

"Well now," he said, "tell me more about this other president named Roosevelt."

"Well," said Beth, "he's a distant cousin to Theodore Roosevelt and will become the longest-serving president in U.S. history, serving for four terms. He'll die in office, after having taken this nation through depression and war, and will create some of the most enduring social programs in history. He was a tremendous supporter of conservation, like his cousin Teddy, and the National Parks of my time owe much to the programs put in place while he was in office. He will see the defeat of Germany and die on the eve of Japan's surrender.

"His image is on the dime, due to his involvement with a charity known as the March of Dimes. The mission of the March of Dimes is to raise money for the research of polio and to assist in the care of people afflicted with it. They will develop a vaccine against polio. FDR will develop a condition that will be mistakenly diagnosed as polio when he is around forty years old. He'll serve his presidency from a wheelchair, although through his own determination, he learns to stand upright with braces and can even make himself walk very short distances with those braces. He too will be greatly admired for his accomplishments and contributions to the people of the world, not just America. He will propel America forward to become the greatest nation in the world, and when he dies, the entire country will fall to their knees and cry. He will be one of the most admired men of the twentieth century. Although I have to admit, this—his New Deal doesn't make him a very popular fellow here in the Hollow."

Liam shook his head in amazement. "I'm impressed with the knowledge that you have of American history. Where did you learn all of this? Does everyone know so much?"

Beth laughed. "Thanks for the compliment! But you keep forgetting that I have an interest in history. Some of it was learned in college, but much of what I know was self-taught. Information on just about anything is readily available, all you have to do is apply yourself."

She paused to cast her line into the water before speaking again. "It does seem a little uncanny now that I should have taken such an interest in history all of my life, only to end up here, on the eve of so many key historic moments. I know that my parents encouraged me to do that, but I think that the interest would have been there even without their support."

"What do you think that it means, if anything?" asked Liam. He continued to cast his line into the river, expertly landing the fly exactly where he wanted it.

Beth watched him, admiring his skill. "I don't know, exactly. I've thought about it over and over again. Sometimes, I think that I must have been sent back here to stop or change an event. Or maybe a series of events. Of course, if I were to change one event, wouldn't they all change? And we've already talked about that."

She had waded over to disentangle her line from an overhanging shrub on the riverbank. "Or maybe, I learned all that I have so that I could fit in here and survive and offer help where I can with what I know. Maybe this is all part of some 'grand plan.'

"But then, perhaps I just ended up here because of some sort of 'atmospheric fluke,' or something, and it has no purpose at all. It simply is what it is, if you know what I mean. But I have to admit that I'm having a hard time believing that this was just a random thing, some sort of wrinkle in time. This is my life, and I can't believe that a change this radical doesn't have any meaning to it—that it was just an accident." She shrugged her shoulders and shook her head. "I honestly don't know what to think of it, Liam. But I intend to face it head-on."

"I would, too," Liam said, nodding. "No matter what. And I think that what you said this morning made good sense. I agree that there will always be people who will keep the good alive. Maybe offering assistance is all that we really can do with all of this knowledge. Maybe that's all that you were meant to do."

He turned and looked at Beth, now trying to tie a new fly onto her line. He reached over and took both the line and fly from her and tied it on without any effort. He handed it back to her and continued talking. "So, all of this being said, it begs the next question: how do we offer that assistance?"

"Thanks for the help. I would've got it, eventually." She smiled at him as she took the line and fly from him. "I think, Liam, that in most cases, we will know how to help. But here's something to think about . . . we have a World War approaching us, if things go according to the history that I know. Soldiers will come home traumatized. It will be labeled battle fatigue, but no one will really address it. People will just assume that time will heal, and now that the boys are home, their bad experiences will fade away. But that isn't the case. They will be suffering from something called post-traumatic stress syndrome, and it is treatable. But the key is that someone who has the ability to help them recognizes the problem and listens to them. Not to mention the huge physical problems that they will have from their injuries and mustard gas.

"Or if you really want to be in the thick of it, you could become a Red Cross doctor and travel to Europe. The need for trained doctors and nurses in field hospitals will be great, but it will be gruesome work under deplorable conditions. Of course, we would probably need help for post-traumatic stress on our return, provided we survived. But I'd go anyway, if I could help." She crossed her line over his in the water and smiled sheepishly at Liam.

"You're right," said Liam as he waded over to the riverbank and set his fishing gear on the ground. "It is food for thought."

Their conversation lagged as he moved to stand behind her, much as he had done the first time that they had fished together, watching her cast.

"Elizabeth, you're still too impatient! Remember, you have to wait a little longer before sending the line forward again." He placed his hand over hers on the rod, as he had done before, his face next to hers as they cast the line together. "You'll have more control of it if you wait."

Beth could feel his breath on her cheek, and she suddenly thought to herself that all she had to do was turn her head and she could kiss him. She felt a tingly sensation travel up and down her spine and forced herself to focus on her fishing. These feelings were unbidden and had snuck up on her. But they weren't unpleasant, and she didn't feel the same shyness that she had when they had occurred the first time earlier that summer.

Leaning into the cast with Beth, Liam could feel the hair that had come free of her braid tickling the side of his face. He had the urge to reach out and tuck those stray locks behind her ear for her, just to feel their softness. It occurred to him that if she were to turn her face toward him, he could kiss her. He cleared his throat and stepped back, reluctantly putting a little distance between them so that he could get his thoughts under control.

Beth turned to look at Liam as he stepped away from her, her eyes locking with his. She didn't look away, and he felt his heart give a sudden lurch in his chest. He gave in to his urge, reaching out to tuck her hair behind her ear. She turned her cheek into his hand as it lingered beside her face, and Liam found himself retracing the step that he had made away from her. With his hand still on her cheek, he bent his face toward hers, hesitating with his lips hovering above her mouth. Beth could feel his breath, warm and intimate against her lips.

"I want to kiss you," he whispered, as though giving her the chance to say no.

Beth looked into his eyes, so close to her face, sparkling with an amber light, and breathlessly whispered, "I want to kiss you back," forgetting completely her resolve of a few weeks ago not to become physically involved with him.

In that instant before kissing her, Liam thought, briefly, that they shouldn't be doing this. He didn't like feeling this need for her when he knew that she could never be his. But he couldn't go through life after she left without at least having this.

Time was suspended as the river gurgled past them while they stood together in the water, with the late summer sun warming their skin and the birds singing nearby. Liam didn't rush their kiss, and Beth's heart skipped over in her breast as she felt his warm, supple lips touch hers. Her whole body felt alive as she felt sensations rippling up and down her skin. She had never reacted to a kiss this way, not even her first kiss when she was sixteen! There was a sweet, gentle pressure that told of things that could be, and she had the impression that he was deliberately holding back a more insistent kiss, simply enjoying the feel of his lips moving on hers. Her heart was pounding in her breast, and she felt as though she would never breathe normal again! She laid her hand on his chest and felt his heart reacting the same way beneath her fingers, felt the warmth of him through his shirt. She drank in the taste and feel of him, enjoying the warm, sweet feeling that had spread throughout her body.

Eventually, she became aware of an insistent tugging on the end of her line. With a start, Beth realized that she must have caught a fish. Reluctantly, she pulled away from Liam and, with a faint smile, nodded toward the end of her fly rod. Liam smiled in understanding. He dropped a quick, firm kiss on her lips before reaching for the line. They were scooping the fish into the net when they heard a voice call out.

"Hello!" called Liam's father. "Bill told me that you were down here scaring the fish, so I thought that I'd come along. Do you mind? Mother's up with Naomi and the babies." He waded out into the river with them. "Lovely outfit, Beth!"

The spell had been broken and, thought Beth, not a moment too soon! She needed to regroup. Her reaction to his kiss had confused her, and she needed some time to sort it out. This was way more than just good chemistry! There had been a connection that went far deeper than hormones, and it was brand new to her. She looked over at Liam, and he gave her a soft smile while he shrugged his shoulders and shook his head.

They fished for another hour, catching a stringer of fish before packing up their gear and heading up river. Beth commented, "I wish that I had my camera with me right now. My Dad would love a picture of me with these fish!"

As it turned out, they stayed for supper at Bill and Naomi's. Mr. and Mrs. Sizer were both there, and there were plenty of fish for a meal, so the three women shooed the men outside while they prepared the supper. Beth and Mrs. Sizer did the cooking while Naomi picked over the green beans that Liam and Beth had gathered in the garden outside the kitchen door. The women chatted comfortably and fussed over the babies while they worked, and soon enough, the meal was ready. It reminded Beth of holidays at her parents' house, when the women all pitched in to cook; of the warm contentment that she always felt working next to the members of her family, with their laughter and gentle voices wrapping around her like a warm, familiar blanket.

Liam sat outside with his father and Bill. Every so often, he would hear the women's happy voices through the open window and thought to himself how quickly his family had taken to Beth. He remembered how it had been when he had brought Lily back here. His family had been accepting of her because of him, but they didn't have the same easy warmth that they obviously felt for Beth. There was just something about her that made it so easy to be comfortable around her.

His mind drifted back to the kiss that they shared earlier. He recalled the softness of her lips against his, and how smooth her skin had felt when he had caressed her cheek with his thumb while he had kissed her. When they had pulled apart, there were spots of red high up on her cheeks, and her dark eyes had shone brightly. For a moment, he had felt as though he could get lost in them, had gotten lost in them. He still felt lost.

It hadn't satisfied his need for something to remember her by; it had only made him want more. He had thought that he could satisfy himself with just one touch, one embrace, one kiss. But now, he wanted just one more touch, one more kiss, one night, just one time. But they couldn't do that. Or could they? What would happen after that? She couldn't commit to a permanent relationship with him, and he had no right to ask it of her. Besides, she didn't love him. What could he offer her compared to the life she had left behind?

He was pulled from his reflection by Beth saying, "Okay, gentlemen, I hate to break up this stimulating conversation about whether or not it's going to start to rain tonight. But supper's on, so get it while it's hot."

Mr. Sizer stood and offered her his arm, saying, "May I escort you to the table, my dear?"

Beth laughed and said, "Why certainly, kind sir!"

Liam's smile was melancholy as he walked behind them, thinking how hard it would be on all of them when she left one day. It was getting harder and harder for him to accept that idea.

CHAPTER XVIII

Beth and Liam were greeted by Anne Mortimer when they walked into the yard after their supper at Bill and Noami's house. Ten-year-old Anne was sitting on the pasture gate, watching Ned and Belle graze nearby. When she saw them, she called out a greeting and jumped off the gate, running toward them.

"Annie, what brings you here this evening?" asked Liam as he placed a hand on top of her head. "Have you been waiting long?"

She stared at Beth with big, shy eyes while she shook her head in answer to Liam. Still taking in every detail of Beth, her words came out in one long breath, "Pa fell from the hay loft this afternoon, and now he's having pain, and Momma sent me for you—if you could please come?" She swung around to look at Liam, clearly proud of herself for having completed this important errand that her mother had sent her on by delivering her message, which she had obviously been rehearsing while she waited for them.

Beth headed quickly toward the barn, calling the horses over as she went. She heard Liam ask Anne where her father's pain was and looked over to see her point to her chest. Soon, they left the yard with Anne sitting in front of Beth in the saddle. She and Beth were chatting away like two old friends by the time they rode into the Mortimer's dooryard, Anne's earlier shyness forgotten under Beth's subtle prodding.

Liam had made the decision to stay the night at the Mortimer's house to keep an eye on Charles, who had cracked several ribs in his fall. He explained to Beth that sometimes, with injuries like this, contusions within the rib cage could develop and cause severe respiratory problems. It was important that they control and monitor his pain so that he could cough in order to allow his lungs to expand and remain clear, keeping the secretions from his injury from collecting in his airway. It was an insightful decision, as Charles did indeed develop some breathing trouble in the early morning hours. After clearing his airway, Liam kept an even closer watch on him. It wasn't until late the following afternoon that he felt it was safe enough to leave for home.

Mr. Sizer had been right, and the rain had begun to fall overnight while they were at the Mortimer's. It had rained steadily the following day, and toward evening, the rain had begun coming down harder than ever as Liam and Beth took their leave to head home. The wind was picking up, and the temperature dropped.

They had only just come back from the Mortimer's when the first storm call for the doctor came at around 5:30 p.m., when a worker from the gristmill rode into the yard calling for Liam. One of the other workers had gone out to adjust the sluice gate at the mill and slipped, catching his foot in the gate. The others had managed to free him, but he was badly injured. Liam and Beth found that his ankle was broken. Beth had ridden back to the house and got the plaster powder and bandages so that she and Liam could set the break.

While she was gathering up the supplies to bring to Liam, another rider appeared. A tree limb had come down in the wind, pinning a man under it and cutting his shoulder deeply. And so it began and continued on thru the night. They rode from call to call in the wind and driving rain, picking their way across roads damaged by washouts and gullies as the rain came down around them in solid sheets like a waterfall.

Now in this hour before dawn, the storm had finally worn itself out. The temperature had dropped almost twenty-five degrees during the storm, and Beth shivered slightly in the predawn gloom. It had been a wild, busy night. She and Liam were heading toward home, at last, and her thoughts were already on getting out of her damp clothes and into a warm bed.

Looking at the slump of his shoulders, Beth could see that Liam was more tired than she was and needed a good rest. They had already put in a full night and day at the Mortimers' before the chaos from the storm hit, but while she had taken a short rest at the Mortimers in the afternoon, he had not. With Charles confined to bed for observation, Liam had taken it upon himself to help the Mortimer children with the chores while Beth had stayed with Charles. After two nights away from home, even he had lost his usual pep.

Beth urged Belle forward, her hooves splatting in the mud, and rode alongside Liam. "If you'll bring our kits in, I'll take care of the horses. And don't worry about the ledger, I'll get that, too." She knew that Liam hated this task and just might agree.

He didn't respond right away, and she knew that he was debating accepting her offer to take care of the horses. It wasn't his nature to leave all of the work for someone else.

"Just this once, Liam. You're beat, so let me do this, okay?"

"It's a deal," was all he said.

"It will be nothing short of a miracle if we don't come down with pneumonia after the night that we've just put in! When we get home, it's a hot meal and warm bed for both of us."

Liam turned to her. "Okay, boss." He smiled tiredly at her. "But maybe I'll take the bed first, and get the hot meal later."

They both rode along in silence, each too tired to talk any more. As they approached the bridge across the river, Belle stepped out ahead of Ned. Crossing the bridge, Beth saw that the water had come down the road with such force that it had washed away the portion where it met with the bridge on the other side. The water was still running heavily thru the gully that it had cut into the dirt road across the end of the bridge and then down into the river, which was swollen and flowing fast from the rain. She urged Belle to jump over it and turned in the saddle to watch Liam and Ned navigate across it.

"Be careful, Liam. It's washed out here!"

Liam nodded back at her as Ned was gathering himself to leap over the washout. Suddenly, the end of the bridge seemed to crumble and disappear before Beth's eyes. Ned let out a quick neigh of surprise and fright and, with Liam on his back, dropped into the river. Ned stumbled and Beth watched, helpless, as the river swept Liam away from the horse. The water was flowing swiftly with the extra rain, and debris was being carried downriver. The lazy amber-colored water of the river had been replaced by a muddy torrent. She watched as Liam tried to get his footing, but the current was too swift, much as it had been when she had been thrown into the water in May. She saw that he was trying to grab at branches hanging into the river or at rocks sticking up from the water, but he was being tossed about too much. She had a terrible feeling of déjà vu.

"Liam! No!" she screamed in horror. "Oh, no, no! Don't take him away!" Beth feared that he would disappear before her very eyes. She realized, in a flash, that she couldn't imagine a life without Liam at the center of it. She had quietly, slowly, fallen deeply in love with him.

Turning Belle downriver, Beth urged her into a gallop and followed Liam from shore, trying not to take her eyes from where he struggled in the water, afraid to lose sight of him for too long. She rode into the field that she had been in when she was thrown into the river. Looking back to the river, she saw that she had moved ahead of Liam. He was still unable to grab hold of anything and was being tossed around in the water. She looked around frantically, hoping in vain that there would be someone around at this early hour to help them but knowing that there wasn't. She was his only chance. She jumped off of Belle's back and tucked the hem of her skirt into her waist. Picking up a stout stick, she waded into the river without a thought for her own safety.

The water came up past her waist, and the force of it pulled at her immediately. Gone was the warm earthy smell that she usually got when she stepped into this water. It had been replaced with a strong muddy odor that filled her nose. She could hear the rolling water roaring in her ears. Or was that her heart pounding? Beth braced herself with the stick and quickly moved toward the spot where she anticipated Liam would be carried to. She stumbled, and the cold water that washed over her sucked the air out of her lungs. Pushing herself up with the stick, she forced herself forward, knowing that this was her only chance to help him. She quickly picked her way across the river, feeling the slippery rocks beneath her feet and the cold water tugging persistently at her.

"Oh, please, please let him be all right," she prayed out loud. "Please let me get him out of here!" Beth had never been more fearful in her life. What if she wasn't able to get him out? She had to—there was no one else around to help. She continued to fight her way through the water, never taking her eyes off Liam. He was being carried toward her swiftly, and she braced herself to grab him as he came closer to her. She recited the same thing that she had said to herself so many other times when faced with a challenge: *Courage, Beth. You know that you can do this!*

"Liam! I'm in front of you! I'll grab you when you get closer!" She saw him look around at the sound of her voice. She had to assume that he had heard what she had said and would be looking for her outstretched hand. Fear made the breath catch in her throat, and she forced herself to breathe normal.

Beth had placed herself in his path, and the river brought him to her. She shoved the stick hard into the riverbed and braced herself against it with her other hand stretched out toward Liam. She saw that he was already reaching toward her with a determined look in his eyes. She nodded to him and lunged toward his outstretched hand as he came within reach. She felt his flesh, wet and slick against hers. His fingers slipped along her forearm, then bit into her wrist with a vicelike grip. His body swung around in the current in front of her, and Beth felt that her arm was going to be pulled out of the socket. She cried out from the sudden pain of it, and her breath came out in a hiss from between her clenched teeth as she ground them together while she fought to ignore the burning pain in her arm and shoulder.

She knew that if she faltered—if she slipped just once—he would be swept from her, and she wouldn't have another chance. She dug deep inside of herself for the strength to hold on to him and focused beyond her pain to pull him in to her. Closing her fingers around his wrist, she hauled backward on his weight, feeling the river pulling at him every inch of the way, determined not to give him up so easily.

Finally, she had pulled him in against her body, and Liam was able to wrap his free arm around her waist while he got his footing and stood up in the water holding onto her tightly. Together, they made their way back to the riverbank and fell down on the ground.

Beth was breathing heavily, each gasping breath coming out of her mouth in white puffs in the cool air. Liam was still choking on river water, and she thumped him on the back while he coughed his lungs clear. She put her arms around him and held him close, gasping, "Don't scare me like that! I thought that I was going to lose you forever to this blasted river!"

Through chattering teeth, Liam said, "Th-thanks for c-coming . . . to my rescue . . . Couldn't g-get my balance . . . out there."

Beth looked at him, noticing with alarm that his lips were blue with cold. He had only been in the water for a short time, but the large amount of rain and runoff into the river had lowered the water temperature along with the air. She forced herself to get up off of the ground.

"I have to get you home and out of those wet clothes. Your body temperature is dropping too low, and you're going to have a real problem if I don't get you warmed up soon!" She looked around and saw that Ned and Belle were both standing in the field. Ned must have followed them downriver after making his way onto shore. Beth called out, and both horses came over to her, Ned whickering softly as she cupped his muzzle in her palm. She looked him over carefully and, satisfied that he wasn't hurt in any way from his fall, led him over to Liam.

Liam's shivering was increasing with each passing minute in the cool dawn air, and it was all that Beth could do to get him up on Ned's back. He had used up his energy fighting the river. She climbed up and put her arms around him, holding him in the saddle from behind. His hands felt like ice, and Beth found that she too was shivering. Clenching her teeth against the cold, she nudged Ned into motion and, with Belle following sedately behind them, set out toward home, taking the river trail to their backyard.

Beth helped Liam in through the back door and into the kitchen, their wet shoes squelching across the wooden floor. Pushing him down into a chair, she ran to get a towel and blanket. When she came back, he was trying to unbutton his shirt, but his shivering was so intense that he couldn't do it. She pushed his hands away without too much effort.

"Turnabout is fair play, Doctor. It's my turn to help you out of your wet clothes and take care of you." He nodded to her, unable to speak.

Beth pulled off his boots and stripped him of his clothes, wrapping him up in the blanket and briskly toweling his wet head. "Let's get you up into bed. Can you get the stairs?"

With her arms and body supporting him, they went upstairs, and she got Liam into the bed. Beth started a small fire in the fireplace stove to take the chill out of the room and to help warm him up. Even after getting out of his wet clothes, he was still shivering uncontrollably.

"I'll be right back," Beth said, putting another blanket over the bed. Without thinking, she reached down and pushed the damp hair back from his forehead. "I have to take care of the horses."

Her mind was racing with all of the things that she needed to do. She stripped the saddles and bridles from the horses, brushing them both quickly. They had also put in a long night and deserved proper care. That was something else that Liam had taught her. Beth said out loud to the horses, "Boy! Do I miss modern transportation right now! Just park the truck and walk away." She quickly gave them both grain and left the barn, leaving the doors to the pasture open for them to come and go as they pleased so that she wouldn't have to worry about them again for the day. She picked up both of their medical kits and hurried back to the house.

Coming into the kitchen, she saw the puddle seeping out from Liam's pile of wet clothes on the floor. She spread them out on the back porch rail and quickly mopped up the floor. She was still soaking wet and, stripping off her own clothes, put them next to his on the porch. Now, shivering in her undergarments, she poured a jar of beef broth into a kettle and, grabbing a mug and spoon, headed back upstairs to Liam's bedroom.

Liam was lying on his side, his eyes tightly closed and still shivering under the blankets in the bed. His lips still had a bluish tint to them. Beth noted that the room had become warm with the fire in the stove. He should have been warming up by now! She put the kettle on top of the stove. She had to get warm broth into him. She stirred it with the spoon, watching that it didn't get hot, only warm.

Crossing the hall, Beth unlocked the door and went into the pharmacy. She restocked both of their kits while the broth was warming, hoping that they wouldn't be needed again for a day or so. They'd had enough excitement over the past couple of days to last for quite a while.

Beth hurried back into the bedroom. Turning away from Liam, she cast a look at him over her shoulder and stripped off her wet underclothes. She took one of his shirts from the peg near the wardrobe and pulled it over her head. She noticed that it had the light, clean smell of his shaving soap on it and breathed in deeply, savoring the unique scent of him.

Pouring the broth into the mug, she turned back to the bed and sat down. "Liam, I have some broth for you. We have to get you sitting up a little bit so that I can get it in you."

He opened his eyes at the sound of her voice and nodded slightly. With Beth's help, he slid up into a slightly reclining position. Beth held the mug to his shaking lips. Slowly, he drank the broth.

"I c-c-can't get w-warm. Have to g-get w-warm," stammered Liam. Beth gave him a little more broth and set the empty mug down on the bedside table next to a framed picture. It was a sketch of her and Liam, and she'd never seen it before, but she didn't have time now to think any more about it. Lifting the blankets, she got into the bed and put her arms around him, pressing her body against his. His skin was still cold but not as bad as it had been. She used her hands to briskly rub his arms and torso, over and over again until she felt as though her arms would fall off her body; and still, she kept on.

At long last, Liam's shivering eased, and Beth heard his breathing change to the rhythmic sound of sleep. She lifted her head and looked at his face. His skin had a reddish tint to it. Laying her hand against his cheek, she felt the warmth coming back into his skin. A wave of intense relief washed over her. She knew that he was out of danger, and she should get out of the bed; but she admitted to herself, it felt nice lying next to him. What would it hurt if she stayed there for a little longer? She placed a light kiss on his cheek and laid her head back down on the pillow next to his.

She thought again about the picture of the two of them on Liam's bedside table and turned slightly in the bed to look again at it. The artist had not drawn them from the front but, rather, at an angle. She was sitting on the ledge of an open window, wisps of hair loose from her braid around her face. Beyond her, Liam was sitting in a chair, his ankle resting on his knee, relaxed. He had a smile on his face, his eyes crinkled up at the corners and that persistent shock of hair falling across his forehead. It was an incredible likeness of him. It was obvious that they were both listening to a third person. Beth looked at the signature in the corner of the drawing, Hugh Locke. She remembered the day now. Hugh was a gifted seventeen-year-old with an incredible ability to draw. He had shown Beth some of his drawings, and they were very good. She had suggested to him that he pursue a career in illustration, and they'd had quite a conversation regarding the possibilities. On the day of this sketch, she and Liam had stopped to visit Shamus Locke, Hugh's great-grandfather, who was now bedridden. Liam would often stop in to see the elderly man, who had been a very good friend of his own grandfather's. The older man would reminisce about their escapades or tell Liam how his grandparents had met. Beth recalled that was the topic of conversation during this particular visit.

Mr. Locke had been telling them how Liam's grandfather hadn't fallen in love until his thirties and how everyone thought that he would always be a bachelor until a pretty young woman moved into the town. She was full of spirit, and Liam's grandfather fell for her almost from the start, although it took him a while to figure it out for himself!

Hugh must have been outside on the porch sketching them while they listened to Mr. Locke. She remembered now how Liam had come out of the house when it was time to leave, stuffing a rolled-up sheet of paper into his shirt. This must have been it. It was curious that he hadn't shown it to her and interesting that he kept it by his bed in a frame with vines and hearts carved into it.

Beth let her mind drift back over the summer. She recalled that first night, waking up in this same bed, so confused and frightened. She smiled at the recollection of Liam's face when he came thru the door as she was trying to get dressed, and she had turned around, pistol in hand. He had tried so hard to ease her mind, and she felt comfortable with him almost immediately. Their friendship had begun that night and grown steadily since. She had never enjoyed a man's company as much as his. She thought about all of the things that he had done to make her life more comfortable and how he had always given her his strength, seeming to know just when she needed it.

Something had changed within her, subtly; and in that moment, she felt a peace of heart and mind that she hadn't really felt in a long time. Maybe never, she admitted to herself with a bit of wonderment. Always, she felt as though she had been reaching for something that she could never quite get. Nothing ever totally satisfied that need for . . . completeness. Suddenly, she felt like she wasn't looking anymore. Somewhere over the past weeks, she had stopped without realizing it. It was as if it was here, all around her; and it showed itself in so many ways, every day, with the people that she interacted with. She was building a history here.

Pictures, like flipping thru a photo album, flashed in Beth's head. There was the image of Liam stepping in front of her when Naomi came into the kitchen that first morning. And pictures of the two of them working together or taking walks or just reading in the evenings. There were pictures of Decoration Day. Liam had, by then, appointed himself her protector. She remembered the joy that she felt dancing with him. She saw the celeidh at the Owens' and felt again the thrill that went through her when he held her in his arms and gave her that impulsive kiss. It had been such a simple, quick thing, just a kiss on the forehead. Why had it done so much to her, then? It brought to mind another kiss that he had given her, the afternoon that they had fallen in the river when he had taught her to fly fish. She saw him standing in the river fishing and realized, suddenly, that she never grew tired of watching him. She recalled the day at the train station, when they had stood looking at each other, and he had taken her hand. The butterflies weren't from her nervousness over being alone. She had fallen in love. She realized now that she must have known this the other afternoon, when he had kissed her while they were fishing in the river. It had confused her, because she had never felt such strong emotions or sensations like that before, and she had been glad that Mr. Sizer had come along when he had.

How could it have taken so long for her to recognize that what she had found in him was love? It had come upon her so quietly and easily, not crashing down with fanfare and fireworks, the way that she had always expected this kind of love to arrive. He was the other half of her that had been missing her whole life. Maybe, this whole thing was as simple as that. Maybe, she had been sent across time just so that she and Liam could find each other. Maybe, there was no other reason; no grand plan for her to alter or prevent some historical event. Perhaps the world was still meant to play out on its own without any deliberate interference from her. Like Liam had said, maybe the future was a blank page waiting to be written.

A sobering thought came to her. What if Liam didn't feel the same as she did? What if she was just overtired and not thinking clearly? No, she was sure that his actions spoke of love. Didn't they? She thought back to the way that she would sometimes catch him looking at her or the way that he was always there for her. And what about the picture of the two of them that he had kept to himself? And the way that he had kissed her in the river? They hadn't had a good opportunity to talk privately since then. Maybe he had just been waiting for her to make her feelings known to him. That must be it. She was sure of it. She couldn't be wrong about this; it felt too good to be one-sided! The adrenaline burst that she was moving on earlier had worn off, and fatigue finally caught up. Beth fell asleep, her body pressed up next to Liam.

Liam awoke slowly. The room was warm, and as he moved his arm, he felt something across his chest. Opening his eyes and raising his head, he saw Beth lying next to him in the bed. Her arm was stretched across his chest and her body pressed against his. In a flash, everything came back to him. The storm, the long night, the river, the intense cold. His bedside clock said that it was just after noon.

He lay still, not wanting to wake her and enjoying the feel of her body next to his. Lying with her like this was something that he had thought about many times. He vaguely recalled opening his eyes earlier to see her stripping off her undergarments and putting his shirt on. In his mind, he saw again the curve of her bare back and bottom as she had stretched her arms to pull the shirt over her head. He felt his body respond to her and prayed that she would not choose this moment to wake up. Even as he thought this silent prayer, he felt her stir beside him.

Beth woke up and lifted her head to look at Liam. She hadn't meant to fall asleep! She saw that his eyes were open, and he was looking back at her. She felt her cheeks flush pink. She should have gotten out of the bed earlier, before she fell asleep. She had been foolish to indulge her desire to lie next to him. She looked aside, feeling a straitjacket of shyness close around her, and moved her body to push away from him. Her leg was draped across his, and as she moved, she felt herself brush up against him. She froze and looked back at him, uncertainty all over her face. Now his face was flushing pink. Their gazes locked together for a long moment.

—

Suddenly, Beth felt her shyness leave her. This was Liam, the man that she had already bonded with in so many other ways. This wasn't simply physical desire that made her want him now. She loved him, and everything about this moment felt right to her. Never before had she been bold enough to make the first move, but she laid her hand on his cheek, running her thumb across his bottom lip and looking him in the eye. She felt his lips move against her thumb in a soft kiss, and she felt her heart stop for a beat. Her eyes followed her fingers as she let her hand trail slowly down his face and on to his neck, to his shoulder and across the expanse of his chest, where she felt the hairs against her fingers. They were springy and soft, just as she had thought they would feel. Bringing her eyes back up to his, she saw hesitation there, but watched as the amber color darkened to a deep gold with desire. Emboldened by his reaction to her touch, Beth smiled as she trailed her fingers down to his flat belly and let her hand lay there for a moment before moving lower, where she brushed him softly with her touch.

As her hand closed around him, Liam closed his eyes and let out the breath that he hadn't realized he had been holding. After a moment, he felt her hand leave him, and he opened his eyes to look at her. Beth sat up and put her leg over him, straddling his stomach. Liam put his hands on her thighs, slowly sliding them up along her smooth skin. Taking hold of the hem of the shirt, he pushed it up over her head and off. She sat looking down at him, her chestnut hair falling around her face and shoulders. He noticed, absently, that the skin on her right shoulder was still a pale pink where the scrapes from her injury in May had healed. He slowly ran his hands up her arms and cupped her breasts. He watched Beth's expressive face as she closed her eyes and sighed lightly, leaning toward him. He moved both hands to her shoulders and pulled her to him, kissing her gently at first then with growing passion, his hands caressing her back and shoulders. He brought his hands down to her waist, wrapping them around it, marveling at the trim shape of it, then over her hips and down to cup her bottom.

He had wanted to touch her for so long, now he couldn't get enough of her as his hands moved greedily over her body. Briefly, he thought at how quickly things were moving. But he didn't care! What happened later could take care of itself. He couldn't resist his desire for her anymore or the passion that he had seen in her eyes before she closed them. She wanted him as much as he did her, and there was no stopping it. He didn't want to.

Beth pulled her lips from his and trailed kisses down the side of his face and to his ear, where she drew his earlobe into her mouth, gently tugging on it with her teeth. She let go of it and kissed her way down his neck and onto his chest. She ran her tongue over his skin and heard him let out a small groan. Lifting her mouth back to his, Beth felt Liam tease her lips with his tongue until they parted. She shivered as his tongue darted into her mouth. They explored each other with eager hands and mouths, touching and teasing, giving and taking.

Pulling back slightly from Liam, Beth lifted her hips and lowered herself onto him. She remained still for a moment, letting herself adjust to him as she let out a long sigh. It had been a long time since she had been with a man, but she had never felt like this before or wanted to please someone like she wanted to please him!

Liam put his hands on her thighs and watched her face. She felt so good, better than he had imagined. Never, in his wildest dreams, had he believed that they would be together like this. Looking into her eyes, he saw his own longing reflected there. His desire for her had pulled at him for weeks, and he had lain awake during nights, burning for her. He ran his hands up her thighs to her hips, rubbing her gently with his thumbs. Suddenly, he put his arms around her and rolled them both over, with Beth's body now under his, his face above hers, their lips almost touching.

They both remained still for a moment, looking at one another. Liam took Beth's face in his hands and covered it with soft kisses. Then, as he began to move slowly, rhythmically, he heard Beth's breathing quicken and found that his had as well. He savored the feel of her body against his as she moved with him, bringing herself up to meet him. He felt like he was balancing on the top of a steep slope and it felt better than anything he had ever felt before. It was a beautiful feeling, and he didn't want it to end, but after a moment he stopped her with his hand on her hip. Beth sighed his name as she ran her hand down his back.

"Elizabeth, sweetheart, it's been a long time for me!" he gasped. "We have to slow down, take our time." Beth's eyes were closed, and her lips were parted. Her hair was fanned out around her head on the pillow, and Liam thought that she was the most beautiful woman that he had ever seen.

"Oh, love, it has been for me too," she sighed softly, "but you feel so good to me." She trailed her fingers up his arms and across his shoulders, and then down his back, her finger nails lightly tracing across his skin. She felt as though she was floating, falling, soaring all at once. She felt alive, awash in beautiful colors and soft textures. Every bit of her that touched him melted into his skin until there was no telling where she ended and he began. She wrapped her leg around him, and he dropped his hand from her hip to slide it beneath her, pulling her even closer to him.

She moaned softly, and Liam asked, "Do you like that?" Her reaction and desire excited him beyond belief, and he wanted to give her more. He wanted to give back to her all of the pleasure that she was giving to him.

"Yes . . . yes! Oh, yes! I could die from it!" She gripped his arms, her nails biting into his flesh as she drew herself still closer to him.

The words came out on a breath, and Liam felt it caress his skin and warm his heart. She opened her eyes to look at him. He saw that they were bright with passion, and he felt himself willingly falling into their heat. He could get lost in those eyes. He wanted to get lost there. He buried his face in her neck, planting hot kisses on her skin.

She sighed, whispering soft words as she wrapped herself around him.

Her breathless words and touch were more than he could take, and he felt himself explode within her. He pulled his head back to watch her and saw Beth's eyes open wider as she felt him and cried out with him, arching her back. Liam heard her whisper his name over and over and, as the blood was pounding in his ears, he thought he heard her whisper on a sigh, "I love you." Eventually, they collapsed together, her heart pounding with his.

They lay together for some time. Beth curled up next to his body and he kept his arms around her. Lifting her head, Beth kissed him softly on the cheek and looked down at him saying, "Well. You're warm now."

Liam smiled and pulled her head back down to his shoulder, holding her tighter. "Yes . . . yes I am, thank you very much." He was quiet for a moment, thinking that he had never been with a woman who gave back as much as she took. But that was how she was with everything.

At length, he spoke again. "Elizabeth, what you did this morning in the river—it was so brave. You saved my life, I'm sure of it. Thank you! But I guess that it wouldn't do me any good to ask you not to put yourself in that kind of danger again, would it?"

Beth raised herself up on an elbow, resting her other hand on his heart, where she could feel its steady beat. She shook her head, saying, "There was nothing else that could be done. I did what I had to do, and I'd do it again if you were in danger. Especially then!" She paused for a moment, thinking. "You could have been killed, or . . . Well, I know that this will sound silly, especially now that we're safe. But I didn't want that river to send you somewhere else, like it did me! That was all that I could think of when you fell in. That you would be taken away from here, from all of these people that need you. Taken away from me! I couldn't stand the thought of living here without you!" Then quietly, simply, she added, "I couldn't do it if you weren't here."

Liam felt emotion surge through him, so compelling it ached. It consumed him with new feeling—feelings of tenderness and wonder—mixed with raw need. He reached up to gently touch the scar on her forehead, his eyes following where his fingers traced over it. He tucked her hair behind her ear as he leaned toward her and gently kissed her forehead, then her lips.

He pulled back slightly and whispered, "What would you say if I told you that I would love to make love with you again, right now?" His hands were busy on her body, touching her, exciting her.

Beth sighed happily and lay back down. "I'd say, 'What took you so long?'"

They lay together quietly. Beth floated off to sleep as Liam held her in his arms. He was thinking of what she had said, and it brought his fears back to the surface again. He knew that he had fallen in love with her. He had fought it all summer, but he couldn't deny it any longer, not after what had just passed between them. And it had been perfect! It wasn't simply a physical need for her. There was an emotional need just as demanding as the physical. She was everything to him, and he was lost to her. But he was afraid of the pain that he would feel when she went away from him. He couldn't forget her tears and the pain she felt over leaving everyone behind in her old life. Could his love ever be enough to take the place of all that she had lost and keep her here? His lifestyle wasn't normal and never would be. He had already learned once before how little he had to offer a woman. He didn't want to live each day wondering if it would be their last together. Wondering when she would go into the river and never return.

How did she feel about him? She had called him love earlier, but that was just passion speaking. And what about the words that he thought he had heard her whisper when she had called out his name during their lovemaking? Had she said 'I love you'? He thought about the way that she had looked at him the other day in the river just before they had kissed. He knew that she cared for him, but he didn't think that she loved him. She was from a different time, where men and women had friendships that were more . . . intimate than they were now.

Carefully, Liam slid his arm out from under her and got out of the bed. She stirred a little but didn't waken. He looked at her and reached down to touch her hair, spread out in an auburn wave on the pillow. It was so soft. She was so soft. So strong, and yet so soft. He felt the desire for her growing again in him, and he turned away from her. He needed to think about this. He got dressed and left the room.

Chapter XIX

Liam came out of the field by the river and walked up toward where the bridge had washed out. There was a group of men there, making temporary repairs so that people could cross the river. The river was still flowing brown and fast. Bill had delivered some lumber for the repair, and Frank Burdett and several other men from the area were working away. They all greeted Liam as he walked up to them, and then turned their attention back to the damage from the storm and injuries incurred around the area.

"That wind blew a gale last night!"

"Cook's lost that big maple tree in their yard. Took out part of the equipment shed with it."

"Weeelll, now it'll make good firewood for next year, I guess."

"Travis lost his best mare—she took off like the old harry when one of them big bolts of lightnin' struck."

"She'll be back when she's hungry."

"You must've been busy last night, Doc, from what I hear."

Liam cleared his throat to speak. He had only been half listening to the talk and now brought his attention back to the men.

"Yes, we were. Elizabeth and me were busy from about five-thirty or so last night until early this morning. In fact, we were crossing this bridge on our way back when the end of it gave out."

"You don't say!"

"Were you?"

"Well!"

Liam went on to tell them how Beth had already crossed when the end gave way just as Ned was about to jump over the gully, dropping them both in the river. He related how fast the water was moving and that he was being tossed around so much he couldn't catch hold of anything.

"What'd you do then, Doc?"

"Elizabeth followed me downriver on her horse and managed to get ahead of me. She waded into the water and caught me as I was going by. I believe that she saved my life."

"That little girl? How'd she manage to do that?"

"He means that she rode that little mare of hers in there after him."

"No," said Liam. "She picked up a stick and waded right in on foot. She dug that stick into the river bottom and held on, then she stuck her hand out to me, and I grabbed it on my way by. She held onto me and pulled me in."

"Brave girl."

"Incredible."

"I always said there was something about that girl. She's not like other girls, no sir!"

"Good, strong stock, that one!"

Frank asked Liam, "Where is she from? What are her people like?"

Liam smiled faintly at the irony. "They were good people, Ulster Scots, like us. They're all gone now. She's alone."

"Well, we'll have to convince her to stay here with us. Won't we, Doc?" he said.

Liam saw Bill smiling at him. He knew too that Beth had been accepted into their community. She would be very pleased when he told her.

Eventually, the talk drifted back to the repair of the bridge, and Liam pitched in with the others to finish the temporary repairs. After a few hours, he and Bill headed back down the river road toward home in Bill's wagon.

Liam said, "I'll ride on with you to your house to see Naomi and the babies, if that's all right."

He wasn't ready to see Elizabeth yet. He couldn't stop thinking of how sweet she had felt to him and knew that he wouldn't be able to resist her if they were alone together. What he really wanted to do was tell her that he loved her with all his heart and beg her to never leave him. But it wasn't fair of him to ask her to give up, forever, everything else that she'd ever had in her life, to make him happy. She wouldn't want to anyway. So instead, he would hold on to his heart so that she wouldn't take it with her when she left.

Beth woke up alone in the bed. She gave a contented stretch and smiled as she remembered all that had just happened between her and Liam. She felt good! Better than she'd ever felt, and it was all because of Liam. It had all been so right . . . his kisses, his touch, their loving. They were friends from the beginning and had shared stories and so many of their deepest thoughts and feeling. Their intimacy had been so natural for them.

She got up and, putting his shirt back on, went looking for him. She checked her clothes draped over the back railing and, finding that they were dry, brought them inside. She took her time getting dressed, then filled out the ledger for their calls from the night before. She saw that Liam's kit wasn't on the table, where she had left it next to hers after refilling both of them earlier, but there was a note where it had been. *"I've gone up to check out the bridge. I'll be back soon. Don't go away. L."*

Beth read his note, thinking, *Gee, how very romantic he is!* She felt a little tug of apprehension but refused to accept it and decided to go see Naomi.

She found her in the house feeding the babies. She was relieved to see Beth.

"I'm so glad you're here! I expect that you had a busy night. These two have been antsy all day and a regular handful! I'll get Pearl off to sleep, and Percy will start to fuss and wake her up. I'll get him off to sleep, and she'll start! All I've had time for is one batch of washing, and even that's still out on the line! And it looks like we're going to get some more rain soon! Would you help me get them bathed and, hopefully, put down for the night?"

Beth listened patiently to Naomi and took Percy from her and began to burp him. Naomi picked up Pearl and began to feed her. "Of course I'll help you with these two sweethearts! And I'll bring in your wash for you too. I'm sorry that I didn't come by sooner to help you. Liam and I were out all night on calls."

"Yes, it was a wild night, wasn't it? I hope that no one was hurt seriously? And not to worry about not coming by. How were you to know that they were having a bad day? I was just feeling sorry for myself! Bill told me that the bridge washed out. He's up there helping to fix it now. I hope that no one was on it when it went."

"Actually," said Beth, "Liam and me were on it. Or rather, I had just gotten off of it, and Liam was about to, when it let go. Liam and Ned went into the water, and Liam got caught in the current. That was early this morning, around dawn. We both got soaked, but he's all right."

"Oh, my! How did you get him out? I don't know as if I would have known what to do! Or I'd have been too scared to do anything."

"I've done water rescue before," Beth said patiently. "So I sort of knew what to expect, although I've never done it without a safety rope tied to me. I had to get Liam out of there. And I wasn't afraid, at least, not of that."

Beth paused for a moment before going on. "I know that this sounds crazy, but I was terrified that if I took my eyes off of Liam for too long, or if I didn't get him out of the river, then he would disappear from here, from me. I don't know what I would do if I lost him. I know, it's silly."

Naomi was watching her while she spoke, holding Pearl against her breast. Beth was lightly patting Percy's back and gently rocking back and forth with him.

"No, Beth, it's not silly, considering how you came to us here. I believe that there is something about that river, and that it's not through with the two of you yet. I think that . . . *something* . . . brought you and Liam together, and it will keep throwing you both at each other until you see that."

She nodded her head at Beth with determination. "There, I've said it! You and my brother are perfect for one another. And if the two of you saw what the rest of us see every time that you're together, well, you would know what I'm talking about!"

At that very moment, Percy chose to let out a belch. Beth pulled him away from her shoulder and looked at him. He looked very satisfied.

Laughing, Naomi said, "Always putting in his two cents, that one is!"

Beth laughed with her. "Why is it that Liam has never married? That is, he's a successful, kind, good-looking man. He's good-natured, responsible, and loves his family. Why is he still alone? I mean, I've noticed the way that some of the young women look at him. But he never seems to be interested."

"Well, I guess that it goes back to when Liam went to medical school out in Boston. In the beginning, he would come home every chance that he had. Then he went away for a year during the war, and we didn't see him." Beth nodded and said that he had told her about having worked on the hospital ship.

Naomi continued, "After that, he came home for a short visit and then went on to finish his schooling. But he started to stay out in Boston more and more during his free time, and he told us that he had met a girl. Lily, her name was." As she said her name, Naomi pulled a face. "As time went by, Mother and Dad encouraged him to bring her home for a visit, but there was always a reason why he couldn't bring her out. We began to get the impression that she was making up his mind for him, if you know what I mean. Eventually, when Liam finished his training, he wrote home that he had asked Lily to marry him and would finally be bringing her home for a long visit. Well, we were thrilled to death, I don't have to tell you! That is, until we met her.

"They came by train into Westford, and Dad met them at the station. By the time that they had arrived up here in Corsehill, she was fit to be tied. It was springtime, you see, and the roads were muddy, which made the going a bit slow. And she was a Boston girl, not at all used to our way of life up here in these hills. She didn't pitch in—not that she was expected to as a guest,—but she could have offered to help, if you know what I mean. And she was bored." Naomi sniffed, "Maybe she wouldn't have been so bored if she had kept herself busy, instead of demanding room service. And she made Liam's life miserable. Always complaining to him."

Beth had gotten up to bathe and change Percy. She listened to Naomi's soft voice as she gently washed the baby, happy to be doing something.

Naomi paused and shifted Pearl to her shoulder, then continued. "One afternoon, she and Liam were sitting outside under that maple tree that Mother and Dad have in the back yard. I was in the kitchen, and suddenly I heard her voice raised, and she was giving Liam the what-for. It seems that Liam had told her of his plans to set up his practice here in Corsehill as soon as he could. You see, it was always his plan to come back here. Well, she told him in no uncertain terms that she would not be the wife of a poor country doctor, nor would she live away out here in this 'backwards wilderness.' She went on to say that he would never amount to anything if he stayed here and that she deserved a better life than that. She told Liam that he had to make a choice, right then and there. It was either her or Corsehill. Well, he stood up without saying a word to her and went right to her room and began packing her things. She was gone from his life by the following morning. I was never more proud of my brother than in that moment."

Naomi sighed. "But it hurt him deeply, I can tell you that. He felt as though he had been betrayed, although he has never said much about it. I only know about this because I was in the kitchen and heard what she said to him and saw the look on his face when he walked past me. I think that he has let himself believe, over the years, that he can't have his profession as well as a wife and family. I think that he actually believed some of what she said and thinks that he's just not worthy of it. She really was quite hateful! So all these years, he's hung on to her horrible words. And he's been about his work and nothing else."

Beth had finished Percy's bath and dressed him for bed. Now she sat, holding the baby close. "But that's absurd to think that way! All he needed to do was find the right woman! Someone who sees what an incredible, wonderful man he is!" She blushed as she realized what she had revealed.

Naomi smiled at her. "So. Are you finally realizing that you love him?"

"I wasn't really implying that it was me!" stammered Beth, embarrassed. "Well, maybe I was. And yes, I do love him. I don't know why it took me so long to see it. But I've never felt like this before! I can't even fully describe what I feel, I'm so full of him."

Naomi laughed and reached across to take her hand. "I'm so glad that you have come here to all of us! But mostly, I'm happy for you and Liam. While he's never come out and said it, I'm certain that he loves you too. I've watched the way that he looks at you! He's been so happy these past months. And that's all because of you! He is a good man, and you deserve each other!"

Beth was out at the clothesline, taking the clean diapers down and folding them as she went. She cast an eye to the ominous black clouds that were moving into the evening sky. More rain!

She heard Bill's wagon come into the yard and saw that Liam was with him. She smiled to herself. She had so much to talk with him about! She waved to them both, calling out a greeting. Bill smiled and returned her greeting as he began to unhitch the horses from the wagon. She saw Naomi come out the back door and walk over to him.

Liam came over to the clothesline. His eyes were on Beth while he approached her. He thought to himself that he must be crazy! She even looked beautiful folding diapers! How was he going to be able to keep his distance from her?

Beth gave him a smile, and then shyly, softly, said, "Hello! I was afraid that you were having second thoughts about us when I woke up and you were gone!"

Liam cleared his throat. "Well, with all that's happened, I thought that you needed rest more than anything else. So I left you alone. I went up and helped to make repairs to the bridge, and all of the boys wanted to know the whole story. I have to tell you that you're now a hero to them. They think you're wonderful!"

Beth smiled at the praise. "Well, I hope that you didn't tell them everything!" He smiled at that, and Beth put her hand on his chest, her fingers caressing him through his shirt as she said, "Liam, I was so afraid! I don't know what I would've done if I'd lost you this morning! I love you!"

She smiled at the astonished look on his face, not wanting to wait any longer to tell him how she felt. "I love you, Liam! I've never felt like this before! I don't know why it took me so long to see it, but I do love you, very much. I think that I always have!" She slipped her arms around his waist, laying her head against him.

Liam caught his breath. He couldn't believe what he was hearing! She said that she loved him! It couldn't be true. It wasn't true! He had decided that he could go on forever loving her from across the yard, but they could never make love again. He couldn't even dare to dream of the life that her love would give him. It would hurt too much when she left him. It already hurt. He was sure that she wasn't here to stay; that she would try one day to go back to her own world when she'd had enough of this one. When she'd had enough of him. He couldn't begin to offer her what she'd had where she came from. It would be better for both of them if he put this fence between them now.

He gripped her arms, pushing her out from him. "Elizabeth, don't say that! You don't mean it! We're in an impossible situation. We both know that you won't be staying here. One day, you'll get the chance to leave. We had no business doing what we did today. What you and I shared this afternoon was . . . good . . . but we should never have let it happen."

"What?" She was bewildered. Her hands fell to her sides.

"It was a mistake. Maybe we both gave in to it because you *will* be leaving one day. Are you sure that your emotions aren't just caught up in all that has happened today?"

Beth stepped back as if she had been slapped. She certainly felt as though she had. "Is that what you think? Is that how you see me?"

He opened his mouth to speak, but she angrily cut him off.

"Do you think that I did this with you because I wanted to take something back with me? Is that why you did it—because I'm leaving, and you wanted something to remember me by? No entanglements with that, are there? Just a nice, tidy memory that you can pull out to look at when you're lonely."

Liam felt his face flush. Her words hit him a little too close for comfort. It sounded shallow and selfish when she said it like that.

Beth drew a shaky breath before continuing, the hurt coming through under the anger as she spoke. "If that were the case, why would I tell you that I love you?"

Liam gathered his thoughts together and said, "Elizabeth, how can you be sure? Are you sure that you aren't confusing gratitude for all that I've done for you over these past weeks with love? What I mean is, a lot has happened in your life over a short period of time. I think that you're still adjusting to all of it." Even to him, it sounded insufficient.

"You conceited so-and-so! I'm not seventeen anymore, Liam. I'm a grown woman!" At the surprised look on his face, she continued. "Do you think that I'm so empty-headed or shortsighted that I would mistake familiarity or gratitude, or lust, for love? That I would have sex with you when the opportunity presented itself just to satisfy a physical need? And if that were the case, then it would have happened a lot sooner, Liam. Because we both know that there have been plenty of opportunities before today!"

The color had drained from her face. "I think that I know my own heart and mind! Did it never occur to you that I made love with you because I felt love for you? The love came before making love, not the other way around! It never would've happened otherwise!" She paused, taking another step further away from him. "I thought that it was the same for you."

Liam watched Beth as she stepped back from him. The distance between them was growing by leaps and bounds. He saw the hurt on her face and in her eyes, heard it in her voice, and it unmanned him. He wanted to stop the pain that he was causing her, to bring her back somehow, but he knew that it was too late. He had never wanted to hurt her, just talk some sense into her.

Beth's voice had been getting thicker with emotion as she spoke, and she choked off the last words on a small sob. She closed her eyes and swallowed hard, thinking *Oh no! Now I'm going to cry!* She felt her face redden with humiliation.

It had been a long night, followed by a long day, as Liam had said; and her emotions had been on a roller coaster ride. She was all used up.

Turning, she began to quickly walk away. Liam called after her, but she simply held her hand up as she continued to walk. "Just leave me alone, will you?"

She was embarrassed that she had shared her feelings with him. How could she have been so wrong about how he felt? All that time, he was just being nice because he had felt sorry for her! And there, this afternoon, she had shamelessly thrown herself at him. Suddenly, she felt like that naive schoolgirl that her old friends, and now Liam, had so often implied.

Some shred of pride made her lift her chin and turn back to him. She steeled her voice, "There won't be anyone else like me to come into your life again, Liam Sizer! One day, you'll miss what could've been."

She saw Naomi and Bill. They had turned from the wagon at the sound of her and Liam's voices, and now they were both looking at her. She felt hot tears begin to roll down her cheeks and angrily flicked them away. She had to get out of there before she made a bigger fool of herself!

Naomi called, "Beth, wait!" as she walked away.

Beth turned to her, shaking her head, and Naomi whispered, "I'm sorry!" Turning back, she continued to walk toward the trail along the river to home. As soon as she was out of sight, she lifted her skirt and ran as fast as she could, hot tears of humiliation and heartache rolling down her cheeks. Her breath was coming out in small gasps, her heart hammering against her breast.

Liam stood where he was, watching her walk away, her back rigid. She was right; he would never know anyone else like her. Her words were still echoing in his head. *"I love you . . . I've never felt this way before . . . I think that I always have . . . I know my own heart and mind . . . I thought that it was the same for you . . . "* He had seen the tears begin to fall down her cheeks as she turned away from him and hated himself for having brought them out in her, but he still believed that in time, it would be for the best.

An insistent voice way in the back of his mind made itself heard: *Better for who?* it asked. *Coward!* it taunted. The thunder rumbled in the distance. He looked toward the darkening sky, then at Naomi and Bill. Naomi was standing with her hands on her hips, glaring at him. Bill was shaking his head, his mouth set in a grim line.

"William Sizer! You are the world's biggest fool!" admonished Naomi.

Liam walked over to her, saying, "You don't understand."

"Yes, I most certainly do. Only too well, you pig-headed mule!"

"Would you, please, stop calling me names? I feel bad enough as it is."

"Well, you're going to feel worse before I'm through with you!" she retorted. "You think that just because you had your heart broken all those years ago, you aren't going to let that happen to you again. Am I right?"

Liam said, "What if she gets taken away from me in the same way that she came here? What about when she tires of this life and leaves? How am I supposed to live then? No woman wants the life that I live." The thunder clapped angrily overhead, but they paid no attention to it.

Naomi snorted at him. "Fool! She already lives the life you live!"

He didn't respond, and Naomi shook her head at him. "So you're going to push her away first, before she gets taken away or leaves? Selfish beast! Don't you think that she would hurt too? Although I'm sure that it couldn't possibly be more than she's hurting now, thanks to you! She gave you her love, and you handed it back to her! You two were friends first, right from the beginning, so the love will last. And besides, dolt, so what if it's one year or fifty that you have together? None of us knows how much time we'll have together. Not even Beth. Part of the price for the joy of love is the pain of loss. You can't have one without the other, so you should enjoy each other for as long as you are given the time to do it in. Beth has already had to adjust to losing all that she loves once. Don't make her do it again. She's not Lily, Liam. You don't have to worry about her never fitting in here or coming to hate you because you love these people! She's grown to love them too."

Her words hung in the air, and they could hear the thunder from the approaching storm. That voice in the back of his head was getting louder, and he was beginning to doubt his belief that he knew what was best for the two of them.

Liam sighed. He looked at both Naomi and Bill, anguish all over his face and in his words. "I love her so much that it's painful. I have never met any woman like her before, someone that I simply enjoy being with. She's willful and proud and strong and, at the same time, gentle and caring. And sometimes she's so unsure of herself that my heart aches to watch her. After what happened between us today . . . how could I ever deserve her? These feelings scare me to death!"

Naomi softened. Gently, she said, "Liam, don't you think that maybe some higher power brought the two of you together? That you may have been meant to be together? You two are so perfect for each other. You are equals who were brought together *across time!* Don't you see that this opportunity for happiness is a gift to both of you? Surely, you don't still believe that this was an accident or that you aren't deserving of each other?"

Liam smiled sadly at Naomi and looked over to Bill, who said, "I have to say that I agree with her!" He put his arm around his wife's waist and continued, "Liam, the two of you are ideal for one another. If you let her go, then you're a damned fool!"

"Liam, Beth told me about the night of the thunderstorm," said Naomi. "She said that she made her decision to stay, then and there. She realized that she didn't want to leave. She traded everything that she could've gone back to so that she could stay here—with you! Stop being afraid of what you feel. Trust the love that she has for you, and let your heart go to her!"

Liam stood quietly for a moment, staring at the blowing treetops in the coming dark. He heard Elizabeth's words again in his head. She was a strong, capable woman. She never would have told him how she felt if she hadn't been sure. How many times had she told him that she could think for herself? He muttered to himself, "Liam, you are a fool!"

Turning to Bill and Naomi, he said, "You're right, of course. She's nothing like Lily was. Nothing! I've been an idiot! I hope that she'll forgive me." He turned away and headed toward the path upriver just as the first raindrops began to fall.

Bill hugged Naomi to his side and said, "I hope that she will too."

Naomi nodded, grimly. As the thunder sounded overhead, she said, "I hope he's not too late."

Beth ran into her apartment and through the door to the bedroom. Sitting on the edge of her bed, she was at a loss and didn't know what to do next. She was angry and embarrassed with herself for having made such a foolish mistake. She had been so careful with her heart for so long. How could she have been so wrong?

Her heart felt like it was in a million pieces. How was she ever going to face him again—she had ruined everything! They'd had such an easy friendship, and now they could never go back to that. She had ruined that friendship with her stupidity. How could she see him every day and pretend that everything was all right? She had made a good fool of herself, that was for sure!

She had been so sure that he had felt the same, and after they had made love, she was more certain of it than ever! It had been so special. At least, that's what she had felt. Could she have misread him because of what she was feeling? Did she just see what she wanted to see? The love that she had felt had been such a powerful revelation to her that she had mistakenly assumed that something so strong had to be reciprocated. What conceit had ever made her think that someone like him would ever look her way or want to return her love? But what about the things that had passed between them? What about today . . . hadn't that meant something to him too? But Beth stopped herself here with harsh reproach. She had, essentially, thrown herself at him without giving him the opportunity to say no, and he could hardly be blamed for what happened next. She felt her face flame scarlet again at her behavior. No wonder he wasn't there when she awoke!

Thinking about it now, seeing everything with new eyes, Beth realized that he had never made any reference to a future with the two of them in it.

Only she had drawn that conclusion. He never had any plans on asking her to stay with him. In fact, he had simply done what he did with everyone . . . offered help when it was needed. Liam had taken her under his wing and had spent these last few months teaching her a skill that she would be able to use to support herself, and when she was ready, he would send her on her way. She was no different than any one of his other patients, and she had completely misread the whole thing.

Had she been clinging too tightly to the words in her parents' letter? Perhaps Liam had been right about the future still being open, and anything could happen. What her mother and father had written in their letter was just one possible ending. The real ending was still out there, somewhere, changing every day.

She had gone from feeling incredible elation over the love that she had discovered within herself and what she and Liam had shared, to this horrible sense of confusion and loss. She felt as though she was sliding uncontrollably down a slippery hill, and she had to put the brakes on this horrible ride, somehow.

Her tears started again, and Beth felt as though they would never stop. She put her face in her hands, her fingers brushing against the scar on her forehead while the tears fell. The thunder sounded loud overhead now. She took her hands from her face and looked outside. Wiping the tears from her eyes, she stood and reached for the trunk at the foot of her bed, pulling it around toward her. She didn't have much time.

Liam reached Beth's door as the raindrops turned into a downpour. It had become dark now, with nightfall and the storm, and the lightning flashed brightly. Both the house and apartment were dark, the windows staring coldly, blankly at him.

He didn't bother to knock; she wouldn't have heard it over the sound of the storm anyway. Flinging open the door, he called her name but could already tell that she wasn't there. The lightning flashed again, and he saw into her bedroom . . . and saw the open trunk in the middle of the floor. Running into the room, he lit a lamp and looked inside the trunk, already knowing what he would find. Everything was gone . . . her uniform, gun, backpack. All of it gone. Her skirt and blouse were lying on the bed. He picked up her blouse, still warm from her body. Rumpling it against his breast, he tilted his head back and closed his eyes and said out loud, "Liam, you idiot!"

The thunder crashed, deafening in its anger, urging him now to hurry even more. Throwing her blouse back onto the bed, Liam ran out the door. He knew where she would have gone. There was only one place. Blindly, he ran through the dark and the rain up the river trail, praying all the while that he would not be too late. The lightning and rain streaked down around him.

Beth had left the apartment just as the first drops of rain began to come down. She took one last quick look around, her eyes briefly coming to rest on the book of Longfellow's poems that Liam had given her. Sadly, she shook her head and turned away, closing the door firmly behind her.

She went into the barn and gave both horses a little grain and kissed Belle softly on the nose. "I wish that I could take you with me!" She patted Ned lightly on the neck and said, "Take good care of Belle for me, will you?"

She slipped silently into the woodlot near Liam's house and headed upriver at a quick trot, making sure to stay off the path on the off chance that someone came along. She couldn't risk anyone seeing her in these clothes! This uniform that had once felt like a second skin was now unfamiliar and awkward on her. The trousers were restrictive after the freedom of her skirts, and she could feel the pull from the weight of her duty belt on her hips. The body armor around her torso felt cumbersome and bulky, where she once had been able to wear it for hours. Falling back on old habits, she closed her mind to the discomfort as she made her way toward the field.

Reaching the edge of the field, Beth looked around. It had turned dark, and the rain was now pouring down around her, pelting her skin, soaking her. She waited for another flash of lightning before taking a deep breath and stepping out, heading toward the rock at the edge of the river. She felt the wet stalks of grass whipping against her pant legs as she resolutely strode across the open field. Stepping up onto the rock, she stood for a moment looking into the river, watching the dark water flow past her, thinking of all the people that she didn't have a chance to say good-bye to. But there was no turning back now.

"Okay, river," she shouted above the rain, "do whatever magic you do, and take me out of here! Please! I don't know why I was sent to this time, but I don't want to go on here any longer. I can't! So please, just send me somewhere, anywhere, else! Do you hear me?"

The storm raged around her, and she tilted her face toward the sky, letting the harsh rain scrub away her tears as she stood with her arms at her sides. She felt the air begin to tingle around her.

Liam burst into the field in a clap of thunder and flash of lightning. The air in the field felt alive, somehow. His eyes went instinctively toward the rock at the river's edge.

"No! Oh, no!" he groaned as the lightning illuminated Beth standing on the rock, her face tilted toward the sky. His heart hammered painfully in his chest. She was leaving, and it was his fault! He had to convince her to stay; he couldn't go back to a life without her if she left. There was nothing to go back to. He ran toward her, slipping across the wet grass, calling her name.

Beth spun around when she heard her name and saw Liam running toward her. "Leave me alone, Liam! I have had enough for one day, do you hear me? I don't belong here, so just let me leave without making any more of a fool of myself than I already have!"

Without hesitation, Liam jumped up onto the rock and wrapped both arms securely around her, shouting to make himself heard above the storm. "If you're leaving, then I'm going with you! Elizabeth, I'm such a fool! Don't go, please! I love you! More than I ever thought I could love anyone! I know that you have every reason to leave. The only reason that I can give you to stay is that I love you. Stay with me. Stay for me . . . or take me with you! Please." He whispered, "Please." It seemed that he would, after all, beg her to stay.

Beth stood motionless in his embrace. He saw lightning flash in her dark eyes. He stepped back but had both hands firmly on her arms. She saw his pleading eyes, the anxious look on his face, but refused to believe—couldn't believe—what he was telling her. Above them, the thunder rolled and split the heavens.

"I don't believe any of what you're saying! Why did you say all of those things to me before, if you love me so much?" She paused as his first words sank in. "You're willing to go with me?" Did he really love her? Could he love her that much, that he would be willing to go wherever this river sent them? To take that leap of faith for her?

Without hesitation, Liam said, "I don't care where we live, as long as we're there together. I don't ever want to be far from your side! I love you! Please believe me. I'm so sorry that I hurt you. Give me a chance to explain!"

Suddenly, there was an earthshaking clap of thunder, causing them both to start. As they looked at each other, Liam leapt from the rock, dragging Beth with him. In an instant, the air lit up with a blue-yellow light, forcing them to close their eyes to its brightness. There was a tremendous crackling sound, and they felt the hair on their arms and necks lift. They pushed themselves up off the ground, brushing off bits of dirt and rock and looked around. The rock had split in two pieces from the lightning strike. The air around them felt heavy and very much alive, carrying the stench of ozone.

Liam looked at Beth with round eyes. He opened his mouth but couldn't find any words.

Beth wasn't having the same difficulty. She looked back at him and stomped her foot, suddenly shouting, "Well, that tears it!" She kicked at a chunk of rock with her booted foot and sent it sailing into the river out of sheer frustration. "I cannot take one more *damned* thing today!"

Sullenly, she sat back down on the ground, folded her arms across her knees, and put her forehead down on her arms.

Liam looked down at her, in her strange clothes, a smile of relief and hope on his face. He found his voice. "I'll bet that felt good—just letting go like that."

Beth lifted her head up, arms still crossed over her knees, and glared at him. "Dammit, Liam! Who do you think you are, pulling me away like that?" She paused, then added, "Do you realize that I almost left here forever?"

She lowered her forehead back to her arms, muttering, "This puts the cap on a full, rich day! I swear!"

Liam's smile widened to a grin. He sat down and put his arms around her, pulling her close. She was shaking slightly, and he found that he was as well.

"It's been quite a day for us both, hasn't it?" The rain continued to fall around them but not as heavily. The storm was letting up.

Liam continued to talk while he held her, in the same soothing voice that she had heard him use so many times with his patients and a few times with her. "I know that you've been through a lot today. It's been a long few days, and you've been wonderful! I couldn't have got through any of it without you. I don't blame you for being upset."

Without pulling away from him, Beth said against his chest, "You still owe me an explanation! I'm very confused. And stop patronizing me!"

"Yes . . . yes I do owe you an explanation." Liam sat for a moment, collecting his thoughts. "Elizabeth, when I told you earlier today that you saved my life, I meant it. But not just this morning. You saved my life when I found you in this river last spring. Until then, I didn't realize it, but I was only half alive. You've brought so much into my life that I never knew was missing, and I would have gone my whole life without ever knowing the feelings that you've awakened in me. I was just existing, looking ahead to days that stretched out in an unending sameness. I used to believe that would be enough, that I was content with living my life through all of these people that I take care of, that the emptiness in my own heart wasn't anything that mattered. But I know now that I can never go back to that again. I can never settle for just existing. I want my own life . . . with you.

"I've been fighting these feelings all summer. I think that I fell in love with you your first night here. Do you remember that night when I left the room, and you tried to get dressed?" Beth nodded her head against his chest. "When I came back and found you standing there and holding onto your gun, I looked into your eyes. You were frightened and brave at the same time and looking so confused, but determined too. I admired you so much. I'm certain that I fell in love with you right then and there.

"As I came to know you, I found a strong and capable woman, but one still unsure of herself in so many ways. And I'm still learning things about you, and in doing so, I'm learning things about myself. You touched me so deep inside that I didn't notice it at first. All I knew was that my life was changed forever! And like a fool, I tried to deny it to myself."

Beth sat quietly against Liam, a small seed of hope beginning to grow within her.

"Elizabeth, years ago, I was engaged to be married. I had met Lily while I was in Boston. She was a beautiful, smart girl. But she was spoiled too. I thought, foolishly, that she understood my dream of being a doctor here. She didn't, and she told me so, in no uncertain terms. Along with some other things. Does this sound familiar?"

Beth smiled. She remembered the way that he had looked at her when she had told him about her own engagement.

"In any event, we had a row, and our engagement was over. I decided then that no woman would want the lifestyle or income of a simple country doctor. Nor would I let someone else try to decide my life for me. So I made up my mind that marriage and family were something that I would never have. That idea has stood for all these years. No one has ever even done more than catch my passing interest . . . until you came along, and I fell in love before I even knew what was happening. I was never completely convinced that you wouldn't be taken away again or just get tired of me and this life and leave, so I told myself that it wouldn't hurt so much if I kept my feelings for you to myself. I guess that I knew that if I shared what I felt with you, then my heart would be ripped away forever when you left. I never thought, in my wildest dreams, that you would love me too! And when we made love today, it was so special, and I knew that you now have my very soul. And it scared the living daylights out of me!"

Beth finally sat up, looking at Liam. He reached over and smoothed the wet tendrils of hair clinging to her face back behind her ear.

"And," he continued, "I haven't been very considerate of your feelings either. I had convinced myself this afternoon that in pushing you away, I was sparing us both more pain in the end. I was a cowardly, selfish, fool. Naomi, in her frank way, was quick to point that out to me after you left her house, by the way. Bill too. And I deserved it! All that and more. But, Elizabeth, it doesn't matter to me how we came to be together or where we end up together. The only thing that matters is that we *are* together, for however long that may be."

Liam picked up both of her hands in his. "Elizabeth, you have never allowed me to talk this long without saying something! Please tell me that I'm forgiven for being the world's biggest fool and hurting you! Please tell me that it's not too late for you and me! I need your optimism and your courage and your heart. I need you! I want to be able to say that I'm your husband, and you're my wife, and I want to love and raise our children with you. I want you to show me the future!" He gripped her hands tighter. "God, sweetheart, please tell me what you want!"

Beth smiled to herself. *Children! Oh, my God, Aaron and Lydia are my children! Our children!* She pulled her hands away from his and cleared her throat.

"Liam, I don't know what to say. I wish that I could still be mad and not let you off the hook so easily. Because, frankly, I've had one crazy day! I've been up and down so much these last couple of days that I need a scorecard to keep track! I've been exhausted, frightened, and exhilarated. I found love, and my heart was full, it was overflowing. Then when I thought that I lost that love, my heart felt empty. Absolutely shattered, as a matter of fact. You've been the cause of all of this. At this moment, I have a funny feeling in the pit of my stomach—butterflies, I think. And I'm tired, hungry, and wet. You're responsible for all that too."

"You hurt me, Liam, plain and simple. It would've been so much better if you'd said nothing at all when I told you that I love you. I'm a big girl, I could've handled that. But to pick that love apart and try to talk me of what I was feeling, well . . . that just devastated me. Not only did that tell me that you didn't want what I was offering you, but that you didn't believe in it either. And now I find out that it was all because you didn't think that you could offer me enough! You need to accept that I'll decide what's best for me. And we'll both decide, together, what's best for us. Liam—I almost left here *forever!*"

She paused before continuing, drawing in an unsteady breath. "I thought that I had ruined everything between us by telling you that I loved you! Our friendship has been closer than any other that I've ever had. After what you said to me earlier, I was sure that I had done irreparable damage to it. I thought that you'd only taken care of me because you felt sorry for me, and then I'd forced myself on you, creating this awkward situation that you had to get yourself out of. I couldn't face you after that, thinking that I had changed everything!"

She sat quietly for a moment. Liam waited her out, knowing that she wasn't through, appreciating her frank honesty. "I love you, Liam, and that won't change. That's the only guarantee that I can offer you. Maybe this river will take me away again. We have no way of knowing that for sure. I told you once before that I don't intend to sit around waiting for some sign of what's next. All I need is your love. If you feel the same, then that's all I need to be happy, for however many days or years that we'll have together. Naomi, I think, is right about this . . . we are meant to be together! I've never loved like this before, and I don't think that everyone gets the chance to experience the kind of love *and* friendship that I feel for you. When I think of it, I'm awed, then amazed, and then humbled. It just blows me away."

Beth drew a long, shaky breath, and then let it out. "But something tells me that this river is through with us now, and I'm here to stay. I think that my last chance to go back to where I came from just disappeared in a flash, so to speak. So you're stuck with me, I'm afraid." He could hear the smile in her voice, "Do you think that you can handle that, William Sizer?"

Liam smiled deeply. He reached for her hands again, and this time, she didn't pull them away. "Ask me in around fifty years or so! Elizabeth, will you marry me? Will you do me the absolute honor of allowing me to call myself your husband and the pride of saying that you are my wife?" The rain had stopped falling, and the rising moon was peeking through the dispersing clouds. The river bounced a watery reflection of it to them.

Beth's face split into a wide smile as she threw her arms around him in answer. Eventually, Liam stood and pulled her up beside him. As she rose up from the ground, Beth turned toward him.

"By the way . . . we'll have two children."

He gave her a long kiss and said, "Two or twenty . . . however many you want."

"No," laughed Beth, linking her fingers behind his neck. "I *know* that we'll have two children. And I'll bet that they're the two who told my parents about me! Their names will be Aaron and Lydia. They'll be our children, and they were a part of my life from the time I was born, right up until they died. They treated me so kindly, and they were both wonderful people! They were the only other people to call me by my full name, besides you. Now I know why!" She laughed again, stepping back and picking up Liam's hands in hers.

Liam's eyes had gone wide, then he laughed with her, pulling her close in a bear hug. "Do you think that I'll ever get used to it?"

"What?"

"These little revelations that you'll be hitting me with for the rest of our lives."

"Are you sorry already?"

"No! I'll never be sorry. That's a promise!" With an arm still around her, they began walking in the moonlight along the river trail toward home.

After a moment, Beth asked, "Would you really have gone back with me? Could you, the scientist, have taken that leap of faith?"

Liam stopped walking and turned to Beth, nodding. "Elizabeth, you have changed my mind about a lot of things! I don't care what century we're in, so long as we're there together! The way I figure it, we'd always be able to help each other through it. And if we had gone back to the time that you came from, you would be able to keep this uniform on and go back to the job that you so obviously enjoyed. Then I could see you at work instead of just imagining how it must have been for you. I have to admit that the thought is somewhat intriguing. I've watched you nearly every day since you came here. I've seen you carry yourself through each day, adjusting to all of the new things around you and taking much of it in stride. I'm very proud of the woman that you are now, and part of me wishes that I could share that part of your old life too."

Beth smiled and slowly shook her head at him. "Liam, I'm glad that I did stay, and that we're here now, in this time. I've been given the extraordinary opportunity of experiencing both ends of the same century, but this is where we *both* belong. While there will certainly continue to be times when I'll miss my family more than I think that I'll be able to bear, I'll never regret staying here with you. I know, without a doubt, that this is what they wanted for me. And you couldn't leave here . . . there are too many people who need you. Not just any doctor, but you. Because you honestly do care about them, and they know this, and I love you all the more for it. And I love these people—our neighbors—too. For the first time, everything feels right to me. I think that I've waited my whole life just to be right here with you."

They were married in the backyard beside the river, with just Liam's family present. It was a beautiful, clear day, and the leaves were just beginning to turn varying shades of gold and red. The air had the crisp, dry smell that one can only find in New England at the end of the summer, carrying with it the promise of cold nights and frost. Beth felt all of the pieces of her life fall into place as Liam slipped the slim band on her finger. Everything that she had done and all that her parents had done for her had led her to this place. She closed her eyes for a moment and breathed deeply, savoring the beauty of the moment. When she opened them again, she saw Liam's smiling face, and everything was perfect in the world.

Taking out her camera one last time, Beth set the timer and took a family picture with her and Liam, his parents, and Naomi and Bill with the babies. She took pictures of the house and barn, as well as Ned and Belle. She showed Bill and Mr. Sizer how to use the camera, and they used up the last of the space on the chip with candid shots of her and Liam and the rest of the family.

Although they had decided that the ceremony would be private, they held a ceilidh afterward, inviting whoever wanted to come. They were happily surprised when the house, and then the yard, filled to overflowing with people from all over, wanting to wish them well. Many of Liam's patients were there, along with their neighbors and people from down in town. He had contacted some of his old shipmates, and they had come as well.

Clare Owen showed up with his new fiddle in hand. "It's about time I got out into the world again, don't you think, Liam?" His scar appeared red, but smooth enough, on his face. In time, the red would fade.

He turned to Beth and said, "I still have my old fiddle. If you would like, I'll teach you to play this winter."

Beth eagerly accepted his offer. Both she and Liam recognized it as a peace offering for his earlier behavior.

Martin and Louisa Harrison sought out Liam and Beth. They had quietly gone back to Boston and gotten married. They both looked happy with one another.

"Doctor and Mrs. Sizer," said Martin, "congratulations are in order, I see."

"And for you too," said Liam as he shook Martin's hand. He turned to Louisa and asked, "How are you feeling? Are you following the special diet that I gave you?"

Louisa smiled prettily, saying, "Yes, I am. And I feel wonderful, Doctor. Thank you."

She turned to Beth and put her hand on her arm, saying, "And I thank you, especially. Your kind words came to me at just the right moment."

Martin added, "Yes, your words did come at exactly the right time. We have much to thank both of you for."

As they walked away, Beth said to Liam, "Maybe Martin is finally growing up. Louisa will be a good wife for him, I think." Liam nodded, his arm around her.

They were greeted by Frank and Ethel, who told them that they too would be getting married soon. Ethel said, "We would like it very much if you would attend our wedding on October 11." Liam smiled warmly at Beth as he accepted the offer for both of them.

The gifts that the guests brought to the newlyweds were music, laughter, and plenty of good food, including hams baked with maple syrup or raisin sauce and sweet potatoes served with maple butter, chicken pie with biscuit on top, meat pies in a flaky crust, or roasts of goose, all served with chutneys and pickles of all kinds.

There was baked rice and cheese with a thick tomato sauce; baked beans with brown bread, anadama, and corn breads; biscuits with jams; pies and tarts of all sorts made with the fruits and vegetables that had ripened all summer; puddings boiled in bags or steamed, with all manner of sauces to pour over them, from molasses, to maple, to lemon or cream. There were cookies such as molasses, hermits, sour cream, or rich madeleines spread with savory fruit jam, and then frosted with a light lemon icing.

The cakes were beautiful masterpieces, ranging from nun's cake to ribbon and harlequin, with their tart lemon filling, to spice and date cakes. There was a jellyroll, covered with the finest powdered sugar, and a devil's food cake—with rich chocolate icing—towering over the table.

Wandering past the tables, Beth thought that it all resembled a savory quilt, pieced together by the talented women of Corsehill, using recipes that were generations old. She smiled as she recognized Ethel's blueberry teacake, her mouth watering in anticipation of a piece of it.

There was a table with beverages, all homemade, with names like cherry bounce, grape shrub, and switchel. There was spiced cider along with punch of all sorts and lemonade.

Beth turned away from the food to look for her husband and found him looking for her. She smiled lovingly at him as he pulled her into his arms among the other dancers.

They looked at each other while they waltzed, and Liam softly kissed her fingertips as he held her hand. Pulling her closer, he said, "I've thought many times over the past couple of weeks how incredible and wonderful it is that the two of us were brought together—two people who believed that they would spend the rest of their lives alone. I still can't believe that we're married!" She felt his arm tighten around her, and his chin brushed against her temple. He whispered softly into her ear, "I want you to know how happy I am, and that I'll spend the rest of my days making you happy."

Beth smiled at his words. She felt exactly the same, and told him so, adding, "My parents were right, after all."

Epilogue

September, 1958

"*. . . And so, Mom and Dad, I come to the end of my journals, as I am coming to the end of my days. My beloved Liam has gone, and I believe that I'll be seeing him again very soon. Not a day has gone by that I haven't thought about all of you with love. My memories of the first thirty years of my life with you are as fresh today as they were when I last saw you fifty years ago. I have lived a happy and full life with my wonderful, loving husband. He gave me two beautiful children who have only added to our joy. They each, in turn, have given us wonderful grandchildren. And so, our lives go on with each new generation. Had it not been for your guidance while I was growing up, and your strength to let me take this adventure, I never would have known this particular contentment. I cannot thank you enough for letting me go the way that you did, knowing how hard it must have been for you. I hope that you have found some comfort over the years in the messages that I have left for you throughout my lifetime. I have never forgotten that I, for some still unknown reason, have been given the privilege of seeing history unfold through new and wondrous eyes. Oh, the things that I have seen! Liam and I both tried to put to use some of the knowledge that I gained growing up at the end of this wonderful century to help our neighbors here in the first half. I hope that, in my lifetime, I have done some good . . .*"

May 15, 2008

Beth's mother closed the journal that she had been reading aloud to her husband. She recalled again that day, almost thirty years ago, when she had opened the door to Aaron and Lydia. She had come to know them and their

---

223

children very well in the years that had followed. On that memorable day, Aaron had handed them a letter from their soon-to-be-born daughter, telling them when she would be born, when she would leave, and where she would be going. In this letter, she begged them to let her go when the time came and asked that they read only the journal from her first year in her new life as proof that she would, indeed, find happiness. She asked that they save the remaining journals to read after she left in 2008. Lydia had given them, on that same day all those years ago, a chain with a locket and cross, as well as an old leather-bound book of Longfellow's poems. The pages were yellowed and much read, and there was an inscription inside the cover. A letter fell out and fluttered to the floor as Mrs. Blodgett opened the cover of the book. Picking it up, she noticed that it was in her own handwriting and dated May 15, 2008. She began to read it . . .

Now, all these years later, she and her husband had opened that trunk that Aaron had carried into their house. Inside was Beth's uniform, neatly folded so long ago and stored away with her other gear. They found her camera, with a note written on yellowed paper, saying simply, "Download these pictures. ♥" And they found all of her journals; fifty years of the life that began anew in 1908. And so, they began to read. And as they read, they came to know their daughter even better as she shared her life and thoughts with them through each day, on every page. Through these memories, they learned what she and Liam had offered during and after many catastrophic events, including going to France with the Red Cross during the Great War to work in a field hospital. She had, in fact, done some good in her lifetime.

LaVergne, TN USA
07 November 2010
203930LV00002B/3/P